Hear Their Story

Angie Freeland

Published by New Generation Publishing in 2022

Copyright © Angie Freeland 2022

First Edition

The author asserts the moral right under the Copyright, Designs and Patents Act 1988 to be identified as the author of this work.

All Rights reserved. No part of this publication may be reproduced, stored in a retrieval system or transmitted, in any form or by any means without the prior consent of the author, nor be otherwise circulated in any form of binding or cover other than that which it is published and without a similar condition being imposed on the subsequent purchaser.

ISBN
    Paperback   978-1-80369-270-8
    Ebook   978-1-80369-271-5

www.newgeneration-publishing.com

New Generation Publishing

Acknowledgements

Firstly, I would like to thank all those who asked me when I would be writing a second book. Without you "Hear Their Story." would never have come into existence. Thank you from the bottom of my heart for the motivation you have given me to write.

I want to say a very big thank you to my wonderful husband Keith who proofread "Hear Their Story." He has tirelessly gone through every chapter, corrected my punctuation, made sense of my way too long sentences, read each story and given me feedback. All of this was no easy task, because when I write I just go with the flow and tend to get my commas and full stops mixed up or miss them out altogether! Keith has encouraged me from the very beginning to write about my journey with spirit. Thank you so much for your support past, present and future.

I also want to thank our children Dave and Jay for accepting me as their crazy mum who talks to dead people! Although that's normal for me, it isn't for most people, so it's quite a thing to say your mum is a medium. You are both my inspiration, always.

I also want to thank my family and friends for supporting me, putting up with me the way they do and for believing in me. You're all a great bunch.

I want to send special thanks to two special people. Firstly Jacqui for the amazing artwork for the front and back covers of Hear Their Story. Also to Paul who always takes awesome pictures, one of which features on the back cover.

Of course, I cannot forget the wonderful spirit world who are always willing to talk to me, teach me and share a little of what it's like in the spirit world. I will always be in awe of you all and with all my heart and gratitude I say thank you so much.

Angie xx

Introduction

When I wrote my first book, "Between Heaven and Hell, a Privileged Life," it was very much about my life story and how spirit had always walked by my side guiding, supporting and inspiring me. It also showed how determined they were that I was going to work with and for them. So, after people read the book, I received feedback from many who grew curious and, along with many others, were starting to ask me questions such as, "What happens when we make our transition over to the spirit world?" "Who were there to meet their loved ones when they died?" The most frequent questions I found people were asking were, "Is there really life after death?" along with "When are you going to write your second book?"

So, I decided to write a book that may help answer some of these questions. "Hear Their Story." is in fact ten short stories about ten different people whose lives and passing are very different. Although each person and their stories are fictional, the stories are based on experiences I have had whilst communicating with the spirit world, giving thousands of readings and demonstrations of mediumship over many years. For those who have not had a reading or seen a demonstration of mediumship, this entails giving information and messages that would be relevant to both the spirit and their loved one who has come to see me. Many years of experience have given me a unique insight into the spirit world which I have woven into the ten stories.

Each chapter reveals a different person who has passed over into the spirit world, how they led their life on earth and, having passed, how their transition and new life back in their spiritual home fans out.

When I started out on my journey as a professional psychic medium, my husband, Keith, and I focused on the world of the paranormal and to this day we still work together in this field. Our very first public paranormal event we ran was in Ireland, the very first of its kind ever held there. Keith and I gave the event the name "Hear Their Story." The name felt so appropriate somehow and it is why I do what I do. What else could I call this book other than "Hear Their Story."

I hope you enjoy it.

Angie xx

Chapter 1

LORRAINE

It feels really weird looking down on your kids at your own funeral, Lorraine thought. Bless 'em, they're good kids, especially when you think I was bringing 'em up without a dad! Lorraine was puffing up her own ego as she looked down on what seemed to be very surreal to her. One minute I was in the kitchen having a drink and the next I'm here, wherever here is! I ain't been able to work that out yet!

Lorraine was born in 1985 and brought up in the East end of London. She had an older brother by two years who she adored because he kept her safe when it all kicked off with her dad when he had had too much to drink, which was quite frequent! Their dad, an Eastender, was an aggressive man who felt the world owed him a living, instead of him going out to work like all her friends' dads did, most of the time he would go down the pub, have a good skinful, and come back to start a row with her mum, and if mum wasn't about, Lorraine or her brother Mark would do! Both Lorraine and her brother were petrified of dad because they knew he was good with his hands and wouldn't be afraid of using them when he had a drink! Mum was pretty scared of him also as she had been his punch bag for many years, and to be honest, as hard as this sounds, if she was out of the way and he lost his temper with one of the kids, then it would be a relief that she didn't have to go through it. Neither mum nor dad had the parenting skills needed to give their kids a decent life.

When Lorraine was just 15 years old she was hanging around the bottom of the flats that her and her friend lived in working out how much money they had, and whether or not they could afford a couple of rides at the fun fair that had come into town. Yep, it was a good result because they could afford to have just a couple of rides. Once they were there they walked around a bit and sussed out who and what was there, and they were particularly interested in the boys. Lorraine looked across from where she was standing and saw this lad staring at her and she thought he must be about 17 or 18 years old. "Very nice" she said out loud as she turned and looked at her mate Charlotte, or Charlie as they called her. "Who you talking about?" "That bloke over there, the tall good looking one with the blonde hair and gorgeous eyes, he's lovely." Charlie looked over, but the only lad she could see was her cousin Adam. Charlie looked at her friend and said "oh him, that's Adam, my cousin. You really think he's good looking?" Lorraine looked at Charlie with a glint in her eye, "course I do, or I wouldn't say it would I you silly mare." "Look Rainy", the nickname Charlie calls her, "I know he's my cousin, but even I know he aint all he's cracked up to be, and my mum says he'll come to no good, so you're better off staying away!" "Blimey Charlie give it a rest, I'm only asking you to introduce me to him, the rest I can do myself." Charlie could see that Lorraine wasn't taking any notice of what she was saying which worried Charlie. "Adam is only 18 years old, but the police know him, and he's got a bit of a reputation in certain circles.", Charlie said in the hope that she may listen to that bit, but no.

The girls walked over to where Adam was standing with his friends. "Ad, this is my mate Rainy, this is my cousin Ad." He was even better close up, and she was determined to get his attention. Adam looked over to her and grunted "alright", meaning hello, "yeah I'm alright, you?" She replied. Adam took a cigarette out of a box he was holding and as he reached over he asked Lorraine if she wanted one. "No thanks I don't smoke", Adam, smirked as he said "what are you a good girl then?" as he was sniggering with his mates. Lorraine immediately felt stupid and she knew he was mocking her like she was a tiny kid, and immediately came back with "alright then, I'll give it a go, ta."

Charlie wasn't happy seeing her mate behaving the way she was, and started to walk away. It was a few minutes before Lorraine realised that Charlie wasn't next to her. "I had better go." she said nervously, "I'm not sure where Charlie has gone." Adam chanced his luck, and said "you don't need to follow her do you? She doesn't like it cos we're getting on so well, and she doesn't want me to take her mate away!" "Is that what you're trying to do? Take me away from my mate? Well, she's the one who's got the money so unless I go and find her I aint gonna be able to go on any rides." Adam answered quickly because he knew the time was right to make his move, and said "that's ok babe, I'll pay for you." Lorraine was over the moon and didn't think anymore about finding her mate Charlie.

Fast forward a year Lorraine is 16 years old, she and Adam are still together much to everyone's concern. "He has a temper and isn't faithful to you mate." Charlie said to her time and time again, but she wasn't listening. It was also clear that he controlled her in every way, even what she should wear. Charlie barely saw Lorraine now, and she believed it was because of Ad not letting her. Lorraine was under the thumb, but she couldn't see it, and she saw their relationship through rose coloured spectacles, as the saying goes.

One day when Charlie was heading towards her local pub to meet her other mates, she ran into Lorraine, who had a big smile on her face. "Get you", Charlie said to her as they got closer, "You look like you're the cat that got the cream. How's it going?" Charlie asked, but she didn't expect the reply! 'Yeah all's good with me and Ad thanks, we're both so happy cos I'm pregnant!" Charlie couldn't help but take a big gasp of breath in disbelief, which Lorraine definitely noticed and went on the defensive straight away! "I suppose you're gonna say the same as my mum and dad that I'm too young!" Charlie gathered her thoughts and answered, "no, no I aint gonna say that, I'm just a bit shocked that's all. I take it you're gonna have the baby then?" Lorraine answered very proudly, "well, what do you fink? Could you imagine what Ad would do if I got rid of it?

He'd kill me!" Charlie could see how life was going to turn out for Rainey but she also knew that Rainey wasn't gonna listen to anyone.

Charlie was right, Lorraine's life did go from bad to worse! By the time she was 35 years old she had 3 kids age 18, 16, and 14 years old. All of the kids belonged to Adam, but he hadn't been around since not long after the third child was born, which meant she was bringing them up on her own, or trying to. Her mate Charlie was still there, supporting her and the kids, but it was getting harder because of Lorraine's heavy drinking, which meant she was out of it most of the time. She was desperately hanging on to the hope that Adam would come back and be her knight in shining armour again, although he was never really that, he was trouble from the word go. All those around her could see there was no way he was coming back because he had moved onto other women, was now very rarely on the right side of the law and was doing dodgy deals regularly. He didn't give two hoots about Lorraine and the kids. But for Lorraine, he was still her Mr Wonderful and she just waited day by day for him to come home.

Very often Charlie would arrive at Lorraine's flat to see the kids, and she found Morgan, her eldest daughter doing dinner to feed the other kids. Although Morgan was 18 years old now, she had been looking after her mum for a very long time in one way or another. Lorraine's middle child, Lacey, had always struggled at school in a number of ways, including coming to terms with being dyslexic. The teachers had asked Lorraine to come in regularly, but sadly she never kept her appointments, and as a result Lacey had no confidence. Charlie totally understood because of the lack of care, love or time she was given by her parents and tried to help her where ever she could. Then there was the youngest son, Harry. He was only 14 years old but he was already showing signs of being a rebel, and in some ways he was just like his father, which concerned Charlie greatly. Again, there wasn't much love, time or care given to him either. He was one angry lad that wouldn't think twice of getting into a punch up if he wanted to, and Charlie believed that he probably deliberately started fights because he needed to vent off his anger.

A lot of people used to judge him for his behaviour, but the truth was there was only one person that ever gave any time to Harry and that was Charlie. Charlie had met her husband when she was 20 years old and knew straight away he was for her, which still stood today. Although her husband and her two sons were her life she always had time for Lorraine's three kids. Charlie was an angel really because no matter what, she was always there for Lorraine and her kids. When Lorraine had had a good drink she would be quite nasty to Charlie, but she always brushed it off because she knew that underneath Lorraine's behaviour she didn't mean what she was saying. She was still very much a child in an adult body, and it showed through her behaviours which could change very fast. The poor kids took the brunt of it, especially Morgan who was always the scapegoat for Lorraine.

Charlie had noticed some worrying changes in Lorraine, her appetite had never been great, especially with the drinking, but it was getting worse. She constantly had bruises on her, and when Charlie asked her where she got them from, she had no idea. Lorraine was skinny, and yet her legs and ankles seem to be swollen a lot now. Charlie repeatedly asked her to go to the doctors to have a check up because she feared that the drinking was taking its toll on her, although she didn't express that to her because she knew Lorraine would get really aggressive towards her, and in the past even threatened that she would stop her from seeing the kids. That she couldn't take a chance on happening, after all the kids didn't have anyone else batting for them in their court. Adam wasn't anywhere to be seen since he picked up with this new girl that he was with at the moment, and even if she could find him he certainly wouldn't want the kids cramping his style. Meanwhile she would try and do her best for her mate Rainey, even though she felt that she had lost her mate many years ago. She had to think of the kids now. It was early one morning when Charlie got the call from Morgan that she had been dreading, Rainey was dead! Just like that her lights had gone out as she poured herself her last drink.

Lorraine was talking to herself out loud, her mind was ticking over ten to the dozen with all these questions. "Oh my God, what's happened? And where is everyone? And more to the point where the bleedin' hell am I? This ain't funny no more, I wanna know what's going on. One minute I'm standing in my kitchen pouring myself a drink and the next fing I know is that I'm here. Weird! There's no-one around, and there ain't anyone I could ask where I am. And what's with this bright white light around me? I feel like I'm in it, like it's part of me. Man that's really spooky, it just seems there's nuffink or no-one here, I can't work it out. Why aint there any furniture around? Or at least can't I have a chair while I'm waiting for someone to come and talk to me, and besides that I wanna sit down. Gawd I could really do with a fag, but I aint got none on me, and I can't see any around neither. I wanna drink as well, that would calm me nerves cos I aint got a bleedin clue what's going on."

It was at that point that Lorraine felt as though someone was drawing near and she strongly had a feeling of someone behind her. Suddenly Lorraine knew that she had experienced that feeling before, "but it can't be" she said out loud. "That feels like my nan's standing behind me, but it can't be cos she's dead and has been for years." "Hello darling", she heard from behind. She knew that voice too, it was her nan! She turned around quickly, and there she was, standing in front of her, it was indeed her nan. Lorraine's grandmother was a typical east ender who took no nonsense. She said it as it was because she wasn't afraid to speak her mind. Her name was Margaret, but was called Marge by most people, yes even in the spirit world her name's been shortened. Immediately Lorraine got a lump in her throat, and the tears were welling up inside her. "Nan, how can you be here, you're dead! I know what it is, I'm dreaming, oh and what a lovely dream it is too." Lorraine's nan had passed away 10 years earlier, and, to Lorraine, her nan was her mum. Nan stepped in to be like a mum to her because Lorraine's parents were not capable of being proper parents because of their selfishness about what they wanted in life, and Lorraine who was an only child didn't fit in. This saddened Marge a lot because she had watched her daughter change so much after she got married to that controlling horrible man. Is it any wonder Lorraine didn't have the greatest of skills when it came to parenting, she very often thought. Everyone apart from Marge and her kids had let her down in life, was the view Lorraine held, but Lorraine's views about people could be quite distorted at times, and what she didn't realise at this time was that her views were going to change in some ways very soon, Lorraine had a big awakening coming to her very shortly.

"Nan, how comes I can see and hear you? I'm confused! Am I imagining this"? "No darling, you aint imagining it, you can see and hear me, and you can even touch me if you want". Lorraine immediately moved forward and grabbed her nan and cuddled her so hard. She immediately felt the warmth of her nan's love, and her big bosom was always a comforting pillow when she was young. For a short while she was a child again and experiencing the strength of that bond she had with her nan when she was a child. Her nan held her tight just like she used to, she knew how scary and confusing this would be for her granddaughter because although her passing was different to Marge, she had time to prepare for her transition, Lorraine didn't, it was still pretty scary to experience. "Poor Rainey" nan said out loud, "you just didn't see this building up did you?" That was more of a statement than a question, because she always knew when she was alive that Lorraine would never be strong enough to cope on her own, and watching her struggle from the spirit world she could see just how bad she had got with her drinking! Lorraine had grown up always looking for her knight in shining armour to come to her aid and in her eyes, Adam was that knight! How wrong she was!

Marge gently pulled Rainey away from her and looked straight into her eyes. "What's going on Nan? I can't work any of this out? Are you coming to me in a dream or is all this real?" Lorraine had so many questions but wasn't waiting to get the answers before she was asking another one. "Stop asking questions and let me talk", said Marge. Lorraine looked sheepish and very much like a small child that has been chastised for being naughty. "Rainey babe, you need to understand what's going on here. The reason why you're here with me is cos you've passed away too. I'm here to meet you and to let you know there ain't nuffink to worry about." Lorraine couldn't believe what her nan was saying, "What do you mean I'm dead? Don't talk rot, I've still got a lot of life to live, it can't be over. What about the kids? How will they cope?" Lorraine was sobbing as she spoke, she felt like she was losing her mind. She knew deep down that her nan wouldn't lie to her, but this can't be true. "There you go with all the questions again, give me time to tell you about what's happened."

Lorraine started to control her sobbing and her breathing as she calmed down. All this felt too much for her to take in, but at least she was hearing it from her nan. "What's the last thing you remembered?" Nan asked. "I remember waking up and feeling sick all day, but that was nothing new, I'm like that most days, cos of all the stress that I've normally got." "You mean you were always feeling sick cos of all the drinking you did", snapped her nan, "don't treat me like a fool, I know what you were like even before I died girl, even though you tried to cover it up, as well as the times I've tried to cover up for you and tell people to back off". Lorraine felt defensive, and started to give a heap of excuses, when nan stopped her in her tracks and said "don't even go there with the excuses, you know you had a drink problem."

"So is this gonna be all that I get now is it? Lecture after lecture? Cos I don't need this, and I'm gonna bugger off if it is." "This time you can't run Rainey, and you can't avoid what you have to face up to by downing a bottle of Vodka." Lorraine didn't like hearing nan's frankness but she knew she couldn't avoid it. Nan changed the tone of her voice and became quite gentle again as she spoke with Lorraine. "Look darling, there's no reason to give a load of excuses cos that's not important anymore. You won't be judged here cos there's no point to it, but you do have to face up to what you were like. It's not about punishing you for what you were like on earth, it's about helping you to understand it and grow spiritually." Marge continued to try and explain it the best way she could, but even though she had been in the spirit world for a decade, she was still struggling. Marge then gestured for Lorraine to follow her, "come on darlin', I need some help with this." Nan and Lorraine started to walk side by side, and as they did Lorraine started to see houses and flats that looked similar to the ones where she lived, and she could see people moving around and getting on with their own business, it all looked so similar and normal to some degree, but yet it felt different.

For a start, she knew almost everyone in her neighbourhood, and yet she didn't recognise anyone. "I know I don't much like where I live cos it's a bit rough and ready, well very rough and ready really, but it's still my home, a place I love and feel safe in, and all this aint got that feeling." Lorraine was weighing up how strange all of this was and was thinking to herself, "I'm actually walking up a road that I've walked countless times before but it aint the same, and the mere fact that I'm walking up this road with my nan confirms that because she's bloody dead!" "Nan none of this is real, you know that don't you?" Nan stopped in her tracks, turned and looked into Lorraines' eyes as she said "I'm afraid it's very real. It's been real for me for a decade now, and now it's going to become your new normal and real." Lorraine just stared as they continued to walk.

The walk they were taking changed very much from a small busy street and town into a beautiful country lane with wooded areas either side. Lorraine was mesmerised by the beauty of the trees either side of her, and the gorgeous glow that seemed to follow her around everywhere, everything appeared to glow so bright, "corr, it's so lovely" she thought. Ahead in the distance Lorraine could see the most amazing white building, it looked very grand and plush. She pointed to the house and shouted "Look nan what's that place?" "That my lovely is where we're going." "It's gorgeous, don't tell me you're rich up here", Lorraine said as she was chuckling. Marge stopped, looked at her, and said, "It's funny you should say that, I am a lot richer now than I ever was before I popped off, and so will you be, in time." As they approached this beautiful building Lorraine's curiosity was getting the better of her and she really wanted to see what was behind that big white door.

As they were approaching the door, Lorraine's mind was full of inquisitive chatter, and then all of a sudden she couldn't help but think that it had a holy feeling to it, or at least that's what it felt like to her. "Nan, is this like a Church?" She asked, "it's just that it has that feeling about it." Marge hesitated and then answered "yeah it's a bit like that but you'll get more of an idea once we get inside." "Oh blimey, I don't do churches!" "I've noticed", said nan rather sharply, but she also had that little cheeky grin on her face that Lorraine always loved because she knew that nan didn't do churches either. Nan looked directly at Lorraine and said, "come on darling, let's go inside."

The front door was massive, it was white with a heavy brass door handle on the left hand side of the door, the door opened and as it did Lorraine whispered "my God, the hallway's massive so God knows what the size of the rooms will be like." What the f*** Lorraine was going to say but when she looked at nan, she knew that was a bad idea. "Yeah change that language right now, it aint nice and it aint respectful either." "Sorry nan I was only going to ask what this place is?" Nan came back at her with a bit of a telling off. "Yeah, well there's better ways of asking and it don't involve swearing." Lorraine had a bit of a silent giggle to herself because nan's not exactly innocent on the language front, and Lorraine remembers her effing and blinding like a goodun most days when she was alive.

The white door closed behind them which freaked Lorraine out a bit because there was no wind, and there was nobody standing behind them. Lorraine was soaking in the atmosphere of the hallway. From the front door there were three steps that took them down and further into the hallway. The floor had large black and white tiles, which you would think would give a cold feel but they didn't. There was a large mahogany door both to the left and right of them, which led onto two large reception rooms, and again they were massive. Ahead of them was a grand flight of stairs, Lorraine was thinking what a great flight of stairs they would be for a bride to have her photos taken on the day of her wedding. She thought better of saying that to her nan though in case she got in trouble with her again.

The door on the right of her opened by itself and this time, Lorraine turned to her nan for some assurance that all was OK. Marge pointed her finger to the room with the open door as she said "go on darling, go on through, you'll be fine." Lorraine was scared, she looked towards the open door, and then back at her nan and said "come with me nan, I'm scared." "No, not this time, but I will be right here waiting for you, and don't worry you're gonna be alright." Lorraine walked towards the door apprehensively, pushed her two shoulders back and went through the door. She was right it was a large room, and somehow it felt familiar to her, like she had been there before. The first thing she noticed was how bright it was, and she loved the windows, the shape of them looked very gothic to her. The room looked onto a beautiful wood or forest with a path for those who wanted to walk through them. The leaves on the trees were so rich in colour, which automatically gave a feel of a good crisp winter's morning and Lorraine loved that feeling. To her, it felt heavenly. When she took a closer look around there were some of her belongings placed about the room. There wasn't much in the way of furniture but there were two chairs facing each other. "At least I can sit down this time" she said out loud.

Contrary to Lorraine's expectations the furnishings although quite minimal weren't dull, dark and dingy. In fact the whole theme in the room was light, beautiful and relaxing. She walked around the room and she could see that on the shelves and sideboards that were around the room there seemed to be items from each year of her life. So for example, her first baby hairbrush, her favourite teddy bear that she took to bed with her every night from the age of about three years old. There was her first school photo and the more she walked around the room the more she saw which really summed up her life. It even had photos of her and Adam on their wedding day. She felt a tad embarrassed when she looked at that photo in particular because she was heavily pregnant at the time. She started to stroke Adam's face in the photograph, "I had forgotten about this picture, look at Ad." she thought, "he really was gorgeous. I see a lot of him in Harry. Oh what I would give to be back there now", she said out loud. Even at that time she wasn't thinking of the beautiful baby she was carrying, instead she was thinking of Adam. So typical of her to think about her and Adam instead of the child she was carrying. One thing's for sure she was still very much a child herself, that's always been the problem. At least now she will be able to reflect on the kinds of childish behaviours and actions she took through her life, and how it impacted others. That familiar feeling came over her again, but she knew instinctively it was nothing to do with the memorabilia that had been placed around this room. No, this familiarity goes far deeper than just recognising some objects.

Lorraine was not only scared but she was also getting impatient. "When's someone gonna come and see me? I can't be doing with all this waiting. Come to think of it, what is the time? It feels like I've been waiting forever." Lorraine was hoping someone was having a laugh at her expense and that someone was gonna pop out from behind the curtains and shout "April fool." Of course that wasn't going to happen, and on one level she knew that. Lorraine was only sitting in her seat for a few moments when she had a feeling that someone was standing behind her. She quickly turned around, and she was right, there was someone else in the room. There was a man in a First World War uniform. He was about the same age as her and quite good looking she thought. "Who are you?" she said in quite a firm tone, he didn't answer. He started to draw close to her and as he did she watched every move he made. He started to walk towards the second chair that was directly in front of her, and as he took his seat, Lorraine couldn't help but think what gorgeous eyes he had. For a few moments her thinking was distracted by the soldier's eyes and she started to go off at a tangent again thinking about Adam because she always thought he had nice eyes.

She went deep into thought at that point, but was soon brought back by the soldier when he replied to her question. "My name is Alfred, and I am your guide." "My guide?" Lorraine's voice became high pitched as she went back at him, "my Guide, what the hell are you talking about? I aint got no guides, cos if I did they would have helped me out all those times I needed 'em, in fact, if you're my guide where the bloody hell were you when I needed you?" she asked in an emotional voice. Alfred kept his voice at a gentle level as he answered her question "I am your birth guide and I was assigned to you when you were born." Lorraine didn't believe all this rot, and she said so. "You must think I was born yesterday." "Okay let me explain" said Alfred, "I agreed to watch over you before you were born and were still in your mother's womb. I have watched over you throughout your life, I was there in the good times as well as the bad." Lorraine was sounding angry as she snapped at Alfred, "ok, two things, what exactly does a guide do? And why haven't I ever met you before if you've always been in my life?" "Oh but we have met before, many times" replied Alfred quite sharply. Lorraine was startled at his answer and just sat and said nothing. All this was too much for her to take and Alfred knew this.

"Look you're really confusing me Alf, and to be honest I just want to go home." Lorraine was becoming emotional as she said this. She missed her home and she had started to miss her kids. Alfred shared the bad news "Lorraine this is your home now, you have made your spiritual transition back home." "Speak plain English will ya, what do you mean? I've made my transition back home? Are you telling me that my nan was right, and I'm dead?" Alfred gently answered "Yes, that was the reason why your nan met you, that was the reason why you could see and hear her. She was there to help you make that first step, and that's the reason why she's waiting outside for you now." Lorraine just sat there taking it all in. After a while she asked who were looking after her children, and was quite pleased when she heard that her long standing friend Charlie was going to have the children, because there wouldn't be anyone else she would want the children to go to. As Lorraine thought about how lovely Charlie is, she felt sad and embarrassed about the way she treated her over the years! She was so lucky that Charlie stuck around and put up with it all. Lorraine took a deep breath and asked "ok then, what's next? Have I gotta repent my sins or somefink?"

Alfred gently answered "no, not quite, but you will be reflecting on the kind of life you led." Lorraine didn't fancy that at all because she knew she wasn't squeaky clean and prim like. "Oh" Lorraine said sheepishly, "ok, I guess I haven't got a choice have I?" "Yes Lorraine, you always have a choice, and you have a free will, but, if you chose not to work with us guides and elders, then you won't be progressing forward to reach your purpose, because you still have a purpose, you just don't know it yet." "What do you mean we all have a purpose? If I'm dead, then I'm dead aint it, I've lived past my purpose, I've expired love. if ever I had a purpose, it's no use working with it now so it's too late to make amends." "It's not quite as simple as that Lorraine", Alfred responded, "as you will see once you start to move forward."

Lorraine dropped her shoulders, "so explain it all to me then. It looks like I haven't got anything else to do", Lorraine said as she looked around. "Ok but don't expect to understand it all straight away", Alfred warned. He started by giving some positive hope for Lorraine to hold on to. "Firstly, let me assure you that although you have passed to spirit, it doesn't mean you are dead, because, you see, it's only our bodies that die, and not our spirit or soul. If we truly die, would I be here, talking to you?" He asked, but he didn't expect an answer so he didn't wait for a reply, and just carried on. "I'm still here to tell the tale, and as you can see I am larger than life, and so are you with your temperament and anger that you have right now. All your feelings are alive, not dead, all that you feel in your heart is very much alive. The love that you feel for your children, and the rest of your family, they will always be in your heart, and you can't lose that." With every word Alfred said he was trying to reassure Lorraine that she was going to be ok. "I know you may not believe this at the moment but if you work with us, you will find the peace and happiness you were looking for in your earthly life." "Oh if only", Lorraine thought out loud! Although this was only the start of Lorraine's lessons, she was starting to take everything in and getting a grasp of what was being said.

Lorraine was still on the defensive and it showed through her voice when she asked "why is there all this stuff around me that reminds me of my childhood, why would you have it? To be honest I find that a bit freaky, it aint right." Lorraine paused in the hope that Alfred would answer her questions, which he did. "I haven't been collecting them for any reason other than to help you to become familiar with your environment and help you to reflect back to your life on earth." Alfred could see Lorraine's mind ticking over. "But why do I need to reflect back? It's too late to do anything about it now." Alfred immediately came back with "it's never too late Lorraine."

"Explain" Lorraine demanded, but this time it wasn't as sharp as it had been before. Alfred decided that was enough for now, and as he stepped back his parting shot was to remind Lorraine that he was there for her, and all she has to do is call for him when she's ready to take learn more. "I know your nan is waiting for you to join her, and I know you have some people here that you would love to see." Alfred stepped back and disappeared as quickly as he arrived. Lorraine sat and pondered for a few moments but then nan came through the door, looked over and said, "come on Rainey, you've finished here for now, and there's plenty of people wanting to say hello."

Lorraine looked inquisitively and followed Marge out. She had already learned that nan is as much in charge here as she was when they lived "downstairs" as Lorraine would say. Again they were walking back along the path that led them to the white house. The glow that embraced not only mother nature but also embraced Lorraine and nan was so warm and beautiful that Lorraine was enjoying every moment of basking in this golden glow. For the first time since she arrived Lorraine realised that actually she felt quite well, and even though she didn't understand and was nervous with all that was going on, she didn't have that horrible headache that she normally woke up with. She was going to share that with nan, but thought better of it because she knew she would call it a hangover and she wasn't gonna give her the pleasure of saying that.

They were approaching a large square courtyard, and Lorraine could see a beautiful fountain, with water that looked so refreshing and cool. On each side of this square courtyard were large mahogany doors, that sat in arched frames. Marge looked directly in front of her, and started to walk towards one of the doors, Lorraine followed behind. As they opened the door and walked in Lorraine couldn't believe it but standing in front of her was her granddad whose name was Bill. Her excitement could be seen by all present as she shouted "Oh my God, Gramps, I can't believe it, you're here, and I can see you." "And if you come over here you can touch me too." said gramps with a real cheekiness in his voice. Lorraine and her gramps were very close, even closer than Lorraine with her nan. She ran into her grandad's arms, and her emotions overwhelmed her for a short while. Once she caught her breath she looked around and there in front of her was her aunt Christine, "bloody hell, I'm getting to see you all. I've thought about you guys very often, three of my favourite people. As lovely as it is to see you guys, I would have preferred to be with you all when I was old and grey, and not as young as I am." Lorraines' tears started to flow. Grandad Bill moved forward and held her tight, which helped a little, but she was still feeling lost and shocked that she has passed over into the Spirit world as she had been told a number of times since she got there.

Lorraine looked at her aunt Christine, or Chrissy as she called her. Chrissy greeted her with, "hi ya babe" Lorraine looked at her aunt and replied with a wink and said with a smile "hi ya Chris, fancy meeting you 'ere." Christine and Lorraine were also close, and in fact there were many similarities between them. "You still listening to the Bee Gees?" asked Lorraine, "yeah course, you know me and my music, and none of that changes just cos I'm ere." "Really?" Lorraine asked. "Yeah, in fact in many ways it's a lot better than life down there." Lorraine found that a strange statement her aunt had just made, and at this point she wasn't sure if she believed it. "Yeah well I'm curious to find out about all this." said Lorraine in a sarcastic voice. "But for now, it's time to enjoy being back with the people that I love so much. I have missed you all. You're all diamonds."

As her loved ones gathered around her, Lorraine was still taking it all in, and she was loving that all her family were gonna look after her. It's been a long time since anyone's looked after me, she thought, but then she felt a tinge of guilt and embarrassment as she remembered how Charlie was always there for her throughout the years no matter what, and looked after her no matter what, and never did she thank her. Her mind was full of questions, but no answers yet, however,

Lorraine was learning one thing for sure and that was that she was a nightmare, and very demanding to be around, especially for Charlie. "Oh if only I could say sorry to her now. I'm gonna miss her." Marge could see Lorraine was reflecting on her life and wondered whether she should open up and talk to her. "Penny for your thoughts Rainey?" said Marge in a gentle tone. Lorraine looked over and just blurted out "oh nan, I was a nightmare to so many people, and that doesn't make me feel good, I must have been hard work. Is that how it's gonna be from now on, you know", she paused and then continued "me realising I'm sad cos of what I was like. I've been told I have as much a purpose 'ere as I did have when I was alive. I can't see that myself, I just fink I'm being punished. They say that we have to face all this when we get up 'ere."

Marge continued to listen without saying a word. She knew that although Lorraine might not see it yet, this was an important breakthrough for her, because she was reflecting, and she was realising what her actions were like and the effect it had on others. Lorraine was still doing all the talking, but as she paused Marge jumped in and said, "blimey Rainey I can't get a word in at all with you!" She said with a wink and a smile. "Realising all this isn't about punishment, it's about taking responsibility and allowing your spirit or soul to evolve. If you take a look at all that you did and all that happened to you, can you really say that you had peace and happiness in your life? Cos if you did you certainly didn't show it while I was there." Both ladies remained silent for a while, but in the end Lorraine defensively started to speak out "Yeah, I was really happy when me and Ad were together, and of course when I had the kids." Marge couldn't help herself when she blurted out, "It's because you weren't happy in the first place that you turned to Adam." "Nan!" Lorraine shouted, "that's not true!" "it is darling", Marge continued "you were searching for a knight in shining armour to race along on his horse, sweep you off your feet look after you for the rest of your life and make you happy. You had rose coloured spectacles on sweetheart."

Deep down Lorraine knew that her nan was right, even if she wasn't admitting it! She did always rely on others to look after her, but it wasn't because she didn't want to be her own person, it was because she didn't know how to be her own person. She didn't have a great sense of self worth due to the way she was brought up. She was never really given any love by her parents, and they certainly never had any time for her. She spent her life feeling as though she wasn't worthy of love, that she didn't exist. Her nan and grandad were more like her parents, and they did all they could but even so, it wasn't enough, and she spent the rest of her life craving for someone to validate that she was worthy of love. Marge looked straight into Lorraine's eyes and gently said, "it's time to be honest and up front and work with your guides, they will help you to find out who you truly are, but you will also learn so much more. It may be hard right now, but trust me, trust us all, you can get through this." Lorraine knew that her nan wouldn't lie to her, so even though she didn't trust all that was happening, she decided that she would go with it.

Lorraine's children had been dreading this day, because it meant they had to say goodbye to their mum. Lorraine was able to watch over the service viewing remotely, and once again nan was with her. "Oh nan, look there are the kids." Lorraine was so excited to see them but she was also hurting, because more than anything she wanted to hug them and tell them that she will always love them. "Oh my God, look at 'em, they're being so strong." "I'm so proud of 'em all." Charlie was there with her family which pleased Lorraine as she knew Charlie would get the kids through it. Lorraine was hoping that Ad would be there, if not to say goodbye to her, then for the kids, but no, there was no sign of him. "The bugger" she said out loud, "he's not even there for our kids. What kind of person is he?" That was more a statement than a question. Her mind was full of all that she was realising. He made so many promises, and not one did he stick to. He let the kids down, big time, and between the pair of us we left the kids feeling pretty crap about themselves.

This was the first time Lorraine had ever dealt with any painful situation like this without a drink inside her. This time she felt her pain, but also for the first time ever she could relate to how the kids felt about their parents and about themselves.

"Oh look at Morgan, she's being so strong for all three of them, bless her. That's my girl, she's really being like their mum don't you think nan?" Lorraine's nan was a bit shocked at that question, as it was always apparent to her that poor Morgan had to be Lacey and Harry's mum, because Lorraine was too busy being the child. "I'm afraid Rainey, Morgan is used to being their mum, she had enough practice when you were incapable, so yes it's lovely she's looking after them, it's just a shame that she felt she had to be like a mum to 'em." Lorraine was gob smacked when her nan said all that, and found herself feeling very embarrassed because she knew it to be true. "Blimey nan, you don't hold any punches do you." she said quite sharply, but again it wasn't a question it was more like a statement. Lorraine continued, "I would have thought that you would be a little bit more thoughtful for me nan, after all it is the day of my funeral. You never used to be like this down there, well at least I never saw this side to you, it's totally different to how I remembered you."

Right at this point Lorraine really needed a hug, but she wasn't going to ask her nan for it because she felt that nan was really angry with her, so she placed her focus back on the children at her funeral. Lorraine could see Charlie hold Harry's hand, yes, thought Lorraine, he's gonna be the one it hits the hardest because we had a special bond, and he was always around me. Not quite true, because a lot of the time Lorraine was too busy being spaced out thanks to the vodka she drank on a day to day basis to build any kind of bond with her kids. Lorraine was starting to learn what she had put the kids through.

Morgan was standing strong, but inside she felt like she was going to collapse. Charlie was keeping an eye on her, and Morgan knew if it gets too much, she can let Charlie know and she will support her. At that point watching Morgan, Lorraine's heart was in bits feeling so much pain because she wasn't with them, that her time had run out, and there was still so much she needed to say. "Oh nan, I just want to reach out to them", she said in a shaky voice. Lorraine's nan turned to her and said "focus on them with all your might, and let them know that you're there." "What do you mean nan? Are you telling me I can get through to them to let them know I'm here?" Lorraine asked. "Can I say something to them now?" Lorraine was full of questions about what had just been said and that she may be able to let the kids know she's with them. "Oh nan that would be great if I can let 'em know." Nan only answered one question out of the barrage that Lorraine was sending her way and said, "yes babe you will be able to speak to them soon, but not today. Today is for them to say goodbye to you, don't confuse them now." Nan had given Lorraine some hope, and something to hang onto.

Naturally as Lorraine continued to watch her own funeral, which, felt really strange to her, her main focus was the children. Her heart truly went out to them as she saw how upset they were and she just wanted to give them the biggest hug she could, and she also wanted to reassure them that everything is going to be OK. But, she couldn't do that, she thought. Or could she? All of a sudden Morgan felt as though her mum was around her, and yes, she was feeling that energy like a hug. Although there had been some pretty dark times with her mum, there were also a lot of lovely times when she was younger, and when mum was a bit more of a mother in her early days. In those times there were an awful lot of cuddles, especially when mum wasn't drinking. She had that feeling again, that feeling that mum was looking after her. She didn't question that it was mum, she just knew it was.

Lorraine was also experiencing this beautiful moment between them both, and she was loving the connection. Lorraine took this moment to whisper gently into Morgan's ear. "You're doing so well darling, stay strong and know that I will always love you." Morgan heard it, she knew mum was looking after them, and just as she heard it one of Lorraine's favourite songs that the children chose for her funeral "I will always Love you" by Whitney Houston was played. Just at that point, that feeling that her mum was standing next to her grew stronger, which gave her so much comfort.

Nan knew what was going on, and she also felt such comfort to know that Morgan felt as though her mum was with her. Lorraine was so excited about what had just happened and could hardly contain herself when she was telling her nan all about it, not that she needed the explanation but she just let Lorraine get on with it. "God nan, I didn't expect that to happen. I was actually talking to Morgan and I know she heard me. That's amazing, I always said I didn't believe in this stuff, but deep down I was always hoping that there was a place where we all congregated and we all got to meet each other again one day, just like how I've met up with you."

Nan was thinking how Lorraine was back to being that excited little girl that she was when she was 10 years old, which she loved. "I know darling, it's lovely when you realise that you can leave different messages for them, just to say you're there." As nan said this, Lorraine was already miles ahead of her with her thinking, how she can let the children know she is with them. "What are the other ways we can do it nan?" "Oh there's plenty of ways", replied Marge "and you will learn them over time. What's important now is that they know you're near them now." Lorraine agreed, "yeah you're right as always." They both continued to watch over the children and Charlie as they all said their goodbyes. Lorraine's heart was breaking as the service started to come to an end because she didn't want to say goodbye just yet. "No, not yet!" she shouted, "I'm not ready to see you go." Marge grabbed Lorraine and gave her the biggest hug as the children were starting to leave. She gave some words of comfort and reassured Lorraine that they will be able to watch over the children, especially when they need to feel her around, and perhaps, one day, Lorraine will get a message to them via a medium. But for now, she still had a lot more work to do and so much more to focus on.

Lorraine was starting to understand what was going on, and she was also starting to think that this aint' such a bad place to be. Yeah she knew that she was going to have to do a lot of work on herself, but now none of this seemed so fearful, in fact, she had received nothing but love from everyone. Yes, she'd had a few sharp words from nan, but she knew that was out of love. She had a little giggle to herself because she knew nan was just trying to keep her on track, and if anyone can, nan can. She also realised that Alf as she called him, was nice as well, even though she wasn't that nice to him. Lorraine's face started feeling quite hot at that point, hot with embarrassment. "Ok nan, I'm ready to start moving forward, what have I got to do?" "Well, you can start by calling Alfred and asking him to work with you, and then you can listen to the guidance he and other guides will give you and work with it. I mean really work with it", continued nan.

"So what did Alf mean when he said 'I still had a purpose", asked Lorraine. Nan started with "Well you always did have a purpose when you were on earth and you still have that purpose here in our spiritual home." She continued "I know life didn't go the way you wanted it too, and I know it was hard, which was why you turned to the drink, but in amongst all that look at what you did achieve." "Like what?" Lorraine asked. "Well, look at the children, you've got three beautiful kids that are so generous, thoughtful and caring, and you were responsible for that." Lorraine replied "Yeah they are pretty great aren't they." Marge agreed and continued "There was a lot more that you did too, because your life wasn't all bad, and you gave me so much joy when you were a child, you were my baby." Lorraine smiled because it was so lovely to hear that.

Nan decided to take this conversation onto a deeper level now as she knew it was sinking in. "When we first get here, we need to reflect back on the kind of life we led, not to be punished but to see how far we grew as a person, as well as how we impacted others. The two worlds are always working together to bring a balanced evolution within the universe. There's a bigger picture that needs to be looked at here, in our own environment how did we treat others? How would that have affected them? We all played a part in either helping others or bringing them down. It doesn't mean that we're bad people though, it just means that we weren't strong enough to change. We are all energy, everything we see is energy even the most solid of items like a table is energy, as well as our emotions, our feelings, our thoughts, and not forgetting the kind of actions we took. How much do you think all of this negative energy affects the universe?" Lorraine went straight back at nan defensively. "I dunno do I." "I'm not talking about you personally Rainey, I'm talking about all of us, we're all guilty. When we pass over we start to realise the part we played in it all, but more importantly it's important to recognise that all of our purpose is to help others, to lift someone up when they're down and struggling, it's our purpose, to learn how we can balance out evolution within the universe to bring peace into the world, and it's extremely important to bring the two worlds together as the family that we are, God's family, and create the peace that's so needed." Nan was on a roll "once we learn how, we can help change negative energies that impacts the universe and brings such sadness to the world, then we can open up people's minds, we can give wisdom, support and love from all that we learn from here. Through the work we do with our guides and elders we have the opportunity to put something back into life, help where we can, and make a difference". Lorraine was motivated and ready, asking "where do I start?"

Lorraine started to see that by working on herself now that she was in the Spirit world she can still give her children the strength and comfort that they need, because she will be able to let them know through a medium that she's ok and is learning so much stuff about herself, but what she wanted to say more than anything in the world was that she loves them more than anything, and that she was so very sorry for the way she treated them.

But there was more to this because for the first time ever Lorraine had realised that she can help others too, which is something that she's never seen in herself before. "I can make a difference." Lorraine said to her nan. "Yes, you can my darling, and you can be proud."

Nan was over the moon because she could see that although Lorraine had a very long way to go, she was ready to work with her guides. She was ready to make difference.

Chapter 2

IAN

Ian opened his eyes and wondered what the hell had hit him. He was with a young and beautiful lady who he doesn't remember meeting before. She was no older than 26 years, beautifully dressed in an orange sari that had gold braid woven into it. She had very long black hair and she looked immaculate. He looked around and recognised nothing, he didn't know where he was, or how he got there, and he certainly didn't remember meeting this young lady before. "Sorry, I don't mean to be rude, but who are you?" he asked. "It's just that I don't remember meeting you before, and for that matter I don't know where I am or how I got here. Do you know how I got here?" he asked. The beautiful young lady looked at him with her gentle eyes and her voice, just as gentle, responded to Ian's question "yes I know how you got here, and yes I know where you are which I will explain to you, but first let's talk about the last thing you remember Ian.?" Ian sat quiet for a few moments, and then it started to come back to him, "I remember walking down by the canal which is a shortcut to get home from my local pub to where I live." Ian was staring intently on the ground as he recalled, "I remember being a bit apprehensive because there were three young guys up ahead, and as soon as they spotted me, they started to fan out and walk towards me. They had thick winter jackets on and they had their hoods up, and because it was also dark I didn't get to see their faces. Shit, they attacked me! I can see them doing it now."

Ian was a 38 year old man who was born and brought up in Coventry with his two younger sisters. He had a good relationship with all of his family, and was very close to them. He had been engaged in his late 20's but it didn't work out for him and his then partner, so they decided to split. Since then

Ian had had a couple of girlfriends for a short while, but nothing serious. He was a forklift truck driver for a big warehouse company based on an industrial estate just outside Coventry, and was a popular guy with all of his workmates. He had his own little flat and kept himself very much to himself. The one pleasure that he enjoyed was to go down to his local pub every Tuesday to play darts with his mate, and as it was Tuesday on the night in question he was on his way home from his local.

It was all coming back to Ian now, he left the pub at closing time and was walking along by the canal and he noticed three lads laughing and joking quite loudly. They were stood there very closely to each other and yes, they did look suspicious. They spotted Ian and started to fan out so that he couldn't pass, they had blocked his path. He tried to stay calm and just said "excuse me please", but they were having none of it. One guy in particular started to push him and started swearing at him. "Give us your f*****g money weirdo" he shouted, and Ian could tell he was the ringleader. Ian just stopped dead and said, "look guys I don't want any trouble, I just want to go home", he was hoping that they would just walk away, but he knew really that wasn't going to happen and realised that this situation was getting very serious. The ringleader started to push him with a lot of force and started to shout obscenities at him. Ian started hitting out as he tried to defend himself, but that only made things worse as two of the lads just grabbed hold of him and pinned his arms behind his back giving the ring leader the opportunity to punch hell out of him until Ian was unconscious. "Go on Brett, knock the shit out of him", shouted one of the other boys. The ringleader he now knew was called Brett, shouted back "keep your f****** mouth shut you moron." Once they realised he had become unconscious they let him drop to the ground and went through his pockets to see what was worth taking, laughing while they did it. Sadly for them Ian never really carried a lot of cash, he just had his phone, a credit card, and a little bit of cash. "Result" said one of them as they pulled the money out of his pocket. At this point, although Ian was unconscious, he still stood a chance if someone found him in time, but these boys took it one step further and rolled him over the edge of the canal and into the water. There was no way he was going to be able to survive that.

Ian had also remembered that even though he was unconscious he knew what was happening as he was tossed into the water. He knew that he was dying. At first he panicked as he felt his life literally being washed away from him and there was nothing he could do, his thoughts went straight to his family and his love for them and how important they always were to him. Once Ian knew there was no going back he quite calmly allowed himself to float over into the spirit world, and the closer he got, the more at peace he became.

Ian's beautiful guide sat there and listened very closely. He looked over at her as she sat with him, and once Ian had finished recalling his passing he looked at her and waited for her to say something, which she duly did. "That was a truly traumatic passing you endured Ian." Ian could tell, as she said this, she had a lot of empathy for him. The young lady continued, "Welcome Ian, I see you have remembered everything so I do not need to explain anything. My name is Nasreen and I am here to welcome you back to your spiritual home." "Spiritual home, you're welcoming me back to my spiritual home" he replied questioningly, "have I been here before then?" Nasreen replied "Yes, you have indeed, but I will explain that all to you later. I am here to help you in any way I can." Ian immediately thought of his family, "have my family been told?" he continued, "yes they have been told and they are doing as well as can be expected."

"Oh my God, I feel for them so much", Ian said with tears in his eyes. "They used to say to me that I shouldn't take that shortcut down by the canal because there are a lot of gangs that hang around there, but I didn't take any notice. I used to tell them that I am a big boy now, and can look after myself." He paused for a moment and then continued, "Obviously I couldn't, I wasn't as good at looking after myself as I thought." There was silence between the two at that point just so that Ian could take in all that had happened. Ian brought his attention back and looked at Nasreen. "Sorry, do we know each other? Or are you an angel coming to look after me or something?" "I'm not an angel but I am your guide." "My guide? Yeah" he said as he nodded his head "I've heard about guides that are meant to help us through our lives, and funnily enough I was reading something about that a few weeks ago, so I understand a little bit of what you're talking. So does that mean you're my birth guide, or whatever it is that means you're with us from birth? I have to say you look too young to be dead." Nasreen had a little smile on her face as she said, "There's no age limit for when we are allowed to die, that's up to our God, but I am glad you understand a little about what happens. Although I am your guide I am not your birth guide. I'm just here to help you at this point." Ian was confused and it showed on his face. "Ok I'll go with this if it's going to help me to settle down to what's happened. Just one question though, who is my birth guide? And when do I get to meet them?" Nasreen didn't answer at that point, but Ian sensed that he could trust all would be revealed through time.

Nasreen stood up and gestured Ian to follow her. They started to walk through a beautiful forest full of nature, full beautiful flowers with all different kinds of insects and bees, butterflies, and so many more different kinds of species flying about. Ian loved it because he loved nature and always took every opportunity to be with it as much as he could which wasn't too easy because he lived in the centre of town. At weekends though he very often took time to get out into the open air on his bike and feel at one with nature. That's where he did his thinking and got things straight in his mind about what was important in life. He found by meditating like this he could work out the important things in life and he learned it certainly wasn't possessions. As they walked Ian brought up how he died and started to ask questions about the way he died. "What happened to me is murder isn't it?" he asked. "They took my life away from me, and although I'm not a vindictive man I do want to know that they are caught so that they don't do this to anyone else. They can't be allowed to do this to another family."

Nasreen understood where Ian was coming from as she had her life taken from her through a hit and run driver, and although it's slightly different to what happened to Ian, the fact remained that both of them had abruptly had their lives taken away from them by someone else within a matter of seconds. Nasreen listened to Ian and decided to share her story about how she passed with him, as she knew it's nice to have someone that understands what you're going through. "I Understand how you feel right now Ian, I had my life taken away from me by a hit and run driver!" Ian stopped in his tracks "Really?" "Yes really" Nasreen replied. "I lived on the outskirts of Leeds in Yorkshire. I had a good job as a human resources manager and was going places. It was about 7pm on a cold winter's eve when I was on my way home. Sadly I was later than usual as I had been busy at work. I had just got off the bus at the top of my road. It was a busy main road and quite dark even though there was some street lightning. As I made my way down the road I heard a screech coming from a car and stopped to look around. All of a sudden the car mounted the pavement and I was hit and died immediately. I didn't get a chance to get out of the way, he just came at me too fast."

Ian listened intently "Did they catch him?" he asked. "Yes, thankfully they did, and that felt good to know he didn't get away with it." "Were you angry Nasreen?" Ian asked. Nasreen turned and looked at Ian and said, "yes I was at first, I had a husband, a child and a big family. I was angry because I was so young and had so much life to live, and he ripped that from me and my family." Nasreen turned to face Ian and asked if he was feeling angry. "I don't know really, I don't think I've had enough time for it all to sink in yet. To be honest I'm too busy worrying about my family and how they're taking it, to worry about how I feel. Do you know how they are Nasreen?" He asked Nasreen tentatively. He continued "they say when we die we can look down and see our families, is that true?" Ian looked at Nasreen and asked "Can I see my family? I really need to see them." he said as he held back the tears. Ian watched her as she said nothing for a few moments but he could see her weighing things up.

Nasreen agreed that Ian could see his family briefly, but that he needed to prepare himself for things, in particular the heartbreak he will see and experience. "Remember she said, your family are grieving your loss which is bad enough, but for you to pass in such a way will be very hard for them to come to terms with." Ian was so grateful that he was going to get this chance. "But first let's make sure we can sit and make ourselves comfortable", requested Nasreen.

Ian was fully expecting to be looking down over his family like you see in the films, but to his surprise it was like he was actually in the room with them and it reminded him of the film "Scrooge" where Spirit takes him into his past, present and future. In that film Scrooge could see and hear the people that were in his life, but they couldn't see or hear him, and they weren't aware that he was there. Well, to Ian that was how it felt which made him have a little chuckle. The chuckling stopped as all of a sudden he saw his mum dad and two sisters sitting in his parent's living room talking about Ian's murder. Ian felt uncomfortable and so emotional, he just wanted to reach out, comfort them and tell them that he was OK. He felt the hurt they felt, and now he felt the anger they felt. Nasreen reassured him that what he was experiencing was quite normal under the circumstances, and also told him that she experienced all of those feelings when she first passed over and watched over her family and felt their grief. For the first time since he arrived in the Spirit world, he was angry.

Chief Superintendant Steven Cooper was very empathic with their loss and tried to keep them in the loop as much as he could without revealing too much of the details until he had all the facts in front of him. Ian's father, Peter, was the main speaker for the family, and at that point they were trying to ascertain what had happened on that night. "Do you know exactly what happened?" Peter asked. The Superintendant looked at Peter, hesitated and then decided to give him all the information they had so far. "I'm afraid your son had been badly beaten up before he went into the water and the coroner felt that by the time he hit the water he was already unconscious so the chances are high that he wouldn't have known very much at that time." "What? What's he saying? That's total rot! I did feel everything as I was going down and dying. I did panic but I wasn't able to do anything. I may have been unconscious, but I was still aware of what was happening." Ian was struggling to stay calm at this point, but thankfully Nasreen was able to calm him down. "Ian, as much as I know it hurts, if you want to continue to look over to see what's happening, you're going to have to listen to some of this. Remember, they are still alive, so they truly have no idea what happens as a person is dying, unless of course they have had near death experiences, which the majority of people don't have on their life CV." Ian looked over at her, nodding and agreeing that he would stay calm whilst they were watching over the family.

Ian's mum Anne, was breaking her heart and sobbing as she heard how Ian died. "How can people do this to another person?" she said, "Don't they have a conscience about what they've done?" "In my experience Mrs Murray, there are many that don't have a conscience I'm afraid" said the Superintendant. Anne Murray looked at him in absolute disbelief. Ian's father continued with his questions, "So, have you got the people that did this yet?" he asked. The Superintendant looked down to the floor as he answered "no, not yet, but we are doing our best to find them." As Peter nodded his head, he asked "have you got any leads yet?" "Yes sir, we have. There was someone walking with his dog along the other side of the canal around that time, but because of it being so dark, he couldn't see much, although he was aware that they were in heavy winter coats that had hoods, which the boys had up so he couldn't get a good look at them. He believes there were maybe two of them, they were loud, swearing and shouting as they walked down the canal path. We also found some footprints that forensics are working with right now, so hopefully that will open up some more options." Ian couldn't believe what the Superintendant had said, about only being two of them. "No, he shouted, no, there were three of them. Three of them" he repeated.

Ian looked over at Nasreen as though she was going to be able to fix this situation. "Well" he asked, "can't you do something about this? I want all three of them caught, not just two of them." Nasreen didn't respond at that point which annoyed Ian, but he turned towards the family and focused again on what was being said. Ian's family sat with the Superintendant for a little while longer as he reassured them that they are doing their best. The family were happy that the police were working hard and doing their best in bringing his killers to justice. Nasreen decided it was time to have a bit of a chat with Ian about natural laws. "Ian, I know you are reacting to the fact that they haven't got your murderers yet, and I know you are feeling like they are going to get away with it, but believe me, they won't." Ian looked inquisitive as Nasreen continued. "When I was killed I was very happy to see that the guy that ran me over didn't get away with it. I wanted justice, I wanted punishment for having my life taken away from me which was a natural reaction to what had happened, there was a big part of me that wanted him to be punished for what he did. I wanted karma. Is that how you feel right now?" Ian thought for a moment, started nodding his head and said, "Yep that's exactly how I feel. I want them to get caught so that they don't hurt anyone else, but I also want them to suffer for what they've done to me and my family. Yeah, I guess I want karma, is that so bad." "No, it's not bad, but it isn't right either." replied Nasreen.

Ian jumped in quickly and defensively. "Oh you're not going to get all holy on me are you Nasreen? I couldn't cope with that." She came back at him. "No, I'm not getting all holy, but I am trying to help you see the effects of your thought process right now." "What do you mean?" asked Ian. "One of the things I have learned since I got here, is that we never get away with anything because if we don't answer to our actions whilst we're living our human life, we sure as hell will once we get here." "I'm not with you." replied Ian. Nasreen continued, "Let me explain. You have led a good life, always with a thought on how to help others and to be there when people needed you, right?" "Right" answered Ian, "Well there will still be things that you reflect on within your life, and learn from them, but on the whole, you led quite a good spiritual life." Ian liked hearing Nasreen saying this and was quite proud of himself. He wasn't quite believing everything Nasreen was saying, but he would go with it he thought. "So what are you getting at about my killers then?" Nasreen continued to explain the best way she could. "Well, even if they never catch your killers, and they live their life on earth without being punished, they will not escape their actions, because they will have to face it when the time comes for them to come back home. Nobody gets away with anything Ian, not even them."

Ian wasn't at all impressed with what he was hearing and he let Nasreen know it. "I'm sorry to sound so blunt but that's a load of old bull. Reflecting back on our actions and feeling bad for the pain we have caused someone else isn't being punished. What happens after that? What happens then? Is there a prison here in the spirit word that they are thrown into? Because that's what's needed." Ian's anger was really coming out in him now, and Nasreen could see that he had a lot of things to mull over right now, which would take time. She decided to carry on trying to explain a little further for him. "No we don't have prisons here, but believe you me, their prison is their own inner fears about what's going to happen to them. Once they have to face up to their bad behaviours the more they become unwilling to work and so they never move forward, and they stay where they are, constantly being stuck in the shame of their own actions. So, in one respect they receive their own bad karma because it comes back to bite them."

Ian wasn't having any of this, because he was so intent on making sure the police keep the investigation going until they have all three of his murderers, "Yeah well, with all due respect, I'm not happy with all that, it sounds good in theory, but it feels like they're just going to get away with what they've done." Ian continued angrily, "to see my family suffer like this gives me reason enough to somehow find a way to make sure justice is done." "Ask yourself though Ian, are you wanting justice or are you out for revenge?" asked Nasreen. Being honest Ian didn't really have an answer to that question because everything felt confusing and upside down. All of a sudden Ian realised how he was speaking to Nasreen. He looked down at the floor and was obviously feeling embarrassed, which he admitted, "I'm sorry that I'm speaking to you in such a bad way, I really don't mean it, it's just that I can't bear to think of them getting away with it. I can't bear to see my family suffer like this and it's hitting me now that my life is over."

The next few days were hard for Ian as he settled into being a spirit person. Nasreen was always close by in case Ian needed her. For Ian, one of the loveliest things that happened was that he was reunited with a few people that were in his life and had passed over. Ian looked at Nasreen as he noticed that someone was walking towards him, it was someone that he knew, and he started to shout. "Oh wow there's my mate who I went to school with. Together we had so many laughs, especially after we both left school. Gray me ole mate, well, I didn't expect to see you here." Graham had a lovely big smile on his face on seeing his best mate. "Oh man, I've been waiting to hook up with you again, I just didn't expect it to be just yet." Even though both were really pleased to see each other, for Ian, as lovely as it was to see his mate it was a reminder that he was in the spirit world with him, and that he was dead.

Graham could finally explain to Ian what happened when he passed into the spirit world all those years before. Ian had loads of questions for Graham, a lot of them about how Graham died, but some of them were about exactly what it means to be in the spirit world. "Whoa, whoa, shouted Graham, stop with all the questions, just one thing at a time. I know you have a lot of questions for me, and I will answer but not quite as fast as you want. And let's not forget there are a few questions I want to ask you as well."

Nasreen walked away as she knew that the men had loads to catch up on, and Ian didn't need her at this time. "So mate what happened?" Graham asked as he looked Ian in the eye. Graham already knew but he also knew that Ian was struggling to come to terms with his death, so he was trying to get him to open up and really talk about how he was feeling. Ian looked down at his feet, and was struggling to start to tell his story. "Come on mate." Graham gently said, "We've always been able to talk about everything, and nothing's changed in that respect." Ian looked over at his school friend and said, "I was murdered! Some bastard took my life." As Ian started explaining, his emotions got the better of him which, although Ian didn't realise it, Graham knew was a positive sign. Ian was quite surprised that he was becoming overwhelmed by his emotions. Ian looked at Graham and say "Geez man, I didn't know that when we kick the bucket we still have all the same kinds of feelings that we had when we were alive. I always thought that once you died that was it, you didn't have to go through that again. And let me tell you, I really don't want to go over all this again. It's enough to come to terms with the fact that I've had my life taken away from me in a heartbeat."

Graham and Ian found themselves walking alongside a stream that had the most beautiful waterfall, and, as they stopped and turned around to admire it's beauty, Graham decided to start talking to Ian about what's entailed going from human being to a spirit being. "Ok so let me explain a few things to you mate.

Firstly, just because we're here doesn't mean to say that we're dead. It means that we have made a transition from the human part of us, into the spirit part of us that lives on; and believe you me we do live on." Ian was listening to Graham very intently, trying to take it all in, but was getting confused, so he repeated back to Graham what he had started to understand. "So we live on, we're still the person we were on earth, and we still have all the emotions that we had down there too?" "Yeah, that's about it bro." replied Graham. Ian was starting to feel angry again. "What the hell use is it to have all these emotions swimming around inside of me, how do I benefit from that?" Graham tried to reassure Ian that all was OK. "I promise that you will grow to understand all that's happening, and that we'll all be by your side."

Graham continued to explain a little bit more to Ian, "We are every bit as intelligent in this world as we were on earth, and that includes our emotions. We love the same, and we can feel just as angry or sad as we did, but this time we can work through our emotions and gain some peace. We can work through our anger and sadness, and if we commit ourselves to reflect on who we are and how we felt we can truly find peace and happiness. By doing this we learn that we can guide our families that are still living on earth, and we can also help others on earth too." Before Ian had chance to open his mouth Graham continued "And yes, this may all seem a bit airy fairy, but I swear to you it's the truth. There's no pressure here, we don't have to live up to anyone's expectations, we still have our free will, and we still enjoy our life with the people that we love that have now passed over." Graham finished what he was saying with "Just hang on in there."

Ian felt overwhelmed with all that Graham was giving him, and he needed to mull all this over. "Graham, I can't listen to any more at the moment, it's just too emotional for me. Can we talk about it all another time? I especially want to talk to you about how I can get through to my family to tell them there was a third person who played a part in my murder, but for now, I just need to think everything over." Ian also wanted to ask Graham a few questions too, especially the one question that had been on the tip of his tongue since he met up with Graham again. "Why Gray? Why did you do it?" Graham turned his head slightly and hesitated "Look mate, it was a hard time for me and I didn't know how to handle all that was happening." He continued, "Me and Lucy had been going through a tough time, and I knew she was seeing someone else, but couldn't prove it." He continued, "I lost my job, I started to drink heavily, and you know me I did like a drink. I was sinking lower and lower and didn't know where to turn. I felt like my life was going down the pan." I didn't want to live anymore, and all I could think was that my anti depressants were a way out of this dark, horrendous hole."

Ian carried on listening to his school mate and he could see that after all these years it still affected him. After the pause between them he couldn't help but ask, "Why didn't you tell me? I was your best mate, I would have helped you where I could, you knew that." Graham responded, "Yeah I know that, but it wasn't as easy as you're making it sound. For starters I didn't know how to express myself, especially not to another bloke. You knew what it was like back then, it wasn't the done thing." Ian was finding himself getting a bit frustrated because he felt Graham wasn't taking responsibility for his actions, and how it left everyone that cared for him feeling. "You knew I would be by your side no matter what you were going through, we would have got through it together." He continued by venting a little bit further and a little bit stronger, "Do you have any idea how guilty I felt when I heard what you had done? Every day I asked myself if there was anything I should have done." Ian was really starting to open up and let go. He was in tears, when he said "I felt like I had let you down." They both stood quiet for quite a while, until Graham tried to console Ian. "I know you did mate, I saw you suffer and I know you felt as though you let me down, but you really didn't, none of you did." Ian smirked as he said "Lucy did didn't she?" Graham looked over at him and replied, "Yep, she was the one person that had let me down, but to be honest I've worked through that and let go, with a lot of help from my guides and family here."

"Yeah my guide said I can work through how I feel about what happened, especially when she let me look over my family to see how they were doing through it all and I heard the police tell mum and dad that there were two that took my life not three." Ian continued "They need to know the truth, and I need you to help me tell them." Graham looked surprised "Blimey that's a tall order. I haven't got that kind of clout around here." Graham started explaining, "Just because we're spirit doesn't mean we can sort everything out from up here." Ian was disappointed but wasn't giving up, "So, do you have any idea what I can do to get the message across?" Graham replied "The only thing I can think of is if a member of the family or a friend goes to see a medium." Ian didn't like that answer much because he knew that relied on one of the family deciding to go to see a medium. "Is that it?" he asked Graham. "Yeah, afraid so mate." "But that relies on one of them going to see a medium, which means they will probably get away with it, and that's not fair." Ian responded.

Graham knew how sensitive Ian felt at this time, so he wanted to be as gentle as he could be, but he also knew that he needed to explain how things work in the spirit world. Graham carried on , "Have a little faith with this, it's probably going to take a while before all this gets sorted out down there, so there is time, and trust me, one way or another they will have to answer for their actions, if not down there, they will have to face their actions up here. Either way they're not going to get away with it." Ian answered sarcastically, "Yeah I know, Nasreen has explained how there is a universal law, that they will have to answer to up here, but I'm sorry that don't sit well with me. I want something done about it now." "Ian!" replied Graham, "You can't go demanding that things happen. That kind of attitude will only hold you back! Trust me, all will fall into place. I tell you, you'll be surprised when you see how things can be guided on a path that will bring justice. As long as it is justice, and not vengeance you want, because that will get you nowhere. Right now you're sounding very vengeful mate." Ian turned towards Graham, "No, no, it's definitely not about revenge, it is about justice." Graham wasn't so sure but decided to keep his mouth shut.

One of the things that Ian had noticed was that there's no concept of time, which was a blessing, as he didn't fancy clock watching to see how long it will take to get a message through to his family. He was also grateful that he didn't have that feeling of boredom, because that would have felt like hell for him. Ian started to see Nasreen as a friend, and someone that would help him sort out a lot of his feelings, not just about how he passed but with other issues as well. Issues such as relationships, which he felt he needed to take a good look at. He often used to think that he was never very lucky in relationships, but couldn't see why. In the end he just kept away from the opposite sex and learned to keep himself to himself. Not much fun, but safe.

Ian was getting used to now residing in the spirit world and he agreed it was now time to do some reflecting, and having Nasreens' support really helped him. She knew what it was like to have your life taken away, she knew what it was like to experience seeing her family grieving over her loss and she knew what it feels like to know that it could have been so different, which is where Ian was at this time.

Although Ian was slowly coming to terms with what had happened, he still felt a desperate need to get a message to his family about the third person also responsible for his death. It was so important to him but not for revenge, it was about justice and also to make sure they didn't devastate another family, tearing them apart. Very often he thought about how he could get through to them, and, in time Graham showed him how to draw close to them so that his sister could feel his presence convincing her that Ian was around them. The first time he started to go this close to his family wasn't long after his death and he wasn't surprised that his youngest sister felt him near because she always used to say she could feel spirit around, which is what Ian was banking on as this may guide her to go to a medium.

Although the police had caught two of the gang neither of them was the gang leader, and it seemed that the police weren't getting any closer to catching the ring leader. Ian's youngest sister Carolyn felt that there was more information to unravel regarding Ian's death but had no proof, just a feeling. Carolyn felt Ian around her strongly and did actually share with her elder sister Denise that she believed Ian was trying to get a message through to her. That feeling was so strong at times that it prompted her to find a reputable medium she should go to see. Ian was watching over Carolyn very closely as he wanted to make sure she did go to see the medium. Ian was so chuffed that in his own way he prompted Carolyn to seek out a medium, "I'm getting quite good at this being a spirit lark", thought Ian with a smile.

Carolyn turned to her sister and said, "Please Den come with me, it'll only be about an hour at the most. I just can't get rid of this feeling at the moment." At first Denise was quite reticent, but she admitted she was feeling a bit like Carolyn was describing. It would also be lovely to see if Ian was with them. In the end Denise gave in and agreed to go. "Alright alright, I give in, I'll go with you. Anything for a quiet life." The day had dawned and Carolyn was really excited about her reading. As Ian watched over her he couldn't help but chuckle because it was always Carolyn who always got excited about things, and as a result could be a real live wire. Denise, who wasn't that much older than Carolyn, never really showed her feelings, she just used to get on with life in a grounded and sometimes detached way. Denise always thought Carolyn was a bit too much over the top, and today was no exception as she saw her running around, getting ready, her mouth working ten to the dozen without taking a breath. "For God sake Carolyn, shut up. You're enough to wear the most patient of people out." "Oh don't be such an old fart Den, I can't wait to see if Ian comes through." Denise looked at her sister and as she did she could see the excitement in her eyes. Denise felt such compassion for her little sister because she knew just how easy it is for Carolyn to feel let down and despondent, which she really didn't want her to feel today. Look Cally, (Carolyn's nickname), I don't want you to pin your hopes on today, because it may not happen, and I couldn't bear to see you hurting." Carolyn was getting really frustrated because she didn't want to hear that, she wasn't even going to think like that. "Do you think I haven't thought of that." Carolyn answered quite sharply. "I know there is a chance that it won't be him, it may be nanny or gramps, but I can still hope. That's why I haven't told mum and dad because I don't want to raise their hopes either."

Carolyn felt quite comfortable booking a reading with Susan because she knew of people that had had a reading from her previously and they were more than happy. She had a damn good reputation who always works ethically and professionally at all times. They knocked on the front door and were greeted by the medium "welcome, please come in. My name is Susan, and I know one of you is Carolyn." "Oh that's me." Carolyn replied, "and this is my sister Denise. Can we go in for our reading together please? It's just that I'm a little nervous." Susan didn't mind at all, and, as the girls took their seats in the little room that Susan had showed them into, she could see that Denise was the grounded one, and was probably there to support Carolyn who wasn't quite as grounded.

The medium asked if they had had a reading before, how long ago, and what their experience was like. Carolyn gave all the answers. She also made it plain that there was someone dear to them that had passed about 6 months previous who they would love to come through. Susan, as professional as always, made no promises, in fact told the girls "I can't guarantee the person you want to come through will, but I can say that the person you need to hear from the most will hopefully come through." It's important to say this up front, so the client understands. "Yes we understand thanks Susan", replied Carolyn.

Ian had been watching over his family closely, especially his little sister because he knew she was the one that felt him the most. Ian also felt a pull towards the medium as she sat and prepared herself to work with the spirit world, which for him was wonderful. He saw this as his chance to let them know about the third person. Susan felt Ian draw close immediately, and started to give accurate information about what he was like, the fact that he passed over quickly, she even gave them his age, and hobbies. Both the girls gasped as they heard all that was being given. Carolyn was so pleased but at the same time she felt very emotional and started to cry, as did Denise, which really surprised them both.

"Oh my God, that's amazing", said Carolyn "I can't believe that." The girls were so grateful that Susan had connected so strongly with their lovely brother and they were being "reunited again" as Carolyn put it. Susan and Ian were communicating very strongly, and Susan was giving in-depth information as well as the lovely memories they all had. But things changed a bit when Susan wanted to relay Ian's message to the girls. Susan realised straight away that she was going to have to handle this situation very gently. "I know that Ian had his life taken away from him very quickly, and I do feel it was close to water." The girls were both shocked at the details Susan was giving them surrounding Ian's death which they all knew happened but were finding a bit painful to hear again. It was important for Ian that Susan continued with the message he was giving her, "he wants you to know that there was a third person involved." Carolyn and Denise looked at each other and then looked over to Susan, "No, no that's wrong, there were only two people involved, and they've got them." said Carolyn. Susan asked Ian the question again and it was the same answer that came back. "Well, I can only give you what

I'm getting, and that is that there was a third person involved who is still running around free. I keep hearing the name Brett, and I'm feeling that this person Brett is linked to your brother's death in some way. He's letting you know that this is important."

Both the girls were very shocked to hear this, and didn't know whether or not Susan was telling the truth that this was from Ian, or was she spinning them a yarn? Up until then they were so overwhelmed with the accuracy of Susan's information. Either way they were going to have to approach this very carefully for their parents' sake, and knew the police wouldn't really take this seriously. As the girls left Susan they were relatively quiet for a few moments trying to take it in. "Well what do you think about that." asked Carolyn. Denise looked at her and as she did Carolyn could see she had tears streaming down her face. "I'm not sure what we should do about it, but we can't ignore what we've been told."

Ian was delighted that he had finally got his message across, and deep down he knew that his sisters were going to try to do something about it, they weren't the kind of girls that would let something like this be ignored. Both Carolyn and Denise thought long and hard before deciding whether or not to take it seriously "After all it's only the word of a medium", said Denise at one stage. Carolyn kept saying that her gut feel was telling her to take this information to the police, because she felt in her stomach all this was true. Against all the odds they decided to talk to their parents first which turned out to be a very difficult conversation. Their mum was very much where Carolyn was but dad was totally the opposite keeping saying "What a load of utter rot, I'm surprised that you're even taking this seriously." Their dad was angry and hurting as well. After much going back and forth with the different reasons why they should or shouldn't say something it was decided that the girls would go to the police.

Although the police didn't laugh directly in their face, Carolyn and Denise felt they weren't taking things seriously, until one of the detectives that was investigating Ian's death asked the name of the medium. Once the girls Had told him he looked at them and started wanting the information that Susan gave them. "You do realise that this is not evidence that can be taken into court don't you, because it's not factual. However we will follow this lead and see where it takes us. Firstly, we will need to see if there was someone called Brett connected to the other two boys." As the girls left, they felt so much relief at being taken seriously and that it was going to be looked into.

What the sisters didn't know was that often psychics and mediums had been known to work with the police with very successful results. Susan was one such medium the police had worked with and trusted, which is why they intended to check out this information. The superintendant that was working on this case was Rob Jack, a fair man known to be a "decent copper" who always lived up to his reputation. Ian felt that it wouldn't be too long before they got the third guy so he could settle down.

Ian was right. A few days later Superintendent Rob Jack was knocking on the front door. He informed the family that they had followed the lead and when they presented the name Brett to the other two suspects, they actually confessed to Ian's murder with Brett, the ringleader who instigated it all. Once they started, they couldn't stop! Ian had led them to the gang leader through Susan, and justice would be done. Now Ian could rest in peace knowing that he will get justice for the loss of his life.

What was interesting was that Nasreen stayed by Ian's side through all that Ian was feeling and experiencing at that time, but as soon as the police had all three attackers Nasreen came to Ian to tell him that her job was now done, that he had accepted his passing and it was time for them both to move forward. This seemed quite frightening at first as Ian really trusted Nasreen, so it was going to be hard to thank her and say goodbye.

Ian had learned the beautiful world of spirit was very similar to when he was on earth. Ian grew to like taking a walk in the peace and quiet. He very often liked to walk by the side of a beautiful stream that was rather like a stream he used to walk near when he visited Ireland to see his pals. The water was as clear as day, and the peace absolutely beautiful. One day he was kneeling by the river and whilst he looked into the beautiful clear water he saw a figure standing beside him. It startled him at first, he turned around quickly, there was a man standing next to him. "Hello Ian, sorry if I startled you. My name is Bernard, I believe you have been waiting to meet me." At first Ian didn't know how to respond, but he finally got the words out "Who are you?" Bernard immediately responded, "I am your birth guide." Ian couldn't help but feel that this line belonged in a soppy chic flick, and wanted to have a little chuckle, but as with everything he was learning, he knew nothing was ever as it seemed.

Ian always being up front and honest said "Oh ok, look I'm not sure what to say." He continued, "Am I supposed to bow to you or something?" Bernard laughed quite loudly, "Nobody ever bowed to me when I was that side of the veil, so I certainly don't expect them to do it now that I am this side." Ian felt as though he was being laughed at. "OK, so what happens now?" he said irritably. Bernard started to explain where they go from here, "That rather depends on you Ian. What I mean is now that you have managed to get your message to your sisters and on to the police you have been settling down quite well, and with the help of Nasreen supporting you, you have come a long way." "Bernard continued, "are you ready to do some work now on your spiritual side?" Ian looked at Bernard as though he had two heads. "I'm not with you", he said, "I thought me and Nasreen were walking my spiritual path. I believed all we were talking about and the insights this brought was me learning about myself and mankind. Now you're kind of saying that's not the case, and that I'm only just starting now." Bernard looked over at Ian, and beckoned Ian to walk with him. As they did so, Bernard continue to explain more. "No, that isn't the case Ian, I have been watching you and Nasreen together. You are coming a long way and gaining some great insight which we can keep going if you agree to work with me. You forget, I have known you from your birth in the lifetime you have just left, so I know everything about you, and it's now time for you to gain so much more knowledge about who you truly are, and how you can help others."

Ian realised that actually it would be nice to know more about himself, and he was intrigued to find out what Bernard had said to him about this lifetime, does that mean he's had more lifetimes? It took time to find out. He was also interested in finding out more about his birth guide as he definitely doesn't look or dress like a native American or a Chinese buddha. In fact he looked very much like a man that worked manually, maybe on a building site or something like that. Oh there was so much for him to find out. Yes, Ian was settling in very nicely now. He was realising what fun he can have in the spirit world, how he can keep guiding his family through their lives, as well as still being able to be a part of all their celebrations that were to come.

Chapter 3

KENNY

Kenny had been dead for about a year after he passed with a heart attack before he was able, in the spirit world, to take responsibility for his behaviour whilst on earth. This wasn't a surprise to anyone because of the lifestyle he led.

For a start he loved to have a drink, he also loved his food, not healthy food though, instead he liked the good old fry up breakfast, as well as his cakes, sweets and anything else he could get his hands on. He was your typical heart attack just waiting to happen, and eventually it got the better of him.

He was also quite unhealthy in his choice of professions! He started off as a petty thief, and by the time he was 18 years old had been caught by the police and given a suspended sentence. However as he was going into his early twenties he started stepping it up and a couple of times he served about 9 months of 18 month sentences, so really, at that point there wasn't anything too serious, but things were about to change in that respect as he was offered an opportunity to earn some big money by being a driver for the big boys who were doing the more dangerous of jobs like armed robbery. He liked to be in with the big boys, so that he could be one of the lads. He wanted to be respected by them as well as all the other guys around them, but the most respect he got from them was for him to be their gofer, and the guy that did the dirtiest of jobs. Some of those dirtier jobs were about being a bouncer for the guys that were right up at the top of the villains ring, which was pretty dangerous in itself as they had quite a few enemies. What was sad was that he couldn't see that's all they were ever going to use him for.

Kenny was born and brought up in Aberdeen, Scotland. He didn't have the easiest of lives as his father left the family home when he was three years old. He was an only child and was brought up between his mum and his nan. Kenny was very close to his nan but not particularly close to his mum as he found her a bitter woman because of her husband leaving her to bring up their child alone, or at least that's how she saw it. His mum, Kathy was a tailor and worked in a clothing factory making jackets, coats and suits. It was a hard way to earn a living, but what it did give her was the ability to learn how to make her own clothes, as well as Kenny's, and she always had loads of work altering clothes or curtains, as well as making clothes for people. But all this made for a very lonely time for Kenny when mum was working either at the factory or when she was working at home in the evening. Kenny always looked smart as a child and his mum used to get complimented all the time about how lovely his clothes were and how he was always dressed so smartly. Kenny liked all the compliments because it made him feel important, and as a result Kenny learned to always be turned out well because he got noticed. As an adult he was always dressed immaculately too, with his polished shoes, smart trousers or jeans, and jackets to suit. He still had a full head of hair when he passed away at the age of 48 and there was never a hair out of place.

To be honest that's what his wife Lynn loved about him when she first met him whilst out clubbing one Friday night. They both fell head over heels for each other as soon as they met, and it wasn't long before they were engaged and getting ready to walk down the aisle. They were both 21 years old when they said "I do". There were a few people that thought that they were a bit too young and Lynn's parents certainly wasn't keen on their new son in law, but they just had to go with it if they wanted to stay close to their daughter. They were practically living on fresh air and promises, mainly from Kenny who was always a bit of a dreamer. Yes they did get the odd bit of help, but on the whole they were on their own. Neither Kathy nor Lynn's parents were able to help out because they didn't have a lot to give. Lynn was very close to her mum and dad as well as her sister, but money was already tight for them all. It wasn't too long before Lynn was pregnant which delighted them both, but it did give Kenny more worry as to how they were going to be able to afford it.

At this point Kenny was a delivery driver for a pet food company, and the pay was crap. They were renting a one bedroomed flat and were just covering the bills. Kenny was getting worried about how they were going to cope and was talking to a friend of his called Mike who was from London but moved up to Aberdeen many years earlier. He was another one that was dressed well, and it was clear to see that he always had a few bob in his pocket. Kenny looked up to Mike quite a lot as he saw him flash the cash and to Kenny that meant he was successful. Kenny was sharing his worries, and Mike listened intently because he could see an opportunity for him earn a few bob even if it was a bit shady. Mike had known Kenny for a number of years and he knew that if there was one thing that Kenny could be relied on it was that he would never open his mouth about anything, so he felt quite comfortable in sharing with him that he was part of a gang that was going rob a jewellers and they needed a driver. "Hey Mike I'm not sure about that. I mean that it's fair dodgy." Mike looked at Kenny "Look Ken there's no real risk for you, because all you've got to do is drive, it's a walk in the park pal." Mike kept talking to Kenny about it all being easy money, and Kenny fell for it hook line and sinker. This was the start of Kenny taking the wrong path in life.

Mike was successful in persuading Kenny to do the job. It was going to be a top Jewellers in the heart of Aberdeen where they had the best of shops. Kenny was excited to be working with the top boys, but he was also scared of getting caught, and the other thing that worried him was how he was going to get around all this with Lynn. She's not a stupid woman, he thought, but he was sure he could talk her round. He stood outside their front door, put a smile on his face and walked through the door like he didn't have a care in the world. "Only me", he shouted, "You'll never guess what, I've got myself another job working as a bouncer outside a nightclub. It's good money, although I'm not sure how much yet, but it's better than nothing." Lynn looked at him with a look on her face that said "I'm not sure about this, and you're lying to me", but she didn't say what she was thinking, instead she greeted him with a kiss and spoke loudly "Well done, that's great, how did you find out about that?" Kenny started stumbling over his words because he knew that Lynn didn't like Mike at all, and was always convinced that he was up to no good. "Oh Kenny you're not gonna work with him are you?" Lynn's voice had a concerned tone with a slightly irritated slant to it, "yes, why not?" Kenny asked "come on love, you know we need the cash." Lynn sat thinking for a while, "Yes but not with him." Kenny looked down to the floor and started the emotional blackmail bit because he knew it always worked. "I thought you would be fair pleased, it's an opportunity to put some more cash in our hands."

"Ok, ok, if you want to but don't say I didn't warn ya. When do ya start?" "Tomorrow at 8pm." At this point Kenny was crossing his fingers behind his back in the hope that Lynn didn't ask any more questions, taking a deep breath when she walked away and started to dish the dinner up. Lynn only had a couple of months left before the baby was due, and Kenny knew that she was stressing out about getting everything they need, so in his mind he could justify why he was doing this job. He could use that to say that he was thinking of his wife and child, but deep down that wasn't the only reason, because he saw this as an easy way to earn cash, and the other bonus was that he was working with the big boys, which would have given him some street cred. Yes, he could see life getting better, or so he thought.

The following evening Kenny arrived at the given time and place, where Mike and two other guys were sitting in a car. They beckoned him to get into the driver seat, which he duly did.

"Good you're on time," said one of the guys. Kenny immediately knew who he was, and almost bowed at him as soon as he recognised them both. These two guys were well known in the area as they were what would be considered to be nasty pieces of work because they were well hard and were known to have seen off a few old time rival gang leaders in the past. They were taking over the area when it came to crime and control. Their names were Joe and Alan, and deep down Kenny knew he should be staying away from them, but he went against his intuition. They gave Kenny clear instructions what he had to do, which he followed to the letter. The job went smoothly and with no dramas, so after a few days, Kenny got the money owing to him. Kenny couldn't help but think what easy money this was, and although he was keeping his mouth shut and a low profile, he was secretly lapping up the thought that he had worked for the big boys.

The money that he earned that night went towards buying the lovely new pram that Lynn wanted, as well as a lot of other things the baby needed, which kept Lynn happy. Kenny thought that was the end of it, but a month after Kenny's daughter Sophie was born Mike contacted Kenny again to see if he was interested in doing another job. Kenny had stuck with doing his day job as a delivery man and although money wasn't flush, life was ticking over nicely, so he was hesitant, but there was still that part of him that still wanted to be in with the villains and get a name for himself with them. So, just as before Kenny agreed to be the driver for them, but this time they wanted him to steal the car as well as drive for them. There was no mention of what the job was, but one thing's for sure there was a lot more tension this time than the last time. Kenny's heart skipped a beat when they told him that they wanted him to steal the car. He could see that he was already getting more involved and he didn't need much intelligence to tell him that things had already become more complicated. Kenny wasn't sure if he wanted all this hassle, but in the end once again he agreed to go ahead.

Kenny spun the same old yarn to Lynn, and this time she believed him straight away because she trusted Kenny. He duly stole the car on the day of the job, and hid it where it would be safe until it was needed. Kenny turned up at the agreed time and waited for Joe, Alan and Mike to get there. Once they all arrived they told Kenny where to drive to which seemed pretty remote, but he did as he was told. They all sat in the car for a while when another car pulled up, and the boys got out telling Kenny to stay in the car no matter what. They met up with another guy who was holding someone so that he couldn't move. Kenny kept his lights on, and what he saw next stayed with him always after that. Joe and Alan walked right up to the guy being held, his hands yanked up behind his back, and after a few words were exchanged, they both stood back whilst Mike moved in, hitting this guy with such force that Kenny knew there was no way he were going to survive the beating he had just been given. Kenny felt sick to the pit of his stomach and he started shaking. He didn't know the guy that got out of the other car and now he didn't want to know, he was scared. This guy's life was over in a minute. Alan, Joe and Mike all got back in the car and said nothing. Mike had blood all over him. No one said anything apart from telling Kenny to drop them off outside their nightclub, which he did. As they got out of the car they told Kenny to get rid of the car, set it alight and not to leave it until it's burned to the ground. Kenny realised that he was now in way above his head.

Kenny tried so hard to just carry on as though nothing had happened, which was really difficult for him, especially around Lynn. He couldn't get away from what he saw that night, and now that it had been confirmed in the papers that a body was found in that area that was so badly beaten they were struggling to identify the victim, Kenny was like a cat on a hot tin roof. The reality was that now he was part of the gang that had killed this man, the police could knock at any time.

The next time he saw Mike he had a word and said that he didn't want anything more to do with him or his mates.

Unfortunately for Kenny Mike told him "Listen pal, you're now a part of this murder, and you could go down just like the rest of us." As soon as Kenny started protesting Mike stared at him. Kenny knew he was warning him to shut up. Once Kenny had shut up Mike quietly but firmly said, "The thing is Kenny you can either work with the lads or you can end up the same way as your pal." Kenny was quick to say, "Hey look Mike I've no idea who your man was, but he was certainly not one of my pals." Mike carried on staring at Kenny, and the coldness of the glare made Kenny shudder. It wasn't what was coming out of Mike's mouth that worried him, it was the body language that told Kenny to just get on with it, or he was going to end up with the same treatment as the poor man he saw Mike kill in front of him. All of this was a big eye opener for Kenny because he had no idea that Mike was so evil, and he genuinely never had seen that side of him.

Kenny knew he was now seen as one of the gang. The hard reality was that Kenny wasn't wanting any part of it, but he knew he couldn't leave, and he was told in no uncertain terms by Joe and Alan that he will do what they want him to or he would be 'fish food'. As time went on Kenny gave up his job of delivery man and started to work for Alan and Joe full time. Yes it was good money, and now he and Lynn had a good life style, but it meant he had to lie to Lynn about what he was doing, and Kenny hated doing this. It also came to the point where Kenny became one of the guys that would hold a guy whilst he was being beaten by others. Sometimes they died and other times they survived but were disfigured for life. Kenny's job went beyond that as well. He was bouncer at the boys night club, which is the story he told Lynn and, after all, it was partially true he thought, but it was all the other stuff that he was struggling to come to terms with. He would go around to the different clubs and pubs and demand money for protection, and if they didn't pay, he was one of the guys that would totally wreck their premises and sometimes they would totally wreck the guys that owned it too. After a while Kenny switched off from his conscience, and just got on with it the best way he could. Each job he did for the boys, got him in deeper and deeper and his fight for survival got harder and harder. In the end what he was prepared to do got nastier and nastier.

Although Kenny hated what he did he was still very loyal to the gang and would never grass them up or lead anyone to them. They always felt secure in that. In fact when he looked at it he was actually more loyal to Joe, Alan and the rest of the firm than he ever was to Lynn. After all he had been lying to her for years. In her eyes he was a bouncer at their clubs and casino's as well as a gofer and sometimes a driver. But no matter what happened, he never brought this stuff home. Yes, he became very good at shutting out what his life was like and how low he had stooped in the way he lived. What was interesting was that the police knew what the boys were like and what they were capable of but they were never able to get the proof they needed. In some ways Kenny wished they would find evidence that was going to nail them all and he knew that would mean life in prison, but it was almost worth it so that he could clear his conscience and be punished for his crimes.

As Kenny grew older naturally he couldn't do the kind of jobs that he used to, and would happily leave that to someone else to do, but he was still useful, and Joe and Alan always liked to have him around because of his loyalty to them. Little did they realise he hated them and only stayed loyal so that he and his family were safe. Kenny was now 42 years old with a daughter that was doing great. She was an only child, but that didn't seem to bother her. She had left school at the age of 18 so that she could get a job and earn some money, and she now worked in a solicitor's office as a secretary/personal assistant and was doing very well. Kenny and Lynn were extremely proud of her. She absolutely adored her mum and dad, especially her "Da", to whom she was his "little princess." Kenny's daughter Sophie had met the man of her dreams where she worked, he was one of the junior solicitors. Their relationship was very similar to Kenny and Lynn's when they first got together, they had got engaged and were busy planning their wedding. Kenny had been saving for this day and was highly delighted that he could also provide them with their deposit on their first home, which they moved into together as soon as they got the keys. Well at least he got to see the some of the money being put to good use before he collapsed and died.

When the fatal day came that his heart had decided to quit on him he was out walking the dog, so the end of his human life was of natural causes, not someone doing him in as a revenge for his actions. So, he may have lived by the gun, but he didn't die by the gun. Some would say he got away with his nasty deeds, and that he didn't get his comeuppance, but they were wrong, very wrong.

When Kenny arrived in the Spirit world he knew straight away where he was and what had happened. He hadn't lost any time that he couldn't account for. He found himself in a beautifully brightly decorated room, it was huge. "This is interesting, what happens next." He said out loud. It wasn't that long before someone was walking towards him.

"What the f*ck" were his first words as he saw a monk walking towards him. "Christ I can't see his face cos he's got that stupid hood pulled over his head." As the monk got closer to him Kenny started to feel a little bit nervous because he didn't know what he was facing. Although he never shared it with anyone he had feared that because he didn't live the purest of lives he would end up in a place like the hell most people imagined. Brother Edward was a gentle man which Kenny could tell by his mannerisms. Brother Edward made the first move, "Hello Kenny, welcome." "Hello Father" replied Kenny, "What am I doing here." "Oh I think you know what you're doing here.", Brother Edward replied. "Yes, I've kicked the bucket pal, what I wanna know is who are you like." "Are you here to give me a good telling off, or to lead me to the furnace like." Brother Edward was intrigued by Kenny's way of thinking. "Now why would I want to do that." Kenny felt like he needed to explain himself to the Brother so that he can get the punishment over with. "Well excuse me Father, but I'm sure you know that I've not lived the best of lives and that I have done a lot of awfully bad things." "Yes I know friend, but you're going to start working with that." "Yes, and are you going to help me?" Kenny said sarcastically. "Where I can, but you will have to do the work", replied Brother Edward rather firmly. "Ok, ok, I'll go along with this." Replied Kenny in a voice that said he was giving up and go along with it all, even though he was convinced that he could do the work.

Kenny and the Brother walked along a beautiful bright path where either side of them there were meadows, and Kenny couldn't help but think that heaven seemed to be a lovely place. As they walked and talked along their path Kenny was conscious of the fact that they had left the path where the meadows had been and were now walking by some beautiful building, which, to Kenny, almost felt like it was church like. Actually, Kenny wasn't far wrong because each and every building in the Spirit world has got a purpose, and at some stage Kenny would visit all these buildings as he reflects, learns and understands what he needs to do to re-balance evolution.

All of a sudden the Brother stopped outside one of the buildings. Kenny's thoughts immediately went to how grand it was, how much it would cost and how lovely it would have been if he could have afforded something this size when he was still alive down on earth. Brother Edward gestured for Kenny to walk in, and nervously Kenny complied with the request. As they approached the front door Kenny wanted to turn and run because he had a feeling this is where he was going to be punished for all his deeds on earth, but he continued walking towards the front door determined not to show his fear but stand strong. Kenny could see that the door was extremely wide, and very heavy. As he was looking at the beautiful ornate hinges and handle that was on the door it gave him a start and he stepped back as the door started to open on its own. Kenny quickly turned to Brother Edward to see what his reaction to this was. He saw that the Father wasn't reacting to it at all asking Kenny to go in. Kenny knew that this was all part of the plan, although he didn't quite know what the plan was.

Once they were inside it was like walking into a massive cinema foyer with wide doors very similar to those he would see at a cinema. These are the doors that Kenny didn't want to go through because he had a strong feeling this is where he would be made to remember his life on earth. Kenny turned to Brother Edward and said "I'm sorry but I'm not going in there." The Brother's tone of voice or his gentle body language didn't change one bit but he did ask Kenny the reason why he wouldn't go inside. Kenny replied, "Let me tell you I'm not going in there to be punished." The Brother looked at him "Why do you feel that you're going to be punished?" "Look father I'm no fool, I know that we don't get away with our behaviours, I had that drummed into me plenty of times when I was a boy, and now it's payback time." "Kenny, let's go through the doors together, I'm not here to punish you, I am here to help you." Kenny wasn't sure if he believed him, or could trust him, which said more about Kenny not trusting anyone, more than it was to do with the brother being a monk.

Kenny had lost faith in people very shortly after working for Joe, Alan and Mike, and all the terrible things that were done, which he had also played a part in. He wanted to pull out after the first time he saw the violence but he knew there was no way out because he was in too deep, so he just had to learn to survive the best way he could because it really was a question of survival, and his survival would, at times depend on the violence he would use. Kenny faltered for a few moments, but decided that he had to go for it and nodded his head in agreement but deep down he agreed to it because he really didn't feel he had a choice!

They both walked through the double doors, and it really was just like a proper cinema with comfy chairs and although there wasn't a screen ahead of him it still had the same feel.

Both Brother Edward and Kenny sat down as Kenny commented "Wow, this really is just like a cinema, am I going to watch a film?" he said laughingly, but the Brother didn't laugh. He started talking to Kenny about how he was about to view his life from beginning to end. Kenny couldn't help but say "Well that's going to take ages then pal." with a smirk on his face, the Brother just answered "There is no such thing as time here my friend, so we're fine." Kenny didn't know what to say or where to look at that point as he didn't quite understand that there is no concept of time in the spirit world, but he wasn't going to ask any questions because that would just complicate things.

The Brother continued to say that they weren't going to go through every day of Kenny's life, just the bits that moulded who Kenny turned out to be. Kenny really wasn't sure that he wanted this, but here goes. The next minute he knew he was looking at him and his mum when he was first born. At that point she did seem to be pouring loads of love on him, and it was plain for all to see that she genuinely loved him, which is something he never felt after the age of 5 years old. He took a good look at her and thought how beautiful she was, which was something else that changed over the years too, as she developed a harsh face, and a hard attitude. "What happened to mum?" He asked out loud as he was watching his mum when she was young and appeared to be happy. The next thing he knew for the first time in years was that he was seeing his father with him and mum. Kenny took a big gasp of breath as he looked at his dad, and again said out loud, "God I can remember him now, I think I was about 4 years old when dad just up and left, never to be mentioned again."

Kenny's mum's mood always changed if he did talk about his dad, or asked a question about him. "I could never work that out and still don't know now." Whilst Kennys life unfolded before him he was already learning so much about his mum and what his father was like. He had put him on a pedestal and thought it was mum's harshness that made him leave. He was learning something very different now, and he couldn't help shouting out angrily "The dirty rotten bastard how could he?" When he found out that not only did his father constantly lie to his mum, he used to hit her, have affairs and even charge her petrol money for him to take her shopping for the food that he would soon be shouting about if it wasn't on the table when he expected it. He just wanted to give him a bit of the old rough treatment that he had become so good at when he was alive, "I tell you if I meet him here, I'll give him what for." Brother Edward turned and looked at him, "Isn't that the life you hated though?" Kenny felt defensive "Yes, that's right, but I'll not let him away with this." Brother Edward just turned and looked at Kenny with a look that didn't need any words. Kenny knew he was saying "You still have a lot to learn", and he would be right thought Kenny. When Kenny's dad decided to leave them, he neglected to say that he hadn't paid the rent for months, because he had spent it on drink, betting and other women and his mum was only just learning that he had left them so deep in debt that if they didn't pay up within the month they would lose their home. Kenny saw how Kath and her mum had to work hard to get the money together and that meant her working right through the night on her sewing machine as well as doing cleaning jobs through the days.

Kenny was now feeling so emotional and tearful that he was finding it hard to hold it all in. "I never knew any of this about mum, she never told me. Oh my God it's no wonder she ended up bitter, resentful and distant." Kenny broke down in tears seeing how she was treated, remembering how he treated her as he was growing into adult years and still treated her in a cold way right up until he died. "I so wish I could say sorry to her, she must have been so disappointed in me." Brother Edward wanted to give Kenny some hope "You will be able to say sorry at some point, don't worry about that, but right now there are a few things I want you to reflect on as you sit here watching your life on earth pass you by like a film." "Hey I'm not sure I want te go any further just now cos if I'm like this wiy just this first part of me life, what the heck am I going to be like with the rest?" After a while the Brother managed to talk Kenny around just to watch some more of his life unfold, but Kenny definitely wasn't happy with it, and was quite vocal about it.

As Kenny sat back to watch where they had left of, he was a bit surprised to see that this movie had moved on to when he was a rebellious teenager of about 15 years old. "Oh God.", said Kenny as he saw who he was then, "I was a nightmare then, and got up to anything and everything." The Brother noticed that Kenny was smiling as he saw himself getting up to the antics he did. "Why do you smile Kenny?" asked the brother. Kenny turned to look at him, "Well things were easier then, not like they were before I croaked it." The Brother asked "In which way?" "Well, for starters, I didn't have the responsibilities I had when I died, and I didn't have to think of anyone else back then." The Brother said nothing for a few moments, the movie also stopped running at that point, Kenny was walking alone down a street after leaving his friends. The brother turned to Kenny, "Take a look at you there, I really want you to remember and feel what was going on at that time."

Kenny's smile turned to a serious and unhappy expression as he remembered all that was going on then. His mum was still working as hard as she always did, so when he went home he didn't get a great welcome, or time out with her because she was too busy. By this point in their lives they had moved into a house and mum was renting out to a lodger, so even when she did finish her work, she had to cook and clean for a total stranger. Oh how Kenny hated this, and was actually quite cold towards his mum because he didn't realise it was just to keep them going. All that he knew was that his mum didn't have much time for him, and when she did there was always a moan about him. How he looked, or what he was up to and why he was wasting time hanging around with his new mates because they were no good. "Hmm, if I'm honest, I felt really lonely and I also felt that I was in the way for my mum to have her life. I felt I didn't fit in, I was a mistake, and no matter what I did I couldn't shake that feeling like. I didn't fit in at school either, cos me mates all had their dad's wiy em like, so I felt like the odd one out. Yes I see what you mean, I was never happy." As Kenny finished his sentence he again broke down because he realised how much he took on board about himself as a person, influenced either by what was said, or more often, what wasn't said.

Kenny started to balance his feelings out because he could now see the struggles that his mum had, and realised that she wasn't completely to blame, he was just an angry, mixed up kid. After a while he once again put a smile on his face when he thought of his nan who he was very close to. The Brother said nothing for quite a while whilst Kenny reminisced about the relationship he had with his nan. All of a sudden Kenny came back from thinking about Nan and looked over at Brother, "Sorry, I was thinking about my gran, she was amazing, but she died when she I was 16 years old. bless her, I always missed her so much." It was then that Kenny said, "Hey if I'm here, is she? Where is she?" The Brother replied "Yes she's here, and you will see her later, but not quite yet." In a panicked voice Kenny said, "Hey, I'm not sure I want to see her yet. I mean she will know how I ended up in the end, and I'm not sure I want her to tell me what she thinks of me because of it." "Kenny your Nan will never turn away from you. She may share her thoughts with you, but she would never reject you for being you." "Yes, well I'm not taking chances just yet." replied Kenny.

Kenny felt awful saying that but he did have a fear of her judging him for his behaviour since she passed away, after all he was the apple of her eye. Deep down he would love to see her but he was scared. "Ok, shall we move on then, I'm guessing that's what you want me to do." Brother Edward just replied, "Well is that what you want to do?" Kenny thought for a moment and said "Yes I do." Kenny really wasn't sure he wanted to do any of this because he was struggling to see what he was like. He carried on watching his life, they were now at the point where Kenny met and fell in love with Lynn, and boy was it pulling on his heart strings. "Wasn't she beautiful?" he said out loud, "So lively, and so innocent." As he was watching the two build their home together and have their beautiful daughter, he started to realise that perhaps it was Lynn that had the strength and courage to carry on everyday even in the toughest times and not him. She never moaned and she always had a smile on her face. Of course at the same time Lynn was pregnant he got mixed up with the heavy boys, and this took its toll on him. As he watched the struggles that they had in the early days, how Lynn kept everything together, he started to see how distant he became with both Lynn and their daughter Sophie. He could even pin a time on when he changed, which was the first time he saw Joe, Alan and Mike use violence and killed whoever got in their way. He knew that he tried to pull away but he was warned what would happen if he did so they always had a hold over him. That was enough for him to behave himself and do what he was told. As the flashback through his life continued he started to see how nasty and cut off he had become. The flashback stopped at the point where Kenny was using violence against another man as per the boys' instructions leaving him severely beaten before walking away. Kenny just stared at this horrible man he didn't know and shouted out "Look what I did to him! I didn't want to but I had to do as I was told like." The Brother again turned to him "Tell me how do you feel as you look at you and the behaviour you used?" "Well, how the f*ck de you think I feel?" Brother Edward said nothing, he could see that Kenny was very affected by what he was seeing, so a swear word didn't mean anything right now. The brother knew he was more angry with himself than anyone else. Kenny immediately regretted swearing at the brother saying quickly "I'm sorry Brother Edward, I didn't mean that, it's just that I don't like to see all this, in fact I don't want to go any further at the moment." "I understand" replied the brother, "we'll hold off for now."

Kenny looked over at Brother Edward nodding thank you. The Brother wasn't going to stop there though, he wanted to see what Kenny was learning by reflecting back on what he had seen. "So tell me Kenny what was going through your head when you saw what you were like back then?" Kenny did feel that this time he could trust the brother with all of the emotions he was feeling. That was a breakthrough on its own, as Kenny would never have done that when he was earth side. "To be honest, I hate myself for it all. I hated myself then and I hate myself now." "Why?" asked the Brother. Kenny sat there for a while looking at the freeze frame of himself. "Well, I would have thought that you could see why, but I'll tell you anyway. Look at the violence I was using, look at how prepared I was to harm someone to save my own skin. That's no good, and he wasn't the only one I did that too. I can see that I left everything to Lynn when it came to the home and the kid. I constantly lied to her about where I was and what I was doing. She must have wondered what she had done by marrying me bless her. Oh my God, Lynn, I've not thought about her until now, she must be distraught." Not thinking about Lynn and her feelings became a natural thing in their marriage throughout the years. Kenny's attitude was that as long as he was putting good food on the table and a very good roof over her head, she should be grateful, because they were doing better than any of the friends that he went to school with.

Neither Kenny or Brother Edward said anything for a while then Kenny looked over and said "Please Brother Edward, can I just see how Lynn and Sophie are doing? It would make me feel a lot better.", he explained. Brother Edward thought for a moment, "Look forward my friend and you will see them." Kenny did so, and there they were, "Oh my God, I forgot all about them until now, how could I do that? I can't believe that." Both Lynn and Sophie were in the kitchen of Kenny and Lynn's home having a cup of tea trying to come to terms with what had happened. Lynn looked over at Sophie "Do you know this, I'm looking around and seeing our lovely big house with it's big kitchen and it's lovely garden but right now none of it means anything to me. I just want your dad home." Sophie moved over to where her mum was sitting, said nothing and put her arms around her to give her a comforting hug, but she could see nothing was going to work at this stage. As mother and daughter sat and hugged each other, there was a ring on the door. Sophie got up to answer it, greeted Lynn's best friend with a hug and beckoned her into the kitchen. Lynn immediately got up as Beverley put her arms out to give her best pal and old school mate the biggest hug. Lynn almost fell into her arms as she let go and started sobbing, "Yes hun you have a good old cry my love."

When Beverley thought it ok to let go of Lynn as she calmed down, she walked over to Sophie and asked how her mother was really doing. "Yes she's not bad on the whole, but it has been an awful shock for her." "Yes I can imagine. Do they know what happened like?" "No not really." said Sophie, "But it looks like he just collapsed as he was walking along the road with the dog." Sophie took a deep breath because she could feel all her emotions building up like a pipe that's ready to burst, but not quite yet she thought. "Aunt Bev, would you stay with mum whilst I nip out to get some errands for me and mum?" "Of course hun, away you go, and don't rush, I'm in no rush to get home." Once Sophie had gone out Lynn felt she could talk more openly about Kenny dying. "I always said this to you didn't I, I always knew this would happen to him even though he always told me to stop nagging." Lynn took a break to catch her breath as she was talking really fast to ensure she got it all out before Sophie got back home. "I mean let's face it, he wasn't exactly the fittest of guys was he? He was overweight, loved his drink, fags and food didn't he?" Bev just kept nodding her head with the odd "Yes, you're right." Lynn, still kept going, "And I was always suspicious of his job with Alan, Joe an Mike. I know he said he was chauffer, gofer and bouncer for them, but if you take a look at the house and the car we have it's not just from doing those kind of jobs. I always used to let him think I believed him, but I never did, and when you see him at home, he was never relaxed. I knew that he was in way over his head, right from the start. I just kept this shut." She said pointing to her mouth. "Why did you not say anything to him?" Bev asked. Lynn just looked at her and replied, "Because it was easier that way, I just let him get on with it. To be honest, I knew very early on that no matter what I said or thought, he would do his own thing like, and I was right, but I never trusted him because he was never honest with me. Remember all the times when I spoke with you about his lying, and his dodgy dealings. I think I was right do you not think Bev?" Bev, did always feel that Kenny led a double life. She felt for her pal because of all of his secrets, and said as much to her.

Again there was that freeze frame and this time it was on Lynn. He just sat and looked at her with tears in his eyes. "Oh God Lynn I'm sorry for all I did or didn't do. You deserved better than me, I swear you did." Brother Edward looked over and said, "there's a lot for you to take in right now, so I think we will leave it for now, and you can have your reflection time." "No" replied Kenny in a loud and firm voice, "I'm not going to sit and watch anymore or reflect back, I can't take all this, it's too heartbreaking to think how little my family trusted me, and with good reason too. I wasn't the best of husbands or a dad for that matter, and I don't want to know any more."

Brother Edward wasn't surprised at Kenny's reaction, but he was surprised at the strength that came from his voice when he said no which concerned Brother Edward. He thought it would be good to leave Kenny for a while in the hope that he would have a think and agree to continue, which he explained to Kenny but it appeared that Kenny wasn't listening. As there is no such thing as time in the Spirit world, Brother Edward had decided to visit Kenny again when he feels that reflection may have taken place within Kenny, and he truly hopes that Kenny would have reflected back on his life because if he doesn't he will be affected by this even in the Spirit world.

Once Brother Edward had left, Kenny just sat and aimlessly stared ahead of him not taking anything in and desperately trying not to think about what he was learning about himself. It was different knowing it when you're on earth, pushing it to one side and just getting on with it, but it's another thing being confronted with it now that he's in spirit because that means he sees the impact he's had on those around him, especially his wife and daughter. Kenny was deep in thought, which meant he was reflecting back as much as he was trying not to, but all this did was break his heart. The brother once again went to see Kenny to see if there was a change in his way of thinking, but unfortunately that wasn't the case.

Kenny turned, saw Brother Edward there, but before the Brother could say anything Kenny stared straight at him, "Brother I don't wish to be rude but just go. Please just go, I don't want to speak with you." The Brother stood firm and asked "Can I just ask you to share with me why you're feeling like this?" Kenny couldn't believe the Brother had said that and wanted to swear at him, not that it would have phased the Brother. Kenny's mouth slipped into quite an aggressive and disfigured smirk as he said "surely you can see why? Do I need to spell it out for you?" Brother Edward replied "yes you do. I want to know what your thought pattern is around this to see if I or anyone can help you." Kenny was making it plain that he didn't want the brother's help, that he would prefer him to go away and leave him alone. The brother wasn't going to give in that easily and he let that be known to Kenny. "I understand that you don't want to talk to me about all of this, but I would like to talk to you if you will allow me to." Kenny stood and stared at the brother. He did think about it for a moment, but he quickly changed his mind when he realised that by working with this he was going to have to face up to how he behaved whilst on the earth. As he said no to the brother, he knew deep down inside that he really wanted to ask for his help, but wasn't ready in that moment.

The brother could see that Kenny was suffering because his conscience had got to him. "Kenny, are you afraid that you will be judged because of the life you led on earth? Or is there something else going on?" Kenny looked down to the floor, "It's a wee bit of that, as well as other things. You wouldn't understand brother, you probably led a very good life when you were alive." The brother didn't say anything, but he thought perhaps in time he would share more of what his life was like when he thought it may be of help. The brother felt there had been a bit of a breakthrough, even if it was only a small one. Kenny was willing to share that judgement was one of his fears, and that he had other fears to. Now to discover those fears and work with them.

Brother Edward started by saying "Kenny, tell me more about your fear of being judged." Kenny said nothing for a moment, he was getting angry with the brother for not letting the judgement thing go. He looked up at the brother and replied, "For Christ's sake, I can see the only way I'm going to get rid of you is to tell you how I'm feeling so that I can get you to leave me alone, I'll tell you shall I?" That wasn't really a question it was just a sarcastic reply. "Right, well you asked for it. I know I wasn't a good person when I was alive, in fact I was f****** awful, I stole, I injured and hurt others on every level, including my family. That's why I didn't want to share it with you. Can you imagine when I end up meeting them up here in the spirit world, I'm going to have to face em, and I don't want to do that." At first the brother listened intently and said nothing, letting Kenny get on with what he was saying, but now it was time that he spoke.

"Kenny, firstly can I just say that you used the term, "when I was alive", and I just want to remind you that you are still alive, just in a very different way now. We're all alive in the spirit world." As the Brother finished speaking, Kenny quickly replied "Yes, yes, I know, you've told me all this before, but it doesn't feel like I'm alive cos I can't see my family, or my mates, I'm just stuck here waiting, and I'm not sure what I'm waiting for. All that's happening is that you keep popping up pestering me and I wish you wouldn't do that, cos I really don't want to go through this." Brother could see this was going to be harder than he thought, and at this point wasn't sure if he was going to be able to help him because his mind was set.

Now that Kenny had spoken his truth it was time for Brother Edward to do the same. "Thank you for sharing all of this with me, now I would like to share something with you. You speak in great depth about not facing up to what you have done, that you don't want to be judged as a result of your behaviour, and yet you are the only person that is judging you, nobody else. Not me, not the people that are on this layer of transition with you, just you." Brother Edward continued, "Take a look around you at the spirit that are here with you, do they appear bothered by you? They're not judging you, they're busy trying to understand their own life, and are slowly learning it isn't their duty to judge others. Please believe me Kenny, I'm only here to help you." The brother was really hoping some of this would sink in, help Kenny to open his eyes and his heart to learn how to cope with all that he needs to work on for his own sake. Kenny looked around and he did notice that other spirit were taking no notice of him, apart from giving him a smile as they continued on with their business. Kenny had a question, "Ok, so if they're on the same level as me, how come, they're still here, and haven't moved up to another level of their transition?" Kenny felt almost smug because he didn't think the brother would be able to answer him. "Many here are due to move up to the next stage very shortly. Those that do move on have done an incredible amount of work and are in a completely different place compared to when they first arrived. This is where you could be if you do the work." Kenny replied "I'm not sure, I bet half of them haven't done the kind of things I have done. I'm not a nice person I'm afraid." The brother reassured Kenny telling him that he wasn't the only person that had led that kind of life, but to no avail, Kenny wasn't having any of it.

The brother decided to have a couple more goes to see if he could break Kenny's defence barrier. "Kenny, you can make the peace with those that you have harmed in your human life because they have moved on and learned the importance of forgiveness. They also now understand just how afraid you were of what might have happened if you hadn't done what was asked of you, or should I say, what you were told to do. Yes, you will come face to face with the people you harmed and are now in the spirit world. Yes, there will be talks, and you will meet more that you harmed, who are still on earth right now but will, at some stage, pass into the spirit world. All of this can be worked out, you will have all the support you need to help you come through it, and you will find some kind of peace within you." Kenny looked straight into the brothers' eyes. "Sorry brother, it's not happening, I'm not meeting up with any of them." Brother Edward felt deflated at Kenny's reply, but he decided to try once more. This time he reminded Kenny that if he stays here and doesn't evolve, the chances are high that when the time comes when his wife and the rest of his family make their transitions, he wouldn't be there to greet them. "Do you want them to realise that you're not with them because you couldn't face up to taking responsibility?" After some time Kenny said "Brother that suits me fine, I don't want to see them because I don't want them to know what I'm really like. No thanks I'm not interested, I'm staying here. I'll stay here and mind me own business. I'm not listening to you anymore."

Brother Edward knew that Kenny wasn't going to change his mind, and although he felt quite sad about that, he also knew that there was always hope. Although Kenny may not be prepared to face up to it at this time, Brother Edward was hoping he would come around at some stage or other. Brother Edward knew only too well that Kenny, as all in spirit, had his own free will. Although the brother had tried in different ways to reach Kenny, at the end of the day he had the right to say no, but as a guide and teacher Brother Edward would never give up on Kenny or others in spirit he supported and worked with because he knew that there was always room for change. He would make it his business to pop in on Kenny on a regular basis to see if he felt differently. As always Brother Edwards would be by his side all the way, he may even share his human life with him because he hadn't been such a good boy either. Meanwhile, Brother Edward knew one thing for sure, when the time comes that Kenny is ready to work, Brother Edward would be there ready and waiting.

Brother Edward's faith was well placed because around a year later Kenny came to see him. "Brother Edward, can we talk?" said Kenny with a new found humility in his voice. "Of course Kenny, what about" was Brother Edward's reply. "Can we pick up where we left off a year ago Brother, I'm ready to move forward now." Brother Edward smiled a little smile to himself as he asked Kenny to take a seat.

Chapter 4

TERRY

Terry is a 70 year old man who recently passed away with cancer of the stomach. He is a very proud man, and especially proud of his family, who were his world. He isn't your typical man's man, in fact he was never happier than when he had all of his four children, their partners and their children around him, and let's not forget his beautiful wife Sue. Their house wasn't overly big and it was extremely noisy as the family gathered, but that didn't bother him at all, the more noise the better. He was married to Sue for 49 years, and between them they made a very happy life together. Neither of them were big into possessions, they never felt like they were chasing after something that was going to make them feel better or make them look richer because both of them were happy, and in their eyes they were already very rich, so their little blessings were big ones to them. In fact, to be honest both Terry and Sue were a very true example of what being a spiritualist is all about, although Terrys' answer to that would probably be something like "I don't know nothing about that, I just know it's important that we all look out for each other and be happy." He very much lived by what he said. He was known for always helping people out and it didn't matter if he knew the person or not he would never walk past someone that was genuinely struggling.

Terry had been diagnosed with cancer of the stomach a few months before, and he was declining quickly. His four children David, Tina, Jackie, and Barbara spent every spare moment with him and their mum who was being very strong as always, but as she saw her husband growing weaker, it was becoming really tough to put a smile on her face. Terry, on the other hand always had a smile on his face and that never changed, no matter what the issues were. He used to say that it was because he had a very tough childhood. His mother had died in childbirth, and his father couldn't look after him, so Terry was passed over to his grandmother who lived in Croydon, Surrey and didn't have a maternal bone in her body. He once shared with Sue and their children that he felt that no matter what he did or didn't do he couldn't win because she would find fault in everything. Terry always used to say that he was resented by his grandmother because she had to look after him, not that he was ever a problem child, in fact he was a saint compared to some. On the odd occasion that his father came to see him they did get on, but he knew never to ask anything of him as he wasn't interested in helping him and he didn't really want to encourage a strong bond between them. So he really left Terry at the hands of his mother's mother, his nan. Even when his dad remarried, he never once invited him over to see his new family, or to meet his little sister when she came along. It was very clear to Terry at a young age that there was no room for him in his fathers' life.

Terry's nan Emily was never physically cruel to Terry, but she certainly was emotionally cruel, and would call him all the useless sods under the sun. She was also very quick to remind him that his dad wasn't interested in so she got lumbered with him. In many cases if a child grows up hearing these cruel words they could well grow to think that they're useless, or that they're unworthy of love or a good life. Not Terry though, he was living proof of the saying "what doesn't break you will only make you stronger", and Terry was a prime example that that is a true statement. Yes, Terry had been affected by his upbringing but not to the degree he was going to let it ruin his life, and no matter what he was always so grateful of his blessings. As he grew into an adult he firmly believed that his mother was helping him from the Spirit world. In fact he knew it, because there were many times when he felt her presence, once he actually saw her at the end of his bed. He knew for sure that it was her and he kept that in his heart as the love that he knew she would have had for him if she had lived. Terry knew from his older cousin that his mum was lovely but Emily was always so hard on her, just as she was with him. So yes, he knew his mum was looking after him as a loving mother, the only difference being that she was doing it from the spirit world.

As soon as Terry was old enough he left home and rented a room. It wasn't the best of rooms but it was definitely a lot better than living with his terrible nan. Once he had left he never went back to visit her, and he never let his experiences affect the path he wanted to take. He knew how terrible she was, but he always felt that his mother was keeping him safe from the emotional abuse she used to throw at him and he recognised it for what it was, just pure bullying and control. When he left, he closed that door for good! Terry had a beautiful talent of doing sign writing as well as being a great artist. He didn't do much with his drawings and paintings, but he did set up his own business as a sign writer. He had amazing patience and spent hours on the orders he had. His business was quite successful and he loved nothing more than working on designs with clients to discuss what they wanted, the layout, design and colours. He loved to allow his mind to flow and create designs that would work on all different kinds of material such as wood, metal and more. Very often his creative art would flow in the design of the signs. He was immensely proud of his work.

Terry may not have earned a high wage but he did bring enough in for a good life for him and his family. He was never trying to "Keep up with the Jones's" as they say. He, his wife and his children were very settled in their life. Mind you, he always encouraged his children to go to college or university, as he could see the world was changing and they were going to need some qualifications behind them to help secure a good life for themselves. At the time he decided he wanted to retire he was diagnosed with cancer, news which, as you can imagine, devastated them all. It was such a cruel blow. They knew he wasn't going to pull through, it was terminal. Terry was determined that the last part of his life would be worthwhile, something that could be remembered with love and laughter by his family that would keep them going through the hard times of their grieving.

Terry's way of thinking showed how determined and open he was. It also showed the strength and courage he had together with his gentleness and his care not just for his family, but for others to. There is no doubt about it Terry was a very special man indeed. It was very clear to all that met Terry even when he was a child and then an adult that he was definitely a wise soul. He was someone that always seemed to know what was needed whenever someone had a problem. He always remained calm and cool in very difficult times and he always gave good advice when people turned to him, which was often. Many people that met him would say that he had lived on earth before, as only a person with that experience would understand what was truly needed in times of crisis. Terry was very rarely wrong.

When Terry was a child he would feel his mothers' love around him, he thought he only felt this because she was his mum, and she wanted to help him, but it was only as he grew older that he started to realise that he could feel the presence of other Spirit around him. This didn't scare him at all, in fact he loved it and very often he would find himself chatting away to spirit which gave him great peace because no matter what, he always felt they were there for him. Terry thought it was amazing he could do this, but yet, he didn't think of himself as a medium let alone a good one. When Terry woke up to the fact that he had mediumistic abilities it was at a time when this kind of thing was only spoken about behind closed doors, any seances that took place were definitely best to be kept secret, but not Terry. He was proud of his relationship with the spirit world and wouldn't hide it at all, even if it did mean that he may lose his friends or that they would label him as mad. Many others would have kept quiet, but not Terry, he just knew that the two worlds combining through mediumship could only be a very positive thing, with knowledge and information being given from the spirit world, that could inspire those in this world. Terry's Spirit was so beautiful and inspiring it definitely got people thinking.

When his children visited him, he liked to see them one at a time first, and then as a group. When he would see them one to one he would point out their strengths that they should work on, (and this included if he thought they had mediumistic abilities), and their weaknesses too. To him each child had something different to offer mankind. This may seem as though Terry was being either critical or controlling, it wasn't, it was just his way of helping his children to stay on their true path. Each of his four children knew this and didn't see it as any other way than to help them. For his wife Sue, he was just as eternally grateful for all that she did for him throughout their life together, not just when he was ill. Now they spent many an hour, her sitting by his bedside, reminiscing about their young days and how they stood by each other through the toughest times.

Don't get me wrong Terry was no angel, and he certainly wasn't perfect. He could be sharp with his tongue if he was pushed too far, or if someone was trying to push their views onto him. He was also stubborn over certain things, especially when it came to seeing doctors and taking his medication as, unusually for a man of his age he believed there was always an alternative and holistic way of being treated for any disease. He would become awkward when they tried to give him treatment, but in the end he continued with his treatment for the sake of his family. As his time grew closer he repeatedly reassured his family that he has always been happy with his lot. He was especially proud of his family, who had always given him the greatest of pleasure, and he knew that as he watches over them he will be just as proud. One of the last things he said as his transition grew closer was "My mother is waiting for me. I'm ready to spend time with her now, so I still have a lot to look forward to, and I will also have the opportunity to tell my grandmother what life was like with her." It was now time for him to leave his earthly life and return back to his spiritual home. All his family were there as he took his last breath, but they all knew it was only his last breath here and that as he left, he would take his first breath back in his spiritual home.

Terry was so pleased as his mother greeted him with open arms. This was something he had dreamt of many times but interestingly he had dreamt it again only the other day and it felt more real than ever before. That to him was the sign to tell him he was on his way. As soon as he arrived he was completely free of pain, and he had his youth back and the strength that went with it. He looked over to his mother and saw how beautiful she was. He had only ever seen one photo of her, and that was a fairly blurred one at that, but he could see her beauty, and she could feel his love and strength. Once they had greeted each other the way they had always dreamed of they sat and spoke for what seemed like an eternity, and of course the reality is that they did have eternity together now to make up for all of those years they had missed out on.

They spent time talking about how proud his mum was of him, and how, against all the odds he didn't allow all that he had experienced at the hands of his grandmother to make him bitter about life. Terry's mum, Nancy, turned to his son with a beaming bright smile and told him how often she felt when he was a child that he instinctively knew how to deal with things, like he had been given that guidance from someone else. Nancy shared this with her son proudly, "I always thought you were an old soul reincarnate that had the knowledge to know what to do next. It wasn't until you were a teenager and I witnessed spirit coming to join you in your sleep and in your quieter moments, that I realised just how close you were to the spirit world, and the wonderful path you were walking with them." "Terry smiled and replied, "I knew it. I knew I wasn't imagining those visitations I used to have. Wow, how blessed am I to have experienced something as wonderful as the two worlds combining together to make each side a better place to be, and to help bring peace and calm to mankind and the world we've lived in. It's a shame it took so long though", he said with a big grin on his face and a cheeky wink.

Terry wasn't surprised to see that life in the spirit world runs parallel with life on earth and it didn't surprise him either that living in the spirit world was just like living a life on earth, well almost. In the spirit world there aren't any of the pressures, or so many foibles the way there was in their human life, so in some ways it was different. In fact Terry would say it would better if it wasn't for the fact that he was missing his family. As he observed how spirit got on with their lives he saw that people were still enjoying the same things they had on earth, had the same hobbies as they had on earth, and some were new hobbies that they had always wanted to do but never had the time, or the money. Terry also found it interesting that although he had the same personality he had always had, it had a very different feel to it because he didn't really have a body to house his personality in. He could have if he wanted, which he would so that he would be recognised should any of his family go to see a medium. This fascinated him as it was how he had always imagined it to be. He also realised that how he imagined it would be like here was more than just his imagination. It felt more like he knew it to be this way somehow, but how? So far he had only had time with his mother, and hadn't seen anyone else but all that was about to change as he saw his grandmother approaching him. He knew who it was straight away as he always felt her vibrations and frequencies were very heavy, much closer to the physical and material world than the spiritual side. Her main concern was always about herself and bringing others down, trying to manipulate those around her for her own gain. Even as a young child he understood the fact that every one of us were just a load of vibrations and frequencies that resonate at certain frequencies. It always fascinated him how we can all tune in to each other's wavelengths. As his mum always believed, Terry had an old soul, full of knowledge and wisdom.

Terry's gran was approaching him. Terry started speaking out loud and as he did he asked himself, "Hmm, how do I deal with this one? I always knew this day would come, and I've asked myself regularly, do I ignore her, or do I give her what for? Let's see." As Emily approached him he looked straight at her, said nothing, and just waited. He knew that she felt uncomfortable as she stared back. Terry decided he will be the first one to say something because he didn't like making anyone feel uncomfortable, not even his Gran. "Hello nan how are you?" he asked, Emily hesitated for a moment, then replied, "Hello, I'm ok, I was hoping to see you when you arrived." "Why?" he asked. Emily "Oh I was just hoping we can make the peace between us that's all." Terry had waited a long time for this conversation so that he could let her have it right between the eyes, but now that it came to it, he didn't feel the same. He did want to have his say, but not in a vindictive way, he just wanted to clear his chest of anything that he was holding against her. "I'm happy to have a conversation with you, but we will have to see how I feel about making the peace between us then." Terry felt quite emotional and turning his emotions into words surprised him. "Why nan?" he asked, "Why did you always pull me apart on everything? Why wasn't I ever good enough for you?" Emily knew it was time to be honest which was something that she had only started learning to do once she passed into Spirit. "Oh Terry I don't know, I think I just felt as though your father had lumbered me with a child to bring up and it was hard." Terry didn't like to hear that but thought, if that's how she felt, then that's how she felt. The only problem was she was exactly the same with his mum when she was growing up.

"Nan, there's a part of me that wants to believe you, but you weren't only like this with me, you were the same with my mum, so it wasn't just that was it?" Emily was getting a little frustrated because she wasn't able to manipulate him using his emotions and she could see how strong he had become as he started sticking up for himself. Terry could see the frustration in her, but didn't say anything, and continued to tell her what it was like for him. "Do you have any idea what it was like for me? In the beginning I tried everything just to get some praise from you, but to no avail because you were too busy moaning and groaning about something that I had or hadn't done, instead of seeing all that I accomplished." Terry was on a roll now and he wasn't going to stop. "The only emotion you ever showed me was anger. God I was glad when I left home, but in some ways I have a lot to thank you for. I knew, because I had always had to depend on myself, I had already started to build up a survival kit to get through life when things got tough, and of course when I met my wife, I really knew what it was to feel loved, a feeling I never lost." Emily looked at Terry and for the first time he saw she had softened the look on her face and even gave him a smile. Emily knew it was no use trying to think up other excuses why she was the way she was, so she decided to stop going on the defensive and finally take responsibility for her behaviour.

Emily looked over at Terry "I'm so sorry son, I have learned since passing over just what my behaviour was like and how it impacted you." Terry was taken aback by Emily's apology he certainly didn't expect that! For a few moments there was silence between them, and Terry in particular didn't know how to deal with this apology, so he said nothing until he could find the right words to fit this momentous moment. When Terry was a teenager and young adult he had spent a lot of time dreaming about receiving an apology from his gran. He had even thought about how he was going to relish the moment and tell her where to stick her apology. But now that the moment was here, he didn't feel the need to say all that. He also didn't feel the need to throw it back in her face because as a mature man he had learned there's no point in doing this, it doesn't change what happened, and by dealing with it in a vindictive way he might damage himself and his spiritual evolution.

Terry looked over at Emily, "I accept your apology, and I do believe that your apology is sincere." He could see that this was a great relief to his gran "Thank you." Emily shared how she had often looked down at Terry and his family to watch them live their lives, and now that she had made a huge leap forward by the way of an apology, she also wanted Terry to know how proud she was of the family, they were a credit to him. Terry's replied "Yes, I'm proud of them too, they're a great bunch and have brought me and my wife Sue great love, joy, and laughter, something you missed out on." Terry continued, "I'm sorry but it does have to be said, because you were never a part of my, or their lives, and I think you have missed out on so much." Emily agreed and it came pretty easy for her to say.. "Yes, you're right and I would like to make up for that now if you will allow me too. I know I'm no longer living a human life, but it doesn't stop me from being able to guide them from here." Terry could see that Emily had done a lot of reflecting since she passed over, and that she had been working with it, so he happily said "Yes, that would be fine with me, and I'm happy for us to build some kind of relationship now that we're both here, but there's just one thing though, don't ever expect me to call you nan, or gran, or any other word of endearment, I will just call you Emily." After this was agreed Emily went off to do whatever it is she does up in the spirit world. She certainly hadn't given any indication what she does, so perhaps that was something to find out the next time they were together.

When Terry was part of mankind he used to do a lot of meditation, and working with guides that he knew were around with him often, so it was no surprise when he saw his main guide walking towards him, as always with a lovely big smile on his face. Terry was keen to greet him. "Hello my friend, I was wondering when I would get to see you.", Terry said in a jolly voice. As the two joined together through their vibrations and frequencies, it was clear for all to see that the pair were very close and comfortable in each other's company. Now, some may think that Terry's guide would be a native American, or an Indian or Peruvian warrior, but no, his guide, Tom was a builder in his earthly life and was in fact a wonderful Irish man living in London who worked hard all his life. Like Terry, was a very gentle and spiritual person. The two of them had so much in common and even before Terry died would spend many an hour together learning from each other and gaining different insights and views. It is through their blending that Terry learned exactly what it did mean to walk a spiritual path, as well as how to help mankind which Terry always put into practice. He would share with others the teachings that this wise guide would give him. Yes, Terry had done a lot of spiritual evolving before he left his physical life.

As the two gentlemen met, they bowed to each other and sat together. Tom started the conversation welcoming Terry back home. "It's so good to see you my friend. I have been watching you with your mother and grandmother, and I have to say you worked with your grandmother very well, especially given that you refused to let her come through to you when she tried through mediums before you died. You have helped to give Emily some purpose that she was looking for since she had started to work on her spiritual self." Terry had a smile on his face "Thank you Tom, yes I did think about refusing to meet with her, but there's no point in that because in the end, I would have remained her victim, and quite unforgiving, which, as you have taught me, does no one any good."

Tom now wanted to talk to Terry on a deeper level about the work he had done both in his earthly life as well as the positive signs he was showing now that he was back in the spirit world. Tom looked at Terry "Come let's walk." Terry felt this was going to be a deep conversation, not that he minded because he had always enjoyed their deep conversations. Tom started the conversation off, "So my friend now that you're back here, I wonder what it is that you have learned from your recent life on earth. I can't help but wonder what will come out of your reflections on life, mankind and the world." Terry replied almost immediately "Oh my goodness, where do I start. It certainly hasn't been the easiest of lifetimes, but perhaps it was the most valuable life in some respects." Tom had a curious look on his face, but said nothing because he knew that Terry would continue, "When I say not the easiest life, I mean that the world and mankind have taken steps back instead of evolving and growing." Tom was intrigued "Continue my friend, I'm keen to hear more." "Well, for a start there are many that claim they are walking their spiritual paths and yet as I observed them, they seemed to be more obsessed with the material side of life, and all that they could own. It appeared they were once again judging people based on what possessions they had, not who they were." Terry was still going strong continuing to share the reflections that he had started to have before he ever left his body and returned home. "There is now so much information and knowledge that can be gained should people decide to turn their thoughts away from the materialistic perspective and give a thought for mankind, and yes there are many that are doing that, but not enough, to make a difference."

Terry seemed quite distressed at this point, and Tom could see this, "Take a deep breath and just sit, as there is no such thing as time here so we have an eternity to work with this." Terry looked at Tom "What do you mean we have an eternity to work with this? "Yes we may have an eternity here, but mankind doesn't have an eternity on earth, and they need our help now." "Yes I agree." replied Tom, "But we can only work at a pace that mankind can deal with otherwise it can all become too overwhelming for them and they will turn back to what they know, to focus on things rather than life which will bring much more damage than we can imagine." Terry calmed himself down and apologised for his sharp words. "There is no apology needed." replied Tom, "I know you care deeply for mankind and having just come back from there I can understand why it stresses you out so much." Terry looked over at Tom, his eyes thanking him for being so understanding. Terry was now speaking more slowly and more gently, "When I was a fit healthy man I was too busy working and raising a family to put much thought into how we treat each other and the earth, but now that I sit here and I look down, I see that there are some positive steps that the world has made, but there is still so much to do, it's unbelievable. If you look at how badly many people treat mother nature it is awful, and in many cases how they treat each other and some animals to. It's just a real mess."

Tom was so pleased to see that Terry cared so deeply for every living being, mother nature and how the world was going, but he also wanted Terry to recognise the good work that had been done. "Terry, thank you for sharing all of this with me, you have definitely made a good study of life, but can I just ask you to think about the way you're thinking?" "What do you mean?" Terry asked rather surprised. Tom continued, "Was everything you saw or did negative, or did you do a lot of things that you felt helped the world when you were living your human life?" "Well, I like to think I always acted in the best interests of mankind and the earth." Terry replied. "Exactly." stated Tom straight away. "There has been so much that you and many others have done to help the world, and I have many other students of life like yourself that always worked for the greatest and highest good. Each and every one of them certainly contributed to making the world a better place." Terry continued to listen to Tom, as always he was soaking everything in because Tom always made Terry look at things from a different perspective, and although he may not have always agreed with it, he did respect him enough to listen and think about it. Tom continued with his thoughts on the matter, "All of my students including you Terry have made a big difference to the world, we just don't always see those differences, basing our judgement on the negatives we can see rather than looking for the positives".

There was a brief pause before Terry asked Tom "Is that what I have been doing? Instead of seeing the good, I was seeing the bad?" "In some ways yes." replied Tom, "but that is quite natural when you live there because you don't always have the time to focus on a deeper level. I want to remind you that you have done some wonderful things in the world, and you were so approachable for so many which helped them through their challenging times. Never forget I have witnessed these wonderful differences you have made in the world, and each good deed that you did for mankind did actually have a knock on effect to help others." "That all sounds great.", replied Terry, "But when you're there you can see what needs doing, and in many cases how to do it." "Yes, this is true." agreed Tom "In my physical life, I experienced all that you did, from the frustration of not being able to stop what was happening, to the hurt that was so damaging to others as a result of other people's actions." Tom continued, "I've been there and on many occasions I felt despairingly worried about how mankind was going to continue in the decades to come, how it would affect our children and their future. But it was only when I returned to my spiritual home that I saw there is also a lot of good being done in the world, even though there is still so much to do."

Tom's words were reeling around in Terry's mind, he knew he had a lot still to do. As he sat with this he could see that for him, he felt he died to soon, because there was still so much that he could do for the world. Terry shared his views and thoughts with Tom who could see that Terry was still coming to terms with his passing and struggling with the fact that he didn't achieve all he wanted to. Tom knew these thoughts were taking Terry to a very set way of thinking and wanted to remind him of this before his thoughts ran away with him. Well here goes, crunch time, thought Tom as he approached his next sentence. "Terry, I know you feel as though you should have been allowed to stayed on earth and continue to do the good work you were doing, but the reality is you were meant to pass when you did. Because of the way you have worked with this through me and other teachers and guides you know that you agreed to the life you had, and you also agreed to the time you would pass before you ever took a breath on earth." Now that Terry was back in his spiritual home he remembered all that Tom was saying, and the agreements he made, but now he felt very different to the way he did then.

"Yes I remember all of that." replied Terry, "But I feel very different now and I can't get it out of my head that I now know more about what I need to do." Tom knew that there was an even more uncomfortable conversation that was needed between the two of them, so he let Terry finish what he was saying as he could see he was rather stressed out. Tom started the next part of the conversation "I know you feel passionate about all of this, but I want you to think about how much you can teach us here with your experiences in your recent lifetime. There is still so much we don't know, and as you know mankind is forever unfolding, so we never stop learning from them. I also have to say that with the work you did down there, we can all help mankind from here with your new found information." Tom stayed silent for just a few moments but then looked straight at Terry "Terry you have so much within you that can continue to help the world and mankind even though you will be doing it up here. We need you up here with us now, please think about that."

Both men had finished what they were saying, each could see the other's opinion, even if they were coming from different perspectives. It was clear that Terry needed to have a good think before they met again. Terry did think long and hard, but still felt the same. He was wondering how he could get this across to his guide. He had done a lot of reflecting and was continuing to do so. Terry was enjoying reflecting back on his life, finding such comfort reflecting back on all the laughter, love, and happiness he had in his life. He became emotional at this point because he was wishing himself back there to when his children were small and he and Sue were building a good life for them all. Gosh he thought, it wasn't an easy life, but it was a great life. "Oh how I miss them, but I know they're doing ok, and the kids will definitely be making sure their mum is ok." Terry was also seeing all the gentleness and support he gave others that he thought nothing of, but now he was seeing the impact a kind thought, a little bit of respect and love for mankind can have, and yes, he was quite proud of that. This reflection back carried on for a few hours and every so often he would speak or laugh out loud forgetting that he wasn't sharing this with anyone else, which felt quite lonely for him.

Terry didn't realise how much he had done for others because he just got on with it saying nothing. He believed that that was what we should all do. Even if Terry only had £10 in his pocket he would give it to someone who needed it more than he did. What used to make his family laugh was that he saw it as his purpose to make others laugh, and feel good about themselves. Now Terry was doing the laughing but with great pride as he looks down and sees that his children are all doing the same. "Well, we certainly did something right with our four children." He said. Terry knew that it wouldn't be long before Tom came to see him again, and he wanted to make sure that his thoughts and beliefs were the same as when they were last together, so he had to search within and find what his truth really was.

Terry used his time wisely weighing up the sacrifices he must make if he decided to go with what was right for him. He needed to make sure that he was aware of the impact it would have on everyone in both worlds. In case you haven't guessed it, what Terry was weighing up was whether to stay and become a guide for those that needed him, or to return back to the physical world and help others from there. Neither of these situations were ideal but he knew he had to go one way or the other, so he had to make his mind up and commit either way. As Terry was thinking, instead of just sitting, he got up and started walking around to see and meet others. One thing he had noticed was that the sun always shined, and that the air was clean. They had woods and forests as well as meadows, which was something he had experienced in meditative state, but to be honest he thought that was just something he experienced then. Now he was seeing that they were real, just in a parallel world. When he met with another Spirit being he acknowledged them and had brief chats with them, which he found so interesting because it confirmed that everything, our likes and dislikes were the same in both worlds and that included food, and hobbies to. In fact Terry was pleased to see that it was very similar to the physical world, so if he stayed he could still enjoy working on old cars, which he loved. He in fact saw some spirit beings doing exactly that which confirmed all that he had been told by Tom and his other guides and teachers. Not that he was questioning them, but it was nice to have all of this confirmed.

Tom approached Terry with his normal gentle smile and bowed in front of Terry, who in turn did the same to Tom. "I see you have been doing a lot of thinking and evaluating what is right for you." Terry smiled "Is there nothing you don't know about me?" Tom smiled back and replied "Very little. I also see that you have made your mind up about whether to stay here with us and be of service this way, or return back into another physical life and continue to help mankind that way. Terry shouldn't have been surprised that Tom knew, but it still managed to do just that. Terry tried to keep his voice firm "Yes, I have decided to do exactly that", and continued to explain things from his perspective. Tom listened intently, and of course he did truly understand because he had been in the same position himself when he passed over, which he decided to share with Terry. "Thank you for explaining what's going through your mind, and believe me I truly understand why you would be thinking this way, but I would like to explain a few things to you before you make that final decision to stay here or return back there." "Of course." replied Terry, "I'm all ears." This was Terrys' attempt to lighten the situation, but at this point Tom didn't feel it was a situation that could be made light of.

Tom started to point out the pros and cons of this situation. "You are a truly evolved spirit, and no matter what you had to go through you didn't allow any of it to turn you bitter, vengeful of tunnel visioned. Throughout it all you responded from a place of spirituality, even when you were going through your toughest times, which is something us guides and elders are so proud of because you never wasted a moment and continued to develop, grow and evolve as the beautiful soul that you are." Terry felt slightly uncomfortable as he heard Tom praising him "There are many that did the same." Tom continued, "Yes there are many that did the same, and there are many that are continuing to do the same on earth. One day they will have to decide what's right for them, but for now this is about you. We believe that you will achieve so much more by staying here with us, and we also believe that it's time for you to come home. You have had many lives and in each of them you have undergone some very difficult times. At the end of each lifetime you have achieved so much more than we ever hoped for, but don't you think it's time for you to have an easier time now. You are more than ready to take this next step and be a guide to someone that really needs you right now."

Terry could see exactly what Tom was saying but thought to himself this wasn't really working as he had made up his mind that it would so there didn't seem to be a real reason to carry on the discussion. Tom, however was determined to finish this conversation in a way that enabled Terry to understand every aspect of his decision, so carried on with the final few words that he wanted to say. "Terry, you also need to understand that if you do this you will never be able to have that reunion with your family that so often happens when they visit a medium. Your family will wonder why you never come through to guide them through their challenging times, because they will be looking for that."

Terry hesitated but then answered, "Yes I have thought long and hard about this and I'm sure that at times, I might wish I had made a different decision, albeit that everything I know tells me that what I will be going through will be as a result of my decision. The other couple of other things that I am also sure of are that as I leave my family behind they will all do well, growing together with the help and support that Sue and I have given them through their childhood as well as everything we have taught them. I know that their guides and teachers will never desert them, they will always have their guidance and support. I hand them over with great gratitude for looking after them and helping them. The final thing that I'm sure of is that they will be part of my soul family, and when we have all decided to continue to help mankind from the spirit world, we will all be together once more. Of that I am really confident." Tom could see that Terry wasn't going to change his mind, so there was only one option now, to arrange for an elder to go through the kind of life that Terry was going to live and the challenges he will face with the intention of bringing more knowledge about how the two worlds can combine, bring peace to love to mankind and the world they live in.

Tom admired the decision that Terry was making, but couldn't help thinking that he could do so much more as a guide working with mankind. As Tom knows and respects there is always a choice, and we all have to choose what's right for us, which is always respected in the spirit world. Terry looked over at Tom, asking hesitantly, "Can I just have a few moments looking down on my family please? I just want to see them one more time before I take my new but different path." Naturally Tom agreed, "Of course, but just for the record, you won't be returning back to your new earthly life just yet, as there is still much to do before you leave." Terry agreed that he had to go through a procedure before he returns, and he understood that the reason for the procedure was to ensure that spirit gains understanding of what mankind, and the earth, needs in order to bring peace and harmony to them all. People like Terry who had just returned from living another life as a human had a lot of information that will help spirit to understand so much more. Spirit were the first to admit that it's not only mankind that is constantly learning, it's them also, and it's the information brought back from those who have just passed that can bring the kind information to help them understand more.

Before he knew it Terry was looking down on his family. His heart melted as soon as he saw them, and it did make him wonder if he was doing the right thing. As he looked over them he was so proud to see his children all supporting their mum, and said out loud, "Bless them, look at them, they're all there supporting their mum. They're good kids bless them." He looked over to Tom and "That's why I know my family will be ok now that I am gone. I know they will support each other, because they're strong." He watched his daughter Tina go into the kitchen to make some tea, and he knew to focus on her for the moment. Tina stood by the sink unit as she was waiting for the kettle to boil and broke down in tears. Through her tears she said "Oh dad, what are we going to do without you? You were such a big part of our lives, and you always gave us strength when we needed it." Tina continued, "Dad, if you can hear me please give us the strength now to get through this, especially looking after mum because she's going to need it." Terry felt his emotions starting to overwhelm him, "I will my lovely girl, I promise." At that point the bond between Terry and Tina was as strong as ever, and she felt it. "Dad are you with me?" she asked. "I can feel you, and I'm sure it's not my imagination." Terry whispered ever so gently, "Yes, it's me my angel, I'm right beside you." Tina felt sad and elated all at once because she could feel her dad, but at the same time it was a reminder that her dad had passed.

Tina didn't say anything in front of her mum, but she did call her sister Jackie over to her and all excited she shared with her what had just happened. Jackie looked very sceptical "I know you think you felt dad around you, but it may only be because you wanted to, so don't read too much into it." As Terry heard Jackie say this to Tina he had a good laugh to himself as that was very typical of her. "She should have been a scientist", he said with a smile on his face. "She was always the logical and analytical one of the family who always thought in the box." Jackie could see that Tina was disappointed by her sisters' reaction. Jackie felt awful, but as she said to Tina "I just don't want you to be disappointed, or imagine that he's still here because we all know he's not." Tina was angry at her sister's way of thinking, but wasn't going to show it, particularly at this time, but she also wasn't going to let her sister's belief ruin what she knew she had experienced for those few brief moments, because it was definitely not her imagination. Terry looked over at his wife as they sat with David and Barbara and went deep into thought about how much Sue had given him over the years. "She was always there for me no matter what, and she is the same with everyone, but sometimes it's to her detriment as often she puts her needs at the bottom of her priority list ending up being exhausted." Tom found all of this interesting as it was clear that Terry adored his family and he felt they reciprocated that, yet he is prepared to miss out on being by their side so that he can continue to help mankind by returning to earth. Tom looked at Terry admiring his strength, courage and willingness to sacrifice everything as he is preparing to step back, leave his family in capable hands, and start all over again. Suddenly Terry looked around and asked if he could do one more thing before he leaves, to squeeze his wife's hand because that's what he always promised he would do if he passed first. Tom agreed and helped Terry to focus on his frequencies and vibrations so that they will match Sue's. Terry drew so close to her that he was standing next to her, so he knew she would feel him. As he blended with her energy he brought his hand down over hers and grabbed and squeezed her hand in the hope that she would feel it. Sue looked down at her hand and felt this tight squeeze on her right hand. She knew immediately that it was Terry trying to let her know that he was with her. She placed her left hand over her right one so that she could squeeze his hand back, and yes, he did feel it. At that moment Terry wanted that moment never to end, but he knew it had to, and he knew he had another purpose to serve now.

Terry looked over at Tom, "Thank you so much, you have given me the world in those few moments, and I will be able to take the love and bonds that I felt in those special moments with me wherever I go." Tom smiled, "You are very courageous my friend. I feel you still have so much work to do on earth so I wish you all the very best. I know we shall meet again, so I won't say goodbye. You and I will always have that connection together and it's because of that connection that I am sure we will be called to work together once more, as we already have after many other lifetimes." As Tom bid farewell to Terry, he reminded him that one of the elders would be coming along to see him shortly to discuss the next stage with him. Terry felt quite sad that he had to say goodbye to Tom even though he felt that they would work together again, but perhaps in a different way. Right now the thing that Terry was missing the most was the support that Tom gave him as well as the comfort and cushioning he brought him in tough times.

Terry sat back and reflected on his lifetime and all that he had experienced because he wanted to work out for himself why he felt the need to go back so quickly. So, he thought about what was the one thing that affected him the most, and why. So much came to mind for him. Things such as the way mankind treats each other as well as not caring for other living beings such as animals. Or was it the greed that many had? God that's a big one he thought, saying out loud, "I don't know how many times I saw people turn ugly because of their ego's and the need to have more materialism in their lives. In some cases there were some that would lie, cheat and do anything to have that. That's not right, it's just pure greed." Whilst Terry was reflecting on all that he had learned he hadn't noticed the elder come forward to be with him. The elder was dressed in a robe with a hood just like a monk, he had the hood up at that point so Terry couldn't see his face no matter how much he tried. "Sorry sir, I didn't realise you were there. I was very much deep in thought about mankind and their behaviours." The elder lifted his head so Terry could see the his face. To Terry's surprise, the elder, who he called father, was younger than he had expected. He really didn't seem to be very old. He was clean shaven and had short blonde hair, which made Terry wonder what had happened in the elder's life to end up in spirit so young. Another thought quickly went through Terry's mind. was, "How come he's an elder? Was he really that evolved whilst on earth?" Terry had so many questions but was sure the answers would unravel themselves in time. Terry could feel the beautiful and peaceful energy that was coming from the elder, and he could tell that this man had a beautiful old soul which had nurtured many people through time. Terry greeted the father "Father I'm pleased to meet you." The elder looked over at Terry acknowledging his greeting. "Thank you, I'm glad to know that you were reflecting upon the behaviours of mankind because it's that kind of knowledge that we need to work with." The elder continued "We now need to look at the biggest thing that has stayed with you about the behaviours, insecurities and greed that you noticed with many." "Oh gosh father there is so much to this. I call it greed, but I really think it's probably more about the insecurities that many in the world have as a result of the media, the competition. I believe the fear of being rejected is at the core of it."

Terry continued, "But there is so much more to this father because it's like the whole world is blind. They can't seem to allow themselves to focus on their inner world and work with it, so instead they focus on the materialistic side of life, and try to find some kind of worth there, but of course we all know that's not possible. From a child I could see this happening, and even though I was very young I could predict where that attitude was taking mankind. I know that there are now more people becoming aware and working with their soul and all that we need to do on a spiritual level, but it's still not enough. Father now that I have come home and reflected on that lifetime I now recognise I can hopefully set an example and show people the way when they want to walk their spiritual path." The Elder said nothing but sat and thought which made Terry feel uncomfortable because he wasn't sure if he had been pushing his luck by asking to go back to live yet another mortal life.

The Elder turned and looked at Terry, smiled and said "Yes I understand what you are saying, and it is truly tempting to allow you to go back, but before you entered the last life you seemed to be in a rush to get back there as you felt that you had more to do. Now again we have the same situation, and I wonder if you will ever be ready to give up your lives on earth and work as a guide from here. I really do feel that you can achieve so much by working from here for those on the earth that are still mortal." The Elder took a brief pause, but decided he wanted to ask one more question before he made his decision. "Let me ask you Terry, are you going back to help mankind and bring balance to the Universe? Or are you just not ready to give up the mortal lives that you have been leading on earth?" Terry was quite surprised at that point because he hadn't thought that was how it looked, so he thought deeply before he replied, and when he did, he surprised himself with the answer. Now he had to admit it openly to the Father. "Well, I guess some of it is because I'm not liking the idea that my time on earth may be finished, but I also realise, and am very aware that if something doesn't happen soon mankind are going to take some great big steps backwards." The Father smiled, "That's already happening, and sometimes it takes drastic and tragic events to happen in order for mankind to become aware of the blessings they truly have in life. Well, regardless of all that, I think you should return to living a mortal life, but we now need to agree where and what your life will be like."

Terry's mind was going ten to the dozen because one part of him was glad to be going back, but the other part said that by doing that his family wouldn't be able to call upon him for help. The other side of him was saying, he needed to go back and continue to do the work that was so important to him. There was also a part of him that was dreading what kind of life he was going to have the next time around. As he thought about this he said "Yes, I will have to talk to the father about that", forgetting that the father was actually standing next to him! "What was that you said Terry", asked the Father. "Oh I was just thinking out loud about the next time I go back. I hope that my life will be a little easier because I have always had the hard ones, or at least it feels like that." The father actually agreed with him because Terry had had some horrible past lives, so perhaps it was time that it all changed for him.

There was a lot to be done now in order to for Terry to return. It wouldn't only involve Terry and the elder, there were other guides and elders that wanted an input to this as they would also be helping him through his life and the different kind of experiences he will have. So it was all hands around the table to work this out. Now, depending on the life that was agreed for Terry he might have an inner knowledge that he chose the life he's living, and he also chose the kind of things he would be up against, the challenges and battles. On the other hand, he might not have a clue about, or belief in, in the spirit world, and how it is our spiritual home. As a result his first set of behaviours in his young life won't be as spiritual as he might expect, although he could be sure that throughout his difficult times his guides will be there.

So after much deliberation it was decided that Terry would be lucky enough to have a better life, although it would bring problems for him. Now he had to choose his parents, understanding that we always choose who our parents are. Terry's parents would serve a purpose with all that he was trying to share with mankind. He could only share these things if he had actually had the experiences in his life. Terry couldn't wait for this, he had visions that he would chose very calm, loving and caring people, who would have a lot of time to give him the love that he needs, and he was right. That was exactly the kind of parents that he and the elders chose for him.

Some may question how it is that if he had a good life, and had a solid sense of self, how could he learn and understand from his experiences? There are some that might believe that it's only those that have bad upbringings and horrible experiences through their lives that would truly understand what it's like and through this stand up for their and others rights. Well, the same can be said of those that have a better upbringing. Many of them will have a strong sense of self, fight whichever way they can in order to keep that strong part of them, and also fight for the injustice towards others. So, they could help make a difference just as much as the people that had been treated badly in life.

As Terry sat around the table with the elders, he was liking the sound of his new parents, and he was getting quite excited. They were both teachers that work in a primary school, named Tanya and Paul. They had been trying for a child for about five years, were starting to think about trying to adopt, and they would have had a good chance, but now it had been agreed that Terry would return back to living a mortal life, all of a sudden they would hit the jackpot and Susan would fall pregnant. Yes, they're going to make great parents, ideal to give Terry the support he will need throughout his life.

After the meeting the father and Terry walked for a while which pleased Terry because he was keen to say thank you to his guide for listening to him, his concerns and the need he has to return back into a mortal life. "Father, thank you so much for all that you have done for me, especially for listening to me about why I need to go back. I didn't think I would be that lucky this time around. Now, I can be of service to mankind again." The Father stared over at Terry, "My friend I can see and feel your excitement as you talk about your future work with mankind, and I'm glad this all went your way, but I do have to tell you that it is very possible the lifetime you're about to be born into will be the last on earth. I know that sounds quite hard but you have already developed to the point that you are a very evolved spiritual soul, who also has work to do here in this world, but don't worry you will be able to help as many here as you have helped back on earth." Terry knew this would be the case so he didn't argue, but it did give him a greater sense of urgency for the work he needed to do back on earth. Terry responded to the father quietly, "Yes I understand ather, and I will respect that."

There was one thing Terry wanted to ask his guide about his family. "Hmm Father, I know I am being cheeky asking this, but I'm wondering if you would keep an eye on my family please? I know it has been me that pushed to return back into a mortal life, and I know I may seem keen to abandon my family and go back as a different person, but that just isn't the case. I just need to do the work I started doing before I died. I'm aware that in one way I'm leaving them in the lurch, but I do feel I don't have much option right now as mankind are really at a point where things have got to change, or there will be a backlash that can't be controlled." The Father agreed telling Terry that he understood. Just as the father and Terry were about to separate, the father looked to Terry, and to put his mind at ease he said. "Your family will be fine, and I promise I will look after them for you, as well as their own guides. Remember, when the time is right you will be meeting up again with your family because they will always be a big part of your life. So, you can live your new life without a worry." "Thank you father, I needed to hear that. That has put my mind at ease immensely."

So, Terry was on his way back to life as a human being. Terry heard his guide wish him luck in his new life and as he turned around the father said "Remember my friend, you will always have a beautiful soul, and your spirit will always be ready to fly, even if it is in a human body."

Chapter 5

AMANDA

Amanda, or Mandy as she was known to her mates, was a young lady who lived in Southend, Essex, and was barely old enough to be earning a living, (she was 20 years old) when she got in with the wrong crowd and started taking drugs along with her new found mates. At first she had it all under control seeing it as a bit of fun, something that many who start on drugs believe. It didn't take too long though before the people that cared for Mandy could see that she was on a downward spiral. Like so many, Mandys' thought process was that it was just party drugs and was quite harmless. At first she was also able to keep that she was taking drugs away from work, but after a while things changed, and was escalating pretty fast. She started desperately seeking a drug that would give her that euphoric feeling, and the loving everyone feeling she felt when experimenting with substances. The kind of drugs she was using at that point was classed as uppers, and she loved that feeling of being happy. Sadly, all too often people start chasing how they felt with that very first fix, trying to reach that euphoria again, so they start to experiment with other drugs, such as cocaine and heroin. Both of these drugs are highly addictive and highly dangerous. Experimenting with these kinds of drugs teaches the drug user that cocaine works as an upper and heroin as a downer, so it's easy to see just how drugs mess with peoples' moods and become mood enhancers. In the end though Mandy was trying every kind of drug she could just to feel some kind of happiness.

Sadly, it wasn't too long before Mandy was well on the way to using the harder stuff to control her moods, but in fact she had totally lost the ability to control her moods and her life as a result. Her family was now aware of just how bad her habit was but sadly the support and help they tried to give her was thrown back at them, she became very defensive and, on some occasions, aggressive to be around. Her mum used to sit and try to talk to her, but it was no use, she wasn't listening, just kept telling her mum she had it all under control and that she could stop at any time. What wasn't helping Mandy was the fact that she started to see a guy that was heavily into drugs as well and because he didn't like to use on his own he encouraged Mandy to do it with him. Mandy, by now, had been sacked from her job because of her late timekeeping over the last few months and, to be honest, they also couldn't afford to keep her on because of how she had started looking. She had lost pride in herself and didn't care about her appearance. She also had sores appearing on her face and if she had a sleeveless t-shirt or top on you could see the injection marks, so she had even stopped trying to hide the marks on her arm.

Naturally her family and her friends were very worried about her because they knew where this was all going. Her mum, dad, sister and brother all tried to help her, but to no avail, although, at this point, they were hanging on to straws. They had a quiet word with Mandy's cousin Julia, or Jules as she was known by the family, who had always been and even recently was still very close to Mandy. When they were young they were called the "terrible twins", and both Mandy and Jules always said they were "soul sisters" which the family always agreed with. Until very recently, even though Jules was saving up, she would always make time to be with Mandy and they were always going clubbing together or they used to pop down the local. Now Mandy was a very different girl toward her cousin and it was breaking her heart to see her going downhill. Mandy's mum Kirsty was hoping that if Jules had a word with Mandy she would listen, so she arranged for her to come around when she knew Mandy was there. Mandy was sitting in the living room when Jules arrived. She walked down the hallway, turned and looked into the sitting room where she saw Mandy sitting on her own on the settee. Jules walked in and said "Hi" in a very upbeat way. Mandy turned around and cracked a smile when she saw her soul sister there. "Hiya babe, how's you?" replied Mandy, "What you doing here?" "I've got the day off so I thought I would come around and have a catch up with you." Jules felt bad because she was lying, she didn't have a day off at all, in fact she had pulled a sickie. Mandy looked over at her looking doubtful, "You sure about that? How did you know I would be here?" she asked because she had recently left home to live with her boyfriend. Jules was getting a bit flustered thinking Mandy surely could see through this, "Well I didn't know you would be here, I just thought I would try, and if you weren't here I knew your mum would be." Mandy accepted her answer and cracked a lovely big smile because deep down she was so pleased to see Julia.

Jules continued "so how's it going? Your mum says you've left your job and are looking for another one." Mandy was irritated by the thought that her mum was telling her family about the job, and that was evident in Mandy's answer. "Blimey she didn't waste time in letting you know what was going on." Jules tried to make light of it, "Oh she only told my mum, in passing I think." "Yeah well, yeah I'm looking hard but there's nothing out there. I need the money now because I'm living with my boyfriend and we're a bit short at the moment." Jules got a strong feeling that Mandy was chancing her luck with trying to get some money out of her, "But that's not going to happen." she thought to herself. "Oh that's a shame, I've got my fingers crossed for you hun." Mandy was a bit despondent because normally Julia would always offer to lend her some money, but not on this occasion

The girls sat there quite awkwardly because their relationship was so different compared to how it used to be. "Tell me about your bloke then, what's his name?" asked Jules. Mandy replied, a big smile on her face "His name is Sam, and he's gorgeous. He's about three years older than me, and he's so gentle and caring for me." Julia was struggling hard at this point because she had heard exactly what he was like, not nice. Mandy quite proudly told Jules, "We're living together now, setting up our new home just like you and Darren are saving up to do". Jules was the same age as Mandy. She had been engaged to Darren for about a year, and they were both living with Jules's parents so that they could save up for their first home together. They both had their heads screwed on right and were planning every stage of life together very carefully. Jules couldn't help but reply "It's not quite the same though is it Mand? You haven't known each other for very long, and you really don't know anything about him." Mandy's body language completely changed, she became defensive. In a sharp tone and raised voice she said "What are you f****** talking about? You don't know anything." Jules reply was also sharp. "You're having a laugh aren't you Mand, everyone knows what he's like, he's into drugs in a big way and for the record all of his girlfriends have ended up taking drugs. If you don't believe me, ask Debbie, she knows a lot more than me because she's his cousin."

Mandy didn't know what to say at that point, so she did what a lot of people do if they haven't got an answer when it comes to home truths and that's to verbally attack. "That bitch, she's always been trouble, I don't know what you see in her as a mate. She's always slagging someone off, and she tells loads of lies to." Mandy continued, "And she stirs the sh** between friends as well. She's always been aggressive towards me since we were all in primary school." Jules was annoyed now and felt she needed to defend her friend Debbie, her voice still raised, "Whoa whoa, watch what you're saying please, that's my mate you're talking about." Jules was gobsmacked that Mandy could be so nasty and Mandy could see that she was very upset, but carried on "What's the matter? Don't you like to hear the truth about your so called mate then." Jules wasn't going to have that "Mandy, you're out of order saying all of this stuff because you know what I'm saying is right." Mandy wasn't listening and was determined to have the last word to end the conversation, "You're talking out of your arse!" Jules stood up, walked out of the sitting room and down the corridor into the into the kitchen to see her aunt who was standing there listening. She couldn't believe how nasty Mandy had got with her cousin.

Kirsty looked at Jules, a pained expression on her face, as Jules walked towards her in the kitchen. Kirsty could see the hurt that this row had caused Jules, and apologetically said, "I'm sorry love for asking you to have a word with her. I heard that it didn't go too well. I've never known you and Mandy to fight. I'm gobsmacked because you guys have always been so close." "Auntie Kirsty, this guy is a nasty piece of work, and he will take her down with him." Both Kirsty and Julia had tears in their eyes as they hugged each other. It was at this point Mandy came out of the living room and saw them together which set her off again. "Oh I see this was all set up wasn't it? "You guys are ganging up against me about Sam when you don't even know him," Jules turned to see Mandy "I do bloody know him, and so does Darren. I'm telling you he's no good." Mandy turned tail and started walking to the door still shouting at her mum and cousin. Just as she got to the door, she turned, looked at them both and said "Go on you guys, now that I'm leaving you can have a pop at me and Sam as much as you like. Oh and by the way your mate Debbie isn't so innocent either. She's known as a bully and a bitch." Jules didn't respond, she just let Mandy walk out the door.

Kirsty broke down and sobbed saying in between each sob, "What are we going to do? I'm losing her Jules," By this time Jules was breaking her heart as well. She leant her head against her aunt's, "I don't know aunt Kirsty, I just don't know." When Kirsty stopped crying, she asked, "What was she going on about your mate Debbie?" Jules replied "Oh I wouldn't worry too much about what Mandy says about Debbie because from the very beginning back in primary school they have never got on. But what's really weird is that I have always felt that I've always known her, and we can very often go for weeks without talking to each other, but when we meet up again we pick up where we let off." "So what's it all about with Mandy and

Debbie then", asked Kirsty again, which gave Jules flashbacks to school days and the amount of rows that Debbie and Mandy had. "Sometimes", she thought, "it felt like Debbie was trying to boss Mandy about, and we all know Mandy won't be bossed about, or at least she never used to be bossed about by anybody, until she met this guy. To be honest aunt Kirsty I haven't got the faintest idea, but there does appear to be a real dislike for each other from both of them, and I think the only reason they are still prepared to be in each other's company is because of me if I want us all to get together."

One thing Mandy was right about was that she and Debbie had never got on. In fact they couldn't stand the sight of each other and it showed, but both of them would try not to make it nasty especially when Jules was around. On many occasions Jules had asked both Mandy and Debbie what the problem was but both didn't really have a good answer. They both just felt that they didn't like each other but for the sake of Jules they would try and get on. Jules often noticed that very often it seemed like Debbie would goad Mandy to a point that Mandy would argue with her. The strange thing was that Debbie didn't do this with anyone else, just Mandy. Even stranger was that although Debbie would wind Mandy up she also felt sorry for her now that she was in this situation, asking Jules how it was all going, and making sure that Mandy got all the info on her cousin in the hope that it would get her to see what he was really like. Sometimes Jules couldn't help but laugh at the way that, although Debbie couldn't stand Mandy, she was really trying to look after Mandy from a distance using Jules.

When the girls were younger in primary school, Mandy, Jules and Debbie always hung around together, together with another girl called Karen. They played together, they fought together and they grew up together. Recently though Mandy hadn't seen Karen because Karen doesn't tolerate drug users so from the moment she heard about Mandy and drugs she wasn't going anywhere near her. For Karen, everything was black or white and there was nothing in-between.

Once Jules went back home she sat and had a good old cry which was much needed. She sat and mulled what had just happened over in her mind again and again, making her feel lousy and stupid that she let Mandy wind her up the way she did. She was trying to convince herself that all she had said to Mandy was necessary, but she knew deep down she didn't feel that strongly about it, in fact it was just the opposite because she had never seen her cousin so vulnerable, and scruffy, which definitely wasn't like Mandy. Jules's boyfriend Darren tried to console his partner but it wasn't working, so he suggested that Jules should go and see Debbie. That was a regular pattern the girls had when they were upset about something, so it was quite natural to go and see Debbie, but the tricky bit is that she couldn't say too much about what the row was really about. "I'll have to fluff around it a bit" she said to Darren.

Once Jules got to Debbie's she immediately broke down in tears. Debbie put her arms around Jules and comforted her the best way she could. Jules started to talk about the row that she had but put the emphasis on the row being about drugs, not about Debbie, which it was really about. If Debbie found out there would be hell to pay. Debbie sat and listened carefully to her mate letting go of her tears and worries. She had to admit that she was now really worried about Mandy. "I mean it's not like I like the girl." she said to Jules at one point, "But I wouldn't wish that on my worst enemy." Jules looked over at Debbie, and could see how worried she really was about Mandy. She couldn't help asking, "What is it with you two? You go on about the fact that you don't like her but if she's in trouble you're so concerned and thoughtful about her. I just can't work it out." With a quizzical look Debbie replied "I don't know. I just think that someone needs to look after her and who better than me. I can't remember a time without her being there and in some kind of trouble so I thought I've just got used to watching out for her because she was part of our little group." Jules looked over at Debbie, cracked a smile and said "You just can't help mothering her can you?" Debbie didn't answer, but that was about the truth of it.

As the year passed by Mandy descended deeper and deeper into her addiction which was awful for all to see. She was barely seeing her family, and although Jules and Mandy had made some kind of peace, there was very little communication between them. Mandy was still with her boyfriend Sam. There was gossip that he was seeing someone else and was losing interest in Mandy which was the normal pattern with his relationships. To Mandy this was devastating as she adored him, but the reality was that she needed him more than wanted him now.

One day whilst out shopping Debbie ran into Mandy who had spotted her and was trying to avoid her, but Debbie wasn't having any of that, promptly walking straight in front of her. "Hi ya Mandy, how's you?" As soon as she asked that question she thought to herself "I'm a silly cow to ask that because I can see how she's doing, she looks a bloody mess! As Mandy answered her it was plain to see that she wasn't really in this world looking drugged up. Mandy tried to answer without slurring, "Oh hello it's you, how's it going?" Debbie asked Mandy if she was ok, but she couldn't get a coherent answer out of her. What Mandy did say though, was that she's out looking for Sam because she hadn't seen him since the day before and she was missing him. Debbie thought to herself it was more like missing her supply of drugs. Debbie's heart broke for her as she could see that Mandy was nose diving into an abyss that she was never going to come out of.

Debbie didn't really know what to say. As she stood there awkwardly, looking at this shell of a person in front of her, she couldn't help but think there was no point in saying anything to try and ease the situation because she could see that the girl couldn't take anything in as she was too high. "Mandy, do you want me to take you home?" Mandy responded immediately "No, I ain't going home till I find him." There was nothing Debbie could do , so she just said "Well I hope you find him

Mand." Debbie couldn't believe it but as she walked away she had a great lump in her throat and her eyes were welling up with tears.

As soon as Debbie got home, she phoned Jules to tell her she had seen Mandy and what she looked like. She couldn't hold back the tears. Jules immediately dropped everything and went around round to Debbie's. Debbie opened the door to Jules and as soon as she had one foot over the threshold Debbie just grabbed hold of her for dear life, "She's in a bad way Jules, have you seen her recently." Jules looked so sad, "No, not recently, but she was in a bad way when I last saw her. She won't let anyone help her and I don't know what to do." Debbie grabbed her mate and gave her the biggest hug. Forever the realist, Debbie said to her closest mate. "You had better brace yourself hun because this is going to have a nasty ending if she doesn't do something to change things and judging by what I saw I get a feeling she's too far gone for that now anyway."

As the girls walked into Debbie's living room to sit down, there was a complete silence around them that was incredibly eerie. After a few moments Jules looked at Debbie, "OK so tell me what she was like today." Debbie wasn't sure this was going to help Jules but if that's what she wanted, so be it. She started hesitantly, "Well, she was as thin as a rake, she had scabs over her face, and her hands were shaking. Her eyes looked like they were coming out of her head, and she could barely put a sentence together." Jules sat there almost trance like, even though the tears were running down her face. As soon as Debbie saw that, she started to cry with her as she grabbed her mate for a hug. Their hug continued for a few moments as they composed themselves once more, both taking the deepest breath.

Jules thought it was so lovely to hear her mate be so caring, especially over a girl that she's never thought much of. She started the conversation off again, "One thing has shocked me, how caring you are about her even though you don't like her, and you never have, not even in primary school." "Me to." replied Debbie, "Normally I would have very little understanding of this kind of thing in people, but with Mandy it's different. I may not like her but strangely enough I do care about her, and I do worry for her. It's really weird." Jules sat there with a smirk on her face. "I know why you care, it's because you're not as hard as you like to think you are".

A few weeks later it got back to Jules that Mandy's boyfriend was definitely seeing someone else, but he was also keeping Mandy dangling on a string, which infuriated Jules. Mandy's mum Kirsty was absolutely devastated because she knew that she was losing her daughter and there was absolutely nothing she could do about it. There had been times when Mandy came around to her mum's full of smiles, pretending she was ok but that was only ever if she needed some cash and she always had a plausible excuse that she knew her mum would believe. After a while Kirsty started to realise that it was all just ways to get money for more drugs, so as much as it hurt her she toughened up on Mandy, but at a cost because Mandy stopped popping around to see her at all. Mandy's dad John was always in the background but he left all of this kind of stuff to Kirsty because he didn't know how to deal with it. There were a couple of occasions when he tried to talk to Mandy but it always ended up in a row, so he felt it was better to leave his wife to sort this out. That didn't mean he cared less for her, or that he didn't worry, but all he ever seemed to do was make it worse, or so he though, so it was best he step back.

In the early hours of June 15th Jules was woken up by her phone ringing. As she answered, blurry eyed and not quite sure what time it was, she heard her mum in tears at the other end of the phone. "It's Mandy, she's dead!" she heard her mum say, "she's dead." Jules sat up and took a sharp breath. "No she can't be. No, that can't be true." Jules's boyfriend Darren was woken up by the phone ringing to. As he lay there listening to the conversation between his fiancée and her mum, he couldn't help but think he knew this was going to happen. We all did. He thought better of actually saying that though because he knew Jules would react. Jules was just ending her phone call with mum and promised she was on her way to her.

When Darren and Jules arrived, they walked through the door and she could hear her dad Billy consoling her mum Christine who was devastated even though she had long prepared herself for this day. Her sister Kirsty couldn't take the terrible news in, and Christine knew that when she did this was going to hit her hard. Jules rushed to her mum and grabbed hold of her tight, "Oh mum, I can't believe it, I have dreaded this for so long, and now that it's here it all feels unreal. Oh God." Jules continued, "How's Auntie Kirsty and Uncle John doing?" Christine managed to stop sobbing long enough to say "She's in bits, so I'm going over there shortly to be with her." "I'm coming to." said Jules "I need to be with them all, I can't do much but I can be there for them."

Christine finally had the courage to ask her sister whether she knew what had happened, it was a drugs overdose. Kirsty finally found the strength to talk without sobbing and started to tell them what the police had figured out from her boyfriend. "Apparently, Mandy and Sam had a row around 4.30pm. Sam told her it was over and then stormed out of the flat. He came home about midnight, found Mandy slumped in her chair, already dead. He told the police that he didn't mean all he said, but it appeared to have been too much for Mandy, and she had either overdosed deliberately or it was just that she gave herself too much. There's no way of knowing the real truth. Either way though the moment she met that so and so Sam, she was finished." As she said that she looked at her husband and said "Yes I blame him, he's the one that caused this." and started crying again. Jules didn't know what to say or do, so she just sat quietly with her other cousins Emma and Paul, Mandy's siblings.

The next day, after Jules had a rest after a sleepless night, she went around to see Debbie. She knew she would be in because it was her day off. When Debbie opened the door she could see that Jules was in a bad way. Her eyes were puffy, and it was easy to see she had been crying. "Jules, what's wrong?" Debbie asked, her voice full of care. Jules looked at her and just burst out crying again. Debbie immediately grabbed her gently and brought her inside. "Haven't you heard?" Jules asked, "heard what?" replied Debbie. "It's Mandy, she's dead." "What?" shouted Debbie her voice shocked, "When? How?" Jules just looked at her "What do you think? It was the drugs." Debbie was shocked at just how upset she was because of their past history, but she found herself crying with Jules and really feeling Mandy's loss. As they sat together Jules shared the story about Mandy and Sam, the argument and how it escalated from there. Debbie couldn't help but speak out about what she thought of Sam. "That bastard I knew he would bring her down one way or another." She continued "He needs hanging for what he's caused." Jules nodded her head in agreement, but beyond that she didn't have the energy to say or think anything.

On the day of the funeral Debbie felt the loss almost as much as Mandy's family she thought, but she couldn't work out why. After all they never got on, and they were always rowing when they were in each other's company. Yet Debbie was devastated. As she was heading to the funeral she thought back to her early childhood, the little arguments they had, always Debbie being the bossy one, and when they played the mothers and fathers game, Debbie always had to be the mum. This didn't go down too well with Mandy and even Jules to a certain degree. Debbie had a smile on her face as she thought "I suppose I was the bossy one even back then." As she continued her thought process she tried to justify her little flaws, always wanting to be boss, but it was more about looking out for Mandy and Jules, seeing herself as their carer. In particularly for Mandy because she always felt the Mandy was a bit lost and needed someone to tell her what to do. Debbie's thoughts came to an abrupt end as they arrived at the crematorium.

When the hearse arrived with the family following behind in the limo Debbie felt pain in the pit of her stomach like she had never experienced before. It was a real soulful feeling of tears, hurt and pain, which took her totally by surprise. Never in a million years did she ever think she would feel this way at the death of anyone, let alone Mandy. It was a total shock to her, and one she couldn't get her head around. Debbie felt so selfish feeling this way when at the end of the day Mandy wasn't related to her, wasn't close to her and, as she had said a million times, "That bloody Mandy gets right on my nerves." The family had got out of the limos and were walking into the church. Debbie could see that they were all struggling with their loss, and her heart went out to them. They still hadn't got used to the fact that Mandy was no longer alive.

In another world, the spirit world, Mandy's spirit was very much alive, being supported by her loved ones who had passed over before her. Mandy was in fact watching over her funeral with great interest. "Who's come along to say goodbye to me." she asked out loud. Her guide, who had been by her side every step of her transition back to her spiritual home looked over to her, "People that truly care for you are all there, which is what's important." "Yes," she replied, "That's really lovely." Mandy had settled back down in her spiritual home very quickly and although she was missing her family, she felt so much more alive when she arrived back home, which was clear to see by her guides and companions. She really didn't want to keep living her earth life the way she was, and although she didn't intend to die that day, she was just so desperate after she had that row with Sam, that she didn't watch what she was doing and injected too much. Even so, soon after her passing, she realised that although Sam wasn't to blame for her death, from the very moment she met him he was always getting at her to chill out the way that he does, by taking drugs.

As Mandy watched over her family walking down the aisle, her heart broke for them and for herself because she was missing them so much. Then, all of a sudden Mandy gasped as she saw Debbie walking behind the family, blurting out, "Oh my god, I know that's Debbie, I can see it's Debbie, but it's not

Debbie. That's not Debbie's spirit." She looked over to her Guide "Help me out here." Her guide Pam responded to her request, calmly saying, "Well if she isn't Debbie who is she?" Mandy hesitated a little as she answered Pam "I think it's my mum and I keep hearing the name Florence, that's who she is, but how can that be? I'm seeing Debbie, but I know her spirit to be my mum Florence." Pam looked at her and asked her to tell her more. Mandy sat down as she tried to make sense of what was happening. "Well." she started saying, "None of this makes any sense at all. Each time I look at Debbie I feel a bond with her as a mother that I had a long time ago." Mandy was sitting there almost shocked at what was happening but Pam could see that the iron was hot so she needed to strike. Pam sat with Mandy as she uncoiled what she was learning. "Tell me more please." she asked Mandy. Looking at Pam, Mandy started to feel herself going into an almost trance like state. It was obvious by the way her eyes were moving that she was having strong memories and visions coming back to her which Pam found encouraging.

Mandy started to talk about what she could remember as well as what she was seeing as her memories came flooding back to her. As she recalled her memories she started sharing them. She spoke quite hesitantly at first because, to her, she sounded barking mad! "Um I'm a young child and my name is Isabel, I'm with my mum who was quite a tough cookie, and never really showed her emotions." Mandy continued, "From what I'm seeing my mum was a bit unusual for that era." "Enlighten me on your mother please Amanda or Isabel depending on what you want to call yourself." said Pam inquisitively. "Well, I don't know how I know this but for a women in that era." Pam interrupted her "What era? You haven't said." Mandy looked over to her "Well it was the 15th century." Pam acknowledged what Mandy had said and asked her to continue, "Please share with me how your mum was different." Mandy continued "She wasn't a skivvy, or anything like how I imagine that era to be, she was a thatcher. When I was down there I didn't know any of this, so why do I now?" she asked Pam. Pam asked her whether she knew what a thatcher was. Mandy hesitated for a while before she answered, and Pam could see her eyes recalling a vision of what a thatcher was by visualising pictures of her mum working and what she was working on. When she was ready Mandy replied, "Yeah I know what a thatcher is, it's someone who works on the roofs on thatched cottages, either by repairing them or completely layering a new roof with dried reed, rye, wheat and straw. It was quite a skilled job and highly sought after but many men at that time didn't believe it was the work for a woman. Women should be at home cleaning and cooking for their husband and children." Mandy never knew that somewhere within her conscious and unconscious mind, she knew this kind of stuff. "Blimey, imagine me knowing something like that." She said with a smile.

Pam decided that it was time for Mandy to understand that what she was experiencing was one of her past lives. As Pam started she warned Mandy that she may find what she was about to tell her quite hard to believe, but Pam asked her to let her finish what she was saying before she asked any questions. "You see Amanda, you have lived many lives and this is just one of them." Pam could see that Mandy was just about to say something so she broke in quickly to interrupt her in order to carry on. "I promise you that you have been more than just Amanda, and this is the start of you finding out. You were absolutely spot on when you told me Debbie was your mum Florence, and that your name was Isabel." Pam continued, "It's time to understand more about yourself, the purpose of all of the lives you have lived as well as the relationship with your mum Florence back then." Mandy looked a little afraid. She was finding it all a bit spooky as she would put it, which she was quite up front about to Pam. "I'm not sure I want to open a can of worms and find out more. After all I can't change anything and I'm not sure I want to see Debbie as my mum after the way we have hated each other all these years." After a while Pam managed to convince Mandy that it would be in her interest to find out so much more about herself. "Mandy I want you to remember your relationship with Florence as it will give you the key to open up your story." Pam continued, "You may find out it was more about love than hate between you and Debbie." Mandy immediately replied "Yeah, right, I can't see that being the case." Pam looked at her so seriously Mandy was getting a bit worried that she was going to tell her off, but all she said was "As we work with this don't rule anything out because all is possible."

Mandy looked down to the ground because she was a bit embarrassed that Pam had to be a bit serious with her. She sat back, did as Pam advised, started to take deep breaths and got her head into the right place for her to recall back to her life in the 15th century. "Well I can see that I used to work with Florence as and when I could, and I remember hanging around waiting for her to finish but I never minded because I could always find something to occupy myself. In fact I quite liked being on my own to day dream about getting away from our little village and go as far as London to find out about life." Deep down she knew that wouldn't happen but she could dream. It always frustrated Florence that her daughter was such a day dreamer because she could see her settling down to be a wife and be ordered around and told what to do by her husband, which was the last thing she wanted for her. Florence wanted so much more for Isabel, or Mandy as we have come to know her. Unlike her daughter Florence was very practical and had a great inner strength which got her through so many hard times since her husband died five years ago. Even when he was here, he always respected her as her own person and not just his wife. He was a rare breed for this era. He felt as though they were equals and they were teaching this to their young daughter. Sadly Florence's husband died quite young after having a fever.

Florence wanted Isabel/Mandy to learn a trade so that she could earn a good wage for herself and learn to cope on her own, but it appeared that her daughter's interests didn't lean towards learning how to thatch a roof, even though she would be paid the same amount as the men were paid which was highly unusual back then. Sometimes Florence felt like she was flogging a dead horse with her daughter because she could see that although she had dreams, she never really put any effort into anything and Florence was worried that Isabel/Mandy was destined to either be a skivvy for a wealthy family which was seen as the lowest kind of job to have back then. Alternatively she would become a down trodden wife with no views of her own.

Mandy was starting to become aware of a few similarities that she saw between Florence and Debbie. For a start they were both very practical people, also they both wouldn't be told what to do and the big thing for Mandy was they were both on her back and having a go at her the minute they clapped eyes on her. Mandy shared this with Pam, but she wasn't expecting her to ask "But do you see similarities between you back then and you in the last life you have just lived." Mandy quietly acknowledged Pam's question, nodding to say yes, but didn't want to go into it any further at that point because she wanted to see herself and what she was like in the 15th century, compared to the girl she was in the 21st Century. Mandy triggered her memory once more to find out the differences between her then and her now.

She could see herself being told off by her mother for not organising any food for them both whilst her mum was working hard. She also heard her mum calling her a day dreamer "Which won't get you anywhere." said Florence. To her dismay she heard Isabel/Mandy saying "I may be a day dreamer, but all my dreams are about moving away from here and building a better life for myself in London, so there's no point in me learning how to thatch rooves, or anything like that. Instead I'm going to marry someone with money who's going to look after me and give me a good life." Isabel/Mandy continued, "So many of the children in this village are happily married and have had at least one baby." (It was legal for girl to marry as young as 12 years old back then, and they didn't need their parents' consent either, a horrifying thought) Florence asked her daughter "Is that all that's important to you?" Isabel replying "Yes, it is." For Florence this was a big blow because she was hoping that she could teach Isabel/Mandy to stand on her own two feet.

Mandy noticed that Florence wasn't tactile towards Isabel at all, which was the same with the mum she just had in the life she had just left, although her mum Kirsty in the 21st Century was a bit more thoughtful and caring towards her than Florence was in the 15th Century.

Mandy brought herself back from watching her previous life unfold and sat quietly for a few moments. She started to tell Pam of the similarities there were between Isabel and Mandy. "When I looked at what I was like as Isabel, I realised that I was no different as Mandy. Instead I have kept the pattern of looking for a knight in shining armour to pick me up and sweep me away. It looks like I found that in both lives, but sadly it wasn't quite how I had imagined it to be." She continued, "In fact I was downtrodden in both of these lives. I allowed men to control me for very different reasons in the both lives. In the first it was because I believed, when I met my husband, that he would be a nice and caring person, which he absolutely was not and in the end I ended up being so scared of him, believing that I couldn't cope with my life on my own because he had battered what we now know today as my self esteem with his constant criticism. When I lived my last life down there as Mandy, it was pretty much the same with Sam in as much as I became dependant on him because I was dependant on drugs. Although I couldn't say it was his fault that I took them, which it wasn't, he was the person that introduced me to them and I realise now that was because he was the insecure one in our relationship and he needed drugs to cope".

"I also see how lazy I was in both lives. I never really did fancy working for a living so both Florence and Kirsty had their work cut out trying to get me to make an effort in life. I can't believe I was really like that. When I think of it now I see how much alike Florence and Kirsty were. For example both worked hard, both could stand on their own two feet, both could run a home, both were very much their own person, which, if all that I have just witnessed in my past life and the life I have just left, I have never conquered. I also realise now that all Debbie was ever trying to do was look out for me and although I always kicked up a fuss and pretended like she was talking rubbish I did take a lot in, even if I didn't always act on it. I can see now that all she was trying to be was my mum." Mandy looked quizzical, so Pam asked what was troubling her, "If she was only ever trying to look after me, then why did she become an enemy and not a friend?" Mandy blurted out, "An interesting question Amanda, maybe if you go back to the day Florence died, you will find an answer." Pam replied.

Mandy sat focussing back on the time when Florence died and it wasn't long before she could see it. Florence had fallen off the roof she was working on and fortunately on that day Isabel/Mandy was with her. As soon as she landed she knew she had broken her back and wasn't going to survive. Isabel/Mandy rushed over to her, knelt down and with tears in her eyes begged her mum to be ok. "Come on mum, you can fight this, you can fight anything." Florence looked into her daughter's eyes, "No matter what I will always be by your side, ready to look after you, but be warned if I have to come back to tell you off, I always will but only because I love you and I want you to be ok." Florence continued, "I may not always be your friend, but I will always be there to support you in whatever you need to learn even if it feels like I am your enemy." "Oh I get it" said Isabel/Mandy, now I understand, she didn't really hate me, she was just trying to get me to listen to her, just like a mum would. I wish I knew that way back then." Pam smiled, "Exactly Amanda, she was only ever trying to be your mum, and who better to have as an enemy than someone that really loved you no matter what." Pam continued, "I think Florence knew exactly what she was doing when she came back as Debbie because being your enemy meant that in some way she was shielding you from other people that were not as spiritual as Florence/Debbie were." Mandy looked over at Pam "All a bit confusing but I guess I'll have time to work with this all now that I'm up here. Can I look after Debbie as well as my own family? It's just that I think she deserves that much." Pam smiled, "Of course you can, yes you do have time to unravel both lifetimes, as well as all the other lifetimes you have lived." Mandy smiled agreeing that this was her time to learn about so much, she really wanted to walk this path with all the guidance that Pam was prepared to offer.

After the funeral had been and gone Debbie still wasn't able to get Mandy out of her mind, Very often she felt as though Mandy was near her, but that was ridiculous, she kept thinking, she was also feeling like she was a bit of a fraud because all she ever did was moan about her. These kind of thoughts were rolling around in Debbie's head most of the time, but she felt she couldn't share this with Jules or the family because it was like taking their grieving away from them and focussing it on herself. This was not what she wanted people to feel, so in the end, every time her thought process went this way, she quickly pushed it away, even if it did make her feel as though she was bottling too much up inside. One evening, 2 or 3 months after Mandy had died, Jules popped around to see Debbie who couldn't help but notice how much more upbeat Jules was, which was so lovely to see. "I must say Jules, you look a lot better hun." said Debbie. "Yeah, I do feel a bit better, I still think about Mandy every day, but it is getting a bit easier. The only thing is that every time I think of her I start to feel really guilty." After Jules finished that sentence she looked down to the floor for a few moments, and the room fell silent. It wasn't long before Debbie piped up, "Oh sod this we've gone all gloomy."

Jules looked up, "Oh by the way, I see there's a medium coming to town next week and they're doing a night of messages so the leaflet says. Do you fancy going along?" she asked, "And you never know a message may come through from Mandy, that would be so cool." Debbie wasn't sure about that, as she wasn't sure about mediums in general, whether they were the real deal or not and shared this with Jules, Deep down more than anything she was more worried about the reaction Jules would have if Mandy did come through and decided she must talk to Jules. "Oh I'm not sure Jules, after all we don't know if the person is the genuine article." Jules quickly responded "But we won't ever know if we don't go." Jules begged Debbie to go and eventually wore her down. Debbie agreed to go.

On the night Jules and Debbie was due to go, Jules was quite hyper. Debbie could see that Jules had pinned her hopes on getting a message, "Oh Debbie, wouldn't it be great if Mandy comes through." Jules said in her hyper voice. Debbie, who was ever the realist, looked at Jules in a gentle and maternal way, "Look Jules, don't rely on hearing from her cos it may not happen and I don't want you to get yourself so upset if she doesn't." Jules didn't like to hear what Debbie was coming out with, "Don't be so negative Deb, why wouldn't she want to come through to us?" Debbie replied, "I don't know, but don't forget she hasn't been dead that long and they say that it takes them six months to a year to come through.", Jules felt such anger go through her when Debbie came out with that, "Oh what stupid rot, who told you that?" Debbie was exhausted and couldn't be bothered to answer. It isn't actually true that spirit needs to wait six months or a year after they have passed. In fact I have communicated with spirit that have only passed away a couple of days or weeks before, so if you hear that from a medium, query it.

When they arrived the auditorium was packed full of excited people who were also hoping to get a message from their loved ones in spirit. Jules couldn't help but ask herself "Blimey, there are so many people so desperate to hear from people that have died'? It wasn't long after they sat down when the medium walked on the stage. There was loud clapping from everywhere in the hall and Jules whispered, "Apparently she's very good, a lot of people go to her for readings." Debbie just gave a little smile and kept her eyes focussed on this woman. Debbie expected her to dress a bit like a witch, but she was very smartly dressed in a lovely light blue dress. As soon as the medium started, Debbie's mouth fell to the floor as she heard her give such in-depth evidence that nobody would have known unless they were related to the spirit person. Debbie was really impressed how she worked and delivered messages at such a great speed. In the interval the girls went to the bar for a quick drink. "Isn't she a good medium?" said Jules excitedly and Debbie had to agree that she was very good and impressive. "Mind you." said Jules in a quizzical tone, "I was hoping to hear from Mandy by now." Debbie felt so sorry for Jules, very gently replying, "Well, you never know, she may come through in the second half," all the while hoping that she wouldn't.

The girls returned to their seats and settled down for the second half of the show. It wasn't long after the medium started to bring through another spirit person that both Jules felt the information she was giving sounded very much like Mandy. Both looked at each other in shock and when the medium asked "Who am I with.", Jules immediately put her hand up. Right at that point she wished she hadn't done it, and wanted to run out of the theatre! Jules was asked to stand up and take the mike that was being offered to her, which she duly did. Mandy came through with some lovely strong memories of their happy childhood holidays and fun days out with the two families. Jules could confirm that everything that the medium was saying was correct. Then came the message that the medium was relaying on to Jules. "She wants you to know how sorry she is for all if the upset and distress she caused both when she was here in this lifetime and now that she is in the spirit world." began the medium, "She is also telling me that her passing was drug related, and that the family have to stop blaming other people because it was her decision to do this.", continued the medium. By now Jules was breaking her heart but wanted the medium to continue, "She is giving me the name Sam, and I feel as though this was her partner." With that Debbie took a deep breath as she realised that this medium was the real deal as she would put it. At that point the medium turned to talk to Debbie, "Can you take the mike please because this lovely young lady wants to talk with you also." Debs reluctantly stood up, took the mike and for a few brief moments held her breath in fear of what was going to be said. "She wants you to know that she gets it now, she understands that you were only trying to look after her in this lifetime, and other lifetimes too." The medium carried on, "There have been other lifetimes in which you have supported her too. She wants you to go with it, check it out and confirm it, Will you do that?" asked the medium. Just for a quiet life Debbie agreed, but had no intention of doing it.

Jules was delighted that both of them got such strong messages and talked about them all the way home. Debbie stayed quiet and let Jules talk away, but her thoughts were very much on what the medium meant when she said, many other lifetimes, and to get it checked out. This thought stayed with her for quite a few days until one night she had a dream that Mandy came to visit her and in this dream she mentioned past lives. The next day when she thought about the vivid dream, she couldn't help but think, if someone told her they had this kind of dream she would say that they are crazy and yet, she couldn't get rid of the idea of delving into a past life. When she saw Jules she shared her dream with her, and of course Jules being Jules encouraged her to find someone who can do it and book a session with them. Little did Debbie realise when she booked her first session with someone who does past life regressions, that she really was opening up to many more lives that she had lived, and the many different worlds that she had lived in. Mandy, Debbie, and Jules for that matter, were on a journey of discovery together once more because somewhere in another time Jules and Mandy shared other lifetimes too

Chapter 6

PHYLLIS

When Phyllis passed away at a good old age, naturally her family were sad that she had passed, but some were also quite relieved that she had passed away. Why? I hear you ask, and some of you may be thinking, do some of her family have emotions of relief that she had passed? Are they not quite strange if not cruel? All will become clear because Phyliss was strange!

So, in order to gain a better understanding I shall take you back to the beginning of her life. Phyllis was born in 1924 to the parents of Kathleen and Peter in a little village in Southern Ireland. She was the oldest of 11 children. Her father Peter was a very quiet and proud man who worked as a farm hand for the local farmer. They lived in a very modest three bedroomed house, which wouldn't have been easy, but they managed it somehow. Peter pretty much left the rearing of the children to his wife, and his wife pretty much left the rearing of some of the children to Phyllis because she couldn't cope by looking after them all in a little house on her own. So she told Phyllis that she had to be the minder for the older ones whilst her mum looked after the smaller ones. Phyllis didn't really mind this at first but as time went on there didn't seem to be any change of her role within the household and she spent most of her times as she grew up looking after her siblings which caused a deep resentment within her towards her mum and her siblings. She never felt that way towards her daddy though, he was her hero in her eyes. He never really put pressure on her to do things, and when he walked through the door every night he always gave her a big smile which meant the world to her because her mother was quite the opposite. Day in and day out her mother would be asking whether she had done this or had you done that? Phyllis felt that her mum only spoke to her when she was telling her off, or telling her which child she had to look after.

Out of the siblings there were 5 boys and 6 girls and Phyllis was the oldest of them all. Very often she would stand and watch her mum treat the boys very differently to how she treated the girls. There was once when Phyllis had had enough of her mother taking more notice of the boys and outright asked her mum why she treats them very differently to the girls, but what she didn't expect was the answer that came back. "The boys will always need to go out and work, so they need to be looked after from the very start and kept strong and healthy, whereas the girls will only be working for a short time before they get married and have a husband, children and a home to look after so you need to get the practice in now, otherwise no one will want you."

Now that may sound hard, but that was very much the way of the world back then in small villages, not only in Ireland but all around the world. Phyllis was so upset about the way her mother had answered her question that day that she never forgot how her mother had practically dismissed her because she was a girl. Phyllis attended school until she was 14 years old. She loved school because it got her out of the house and gave her a break from looking after the kids. As she used to walk along the country lanes she could see the sea in the distance, and she used to quietly say to herself "One day I will leave Ireland by boat and travel all the way over to England. I already have cousins over there so they will allow me to stay until I find myself a job." Day in day out when she would walk to school, as well as when she walked into the village to get the messages, she would daydream about when she was going to leave her little village and move on to pastures new "Where no one will tell me what to do and I won't have to look after stupid kids." In many ways this dream kept Phyllis going through the tough times, but now that she was 14 years old she would have to go out to work. Again this wasn't unusual for children to go out to work so early, and the children pretty much realised that as they were growing up. If a child belonged to a wealthy or middle class family there would be a high chance that they may have the privilege of going to boarding school, or even being able to go to college to study for the choice of job they wanted to focus on. But when you are one of 11 children, live in a small village and your family is only just making ends meet, your choice of career will be limited. Many of the men would do physical work very often on the local farm and some may be brave and move through to a big town or city like Dublin to find work, but for the girls, their options were a lot more limited. So when the time came that Phyllis had to consider what she wanted to do for a job, there was only one job that she thought she could be good at which was looking after children.

So, Phyllis applied for a job working for a family that had a chemist in the local town. It wouldn't be too far for her to walk to and from work, the money was good. But Phyllis was kidding herself that she would be able to save up enough money to move away and make a life for herself. As luck would have it she got the job so was now a nanny to three young children aged between 18 months and 8 years. Although Phyllis wasn't best pleased that she was now a childrens' nanny, she knew she had landed on her feet because the money was good which excited her so much that she almost skipped the whole way home. As she walked in she shouted to say she was back and that she got the job. Immediately her mother smiled and said "Well now, that's grand, we can do with the extra money that you bring in, and of course you'll have to pay board." Phyllis hadn't even taken that into consideration that her mother would be wanting money from her, shocked she replied "My board?" Her mother looked up from what she was doing, "Well surely you would expect that we need what you earn to keep our heads above water?" Phyllis spluttered her answer "Yes naturally I expected to pay something, how much are you wanting from me?" Her mother replied firmly "Well now, you can keep enough to bide you over the week, and the rest can come to us." Phyllis was horrified because that meant she would be handing most of her money over to her mother. This surprise that her mother had just landed on her was devastating to Phyllis. She walked out to the country lane that they lived on and looked over to the sea thinking, I'm never going to get away from here, I just know it.

Phyllis felt so desperate at that point because she knew she wanted to be move away from home but just couldn't find out how she could manage to find her way to England. So she decided that she would do her job well, and at some stage whilst doing this she would find her way around this, even if it did mean she would live in a country that was heading for war. In a strange way she enjoyed her work with the children because their house was bigger, and there were only 3 children so that was easier to control unlike the way she had to control all of her little siblings running around in a three bedroom house. As I have stated before, back in those days it wasn't unusual for children of working age to go out to work and hand over most of their money to help support the family. They would continue to support their families even if they didn't live at home anymore, in fact it would really only stop when they got married.

By the time Phyllis was 18 years old she had found a little room above a shop in the nearby town where she worked. She was still a nanny, although not to the same family, and she had resigned herself to the fact that she would have to wait until she was a bit older before she could afford to leave Ireland. She wasn't wanting to leave because she didn't like Ireland because she absolutely loved Ireland and was proud to be Irish, it was because she wanted to be free of the restrictions that she felt by not having her own money to buy nice clothes with. The other reason was she believed that there were more job prospects over in England which excited her.

One night in 1942 she and a friend of hers went along to the local dance. She never in a million years thought that she would meet her future husband because she thought she would know all the boys that would be there, and probably went to school with some of them. But, on that night in 1942 she glimpsed a man in a sailor's uniform on the opposite side of the hall who was staring at her. She coyly smiled as she turned her gaze to her friend, "Hey Nancy who would those two men over there be do you think? Do you know him, because I certainly don't." Nancy went to look towards him when Phyllis nudged her "Don't be looking over to him and making it obvious that you are looking. Do it when he's talking to his friend."

Once Nancy had had a good look she told Phyllis that she didn't know him either. "He must be new here. My they are both so handsome." she said to Phyllis, "He's certainly not anyone I have ever seen before and I think the one on the left is quite handsome in a strange sort of way." Nancy turned to her friend "Why don't we go over to welcome him to the town? They're both so handsome, especially in uniform." In a sharp voice Phyllis said "I will not, he can come to me if he's interested." Well, it wasn't long before this lovely young and good looking man came across to Phyllis and Nancy. "Hello there, my friend and myself were wondering if you would both care to join us for a drink, and perhaps a dance later?" Phyllis and Nancy wanted to go straight away but they weren't going to make it easy for them. Phyllis in particular answered his question "You're a bold man, so you are. We don't even know your name and we know you're not from around these parts. Besides you'll be having people talking about us mixing with you strangers, and being sailors too." Both the girls smiled to each other. The young man replied "Well, my name's Peter, my friend's name is David, and you would be right, we're not from around here. I'm from Wexford, and David is from England, so he's a long way from home." Phyllis immediately became very keen to talk to the boys if they had knowledge of England, so both the girls agreed to join them. Phyllis saw it as a good sign that this young good looking boy had the same name as her daddy which she wanted to share with him. "Peter's a grand name, it's my daddy's name." The ice was broken and the four of them were soon laughing and joking together.

Although Peter was interested in Phyllis and indeed she was interested in him, but she spent most of the evening talking to his friend David at that point because she could ask him questions about living in London and what that was like. David felt as though he was being bombarded with all the questions Phyllis was asking and decided to try and escape by seeing if Nancy wanted to have a dance. Nancy liked that idea a lot as she liked David and quite fancied him. Peter grabbed the bull by the horns and asked Phyllis to dance with him. As they were dancing Phyllis could feel her heart fluttering. Phyllis started the conversation, "Your friend has lots of tales to tell about England, and I should imagine you have some interesting stories to tell, you being a sailor." Peter nodded his head "I have some interesting stories to tell to. Maybe we can meet tomorrow evening and I'll tell you some of them. I'm on leave for a few days and it would be great to spend that time with you. Phyllis looked uncertainly at him, but before she could answer Peter butted in "Don't you worry, I'll not do anything that will get you talked about, I promise." He continued, "Perhaps we can go down by the beach and walk along there." Phyllis agreed to meet up the next evening, and then the following evening, and then the one after that. It was plain to see that they were very quickly falling in love with each other, and at that point Phyllis had no thoughts about moving over to England and working over there, because all she could think about was Peter.

Peter's last day of leave had arrived, he would soon have to start the journey to England to meet his ship, go back into the war, and into battle again soon. Peter didn't want to leave his girl (that's how he saw her now) and as they walked and held hands Peter stopped, looked straight into Phyllis's eyes, "It's been a great week, and being back home in Ireland has felt like there is no war.", in fact to them both it felt like nothing and no-one existed apart from them. They were both in a world of their own. "It's been really wonderful Peter, and it has gone so fast, but now you are going back to England and on from there

I've no doubt that I'll not see you again." Peter was totally shocked by Phyllis's statement "I couldn't forget you, because you're my girl. How could you even think I would walk away from you." Phyllis tried to make light of it, "Well isn't that what you sailors are supposed to do?" "Not this sailor," replied Peter, "Phyllis, I know we haven't known each other for long, but I'm in love with you, and I want to marry you, if you'll have me." Phyllis was taken aback but was so happy that he felt the same as she did. "Do you feel the same Phyllis?" asked Peter. "Oh yes Peter I feel exactly the same, and yes I will be happy to marry you, but you will have to speak to my father before we agree for good."

Phyllis's parents thought it was too soon, but they liked Peter so agreed to them getting engaged for now, to see how things go. So, by the time Peter went back to England to set sail again he was an engaged man. Once Peter had gone back to sea, Phyllis arranged to see Nancy, who had also been seeing David, although their relationship wasn't moving as fast as their friends'. Phyllis almost skipped up to Nancy with a smile on her face that said it all to her friend. "I See you're happy. It wouldn't have anything to do with a certain gentlemen I suppose?" said Nancy teasingly. "Well as a matter of fact it is." said Phyllis calmly, but she couldn't contain her excitement any longer "We're engaged to be married!" Nancy was in total shock "What, really?" Nancy couldn't help but say, "That's a bit quick isn't it? I mean you haven't known him more than five minutes." Phyllis wasn't best pleased at her friend's reaction and couldn't help but say "Trust you to spoil it for me. Well mammy and pappy have agreed that it's ok to be getting engaged, so if they're happy you should be happy for me too." Nancy felt a bit ashamed now about her reaction to her friend's news, but she couldn't help but feel this match wasn't going to be made in heaven. But she needed to calm the waters, "I'm sorry Phyllis, I didn't mean to upset you, it was just a bit of a shock, that's all. I'm very happy for you." With that she grabbed her friend and gave her the biggest hug.

Peter and Phyllis wrote to each other most days and naturally the talk would be about when the war was over how they can be together as man and wife and building up their own home together. But there was no real conversation about where they were going to live or what they were going to do. They just allowed their love, or more to the point their lustful chemistry sweep them along. Peter had been away for almost a year, and it had been a very hard year at that when he lost some of his close friends, but finally he had been given dates when his next leave would be. He immediately wrote to Phyllis and told her when he was due home. He wanted her to get her parent's permission to marry on the date that he had given her, so they could wed as soon as he got back. Her parents weren't 100% sure that this was going to work but they agreed anyway as their eldest daughter could be very persuasive. Phyllis being the person that she was had organised everything very well. She would wear her mother's wedding dress, even if it was outdated. She could do something with it as she was very good at designing, making and altering clothes. She was always very proud that she could work wonders with a piece of material. Naturally the wedding would be in their tiny church in the village and her maid of honour was going to be Nancy. Peter's friend David would be best man. Phyllis and her mum had agreed not to have any of the children as bridesmaids, but they would be dressed in their Sunday best.

Everything was thought of including getting permission from her landlord of the little room she rented for her new husband to stay there whilst Peter was on leave. Peter had arrived home, the date was set, and Phyllis was just about to marry the man of her dreams, which by the way was the only dream she had now. Everything she ever dreamt before about leaving Ireland and becoming independent had gone right out of the window. Peter watched Phyllis walk down the aisle and he couldn't help but think how lucky he was that he was marring such a beautiful colleen (girl). Their wedding day was wonderful, her mother had made a wonderful spread of food for the few guests they had, even though they had very little to spend on it. The wedding cake was a gift from Nancy, and the small amount of drink they had was a wedding gift from the publican of the small pub in the village. Phyllis's father had a quick pint or two in there on his way home from work most nights. Peter had two wonderful weeks leave and naturally most of the time the couple spent time just with each other. Phyllis did have to go back to work after a week off, but rushed home as soon as she finished work each day.

Nancy and David appeared to be growing closer to each other, and it was easy to see that these two were suited. Phyllis couldn't help but tell her friend, who, in turn would blush and tell her it's all nonsense. Nancy knew that her friend was right, she and David were planning to marry after the war was over. Nancy wasn't a person to rush, and neither was David for that matter. Life resumed back to some kind of normality for both Phyllis and Nancy once the men went back to sea, well at least for the first couple of months after which Phyllis found out the she was pregnant. Apart from the fact that she was shocked, she seemed pleased, and because she was used to looking after children she really didn't think that one child would be a problem. Phyllis had a beautiful little boy, whom they named after her grandfather James.

Throughout the next three years Peter had the odd bit of leave here and there, and by the time the war was over in 1945 Phyllis was pregnant again with their second child. She didn't mind too much because it wouldn't be long before Peter would return home and help her with the family. She also had it in her mind that because Peter had travelled the world he would be more than happy to leave the navy and move over to England where there would be more job opportunities for him. The problem was that she had never had this conversation with her husband. Peter had no intention of leaving the navy and no intention to base his family in England as he wanted all of his children to be born, brought up and educated in Ireland. So it looked like Peter would be away a lot of the time and Phyllis would end up practically bringing the kids up on her own. Of course, the other problem here was that once married, forever married, especially in Ireland, so yet again Phyllis was feeling trapped.

Nancy and David meanwhile were planning their wedding which was going to be quite a bit bigger than Peter and Phyllis's. They had also talked everything through and Nancy was moving back over to England once they were married. David also had no plans of leaving the navy but that didn't matter to Nancy, she knew when she met him he was devoted to being a sailor and she wasn't going to change him. Phyllis couldn't help but feel jealous of Nancy, and at one point she blurted out, "This is so unfair because you will be living my dream. I dreamed that we would move to England, but Peter, but doesn't want to." Nancy could see the jealousy in her friend's eyes. "I feel for you, but I would have thought you both would have worked all this out before getting married." Phyllis just stared at her "Well, we didn't." Although Phyllis was pregnant and was showing slightly, she had agreed to be the maid of honour for Nancy. It was clear with she was taking on the role with great resentment because she just wanted the day to be over. Phyllis's resentment towards Nancy showed even to their husbands, they could see the friendship become strained but both felt that the girls would sort it out. It wasn't too much of a problem for Peter and David as they would still be in the same unit for a while at least, and as far as they were concerned the strain on the girls' relationship was their own affair to sort out.

By the end of the 1950's Peter and Phyllis had 6 children, and yes, Peter was still in the navy and still loving every minute of it. It seemed to be for quite a while that every time Peter came home, Phyllis fell pregnant. Phyllis's resentment grew stronger and stronger to the point that when Peter came home they would barely speak two words to each other. It was pretty clear to see that their marriage was based more on lust, chemistry and Phyllis's idea that Peter was the ticket out of Ireland. Oh Phyllis was the dutiful wife who would be there for her husband when he was home, and would cook, clean and bring the kids up but beyond that she was bored of the man he became and the thought of spending the rest of their life together just filled her with dread.

As each year passed Phyllis became more and more resentful and actually quite spiteful to her children as well as Peter when he was home. Things weren't made any easier when she used to see her friend Nancy visit home with her "2.4 children" wearing some very nice expensive clothes. Phyllis knew that David had built up a very good career in the navy, and she resented the fact that Peter didn't want to do the same. It was clear to Phyllis very early on in her marriage that in her eyes she wasn't going to live her dream to live in England and now she felt there was no way out for her. She did approach the subject of moving over to England a couple of times with Peter but he was adamant that when he was not at sea and was at home, it would always be in Ireland, as to him Ireland was home.

Eventually the time came for Peter to retire. Both Phyllis and Peter were dreading this happening because, although they weren't saying anything to each other they were both worrying how the two of them were going to get along. They had very little to say to each other, and to be honest the only time they stayed in the same room with each other for any length of time was when their children and grandchildren visited. So the question they were both asking themselves was how they were going to cope with all of this for however many years they both still had together. The really sad part of this was that Peter didn't need to worry on that score because within six months of him retiring he was diagnosed with lung cancer and his prognosis wasn't good!

Peter's cancer was taking him down fast, and it wasn't long after his prognosis that he became well and truly an invalid, reliant on Phyllis and the family to look after him. Oh Phyllis looked after Peter very dutifully and made sure she was there for him. She was sad to see Peter suffer the way he was, but she didn't feel the devastation that perhaps she thought she should. She didn't want to see him suffer the way he was, and she even had a great deal of empathy for him towards the end. Their children were devastated because they were all so looking forward to sharing some part of their dad's life with him. This, as you can imagine, rocked their world. Very often the people you would see sitting around Peter were his children, but not his wife. Instead she was downstairs finding other things to do.

When Peter passed over Phyllis and their children arranged a lovely send off. There were so many that turned out that day to say goodbye, which Phyllis was shocked to see because of the time he was away. When she shared this with the children her son James reminded her that when he was home, Peter would always go for a nice long walk and stop to say hello to neighbours and friends that he would run into en- route to the pub, or as he walked down to get his morning paper. This brought a smile to James's face and as he smiled he looked over to his mother "Our father was well liked because he liked to share his time with people of all ages and when he was home he would always put himself out to say hello to everyone." Phyllis looked at her son with a cold look "Well I don't remember all that, so where was I when all this was going on?" James bit his tongue very quickly "You were always busy doing something for the church, the fete or for the priest." but under his breath he muttered "Because you were never around when he was and you didn't take an interest in what he was doing." Shh." said his sister Claire, "She will hear you, and we don't want her turning this day into her day because she feels she's a victim or something like that."

After the church service there was a small gathering at the local hotel and many a tale was being told about Peter, always with the affection he earned from everyone. Naturally David and Nancy were there, and as always Nancy looked beautiful even though she was now in her more mature years like Phyllis. As she walked over to Phyllis she smiled caringly as she passed on her condolences, "I'm so sorry for your loss Phyllis, Peter was a lovely man, David is so upset and will miss his pint with Peter when we come back for a visit." Phyllis really didn't want to talk to Nancy but in the end she did acknowledge Nancy's condolences. "Thank you Nancy that's very kind of you and yes it was nice that they stayed friends for so long." Nancy asked "How are you and the family holding up?" When Phyllis was asked this question by Nancy, she immediately went into the "woe is me" mode "Well as you can imagine it's been a tough few months and to see him go downhill the way he did was heartbreaking for me, and of course the children. Still I did my best for him, no one can say any different." Phyllis felt she needed to ask how Nancy and David's children were, not that she was really interested in Nancy's family Nancy answered with such pride as she told them how well both of the children were doing in life. Phyllis couldn't help but give a sharp answer to Nancy, "Well it's all so very different if you have the money to give to the children for them to do well in life." Nancy looked at Phyllis with a "here we go again" kind of look and didn't respond to what she had just said. Poor Nancy had always just stepped back when Phyllis got like that, but, as she said to her husband David after that last remark "I swear if she has one more dig at me I will sweep the floor with her." David had a little laugh at his wife, "Now you know she will say something spiteful again because that's what she has always done. Just ignore her my love, she's never going to change and it's just jealousy that keeps her like that." Nancy knew David was right, but just once she would love to have her say.

When the funeral was over the family all went back to Phyllis's for a cup of tea and a slice of brack. As they sat and pondered about the day, the children all talked about the lovely memories they had of Peter with them whilst they were growing up. Claire bless her said as she looked over to her mum "I tell you mammy, he may have spent a lot of time away but when he was home he gave us all so much time." Phyllis wasn't best pleased with what her daughter had said, and felt she needed to give a sharp answer "Yes it's fine if you have the time to do that the way your father did when he was home.", she said aggressively. Phyllis was determined she was going to have the last word, "It was alright for him because he didn't have a lot to do, whereas with me I was forever busy bringing you kids up, and looking after you. I tell you, I would have loved to have had such free time that your father had with you." Immediately the room went very quiet and the energy completely changed as a result. Claire mumbled under her breath "You wouldn't have spent the time with us even if you could." Phyllis was aware that Claire said something quietly so asked what it was she had just said, "It's nothing mammy, I'm just thinking of the memories I have with daddy." Silence reigned again!

As the years passed Phyllis became frail and had to depend on her family a lot by this time. It had to be said her family were wonderful, they always made sure she was looked after and needed nothing. They set up a rota system to make sure she always had someone on hand if she needed them. The children took turns in looking after her and when it was their turn their first thought was to make sure they popped into see if she needed anything. True to form she would have a list waiting for them when they arrived and God help them if they bought the wrong thing, got the wrong size or just forgot because they would never hear the end of it.

Phyllis wasn't helping herself either as she would completely ignore the doctor's advice and would also refuse to take the tablets she needed for her high blood pressure and other ailments she had. Over the years Phyllis grew worse with her moaning and scolding the children like they were young kids again but for the sake of their own sanity the children used to just ignore it. One morning when it was James's turn to look after his mum he pulled up in the drive and noticed that the kitchen blinds were still drawn which alarmed him as he knew his mum hated drawn blinds and curtains during the day because she saw it as a sign of being lazy. He quickly got out of the car, opened the front door and shouted "Mammy are you up yet?" There was no answer so he immediately rushed to

Phyllis's bedroom and there he found her on the floor unconscious. After he called the ambulance and while he waited he sat by her on the floor and started to phone his siblings. All of them dropped what they were doing and started to head towards the local hospital where they knew she would be sent. As they arrived one by one James told them "It looks like she's had a stroke and it didn't look good." It really wasn't that much longer after the siblings arrived at the hospital when the doctor came out to tell them that their mother had passed away and that it looked like she had been lying on the floor for quite a while before she was found which created complications.

Naturally the family went into shock and as they were taking in the news some of them were surprised that they were more upset than they thought they would be because of the way Phyllis had treated them. After they had left the hospital they all decided to go straight to Phyllis's home so that they could sit and talk. As they all sat around the kitchen table they were all pretty quiet. They seemed to be staring into their cups of tea they had just made. Annie broke the silence, "OK, we need to get our thinking caps on so that we can organise mammy's funeral." They all looked up. Deirdre had a little smile on her face that Annie noticed and asked her what was the smirk for. Deirdre replied quite sharply "It's not a smirk, it's a smile because you reminded me so much of mammy when you started to organise us all." Annie laughed "God forbid I'll be like mammy, she was a fecking pain." Annie's answer had broken the solemn mood and brought the others around by making them laugh.

As Phyllis had made her transition back into the Spirit world she was greeted by her mother and father as well as some of her siblings who had also passed away. Phyllis couldn't contain her excitement as she saw them all, but in particular her parents, "Mammy, daddy, I can't believe you are here. This is a dream come true because when I used to think of the day that we would be re-united, all I wanted was to be met and cuddled by you both." Phyllis started walking towards her parents and as she was giving them both a big hug she saw Peter standing behind them. Phyllis was shocked because she hadn't even given Peter a thought about whether he would be there to meet her, and she never gave it a thought that they would be together again. The only thing that she was interested in was that she saw her mammy and daddy, yes, especially daddy.

Peter continued to smile at Phyllis, and as he did he said, "Are you surprised I'm here to meet you?" Immediately Phyllis replied "To be honest Peter yes I am." She continued, "I didn't think we had anything to say to each other the last few months or years of our lives together." Peter was silent for a while, then looked her straight in the eye, "Oh I had a lot to say to you, but you just wasn't interested." Phyllis retaliated "Oh Peter that's not fair, I was always there for you. I looked after you didn't I both before you became ill and during, so how could you say that?" Peter knew that although it was important to say his piece, it is important also not to get worked up or angry as this wouldn't solve anything. He always had that attitude towards things when he was living a human life which was quite wise, and now that he was back in his spiritual home, he realised it was even more important to stay calm but at the same time be able to speak to Phyllis in a way that would help them to find peace between them. Peter urged Phyllis to look down over the children and watch them for a while. "Phyllis, please just look over at our children and how they're trying to do the best they can to give you a decent send off." Phyllis folded her arms, closing her heart of from her feelings. She immediately replied, "Well I should think so, I spent my life being devoted to them, so it's the least they could do." Peter looked disappointed "There you go again, never a good word to say about them, just how they should be so grateful to you for sacrificing your life." Phyllis looked over at her parents looking for them to support and stick up for her, but they weren't saying anything. "Mammy, daddy, please help me here." begged Phyllis but her father didn't come to her aid, "I suggest you listen to Peter because he is right in what he is saying." Phyllis was shocked and upset that she didn't get any support from her parents. She now felt she was in a corner and didn't have much of a choice.

Both Phyllis and Peter stood together as they watched over their children. "Well." said Phyllis, "What next." Peter didn't take his gaze off of the kids, "Just listen." The children were all in Annie's house. Phyllis watched as they were sorting out the prayer and hymns that they wanted to have played. Annie looked a bit lost "Does any of you know what kind of music mammy liked? We're going to need to know what songs she would have liked." The other siblings looked around the table to see who was going to answer this but the reality was that none of them knew! "Oh how bad is it that we didn't know what she liked and disliked." said one of the brothers. Deirdre quickly replied "No, it's not bad on us, it's bad on her that she never shared anything like this with us. In fact." said Deirdre, "We don't know very much about her at all apart from the fact that she was a real moaning cow most of the time." "Oh my God Deirdre why don't you say it as it is." shouted her sister Claire. Deirdre wasn't going to defend what she had just said, "Come on guys you all know that's what she was like, it's just that no one wants to say it." They all went quiet, until James spoke up "You're right Claire, she kept herself closed off from us and never really told us anything positive about her life. Instead it was always either being told off by her or her moaning about something or someone else." James was on a roll, "I don't know about you guys but I always felt like everything was my fault." Phyllis couldn't believe what she was hearing and tried to defend herself "Well that's nice isn't it. They turn on me as soon as I have gone which just goes to show what they're really like. They must get that from your side of the family Peter." Peter turned to look at her "You never learn do you?" That was more of a statement than a question. Peter said it again, "You never learn do you. It's all about you isn't it and how you are such a victim, when the reality is that you are a victim of your own jealousy, greed, hate, resentment and so much more."

At this point Phyllis really felt like she needed someone to show some tenderness to her. She looked at each one of her family in turn but they said nothing. Phyllis said out loud "Oh for God's sake will someone please help me with this." No sooner had Phyllis said, she felt someone standing behind her. As she turned around she saw a lady standing there. She was young, pretty and beautifully dressed in a long flowing dress that would be fitting in the Victorian era. Phyllis sounded almost disappointed as she said hello to this lady whose name she discovered was Helen. Helen was Phyllis's Guide who greeted her when she first passed over and before she met up with her family. Phyllis wasn't too taken by Helen because Helen had also told her a few home truths which didn't go down to well and it showed in the way she spoke to Helen. "So you're back here, and I bet you would have been talking to my family here about what I was like when I was down there on Earth."

Helen looked at Phyllis disapprovingly, "Do you think I only have you to think about? You are not the only person I guide and you are not the only person that exists in either this world or the physical world that you have just left." Well, that told Phyllis! Helen continued before Phyllis had a chance to say anything. "As I said to you when you first returned home, I am here to support you, but I make it very clear that I will not pander to your tantrums and moods." Peter laughed, "Well you have met your match." Phyllis gave him an indignant look but said nothing. She had to admit to herself that she did feel she had been put in her place and was embarrassed by this. This isn't uncommon for a guide or teacher to be firm and blunt at times, as they know this will help those they care about and support to realise what they were like. Although Phyllis was hard work Helen cared deeply about her because she knew this harsh selfish facade that Phyllis has now got used to isn't the real Phyllis, it's just how she learned how to keep control of her life. Helen saw the embarrassment in Phyllis's eyes and softened her tone a little. "It may help you to watch over your children without judgement to really get to know them. After all you helped to create them and you can take pride in who they have become." Phyllis wasn't keen on this idea because she knew that there may be some harsh words used about her from her family, but in the end agreed to watch them.

Peter stepped closer to Phyllis and both looked down at their children together. As they joined them there was a lot of laughter taking place around the table. Phyllis automatically assumed that they were remembering happier times with their mum, but the longer she looked over and the longer she listened she realised that they were in fact laughing at her, about her personality and how she always pretended to be someone that she wasn't. The laughing stopped at this point because they started to remember how it affected their childhood and the difficulties of being accepted into the community. Apart from anything else they lived in fear of getting things wrong because of the harsh way she would deal with them and then turn the blame onto them and their father. Yes even though Peter was away most of the time it didn't stop her from blaming him. As they continued to talk Phyllis piped up, "See I told you what they were like" as she looked over to Peter, "You just never saw them this way because to you they were perfect." Peter gave it a moment before responding, "I never said they weren't a handful, they would be of course but they were kids and sometimes they just needed to rebel against you because of the way you behaved towards them." Phyllis shouted at Peter, "And what do you mean by that? I was never unfair to them I just knew they needed the rod to keep them straight."

At this point Phyllis's mother decided to speak up and talk to Phyllis in the hope that it would help. "Phyllis, until I returned back here I didn't understand how I treated you, and how distant I was towards you when you were young. I had to do some real soul searching about why I behaved that way. The truth is that I invented excuse after excuse believing that I treated you like that because I was always busy with the other children, or that I didn't have the time to be tactile and caring because life was hard, which it was back then. But that wasn't the real reason." Kathy hesitated for a moment, "It was because I was envious of your youth, your dreams, your excitement of life. You see I was young once and I had dreams but before I knew where I was, I was married, having children with no money to speak of and I resented you starting out on your path. I didn't want you to leave me and live your life because I didn't feel I had lived my life." Well, that was quite a revelation and Phyllis didn't know what to do with this confession so she said nothing, at least until she got her breath back.

Phyllis had tears in her eyes as she stared at her mother and father. She particularly looked at her dad for the reassurance she always found in his eyes whenever times were tough. Yes, that reassurance was there, but she found herself drawn to her mother's eyes. She saw the pain that she must be feeling by having to admit that. When Phyllis gathered her thoughts together and composed herself she walked up to her mum, "Mammy, I want to be angry at you because I always thought there was something wrong with me and that was why you didn't love me. But the truth is I can't be angry with you because I love you and that will never change." With that she gave her mum one of the biggest hugs she could. Peter looked over at Phyllis with that glint in his eye that he had when they first met. He was seeing that soft side to her that she used to show when she was young. He didn't know if Phyllis would react to him giving her a hug but he thought he would chance it, and as he did he said to her, "Now that's my Phyllis, the one I knew all those years ago." The hug had taken her breath away but she didn't fight it.

Peter and Phyllis had agreed that they should work together and support each other. Well, it would really be a case of Peter supporting Phyllis because she was the one that had a lot of reflecting to do. They were talking and together they could find peace about certain things that they had held onto when they were living a human life. Peter saw a smile crack on Phyllis face, "Don't they have lovely strong personalities, and don't they have a real sense of right and wrong, well you gave them that. It was you that kept them on the straight and narrow and it was you that taught them most of what they know." Peter finished with "You see, it wasn't all bad." With that Phyllis turned, looked at him and softly said, "The first chance I get I will make sure they get a message telling them how sorry I am to have treated them so badly. I will also let them know that I am proud of them." Peter smiled, "Now that's my colleen." Phyllis's guide Helen was so pleased to hear the conversation between Peter and Phyllis. She could see that Phyllis was going to respond to the help and support she is being given from Peter and the rest of her family who are in spirit.

So, the relief Phyllis and Peters' children felt after Phyllis had passed away wasn't because they wanted her dead, it was more because now they could live their lives without constantly being moaned at, being told that they couldn't do anything right or were useless. Now Phyllis had to face up to her earthly actions and behaviours.

From a guide's point of view it is always lovely to hear and see a person who has just passed over that is prepared to do the work in order to help spiritual evolution take place through change of attitude, thoughts and actions. No guide can ever force a person to change as everybody has a free will, both when we're living a human life as well as when we pass over to the spirit world. At the end of the day, we all have a right to choose what we want to do, but we must always remember that there are consequences to decisions we make, and that goes for both worlds. We can either help ourselves to find peace within us now, or we can carry on avoiding the responsibility of what we need to do. The choice is always ours and with the knowledge that we can help evolution take place whilst we're still living a human life we can make it so much easier for us in both worlds.

Chapter 7

EVAN

Evan was a 16 year old boy who had the world at his feet, but the saddest thing was that he didn't see that. For a long time he had been spending time on his own in his bedroom completely cutting himself of from his mum and sister Sophie, three years older than him, with a 2 year old son called Caleb, all living under one council roof in Birmingham. He always felt that he didn't have very much in common with his sister so they hardly spoke to each other unless it was to have an argument or because Sophie's little boy was getting in Evan's way. His mum was a cleaner so was out very early in the morning and didn't get home until after 7pm in the evening as she used to clean office blocks as well as people's homes. His dad had left his mum Tricia just after she had found out that she was pregnant with Evan, so he hadn't had any contact with him at all throughout his life.

Evan was always a bit like his dad in some ways, one way being his dark moods. His mum had always said that his dad was always having dark moods "Just like Evan." In fact she never really had anything positive to say about her ex husband, but that would be understandable as he hadn't wanted to know them from the moment he walked away. His mum used to tell Evan that his dad "Didn't want to know about them from the moment he found out that he was going to be a dad again, and he's never asked how any of them were doing since he was born.". Evan always shrugged it off saying "Oh well it's his loss." but he didn't feel that really. He felt abandoned or not good enough, although he wasn't able to word how he felt properly but that's the impression everyone got when he spoke about the situation.

Although it was hard Tricia thought that both the kids were happy with their lives living at home. She was forever asking if they were both ok especially Evan because of how dark his moods could get. Sophie was totally the opposite in her moods and was known as "The life and soul of the party." Even when she found out she was pregnant she was pleased and happy even if she didn't have any money, had split up from her partner, the baby's father. She knew she didn't want a relationship with her son's father but she wanted her baby. At first Tricia wasn't happy about the pregnancy but as the time got closer for Sophie to have the baby she was one very happy Nan to be. Little Caleb was a beautiful little boy and quite a handful so Sophie was very pleased that she still lived at home with mum so that she could get the help and support she needed and even three years on she had no ideas of moving out, especially being that she had 2 built in babysitter's.

Evan loved his sister and his little nephew, but he did feel that in such a small house there was no quiet time, no time to catch your breath as the house was always one noisy and untidy tip. Evan's family always saw him as a shy and sensitive child, now a young adult and could see that it wouldn't take a lot to hurt him. He was an amazing artist and people always thought he should do something with his creativity which was the plan in the beginning. He had intended to go to college and develop his artistic flare further and was quite motivated to do this. He often talked of a dream of his that he would love to be an illustrator for books, especially children's books because in his words "You can leave this world behind for a short while and live in a fantasy where your best friends are animals and they are able to talk to you." He also used to say "In this dream world the wicked people would always get caught out and punished and everybody lived happy ever after." Even for someone as young as 16 years old these kind of words weren't coming from a teenager, they were coming from someone that is so much younger of mind. Tricia always felt that even though Evan was intelligent and artistic he was also a bit immature of mind. She did approach the school about this but they weren't too concerned about his lack of progress. Tricia felt that they had labelled him as "Stupid" from the beginning, and even now they weren't going to offer her any help, support or advice with an art course that he had signed up for that year which was right up Evan's alley. It wasn't too long before he became friends with two lads named Tony and Alfie who were both the same age as Evan. At first Tricia and Sophie thought this was the best thing that could have happened to Evan as he was smiling a lot more and he was far more cheerful. There were a couple of little niggles for Tricia like the lack of school work that Evan was doing. At the moment though she didn't want to spoil the confidence that he was building, and it was so nice to see him interacting with other kids of his own age. Until recently Evan had very little in the way of social skills, but now this appeared to be changing. All Evan could talk about was Tony and Alfie and how they have such great laughs together which made Tricia's heart sing, and to see him sitting on his mobile phone texting back and forth with his friends made Tricia feel as though Evan was a normal teenager just like everybody else's teenage kids.

After a few months Tricia was still concerned about the lack of school work Evan was doing. It seemed to her that he was losing interest in so many things to do with school including the new art course that they had all signed up for. It wasn't too long before the little group of three lads hanging around together became a gang of six young lads hanging around together and sometimes could be even more. At first this was great for Evan because he felt like he belonged to a little club which was great for him, but his mum was worried. Evan's temperament had changed quite dramatically. He became argumentative every time she approached the subject of school and the work that he was missing out on. One particular day when she mentioned it he flipped and started shouting "Leave me alone will ya, you're never happy unless I'm doing exactly as you tell me to do. Well, I'm not 7 years old anymore so you can't order me about." It wasn't long before Sophie got caught up in the row as well trying to defend her mum, but now Evan was on the war path and wasn't listening to either his mum or his sister. Evan started shouting some harsh things at Sophie, "And as for you, you haven't got any room to talk being a mother at 17 years old. I didn't see you doing too much when you were hanging around with that bloke and screwing him." Sophie so wanted to hit him but thought better of it in front of her son, and anyway by the time Sophie got over the shock of what her brother had said, he had already marched out of the house.

Tricia and Sophie stood looking at each other and with tears in her eyes Tricia said, "If I thought it would work I would tell him that if he didn't pull his socks up I would throw him out, but I know that he wouldn't be able to cope and he would probably walk out with nowhere to go. I would dread to think what could happen to him then." As soon as Evan walked out of the house, he regretted what he had said to his sister because he knew that would really hurt her. To be fair to her, since she had the baby she had held down a part time job whilst trying to look after her son, with a little bit of help from Evan and mum of course. Evan walked over to the local car park at the edge of his little town where his friends and other gangs would meet up and hang out. Sometimes there would be some speed racing done up and down the road at the side of the car park with some other gangs that were there to but Evan and his mates steered well clear.

As Evan got closer to the car park he was hoping that the rest of the group would already be there so that he could take his mind of off what had just happened. As he approached he saw one of the newest members of the group, Mark, who Evan thought was a really nice guy. As they approached they both smiled at each other saying hi in their own way. "How you doing?" Asked Mark, "Yeah, I'm good thanks, what about you?" Evan didn't really want to talk about what had happened at home so he just acted like life was good. They both waited there for a while but it looked like no one was going to turn up until later, so they decided to walk up to the local fish and chip shop to get some chips. This was the first time that Mark and Evan had ever really had a conversation, and they found they had a lot in common including the love of motor bikes which Evan had been fascinated with since he was a child. They also both loved tattoo's and ended up discussing what kind of tattoos they were going to get.

As they walked towards the fish shop Evan decided he felt comfortable enough around Mark to open up about what happened at home. Mark sat and listened without saying a word which Evan thought was great, as normally at home someone was always butting in when he tried to express himself. Or so he thought. Mark looked at Evan with a smile "Mate I know where you're at with this, it's a bit like that at my house. Don't worry it will calm down, because nothing lasts forever, especially not rows with the family." Evan laughed "You don't know my family, they're a nightmare." Both the boys went quiet for a while.

Once they got their fish and chips they found a wall to sit on in a little side road just off the beaten track, they sat and talked about how long they had known the rest of the group, and what they both thought of the rest of them Evan listened to Mark and noticed he wasn't your typical guy, as he was quite sensitive and had a very gentle personality, with never a nasty word to say about anyone. The more they both talked it struck Evan that Mark was very confident within himself which was something Evan had never been able to develop within himself. By the end of the night they had discussed just about everything they could think of and Evan felt so much better after the laughs they both had together. As they left to go home he asked Mark if they could do that again one night when it's just the two of them. Mark was happy for that to happen "Yeah man that's no problem."

Evan felt very different on his way home compared to how he had been feeling when he stormed out. After talking to Mark about it all he had suggested that he should go home and apologise for the things he said because it was about being mature when dealing with these things. "I can promise you Ev that it will all be sorted in no time." Well here goes, he thought as he put his key in his front door. Both Tricia and Sophie were sitting in the living room pretending to be watching television, neither of them looked at Evan as he walked into the room. "I'm sorry mum, I'm sorry sis, I didn't mean to say all those things, I was just angry at the time." Sophie looked at him "You mean you didn't like to hear a few home truths?" Evan had to bite his tongue because he knew that if he opened his mouth, things would get out of control again, so he just looked at them both and said, "Look I'm sorry I hurt you both, I really am, and I won't do it again." Tricia felt as though there was some sincerity in his voice, "OK, but before we can move forward you need to start putting some extra work into your school work, because this is an important time for you." Evan looked over at his mum and nodded his head in agreement. Tricia wanted to give her son a big hug, and did so. As she was hugging him she said to Evan "When you're like that you remind me of your dad, and I really don't want you to turn out like him." At that moment Evan felt let down because his mum had thrown up in his face yet again that he was like his father in a negative way but he decided to say nothing.

Over the following few weeks Evan did commit more time to his studies and stepped back a bit from all of his mates except for Mark. When it came to those two the relationship was growing stronger and Evan would always be looking forward to the two of them getting together. Both Tricia and Sophie noticed that Evans moods were brighter, and that they could have more of a laugh with him. They all noticed Evan was finally knuckling down and getting on with his schoolwork more. So all in all things were going well for Evan and his family at long last. Over the following few months, the two boys really just hung around with each other and stepping back from the rest of the crowd. To some degree that didn't go down too well with Tony and Alfie, and when they bumped into them both one day Tony was very vocal in saying what he thought of them. Evan was just about to lose his rag but Mark stopped him "Just ignore them, it's not worth it." Once again Mark was the voice of reason and calmed the situation down without any big fall out.

The friendship between Mark and Evan grew stronger and for quite a few months it was only ever the two of them, but as is usual there were small minded people were starting to talk about them saying they were gay, although they didn't let it get them down and just carried on being good mates. They both had the same taste in music and would love going to different concerts. They also loved taking time out doing things that interested them. Evan would always come home full of different stories to tell his mum and sister about their day, but it does have to be said the more Evan and Mark saw each other the more the girls wondered if they were in fact a couple. As Sophie said to her mum, "After all mum I don't know of any fellas that buddy up like those two and don't really mix with any other mates. I mean, if you think about it they dropped the other guys in the gang pretty quickly, and you never see anyone else being with them as mates." Sophie stood looking at her mum, "Don't you think I'm right?" Tricia didn't know what to think, but she knew one thing, "It really isn't a problem if Evan is gay, as long as he's happy. That's what's important to me." The sad thing about this conversation was they hadn't realised Evan had heard every word of it because he had been home for quite a few minutes and Tricia and Sophie hadn't heard him come in. When Tricia said that his happiness was the most important thing, for a few short moments Evan felt loved, accepted and confident that his family would be there for him through anything he had to face in life. Those few short moments ended when Tricia said, "Mind you I'm so glad that your dad's not about to see this, because he was homophobic, very much a man's man and macho. He would have given Evan a bloody hard time."

What Evan heard his mum say hurt him so much because yet again he was made to feel not good enough, this time by his father's standards. He just couldn't win. Evan knew deep down that he was gay and that he was very much in love with Mark and he was sure Mark felt the same about him, although at that point they hadn't spoken about it. Evan crept up to his room without saying a word and closed the door without a noise because he didn't want his mum and sister to know he had heard them as it would probably start up another big row. As he lay on his bed he felt the tears rolling down his face, and once again he felt alone in his little room that until recently was his prison. After a few moments once he had stopped crying he layed back and thought of Mark saying out loud to himself, "Well it doesn't matter what anyone thinks of me, at least I have Mark and I just know he feels the same way about me as I do him." Even though Evan believed on one level that Mark felt the same he was still frightened to approach him at that point because it didn't feel right at this time, but he didn't know why, just as long as they could still see each other he didn't mind.

Even though Evan was far happier in life and much more approachable, it became clear to Tricia that he wasn't going to succeed in any studies that he was doing because he didn't want to. Tricia was concerned that, although he was a lot better doing his course work, he still wasn't focussing on it the way he could and she started to feel that he will forever drift through life. Instead of having a career he would only ever have a job which probably means he wouldn't earn a lot and he wouldn't have any great opportunities. She would very often say this to Sophie and was naturally quite worried about it. Tricia started warning Evan that it wouldn't be too much longer before he was going to have to get job and if he didn't knuckle down he would end up with no real future. Evan felt ok about this because he wasn't a lover of school and just wanted to earn a bit of money for him to save for a flat and a car.

Today it was crunch time! Both Evan and Mark were due to get their exam results today. For Evan it was pretty clear cut.

Even though he got good marks for art he knew he could have done better. He knew he didn't have the commitment and he knew now that he still hadn't got that commitment so his choice was to leave and get a job. Mark on the other hand had got great marks even though he didn't have to knuckle down too much to study for them as it all came easy for him. He decided that as he got all the qualifications he needed to get a place in the college of his choice, he was going to study hard and make something of himself. On the evening of receiving their exam results Evan and Mark had arranged to meet up and see a film they had both been waiting for to be released and was finally being shown at their local cinema.

As the boys met outside the cinema they both had big smiles on their faces for completely different reasons after the decisions they had made after receiving their results. They both knew what the other one had decided because they had texted each other with their results. After the film had finished they both wanted some fish and chips so they walked in that direction and as they walked they were both talking excitedly about their decisions. Evan in particular was full of his plans. "I tell you Mark, I can't wait to find a job and leave school behind. Once I have a job I can start saving up for the things that I want like a car, or renting a flat and having my own space. I can even see me being able to go abroad on a holiday. Won't that be great and we will have our own place to chill and veg out." Mark replied, "Yeah that will be great mate, but you've got to remember that I'm gonna be studying hard and I probably won't have that much free time. You have to remember that I won't be living here most of the time because the college I want to go to is in London." Evan's mouth dropped in shock. It hadn't even crossed his mind that Mark would be busy studying and worse still he honestly thought that Mark would choose the local college and not one that far away. Mark could see how this had hit Evan which is why he hadn't told him any of this sooner. "I'm sorry mate, but you must realise that things are going to change for us now."

Once Evan got home he went straight up to his room and sat on the edge of his bed with tears running down his face. He couldn't believe that Mark hadn't pre-warned him about moving away. Now all he could think about was that Mark will be leading the high life with his new friends while Evan is sitting in his bedroom with just his own thoughts to deal with. This scared him because he remembers only too well how dark his moods can get when he's alone. As the next day came around Evan's mood didn't get any better, in fact it got worse because the dark thoughts that he was already having had kept him awake until the early hours of the morning. Evan texted Mark and asked if they could meet up that evening. Although Mark didn't want to because he knew the conversation might get heavy, he knew that if he didn't Evan would read something into it. Maybe he would be right because the truth was that Mark had felt suffocated by Evan for quite a while and it was getting worse.

You see the truth was that Mark always felt a bit sorry for Evan and how alone he was. Even when they were hanging around with the gang it was clear to Mark that Evan struggled to interact with people very easily and his social skills were very immature. Mark always felt like he should look out for him and genuinely did like Evan. They had a lot in common such as music and going to concerts, as well as being interested in motorbikes. In the beginning it wasn't too hard being around him but the more time they spent together the more Evan expected from him, which felt a bit like being in an intimate relationship with him. There were also times when Mark felt that's what Evan really wanted, but it definitely wasn't what he wanted, not with Evan or any other man, because, as Mark put it, "I'm definitely into women." He didn't even want a relationship with a woman at that time because he didn't want a conflict with his choice of going to college. It was quite awkward when they met up that night because neither of them knew what to say really. Evan started the conversation off by saying "Sorry about my mood last night mate, it was just a bit of a shock because I didn't expect you to move as far away as London and not be home very often." Mark looked at Evan "No worries mate, now we've cleared the air about it we can just carry on as normal." Evan smiled and "Yeah, you're right." and no more was said that night.

For a while things seemed to return back to normal for them both and there wasn't much discussion about Mark going to college in London. Evan had gone for a few job interviews in factories and workshops, and he even tried for an apprenticeship in a garage and was so pleased that they decided to give him a try. Evan excitedly sent a text to Mark telling him the good news adding that he would tell him all about it that evening when they got together and go back to Marks house for a pizza and an Xbox game. Evan was so chuffed that he had been given this chance and again things were back to normal with Mark. In his eyes all was good and he was full of chat, but it was so obvious the one conversation that Evan, and Mark for that matter, were avoiding was about Mark moving down to London for college. Before Evan arrived Mark had decided that he wanted to have the conversation about him moving again as he didn't want to have irate texts from Evan asking when he was due home demanding they spend all his free time home with Evan Mark was really feeling the pressure of the relationship and would sometimes think to himself that this relationship was a lot like being married.

After they had their pizza and before they started their Xbox game Mark looked at Evan and said, "You do realise that it's only a couple of weeks before I head off to college?" Evan didn't say anything for a few seconds but then responded "Yeah, I know, but it won't be too bad because you'll be home most weekends won't you and of course there will be the holiday times when you're home." Looking at Mark questioningly way Evan continued, "And we've still got the next two weeks to enjoy before it all changes for us don't we?" As he finished that sentence Evan really hoped that Mark would give him a reassuring answer but it didn't happen, instead Mark ignored the question and looked away. Those two weeks went really fast and before they knew it the day had arrived for Mark to be driven down to London by his dad to start his new adventure. That was exactly how Mark saw it, a new adventure, but this new adventure wouldn't include Evan as Mark had already made up his mind that he was going to cool it with him, but he would do it slowly so as not to hurt Evan too much.

Mark had settled into college really well and he started making friends really quickly. Evan had also settled into his new job to and although he didn't get on with everyone there he was enjoying it. Every day he would excitedly text Mark to tell him what he had learned and also who had annoyed him that day, because you could guarantee that there would be someone that Evan didn't get on with there. Tricia and Sophie were getting a bit concerned because although Evan appeared to be enjoying his new job, when he came home he kept himself in his bedroom again, but this time constantly staring at his phone in case Mark had tried to get in touch. They were also concerned because it was obvious Evan was always checking his phone and Mark wasn't answering his texts as much as he wanted. Evan was panicking because he started to think that he was losing Mark and sadly this was really starting to affect him.

Whilst Evan was at home panicking, Mark was in fact thoroughly enjoying college life. He had even met a girl that he fell for hook, line and sinker. Her name was Samantha although everyone called her Sammy. They were were both into science which is why they were studying physics and driven and motivated to walk their paths as scientists. They spent most of their free time together, and because they were both on the same course they could do their studying together, and couldn't ignore sexual chemistry between them was electrifying. Naturally all of this took Mark's mind away from his mate Evan, and he was texting less and less which caused Evan to panic all the more. He completely bombard Mark with loads of texts and also tried to phone him quite a few times to.

One evening whilst Mark and Sam were together Evan was doing his normal trick of sending text after text after text. Mark got to the point he wanted to throw the phone across the room but instead turned it off so that he could have some peace. Sammy noticed that Mark was distracted and asked if everything was ok prompting Mark to let his mouth run riot talking about how much Evan was getting him down. "I mean, it feels like he sees us as a couple and that he's the only one I can mix with." Sam listened intently as Mark carried on. "To be honest I only ever really befriended him because someone needed to look out for him otherwise the group he was hanging around would lead him astray, and I couldn't stand by and see that happen." Sam moved closer to him "You need to talk to him, especially if he is gay and he's hoping for a relationship with you. The sooner you talk to him the better." Mark nodded his head and agreed that's what needed to happen.

The following morning Mark text Evan to let him know that he was going to be home for a few days at the end of the week so they can get together. Evan was over the moon that his mate was coming home for a few days. When he got home he excitedly told Tricia and Sophie the good news including not to include him in any arrangements for the weekend or cook him dinner as he was going to be with Mark. For Tricia and Sophie it was really lovely to see Evan so up-beat looking forward to something again and were both so pleased. After dinner that evening Evan went up to his room but this time he didn't have any dark thoughts the way he had been for a while, instead he was thinking about all the things that they were going to do together. (If his behaviour sounds rather immature it's worth remembering that Evan was in fact comparatively younger in his years as far as close relationships are concerned compared to other aspects of his life.). For Evan the days couldn't go quick enough but for Mark they were going too quickly, he was dreading how the weekend was going to turn out.

Mark arrived home on the Friday evening but said to Evan that he would see him on Saturday because he wanted to spend time with his family. As the excitement was building within Evan he made the decision that he needed to tell Mark how he felt about him on Saturday. He was sure that Mark would feel the same otherwise he wouldn't have hung around with him so much before he went to college. He knew things had changed but Evan was under the false impression that because Mark had contacted him to say he was coming home and wanted to see him things were going to be ok again. Throughout the whole of the day Mark was dreading the meeting with Evan and nearly backed out by pretending to be ill but when he spoke to Sammy she persuaded him that he couldn't do that because it wasn't fair on Evan. "Always the voice of reason." he jokingly said, "Yeah I do need to do this because I can't keep being bombarded with texts and questions about where I am? Who am I with? What am I doing? When will I call him?" Mark took a deep breath and said, "OK, I'm ready now, wish me luck." he said to Sammy as he ended the call.

They met in their usual place which was by the car park. When Evan saw Mark walking towards him he wanted to run up and hug him but managed to refrain himself from doing that. Instead he smiled and shouted "Hi ya mate great to see you". Mark smiled and tried to look pleased to see Evan. Most people however would have seen that wasn't how Mark really felt, but no, not Evan. He saw a smile that said it's great to see you. They decided to go and get a few cans of beer, a pizza and head back to Mark's for an Xbox game. Evan was full of what his job was like and the people he liked and disliked, but he liked the boss. Whilst Evan was chatting away Mark couldn't help but feel Evan wasn't interested in what college was like for him, but the truth was that Evan was scared of what Mark had to say. After a good hour or so of listening to Evan and all his news Mark deliberately brought the conversation back to college and all that was happening there. Evan listened quite intensely, although sometimes he would be a bit lost when

Mark spoke of the work that he was doing with experiments and the like. Then Mark brought it around to making new friends. It was here that Evan wanted to tell Mark how he felt about him and he did actually try to cut across Mark whilst he was talking but Mark asked him to hang on for a minute because he had something to say. Evan sat back and let Mark continue. "The thing is said Mark hesitantly, I've met someone at college that I'm pretty keen on." Evan stared at him, responding with a bit of a stutter, "Wa wa what do you mean you've met someone? Do you mean with someone that's like a good mate, or do you mean someone that you want to go out with?" Mark treaded delicately, "I mean someone I'm in an intimate relationship with." Evan turned his head to the side and stared at the bedroom wall. Mark tried to get Evan to look at him but he wasn't having any of that continuing to stare at the wall. "Her name is Sammy and she….." Evan broke in "She, what do you mean she? You mean it's a girl?" Mark was very surprised by Evan's response, "Yes, her name is Sammy which is short for Samantha and it's pretty serious."

Silence fell between the two of them for quite a while until Mark decided to speak "Why are you being like this Ev? I mean I know we're good mates but I thought you would have been happy for me," Evan thought it was now or never to tell him how he feels. "I thought you felt the same about me as I feel for you, I love you." Now Mark was really stunned, "Whoah mate." Mark said, "What on earth made you think I had feelings like that for you? To me all you ever were and ever will be is a mate and nothing else." There was silence between the two of them for a few short moments, "Look Ev, yeah we're mates, and yeah we're good mates but that's it, there's never been any other feelings for you so I'm so sorry if you thought different. I really don't think I behaved in a way that would lead you up the garden path only to let you down now." Evan didn't quite know what to do next, and for a short while he just stared at the floor like he was asking the ground to open up and swallow him. In the end though he looked at Mark, got up, turned around, walked out of the bedroom door and then the house.

To say that Evan was devastated was an understatement. As he walked home he was trying hard not to break down and fall to the floor where everyone could see him and probably make fun of him. He rushed home as quick as he could, ran up to his bedroom, locked the door sat with his emotions. His mum heard the latch on the door go as Evan opened it and could tell by the way he banged it that something was wrong. "Ev, is that you?" she shouted and all she heard back was "Leave me alone, I don't want to talk to anyone." Although Tricia knew something was wrong, she knew that she needed to leave him alone because she knew her son and how he reacts when he's upset or angry. For most of that evening Evan lay on his bed looking up at the ceiling as he recalled that last conversation with Mark time and time again. The next morning Tricia took Evan up a cup of tea, knocked on his door and called his name gently. "Ev can I come in love?" she asked, but there was no response, so the second time she opened the door as she shouted "I'm coming in so I hope you're decent." When she walked in Evan was laying in bed staring at her as she laid the tea down beside him "Good morning son, how's you this morning?" she asked. There was no reply so she continued what she was saying as she sat on the edge of his bed, "You seemed pretty upset last night hun, what's wrong?" There was still no response from him but she could see he had been crying by the redness and they puffiness of his eyes. At this point Tricia was almost begging Evan to tell her what's wrong, "Ev please talk to me, I'm worried about you." but again he said nothing, and turned his back to her.

A few months went by. Evan and Mark hadn't spoken since that night and although Mark wanted to check out he was ok, he was concerned that if he called or texted Evan he would take that gesture as a sign of him wanting to be more than friends with him so he left it. He had college and Sammy to concentrate on now so his life was good and pretty packed, which was a contrast to how Evan's life was going at that time. Yes, he would get up and go to work, but he kept himself to himself and if somebody said something he would answer aggressively which didn't make for good teamwork. He also wasn't focussing on his work, so one Friday afternoon Evan's boss Mike called him into his office, "Ev I've done some thinking about your apprenticeship and how it's going and to be honest I'm wondering if you're enjoying your work here because it seems that lately your mind isn't on the job. I know also that you have skipped a couple of days college that I signed you onto." Evan looked at Mike, surprise on his face, more or less shouting his response, "You can't do that, that's not fair. I need this job and I like it too." Mike jumped in quickly "Come on Ev, you know and I know that your heart isn't in being a mechanic and I want to give this opportunity of learning the trade to someone that's passionate about it. I'm sorry mate, I'm going to have to let you go, but I will see you right with your wages and a bit extra to make sure you're ok. Now that's a fair deal isn't it?" It was plain to see by the look on Evans face that he was furious and as usual he didn't want to talk about it. He did what he always does, walking out muttering a few swear words under his breath.

Evan didn't want to go home just yet because he knew his mum wouldn't be happy about him loosing his apprenticeship, so he texted her and told her that he was meeting a friend for a few hours and not to worry. The first place he went was the chip shop that he and Mark used to go to and grabbed something to eat. He hadn't been there since the row with Mark but he heard the other day that he was home from college so there was a big part of him that was hoping he would bump into him. His wish came true as Mark was already in the queue. Evan's face lit up when he saw him, but then he realised that Mark wasn't on his own, because beside him was his girlfriend Sammy and they were holding hands and laughing. When Evan saw this it did cross his mind that they were laughing about him. Evan had always suffered different levels of paranoia and was going through some pretty dark times at the moment which in turn brought back the paranoia on quite a high level. At first Evan was going to run, but then he decided to stay put and see what happened. As Mark turned around he spotted Evan. He must have said something to Sammy as she turned around too. Evan's heart was beating fast. He was hoping Mark would acknowledge him, which he did, quickly starting to walk towards Evan. As he got closer he smiled and said "Alright Ev?" "Yeah." replied Evan and for an awkward moment he didn't know what to say or do, but finally he looked up at Mark, "What you doing here then?" he continued "Do you have a holiday or something?" Mark felt just as awkward and even felt like Evan was checking up on him again, but managed a reply "Yeah we're home for a week here and then we go to Sammy's family for a week so it's going to be a busy couple of weeks for us." Evan had to acknowledge Sammy even though he didn't want to, "Is that your girlfriend?" he asked Mark, turning as he looked at her, a smile on his face, standing proudly, "Oh I see." said Ev, "She's very pretty Mark." "Oh thanks Ev, I'll tell her you said that. Would you like to meet her?" asked Mark. Evan had started to feel panicky at that point replying quickly, "No, no you're alright, I'll meet her another time." The queue was getting shorter now and it was soon Mark and Sammy's turn to order their fish and chips so Mark said goodbye to Evan and walked back to where Sammy was. After they got their order the two of them said goodbye to Evan as they passed him and walked on.

The next day Evan was trying to avoid his mum as much as he could because she wasn't happy about Evan losing his job and he didn't want all that nagging again so he took himself on the bus into the town. As soon as he got there he was hungry because he didn't have any breakfast so he decided to stop off at a café and order a full English breakfast. Whilst he was waiting who should walk in but Mark and Sammy! Evan couldn't believe this was happening again. This time he tried to avoid their gaze by not looking over at them. At first they didn't see him as they ordered their coffees which arrived quite quickly, but when Sammy turned around and saw who she thought was Evan she brought Mark's attention to him. "Babe is that Evan over there?" Mark looked over and panicked "Oh shit, yes it is. Hurry up and finish your coffee so we can get out of here because I don't want another embarrassing moment like last time." The more Mark tried not to look over to Evan, the more he kept directing his gaze to him which is exactly what Evan was doing until in the end they both looked up at the same time, looking directly at each other. Mark smiled and acknowledged Evan but he didn't respond back turning his head away from his best mate that was.

It was so hard for Evan to sit and eat knowing that a guy he loved so much was sitting a short space apart with his girlfriend. Evan couldn't cope with what was happening and he had lost his appetite so he paid the bill and walked out of the café without looking or saying goodbye to them. Evan had tears rolling down his cheeks as he walked towards the bus stop to catch his bus home. His thoughts were all over the place and he didn't know what to do with all of the emotions that were rumbling around inside him. He had never been able to express or understand his feelings and emotions properly which had always concerned his mother because she knew that he could flip at any time. Recently she was more worried than normal because no matter how much she and Sophie talked to him he would completely freak out and throw a tantrum, or he would go into his room, lock the door and not come out until the following day. Recently he had been doing this more and more which concerned both Tricia and Sophie. They worried that this would tip him over the edge. Sophie had decided to see if she could coax her brother out of his room and asked him if he fancied going to the cinema with her because there was a film she wanted to see but didn't want to go on her own, "And mum has agreed to have Caleb for me." After what felt like hours of pleading Evan finally agreed to go with her.

That evening when they arrived at the cinema Sophie told Evan to wait by the sweet and coffee shop whilst she went and printed off their tickets that she reserved. It was while Sophie was doing this that yet again Evan saw Mark and Sammy together, arm in arm, laughing and cuddling as they walked through the doors into the foyer. Evan had enough of this, turned around and stormed out leaving Sophie catching the tail end of her brother as he left the building. "Evan, Evan." she shouted loudly as she run after him. When she caught up with him she grabbed his arm and gently tried to persuade him to come back to the cinema with her, or if he wanted they could go straight home, but Evan was having none of it. As Evan was walking away from his sister he said "Leave me alone sis, I just want to be by myself." Sophie knew there was nothing she could do that would change his mind so she headed home to mum. Evan eventually ran out of steam and as he sat down in a local park his feelings were so strong that he was actually thinking to himself that he wanted to die. It was at that point he decided dying really was what he wanted so he did no more than stand up, turn, and walk towards the bus stop that he could catch a bus from and calmly waited. It looked as though nothing was wrong with no sign that his thoughts were as dark as they really were. Once home his mum ran towards him to give him a big hug, gratefully saying "Thank God you're home, I have been so worried about you. Where have you been?" Evan pulled back from her, looked down at the carpet and said "I just went for long walk that's all, mum, stop fussing, I'm ok." Once mum had let go of him and he got the chance he went up to his room, sat and thought about the release of the pain he was feeling if he were to commit suicide. The more he thought about it the more he wanted that peace he had never been able to find on this earth. He felt so useless and insignificant, he was fed up with feeling so low about everything and he decided that this was the only way forward for him. Now it was just a question of when mum and Sophie were out and he had the house to himself.

A couple of days later Tricia managed to finish work early. She shot home as quickly as she could so that she could sit and have a cuppa and as normal she called out to Evan to say she was back. She knew that Sophie would be out with Caleb. She had arranged to go and spend time with her friend at the park who also had a little boy of the same age to let them play together. Tricia felt uneasy because Evan hadn't answered and although this wasn't unusual just lately, she had a really strange feeling come over her. She quickly turned and ran up the stairs, and what she found there no one should ever experience because Evan was hanging from the rafters of the loft. He had opened the loft door, climbed up, tied a rope over a rafter, put the noose around his neck and jumped through the hole. Evan had hung himself!

The next couple of weeks were a blur for Tricia and Sophie, post mortem, arranging the funeral and of course letting everyone know what had happened. Sophie wanted to be the one to tell Mark before anyone else did. She quickly went around to his parents' home not even sure if he was still there or had he gone back to college, but thankfully he was still there. When she told him what had happened Mark couldn't take it in. He fell into the chair with Sammy kneeling at his side holding his hand. "No, no." he said "It can't be, he wouldn't do that." Sophie was sitting opposite, tears running down her face. She confirmed she wasn't joking, "I only wish I was." Sophie said, looking at the couple. All of a sudden Mark wanted to know if he left a suicide note to say why he did it. Sophie answered "Yes he did, but he just said that he didn't feel as though he belonged anywhere and had had enough of struggling." Although Evan hadn't mentioned him in his letter, Mark was already feeling like it was his fault. It didn't matter what anyone said to him, his mind was still locked on to blaming himself. Even when he went to see Tricia, she reassured him that it wasn't his fault but he still blamed himself. "Mark, none of us blame you, this wasn't anything to do with you, in fact if anyone brought him any happiness it was you, and at least you gave him that before he died." Tricia reassured him.

None of those first few weeks after Evan's death made any sense to Mark. Day by day he was struggling. He would say to Sammy, "He did this because of me. I let him down and somehow I made him believe that we could be a couple." Sammy would sit next to him, hold his hand and did everything to try and reassure him that it wasn't his fault, and that no one was blaming him. "He was a complex character babe, you know that, and so does his mum." The funeral was a quiet affair with just a few family members, Mark, Sammy and Marks parents which Tricia really appreciated. That evening Mark sat in his parents living room with Sammy going through that last weekend when they kept running into each other and were equally trying to avoid each other. "I should have done something then." Mark kept saying and each time Sammy and his parents tried to reassure him that there wasn't anything he could have done.

That night when Mark and Sam went to bed Mark was so exhausted that he fell off to sleep almost straight away. It was while he was in a deep sleep that Evan could finally get through to talk to him, so he took Mark to a beautiful green field where there was no noise and no people rushing around, it was just the two of them. Evan looked over at Mark, a big smile on his face "I thought I would bring you here for a chat, you know how I like it to be just us two." Mark was lost for words for a few moments as he was trying to take everything in. "Is this real?" he asked Evan, "am I really with you or is this just a dream?" Evan tried to reassure him that it was real, "When you wake up in the morning you may feel it was just a dream but yes, this is real, we are together again, even though it's just for a very short time." Mark was full of questions, "Why did you do it? Why have you brought me here? Not that it's not lovely to see that you're ok, but from where I'm standing all this is a bit spooky." He continued "I mean we've only just buried you and now you've brought me here to have a chat, it's all a bit hard to take in." "I know." replied Evan," But when I looked over you at my funeral I could see how much you were suffering and questioning if it was all your fault. I listened into your and Sammys' conversation about it, so I decided to come down and tell you for myself that none of this is your fault."

Evan started to share with Mark why he shouldn't blame himself. "Firstly in answer to a question I've heard you ask yourself so many times since I left, no you didn't lead me on in anyway at all, I just didn't read the signs right. Since I passed over my guide has been helping me to understand things about what was really going on for me. He's also helping me to understand more about who I am and how I/my spirit lives on in a place where I don't have the stresses I had down there because I could never cope well with stress as you know. From the day I was born I have struggled to express my feelings and to socially interact with other people which is why so many people used to avoid me because they didn't know how to treat me. I had no self-esteem and I felt as though I was worthless, which is something I never want you to experience, so if ever you're in that place remember what you did for me. You gave me something very special which was your friendship, your time, your patience and your respect. The only time I have ever really been respected is when I became mates with you, so you could never be worthless, because you have such a caring soul, and you did everything in your power to make sure I was ok. I understand now that because of how our lives were changing and you were heading off to college as I was starting my training as a mechanic things between us would change because they were meant to, but I couldn't see that then. I just saw you moving away from me and once again my bedroom became where I would spend most of my time alone. None of that is your fault so you need to stop blaming yourself. In the short time that we were mates we made some great memories that I will always cherish and I will always be looking over you watching you enjoy the life that you and Sammy are creating, because you both deserve to be happy, and Mark, Sammy's a lovely girl. Tell her I said so".

Evan knew that it was time for him to take Mark back into his human life, but before he did he just wanted to say a couple of things to Mark, "Please keep an eye on my mum and sister for me because they're really struggling and in the very near future I will be visiting them also to have a little chat. The other thing is I want you all to know that I am fine and much happier because stress and people's expectations don't exist here and I love the peace, acceptance and love that's given to me. Oh and I am having a great time meeting up with my grandparents again, and as always they're spoiling me rotten". Evan had a great big smile again as he finished.

The next thing that Mark knew was that it was 6.35am and he was now wide awake. Sammy woke up as Mark sat up and asked if he was ok. Mark turned around and looked at her looking confused. He started to unravel his dream or what he thought was a dream. "I had the weirdest dream about Evan but it felt so real. Sammy listened intensely as Mark shared his dream with her and at the end when Mark had finished she said "Mark, that's not a dream, that was Evan talking to you, I just know it was I can feel it was." Mark was silent for a few seconds while he digested what Sammy has just said. Although he didn't like to admit it, in case someone called the men in the white coat to come get him, he had to say that for him it was definitely real, and thanks to Evan he felt a whole heap better because he knew that Evan was very settled and happy, which, at the right time he would share with Tricia and Sophie.

A little note from the author: It's been my experience and my belief that if Spirit needs to speak with us then they will find a way to do so and sometimes the only way to do it is through our dream because that's very often the only time we are quiet and still!

Chapter 8

Lilly

Lilly was the most beautiful little 11 year old girl that was full of energy, love and vibrancy that was contagious when you were around her. "She was also a mischievous little monkey, strong minded and determined" was how her mum would describe her and still does when she's talking about her to anyone and everyone that will listen, which is totally understandable as this beautiful little girl died one year ago almost to the day!

Little Lilly was the youngest child of Trevor and Trudy Hall. They also had a 13 year old son called Monty. They say that sometimes siblings can be so different in their personalities and Lilly and Monty proved that this was right as Monty was quiet, very studious, and happy to be in the background, whereas Lilly was outspoken and always wanted to be noticed, which she was both at home as well as at school. Monty never minded being in the background because he absolutely adored his little sister and sometimes wished that he had the same confidence that she had. Everyone in the family always used to say that Monty took after Trevor who was quiet and happy to blend in, and Lilly took after her mum Trudy who was very focussed, organised, confident and had a zest for life. Sadly though, since Lilly passed over her mum is now a completely different person, riddled with guilt because she was driving the car the day the accident happened. But before we go there, I want you to really get to know this lovely family so I'm going to take you back to a time when Trevor and Trudy was just building their lives together and creating a beautiful family.

Trevor worked in human resources for a large bank and his main focus was creating policies, writing them and implementing them within all branches that belonged to the bank. He was well respected and known as a quiet but dynamic man in business. Kirsty was in public relations for a large company and until she had children travelled all over the world organising and controlling the large shows as well as the media which was no easy task. When they met through another friend's birthday bash, it was easy to see that they were ying to each other's yang. From the word go Trevor knew that he wanted to see more of Kirsty although Kirsty wasn't too sure at the time because he was too quiet for her, however, she decided to give him a chance and boy was she happy she did.

They found out they both had so much in common in their taste of music, their taste of food, and in so many other ways. Trudy was very into sport and exercises and at that time would regularly run half marathons, she would arrange long walks for her and her pals at the weekends and you could guarantee that the walk would be around about a 10 mile hike. As she was telling Trevor how she loved to be outside and do physical exercise she managed to coax him into coming for a long walk the following weekend which she told her flat mate about when she got home. She actually said to her pal, "I want to test him out to see if he's really up to my kind of lifestyle.", which when she thinks back now she gets embarrassed because she realises now just how conceited she was back then.

It turned out that Trevor loved the weekend hike and when they found a nice quaint little pub he shared that he would love to do more workouts such as run, cycle, swim, etc. Trevor was wondering if he had just made a mistake by telling her this because already she was trying to coax him to go for a run with her the following day, which in his infinite wisdom he agreed to. It was plain to see by all those around them that these two complimented each other and that they were meant to be together. Each time they got together Kirsty was up for Trevor trying something new and she won every time but that was mainly because Trevor really did enjoy the different activities they were doing, which was a bit of a surprise for him too because he never had the urge to run, walk, or climb distances before. The first six months was a bit of a whirlwind for them, because they were both so wrapped up in each other and both had started to realise that they had met their soul mate. The next stage was for them to move in together which, to be honest scared the pair of them because they were concerned that the dynamics would change between them and the fun would stop. So in typical Kirsty style she decided that this should be brought out into the open and needed to be discussed which Trevor agreed was the right thing to do and they should make a pact to always do that regardless of any worries they had.

Life just seemed to float by for Trevor and Trudy, they were both settling in very well, they were doing well in their jobs and they just loved being around each other. Trudy was probably the most hesitant about getting serious within their relationship at first because of a bad relationship she had had in the past, but Trevor was quite sure that she was the one for him. A year after the happy couple had moved in with each other Trevor nervously asked Trudy to marry him which took her aback but she jumped for joy and immediately said yes which both sides of the family were happy about as they were so well suited. They had also decided that they didn't want a long engagement or a big wedding because they really just wanted their close family and friends to witness them getting married in a hotel somewhere. So they set the date for December that year which was approximately six months away, and they were so lucky when booking their date because they wanted it as close to Christmas as possible and the date that the hotel had free was on 22nd December at 4pm in the afternoon which they both excitedly jumped at. As always Trudy was the one with the ideas but in fairness to her she always discussed her ideas with Trevor, and as always, he would go with the flow when it came to it because he knew that Trudy would make it so special as she does with everything that she plans. By now I think you will probably be getting the picture that Trudy plans their lives and Trevor just plods along quite happily.

December the 22nd came and the day was truly beautiful. It was almost like a Christmas fairy tale film where everyone lived happily after, and for many years that was the case. It was just over a year after their wedding that they found out they were going to be parents, which both were naturally over the moon about, and yes this baby was planned and thankfully they didn't have any challenges conceiving. Little Monty was born and was not only a very handsome little baby, he was calm and placid, very rarely cried and wasn't an ounce of trouble. Both sides of the family would not only say how much Monty looked like his dad, they would also say that he had Trevors' ways too. Although Trudy would have a little moan about that, deep down she was quite pleased that he took after Trevor more than her because she was always told what a nightmare she was as a baby and a young child. In fact her mum often said, "She hasn't changed, she is still a nightmare.", which Trevor would jokingly agree with. Although Trudy stayed at home for her maternity leave entitlement, she soon wanted to be back at work on a part time basis so that she kept on top of her job, and because it was Trudy's mum that was looking after Monty. They didn't have any childcare worries and she knew Monty would be a happy little boy being with his nana.

When Monty was just over a year old Trudy decided that she wanted to try for another baby so that they can grow up together, the way she did with her sister. Trevor wasn't too sure at the time because, as he would say, "Having a second one so soon after would be tough for a couple of reasons like your mum might not appreciate having both the kids while we work, and also you do need to keep in mind that not every child has the same temperament." He continued "So for example Monty may be an easy going child but the next one might not be." Trudy wasn't having any of this and had made up her mind that she must follow her plan to start trying to conceive once again. In the end she did manage to get Trevor to give in and agree, and in true Trudy style her plan had come into fruition quickly, she was pregnant again. This time she wanted a baby girl so she was absolutely delighted when she had her scan and they told her she was carrying a little girl. Her friends would say to her, "You really do have a charmed life don't you because everything seems to go your way doesn't it." Sometimes when they said this to her she couldn't help but think that they were jealous her life was working out pretty much as she has planned. She used to say to Trevor, "I'm sure Denise and Avril are jealous of us because our plans seem to work out every time, they should take a leaf out of my book and start planning what they want instead of moaning about what they haven't got."

Both Trevor and Trudy were so over the moon that after a difficult pregnancy and a very long labour with some complications their little baby daughter was born weighing in at 8lb 6oz who they named Lilly after Trevor's grandmother. She was such a beautiful little girl and had a good pair of lungs on her which she showed them on more than one occasion. The bonding between Trudy and Lilly was a bit difficult at first as Lilly seemed to be quite an impatient and demanding child who wasn't settling down quite as quickly as Monty did. Breast feeding became a big issue also and Trudy needed a lot of support not only from her mum but from the health nurse who would visit to check all was well with mother and baby. Lilly also didn't sleep quite as much as Monty did which was quite a rude awakening for them both. They realised just how different the two children were, and it was getting to the point where Trudy had started to regret having another child. At her lowest points she would say either to Trevor or her mum "I wish we had decided not to have anymore after Monty." Trudy didn't suffer with post natal depression after Monty was born, but with Lilly it was a whole different ball game. Everyone could see that Kirsty was tired and sinking into depression. She would spend many days crying or wanting to run away, but deep down she knew she loved her new baby, it's just that it seemed to her that nothing she did was right for Lilly and in the end she started to feel like she was a useless mum. Thankfully she had the sense to speak to Trevor, her mum and her health care worker to get the support she needed. As always, they were all so supportive and they helped her to realise that she wasn't a bad mum she just needed more support than she did with Monty. They also helped her to realise how difficult her pregnancy had been with Lilly which made her drained and tired before the baby was born and because of all this the bonding between the two of them was more difficult than it had been with Monty. However, now that Trudy had the support she needed and as she gained more understanding of what was needed for both herself and Lilly the bonding started to take place.

Both Trudy and Trevor knew they would have to keep a close on eye this little monkey as she was so ahead of herself with walking, speaking, and exploring her world. She was always into something or up to something. "Lilly isn't a naughty child." Trudy would very often say, "She's curious and likes to explore.", but the problem with that was sometimes Lilly would do something that was funny, and they all had a little giggle, and the next minute she was doing something that causes your heart to jump and make you anxious that she was going to hurt herself. Although the family did have their challenges with this beautiful little girl, they were all so happy together and as a family they were extremely close. One of the things that both Trevor and Trudy would laugh about and was quite pleased about was how frank Lilly could be when she wasn't happy or if didn't want to talk to anyone. Trevor would very often say "Lilly will never do anything she doesn't want to do." She certainly wouldn't mix with people she didn't feel comfortable with. She would simply tell them that "She felt like that." To both her parents and her grandparents she was like an old soul that had been on this earth before. She could always weigh people up and work out what kind of person they were. The house rang out with laughter from the children who were both happy to be together and play together. It was interesting that Lilly was always the one who decided what game they were going to play and she would also make sure she would play the part that she wanted to. Deep down Monty didn't mind this even if he did kick up a bit of a stink at the time. Lilly would always talk him around.

As the years went on life was treating the whole family very well indeed. Trevor had been promoted a couple of times which made for a good increase in his wages. Trudy was still in public relations, not quite in the same way that she was years ago, but her job did sometimes involve her flying to different countries for a couple of days for meetings as well as make sure there were no hitches in setting up different events she had planned for the different companies that were her clients. Trudy wasn't the kind of person that would be happy staying at home and would very often say "As much as I love being a mum, to spend most of my time at home with a baby or in a job that wasn't exciting would totally depress me." So, the grandparents became great child minders, especially Trudys' parents who only lived around the corner and was always doing one thing or another for the children or for Trudy. Naturally Trevor would take over when he got home if Trudy wasn't about, which to him was a real treat as he valued every moment with them. He did sometimes wish Trudy was a bit more maternal towards them and not always letting other things get in the way of the family but he always knew that if he wanted a stay at home wife and mother then he shouldn't have chosen Trudy. Not that she wasn't a good mum because she was, and she built her life as much around the children as she could with such a high pressure job. She made sure she was there for most of the important events in the children's lives. She always loved coming home to Trevor and the children and would be excited to see what they had done at school that day and what they had been up to around nanny and granddads. Come weekends she would love them all going out as a family for bike rides in the local forest or any other activities the children wanted to do. Both the children had after school activities which for Monty was, football and judo, whereas for Lilly she wanted to do dance, horse riding and learn how to play the piano. It seemed like she was trying to pack everything into her young life. Trevor put it down to her being just like her mum, but in the back of his mind he used to have worrying thoughts about how urgently Lilly wanted to be doing everything all the time. It used to scare him a little bit, but he put it down to him being an anxious father.

Because this household was always busy, it sometimes caused tension between the family. They didn't always get on, especially now that Lilly was finding her feet, answering back on what she was going to wear and what she wanted for dinner which you could guarantee wouldn't be anything that Trudy was cooking which caused mayhem at the dinner table. She would always have the last say which frustrated the hell out of Trudy but, when Trevor pointed out that she was exactly like her mother, Trudy would accuse him of sticking up for Lilly instead of supporting her which meant Trevor was getting the blame for everything. Really all of this was very typical of many households, I can imagine that some readers will be thinking, this is very typical of their family and household. Trudy had noticed that poor old Monty wasn't really getting any time away from the busyness of family life and the outbursts from his little sister and his mum. It was clear to see that Monty was getting more and more withdrawn as time went on, so Trevor and Trudy decided that Trevor should have time out with Monty by taking him fishing which would give him time to talk about anything that was going on in his life. Trevor absolutely loved this idea because it also took him away from all the chaos.

One day whilst out fishing with dad Monty decided to have a chat about how he feels about Lilly always gets her own way which, it did have to be said, was pretty much the norm in their house. This was quite a brave step for Monty as he wasn't normally someone that says anything and plods along putting up with it all, but this time he had had enough. "Dad can I talk to you about something but you've got to promise that you won't tell mum or Lilly." Trevor turned to look at him, "Well son it depends what it's about, I mean I can't keep your mum in the dark about something if it's worrying you." This didn't please Monty at all, "Yeah but if you tell mum it will turn it into a debate like she always does and then nothing will get sorted." Trevor knew that if he didn't make that promise Monty wasn't going to tell him anything. "Ok son, I promise I won't say anything." "Cross your heart." Monty said, and Trevor crossed his heart in agreement. This wasn't a comfortable feeling for Trevor because he and Trudy had kept to the pact that they made about always being up front about things, and in the 12 years they had been together they had never broken that pact until now. "So what is it son?" Trevor asked, "Well, it's nothing really but I just sometimes feel like Lilly gets all the attention and I don't, especially from mum." He continued, "I mean, if Lilly needs help with her homework she gets it, but neither you or mum ask me if I need anything, and she always gets exactly what she wants like horse riding lessons, dance lessons and now she's gonna start having piano lessons. It's just not fair." Monty started to have a few tears in his eyes and so for that matter did Trevor because he could see the hurt in his son's eyes. There was silence for a few seconds but then Trevor spoke very gently "Oh Monty I'm so sorry, how long have you been feeling like this?" Monty was a bit embarrassed about having tears in his eyes so he looked down to the floor as he answered his dad, "I've felt like this for a long time dad, and neither of you noticed which makes me feel as though you don't care about me as much as your care about her." "Oh Monty that's just not true replied his dad quickly, we've just always thought you had it all together, and we've been so wrong, I'm so sorry son."

Over the course of the afternoon Monty really opened up about how he felt about different things and how Lilly seems to have attention pretty much all of the time, whereas no one ever checks how he feels. Now, Trevor was in a position where he had promised that he wouldn't say anything but this really needed addressing because although Monty was only ten years old he was actually right in what he was saying. Lilly does seem to always get her own way, and very often it's at the sacrifice of what Monty wants to do which Trevor could relate to as it was pretty similar in his family. Because he was the placid one no one ever thought to check how he was doing. When the boys got home they both acted like everything was fine and that they had had a great day together, which they had. Trevor had decided that although he couldn't say anything because of his promise, what he would do was become more vigilant what was happening at that time and make sure Monty wasn't pushed to the side anymore. He was also going to encourage Trudy to have more time with her son because it sounded like Monty was really hurting over that. So Trevor's way around this was to suggest Monty had mum and son days on a regular basis which Monty would love and he would have Lilly and dad days, which I'm sure they would both enjoy. Now Trudy was not someone that would like to go fishing, but she did love bike riding and so did Monty, and once Trudy could see what fun it could be she was excited and even thought about having picnics on their day out.

Over the course of the next few months, without the family even realising it Trevor was slowly and gently changing the family dynamic including Monty in far more "stuff" that they could all enjoy, both Trevor and Trudy started to regularly ask Monty how he was doing, What was his day like, What homework does he have and does he need any help with it. Also if Lily got a treat so did Monty. On family days out it wasn't only Lilly that got to choose, Monty was also asked about what he would like to do. This didn't always go down too well with Lilly and she would throw a tantrum, but she soon got over it, and what was really lovely was to see how Monty started to stick up for himself if his sister tried to be top boss. Even Trudy had noticed how much happier Monty looked and how different Lilly is now that the whole family has stopped tip toeing around her. "She's beautiful but she's a little diva." Trudy would very often say with a great big smile on her face, and how true that was but she was a lovely little diva bless her, even though she had her moments. To Trevor and Trudy it seemed like time was now flying by too quickly. It seemed like it was only yesterday that the kids were little ones and now Monty was settling down in his secondary school and Lilly wasn't too far away from choosing what secondary school she wanted to go to. Yes life was idyllic for them all. That was until that fateful day when things would never be the same again.

Trudy had been busy all week trying to sort out a business issue that one of her clients was having with an up and coming event that was taking all week to get sorted and her time was becoming totally absorbed on this issue. It was a Friday afternoon, the kids had finished school and Monty had gone straight around to his pal Henry's house for dinner. Trevor was on his way home battling the rush hour, and Lilly was with Trudy waiting patiently for her mum to take her around for her sleep over that she was having at her best friend Alice's house. Lilly's patience was coming to an end and she started to tug her mum's sleeve who was sitting at the table in the kitchen to tell her to hurry up. Trudy was feeling pressured by her client as well as Lilly so she told Lilly quietly to go and wait in the living room for her "And don't be so rude." she mouthed to Lilly as her client was doing all the talking. "I'm never going to get there at this rate." shouted Lilly as she walked out of the kitchen and walked towards the living room. After about 15 minutes Trudy appeared at the door of the living room, "Right young lady, I'm ready to take you to Alice's now." Lilly looked at her mum and gave a deep sigh, "It's about time, I've been waiting ages." Trudy acknowledged this, "I know poppet, but I'm here now, and it won't hurt you to wait for a while anyway. Sometimes we have to have some patience." Lilly didn't like this but didn't argue because she didn't want her mum to stop her from going over to her friend.

Alice lived in a very rural area which involved driving down some narrow and windy roads that Trudy hated driving down. In the car mum and daughter were having a lovely conversation about how excited Lilly was to be going to her friend's house and that Alice's mum was taking them swimming the following day. Lilly loved swimming and would jump at every chance to go, she was also top of her class for swimming. Maybe in a year or two Trevor and Trudy always thought that perhaps Lilly had a career in that area because she was so good, but then they used to laugh and remember that perhaps they were biased. The weather had started to change, rain started to come down heavily which didn't make for easy driving but it didn't phase Trudy at all as she was used to these roads. However, although Trudy may have felt confident in her own driving, she couldn't be confident that other drivers would be responsible, which was exactly the case that afternoon as they were approaching a blind bend. In the opposite direction a guy in a Mercedes overtook a car he was behind right on the bend leaving Trudy no room to brake or to get out of the way. There were massive screeches, and her car went headlong into the oncoming vehicle that she met on the bend. The impact caused her car to flip up in the air coming down on the side that Lilly was sitting on, killing Lilly immediately and injuring Trudy, a broken leg, broken ribs, broken arm and other injuries were sustained. The guy in the Mercedes also had quite bad injuries, but not life threatening. Thankfully the car that was behind her had managed to stop, and it was a blessing that the driver was an off-duty police officer who knew exactly what to do in a crisis like this. The policeman, he told Trudy that his name was Scott, was very focussed on trying to keep her calm. When he looked in the car he realised straight away that the little girl in the back was almost definitely dead, but naturally wasn't going to say anything to Trudy who was becoming incoherent at times. Trudy layed badly injured trying to mumble to Scott to get help for her daughter, but sadly all he could do was try and reassure her that help was on its way. Sadly the help, Scott thought, was primarily intended for Trudy. He had failed to get any response from Lilly, could not move her and felt that once the ambulance arrived, she would be pronounced dead. There was no way Scott could tell Trudy this in her condition.

By the time that Trudy reached the hospital she was unconscious, caused by concussion as a result of the amount of times her head was hit as the car rolled. Trevor had only just reached home when his mobile phone rang to say that Trudy and Lilly had been in an accident. Trevor immediately dropped everything and rushed to the hospital to be with them. Enroute he called Trudy's parents Janet and Aiden to break the bad news to them. Eventually he found where they were (or at least he thought both of them were there) when a nurse came out and asked him to take a seat. He knew then that it was going to be bad news, but he didn't expect to hear that his beautiful daughter was dead. He held his head in his hands and started shouting "No, no, no, it's not true. She can't be dead." as he sobbed. He looked up and saw Janet and Aiden walking down the corridor who, on seeing Trevor in tears started to realise how serious this accident was. Janet could hardly walk, having to be aided by her husband as they approached the nurse and Trevor. Janet was pleading "Please don't tell me they're dead, please." Trevor stood up, looked at them placing his arms around them, "Trudy is alive, but Lilly is dead." "Oh dear Lord no." shouted Janet as her legs started to buckle under her "That can't be right, not someone as beautiful and precious as our Lilly." Once Janet had composed herself, she realised she hadn't asked about Trudy, "What about Trudy, how is she? Where is she" Janet asked. Trevor told her that she was holding on in there, "She was seriously injured but she's ok and stable." Trevor sat and paused for a few moments, then, looking up at the nurse, said ,"How am I going to tell her this? How can I tell her that little Lilly is dead." Trevor then realised he hadn't told his parents. He immediately phoned them to tell them what had happened, and to also ask if they would collect Monty from Henry's because he needed to be told what's happened.

Whilst all of this was going on Monty was with his pal playing on the Play Station but around the time of the accident he started having an uneasy feeling in his stomach. He thought he was being stupid and continued to enjoy his time with his mate. It was planned for Monty to be dropped off back home by Henry's mum, but already his grandparents were rushing to the house to give him the bad news and to take him home. As Henry's mum Anita opened the door Monty's grandmother Elsie told her what had happened "Would you mind if we borrowed one of your rooms to sit Monty down and tell him?" "Of course." replied Anita "Take as long as you need, I will make you and your husband a cup of tea." Although it was a lovely offer, Elsie thanked Anita but declined the offer because she felt it would be better to get Monty back home as soon as possible. Monty knew as soon as he heard the doorbell that something was wrong. He immediately stopped what he was doing to see if he could hear what was being said but he couldn't which was a blessing in disguise. Overhearing that your sister was dead and your mum was in hospital unconscious would not be nice. After Elsie had spoken to Monty he didn't cry, but he went very quiet and kept looking at the floor. Elsie put her arm around Monty like she trying to protect and comfort him, but there was no way she could protect him from this news. "Sweetheart, I'm not going to ask if you're ok because I already know the answer to that, but I do want to say don't bottle anything up, it's ok to have tears and cry at a time like this." Monty turned toward his nan, "Where's dad?" Elsie explained that Trevor was at the hospital and Monty immediately said "Can you take me there please nan?" Elsie hesitated for a couple of seconds "Oh darling I don't think they will allow you in to see your mum so I'm not sure if it would be worth going there." "Of course it's worth it nan, I want to see dad and be with him so we can wait together." Elsie could see that there was no way she was going to stop him from going so she agreed. Once they got to the hospital Trudy had been transferred to the intensive care unit as there had been a few complications with her injuries so they were keeping a close eye on her.

At this point Trevor hadn't even been allowed to be in with Trudy and he was restlessly waiting outside for some news. As he turned and saw Monty he immediately stood up and put his arms out towards Monty and together they hugged and cried together. "Dad don't send me home, not yet." Trevor's heart broke to see Monty begging him not to send him home. "I'll let you stay for a while but then I want you to go home with nan and grandad." he said. Up until then Trevor's father William had been there saying very little but at that point he sat next to Trevor, wrapped his arms around Trevor and Monty and through his tears reassured both Trevor and Monty that he was there for them both. For the next day or so there wasn't much of a change in Trudy although thankfully she turned the corner, opened her eyes to see Trevor sitting there. Trevor immediately called for a nurse to come as soon as he saw her eyes flickering. Straight away Trevor was told to wait outside whilst they checked her, informing her she had been in a road traffic accident. Once that was completed Trevor was allowed straight in again to be with Trudy. Thankfully Trudy was coherent but now she had to learn the truth about Lilly. Trevor had decided that he wouldn't tell her about Lilly until he had spoken to the doctor so he fobbed her off with "She's ok." when she asked how Lilly was doing. It was getting really difficult to keep fobbing her off every time she asked a question about how her daughter was doing, so he spoke to the doctor "Doctor my wife isn't stupid and she is starting to suspect that something is very wrong so I think it's time she should be told." The doctor agreed that she now needed to know.

It was Trevor that broke the news to Trudy and when she was told they had to give her some medication to help calm her down. She had started to become hysterical and that wasn't any good for her given her condition. Trevor stayed by her throughout, and Monty was at home being looked after by his grandparents. Trudy was making a fairly good physical recovery so they wanted to move her from the intensive care unit to an ordinary ward. Janet, Aiden, Elsie and William however decided that between them they would pay for her to go into a private ward in the hospital as they didn't feel that she was up to talking to the other patients and they were right. Repeatedly Monty had asked if he could see his mum but for the first few days it was a definite no. When the doctor and Trevor felt that if she saw Monty she may feel a little better, it was fixed that he came along one afternoon to see his mum. As he walked into her room and she saw him standing there she completely broke down. She wanted to reach her arms out towards him but because of her injuries she couldn't. Repeatedly she kept saying "I'm so sorry, I'm so sorry." like it was all her fault. Monty ran over to her and got as close to her as he could without hurting her, "Mum, why do you keep saying sorry? dad says it's not your fault it was the other mans fault". Trudy didn't answer, instead she just kept crying.

"Well Trudy how are you feeling today?" asked her doctor when he came to see her. "They say that time heals." she replied, "but I don't think this pain inside me will ever go away." The doctor said nothing, he just listened to her as she spoke of her pain. At least she was talking about it he thought, and he really did have a lot of sympathy for what she was going through. He knew there was help out there for her to come to terms with her grief, it was just going to take it's time. Trudy had been in the hospital for 2 weeks and on a physical level she was doing well, so much so that in fact the doctor had decided it was time to talk to Trudy about going home. Trudy was dreading this day as she knew that as soon as she had a date to go home she was going to have to arrange Lilly's funeral. The pain was just too much to bear because it made it all very real. So, between the doctor, Trudy and Trevor it was agreed that she should go home by the end of the week. Now, Lilly's funeral could be organised. Like Trudy, Trevor was dreading it, but he knew it had to be done. He kept thinking that Lilly deserved a good send off.

The funeral directors had been on hold organising Lillys funeral because Trudy was in hospital, but now that they could go ahead there were questions that needed to be asked in order to ensure that the funeral was exactly how the family wanted it to be. Lilly was your typical little girl, loved her dolls, teddy bears and anything pink, so her flowers needed to be a mass of pink and white flowers in the shape of a teddy bear. They also decided that they were going to bury her favourite teddy bear and her unicorn fluffy toy with her as she very often used to have them both in her arms as she fell asleep at night. Trudy felt that they would keep her calm for the next part of her journey. Trudy always believed that there was life after death because she had experiences of seeing spirit on a regular basis when she was a child. When her grandmother passed away she knew about it before she got told because her nan came to her to say goodbye, and to tell her how much she loved her. Naturally Monty was feeling the loss of bossy little sister too and he wanted to give her something of his to remember him by when she gets to the other end of her journey. He also wanted to make sure that she kept warm on the journey so he gave her his favourite hoodie to wrap herself in. It wasn't pink like she would have liked but it will keep her warm he thought'.

The dreaded day loomed and as you can imagine the family were struggling with what this day would bring. Monty stayed in his room most of the time because he didn't want to see his mum crying again as it broke his heart. Poor old Monty, in amongst the family grief, there he was trying to make sense of no longer having a sister and in some ways he also blamed himself for being such a horrible brother to her by shouting at her or telling her to get out of his room when he was on the Play Station. For the last couple of weeks Monty had been sitting in his room feeling guilty and worthless. The problem was he wasn't sharing this with anyone else, even when he was asked how he was feeling which his parents did quite regularly, well, it was more his dad that was keeping an eye on him really because Trudy hadn't been engaging much with anyone since she got home. Monty just wasn't opening up about his feelings. The church was packed with friends and family as well as the parents of some of the children that went to school with Lilly. Trudy hobbled down the aisle with her crutches and as she did, she could see everyones' faces looking at her, feeling sorry for her, she thought, which she hated. Trevor walked beside her and also had his arm around Monty who felt very overwhelmed by the amount of people that were there. The tiny little coffin commanded the attention of everyone as it lay proud at the front and the family had placed a beautifully framed photo of Lilly with that big beautiful smile she was known for on top. No funeral is enjoyable but the funeral directors had done the family proud and at the end of the service both Trevor and Trudy thanked them.

The wake was held in a nice hotel that wasn't far from their home. Once they arrived there Trudy knew she couldn't go through the motions the way she was expected to do so she asked her parents as well as Trevor's parents if they would represent both Trevor and herself at the wake. Neither one of them could cope being with anyone at the moment and wanted simply to go home. Naturally both couples agreed. Monty decided to stay at the wake with his grandparents because the truth was that he couldn't face being at home now that Lilly was buried. For him this felt so final but deep down he was hoping that his mum is right when she said that Lilly would be watching down over them. There was one point when he left the room where the wake was being held. He walked into the garden looking up at the sky thinking of his sister. "Lilly if you really are looking down on us please let me know." He waited, but nothing happened, so again he said, "Come on Lil, if you're really with us like mum says you are, let me see you, or do something so I know it's you." Again nothing happened and he didn't feel anything around him to confirm Lilly was there. Monty was disappointed and heartbroken because he had always believed what his mum had always said to him "Monty, we all go off to a lovely place when we die". He didn't think that his mum had lied to him, he just thought she had got it wrong.

By the time the gathering had come to an end, Monty felt ready to go home to find peace and quiet in his room. When he got home with his grandparents Trudy and Trevor were sitting in the living room. Trudy immediately asked Monty to sit beside her. Now that she was capable of giving hugs again she grabbed hold of Monty for dear life, "You did very well today sweetie, thank you for being so strong." Monty was a little bit taken aback because this was really the first time she had wanted to embrace him. It sometimes made him feel that she didn't love him the way she loved Lilly, which of course was absolute nonsense. What nobody knew was that when Trevor and Trudy got home after the funeral Trevor spoke quite honestly to Trudy about the lack of attention she had been giving to Monty which was having an effect on him. Trevor was exhausted and it was because of that he had got irritable with her, "Look I have tried so hard to be mum and dad to Monty since it happened but I can't do it all. Remember he still needs a mother." At first Trudy nearly lost her cool but she knew deep down Trevor was right, she had been very focussed on her hurt and not really taking into account how anyone else felt. She needed to let Monty know that she loved him as much as she loved Lilly. Monty broke down in her arms so she held him as tight as she could to let him know that it was ok to let the tears flow. After a while once Monty had calmed down Trevor, Trudy and Monty sat down and spoke about Lilly and the love and laughter she gave them all. They spoke about how her passing had left them feeling. Trudy told the boys that she could sometimes feel Lilly around her playing with her mums hair like she loved to do when they played hairdressers. Trevor shared that he very often felt Lilly was with him first thing in the morning before anyone else was up. She used to love sneaking downstairs when she knew dad was up and ask him to read to her, which he always did. Oh how he missed that. Monty didn't share that he had asked Lilly to give him a sign that she was there. He stopped believing that she was still living somewhere else, and could come to visit them. Let them think he could sense Lilly was around him he thought, after all it wasn't hurting anyone else was it? It was Monty's ways of coping with the fact that he hadn't experienced Lilly around him.

After an exhausting couple of hours talking about emotions and having a take-away pizza Monty was ready to go up to his room to sit and play his Play Station. When he opened the door he hadn't noticed that the controller for the Play Station had been moved from his desk where his Play Station was and was now sitting in the middle of his bed. When he started looking for it and found it on his bed, he did think how strange that was because he always put the remote control on his desk. He was so keen though to play his new game he pushed it aside and got on with his game. After a good time on the Play Station, Monty got ready for bed, and as he lay there he thought of his little sister but he was so tired he fell off to sleep almost immediately. Once he was in a deep sleep Lilly decided to pay him a visit. "Hi Monty thank you for your hoodie you gave me, it really did keep me warm. I've been watching you all day but I didn't want to talk to you whilst you were with all those people. Wasn't there lots of them?. I was really liked wasn't I? Mummy cried lots and daddy did too but not as much as mummy. I've got my teddy and my unicorn too so I'm not alone. Did you know that we have got a great grandma? I think that's what she said, but anyhow she's coming to look after me again so I had better go and meet her. She's ever so nice, I will come visit you again cos I know you're lonely." Monty didn't wake after that, in fact he slept very deeply, but when he woke in the morning he remembered what Lilly had said in his dream or what he thought was a dream, and it unsettled him for the day. In true Monty style he didn't speak about it to his parents or anyone else for that matter. As the day progressed Monty started to let it go and stop thinking about it. He just put it down to an odd dream.

Between the three of them they were starting to find a new way of living without Lilly in their lives, but there were still reminders of that dreadful day. The driver of the other vehicle was charged with drunk driving and due to appear in court very soon. Lilly's teacher also contacted Trudy to ask if she wanted Lillys books from school. "She had done some tremendous work this year and was constantly being awarded stars." explained the teacher, "I thought you might like to keep them." Trudy jumped at the chance of having her schoolwork and was so grateful to her teacher. Trudy was bottling up the guilt that she was carrying because she didn't leave the house when Lilly wanted her to on that day. If she had done that her baby girl would still be here, she constantly thought and had shed many a tear over it. This was also one of the reasons why she had been keeping a distance from Monty. In her eyes she was a failure.

This dream Monty had about Lilly was becoming a regular thing and was starting to freak him out a little bit. He didn't want to talk to his mum about it in case it really upset her so he thought he would have a quiet word with his dad when the time was right. Monty was also noticing that things in his bedroom were being moved, he was often finding things weren't in the place he had left them. Like his trainers for example, he always put his trainers in his wardrobe otherwise his mum said she was going to "Throw them away." Every day that week they kept getting moved when he went downstairs for his dinner, so when he came back up to his room his trainers would be out on the floor, and not in the wardrobe where he put them. Every day yet again his trainers had been moved and his school bag kept on moving from the place he normally kept it. Monty couldn't help but think how strange it was that all of this started on the day of Lilly's funeral after he had said that he didn't believe in Life after Death. I wonder, he thought, it's time to talk to dad. Monty ran down the stairs when he heard Trevor opening the front door. First though he knew that dad would want to say hi to mum, and then he could talk to him, so he waited patiently. It was quite a while after dinner before he could speak to dad without mum around. Now that he had got his dad's attention he didn't know whether to continue or not because it all sounded crazy. "So son, what did you want to talk to me about?" Asked his dad. Hesitantly Monty started to tell Trevor the story of the day of Lilly's funeral when he asked her to talk to him to let him know that she was in heaven, and there was silence. From that moment he had stopped believing what mum had always said about there being a heaven where we continue to live. Since then, Monty explained, some strange things had kept on happening in his dreams or what he thought were his dreams. Trevor was listening intently and when Monty stopped he asked "Like what." Monty explained it all to him, "Well, I'm constantly dreaming about her but this dream feels so real because she's thanking me for my hoodie that I placed in the coffin with her to keep her warm on her journey." Trevor was just about to speak when Monty, who was now on a roll said, "Hang on dad I haven't finished, my school bag keeps getting moved and so do my trainers, I know where I put this stuff so it isn't me". As Monty finished he took a deep breath because he had blurted it all out so quickly he had run out of air!

Trevor gently hugged Monty, "Have you spoke to mum about this?" "No I haven't dad." answered Monty, "Why?". "I was curious that's all.", Trevor immediately replied "No, that's not true, I'm more than curious because your mum has been having dreams, weird dreams, that Lilly is with her saying that the accident wasn't her fault, she mustn't blame herself." Monty was shocked that his mum was having similar kinds of dreams. Both Trudy and Monty had told Trevor how the dreams feel so real. "I can't tell mum." said Monty immediately. Trevor looked at him surprised, "Why son, you know she believes in the afterlife, and she would be so pleased to hear you're getting similar dreams to her." Monty looked down at the floor, "I know dad but she cries so much, I'm frightened of making her cry even more." Trevor looked at Monty with pride in his eyes, "Son you won't make her cry, and if she does cry it would be tears of joy that Lilly is near us all." Monty wasn't ready to talk to mum about it and told his dad so, "No I'm not ready to talk to her about it yet dad." The weeks and months went by during which the driver of the other car that caused the accident had been sentenced to four years imprisonment for causing death by dangerous driving and driving whilst under the influence of alcohol. To be honest this didn't bring much comfort to Trevor, Trudy, or Monty. What was four years without his freedom compared to the loss of their darling daughter/sister?. Trevor and Trudy stayed away from the court hearing, both of their parents attended representing the family. It appeared there was very little remorse shown by the other driver which the family couldn't believe.

For a while Monty hadn't had anything going missing or things being put in different places, which to him felt a bit strange as he had started to believe that it was Lilly doing all of this and he quite liked that she was around him. On the first anniversary of Lilly's death the family decided to honour it by going to the park where Lilly loved to play and place some flowers there for her. Both sets of grandparents joined them, and after that they went to the local burger bar where they used to go after they had done the week's shopping on a Friday night. Lilly didn't like burgers but she loved the chicken nuggets they did there, and she would eat the lot as well as the portion of chips that would come with it. As they sat there that day they all laughed at how Lilly had a great appetite for such a little thing, and she would eat them so fast because she would be in a rush to be getting onto the next thing she wanted to get up to. Although the day was a struggle to get through, they managed it including some lovely laughs remembering how lively Lilly was, and as Trudy said whilst they were in the burger bar earlier "She will still be as lively as ever and driving everyone mad up there." Monty couldn't help it but it slipped out, "I wish she was here right now driving me mad." Trudy immediately gave him a big hug which lasted quite a while before she released her hold.

One of the positive things about the last few months of that first year after Lilly died was that Trudy was getting back into the swing of things again. She was being an attentive mum to Monty again which Monty loved but also felt a bit guilty for enjoying his time with his mum because there was no Lilly taking up all of her time. He also worried that if Lilly was looking over and saw this she would be upset. Lilly was a bit like that and could get quite jealous if she saw her mum and brother together having fun. After getting through the first anniversary of Lilly's loss, once they had all gone to bed, Trevor had a vivid dream that he was back in Lilly's favourite park sitting on a bench. Lilly was holding her dad's hand as she spoke to him "Thank you for today daddy. I loved that you came and spent time here and I know that you couldn't see me, but I did have a go on the swings and the see saw as well." Trevor looked down at Lilly's hand in his. He could actually feel her beautiful little hand the way he could when she was alive walking down the street together. In this dream Trevor looked down at her little face and as he saw that little cheeky grin she always gave when she wanted her own way, he reached out and held her "Oh Lilly mummy, daddy and Monty love and miss you so much that it hurts. We think of you every day and so does both grans and grandpops." "I know." Lilly replied, "I visit you all a lot, but I have been very good lately and haven't moved Monty's things or mummy's either. Mummy still cries a lot and I feel so sad for her, you must tell her that I am alright and happy." In Trevor's dream Lilly was on a roll continuing to chatter away the way she did when she was alive, "You must tell mummy that I see her crying so much and it makes me so sad because I don't like to see her upset. Sometimes I sit next to her when she looks at my photo by the side of your bed and I always say goodnight when mummy kisses my photo when she's going to bed. You must tell mummy this because she needs to know that I'm with great granny now and even though she's very old she's funny. I can twist her round my little finger the way you used to say I could with you." With that Lilly gave a little chuckle and disappeared. When Trevor woke up he was in shock because the dream was so real. Up until that point he hadn't had any dreams about Lilly or felt her presence or anything and yet now he felt as though she was with him.

"It was so real and it felt so true if that makes sense Trudy." Trevor said as he was telling her all about it. "I could feel her hand, I could touch her face and I just know it wasn't a dream. Now I know what you and Monty have been talking about over this last year." Trudy smiled, reached out her hand to him and as they sat at the end of the bed said, "I know you were with her, and I know it was real because I was there too. I was watching you two meet again for the first time and I felt the love that you both have for each other." Trevor looked at Trudy dumbfounded in shock that she had experienced what he saw as a dream state, but now it was looking like he was with Lilly, and she wanted to be with her dad for a short while. They both sat holding each other's hand and sobbed so hard it felt like they were never going to stop. Meanwhile, Monty could hear them talking in their room and when he heard them both crying he rushed in without knocking. "What's wrong?" he asked as he saw them both in tears. Trudy looked at him and held her hand out for him to join them. "It's ok sweetie." she said reassuringly, "It's only your dad letting go of all the tears he had after he met with Lilly in a dream last night, only I don't believe it was a dream. I know she came to him because I was there to, and she came to me as well." "And so was I." replied Monty." I was going to talk to you both today about it because it was so real and I knew it wasn't a dream, it was Lilly wanting to be with her big brother. Dad I saw you with her, it wasn't a dream, she just wanted us all to be close to her on the anniversary of her death, she wanted us to know that she was ok."

Trevor sat quiet for a few moments "So why didn't I see you guys there?" "I believe it's because she just wanted you to herself for a while only. We could watch but not interact." replied Trudy. Trevor really didn't know what to make of all this but he was beginning to realise what had always seemed illogical to him about there being a spirit world where we go when we die, now seemed absolutely possible after what he experienced last night. Never again would he knock it, in fact his way of thinking now was that if it brings Lilly closer to them he will encourage her to meet them in their dreams, or move things or make a sound. It may not be the best way of looking after oneself mentally or emotionally but it was a start for Trevor to come to terms with the loss of Lilly and start grieving. For them as a family now, they know that Lilly may not be physically with them, but she certainly is with them spiritually, and as a family they can work through their loss together!

Chapter 9

Arthur

In Arthur's heyday he was a very good looking man. He "Could charm the birds out of the trees.", or so they all used to say and he was considered quite a catch by many people. In the 1950's Arthur was in his twenties and had moved from Ireland where he was born and brought up to London where he hoped he could make his dreams come true. At that time he seemed to have simple dreams like learning a skill, finding a job that was going to pay well with good opportunities, and work his way up the ladder. Sadly however, once he arrived in England and started job hunting, the more he looked the more he realised that the only kind of jobs that were suitable for him were as a lorry driver. He didn't mind too much and kept telling himself that the next job would be the one that was right for him, but unfortunately the next one was also as a lorry driver so fairly early on he abandoned his ambitions and just get on with the job, so to speak.

Arthur worked long hard hours and did start earning a good wage. He also seemed to get on with the other guys that he worked with which was a blessing because back then the Irish weren't accepted so easily in London. Very often they were seen as "Skivvies" and not human beings, but thankfully that wasn't happening where he worked. One thing that Arthur always loved was at the end of the day, when it was knocking off time the lads would go straight across the road to the pub. Up until then Arthur really didn't drink much as life was far tougher in Ireland where finding work was hard and earning enough just to keep going was harder still, let alone go to the pub. So, he started building a life for himself and at that time he seemed to be happy with his life. Arthur always had an eye for the young ladies and the more he settled down in his new life and felt comfortable, the more he started to turn his head to some very pretty ladies. He soon became known as a love them and leave them kind of guy because he was never really with any of them that long, until he met Muriel that was. Muriel was a very pretty nineteen year old innocent girl who was London born and bred. As soon as she met Arthur she fell head over heels for him and his charm, and it appeared the same had to be said for Arthur. Because he was such a sweet talker, he had even convinced Muriel's parents that he was a loyal, hardworking and stable young man, and at that time he may have believed that about himself as well. Up until recently he hadn't had much experience with women, although in the brief time he had been in London he had certainly started to carve notches on his bedpost, however when he met Muriel he started to behave himself.

Within a matter of about six months Arthur and Muriel were married, and for a short time things were going great for them, or at least on the surface it seemed that way. However there did seem to be a spot of trouble ahead for the happy couple when Muriel asked Arthur to come home straight from work instead of going to the pub because they couldn't afford it, he was spending more and more time at the pub than at home with his new bride and his drinking was becoming heavier and heavier. Arthur didn't like being told what to do as he put it and out of pure devilment he started to spend even longer hours in the pub. They didn't have any money at the end of each week because he had to pay his slate off for all the drinks he had had during the week and there was no money left for anything else. When Muriel complained to Arthur about not having enough money to go around his answer was get a job, which was exactly what she did. The only problem was that within a few months of working she found that she was pregnant. She was terrified of telling Arthur because she didn't know how he would react. It turned out that he was overjoyed at the news and the first thing he wanted to do was to go out and have a few drinks to celebrate. He promptly left Muriel at home while he went down to the pub!

Muriel really hoped that having a baby would make a difference and she had convinced herself that once he saw the baby he would just want to be at home with them. They had a beautiful little son named Arthur junior. Arthur senior seemed to be so proud of his son and for a short time he did become the attentive father and husband that he should be. Within a few months he was back to his old ways and he pretty much left the raising of their son to Muriel. Even though they now had a little person to look after and raise, Arthur still expected Muriel to somehow find the money to feed and clothe them all. He did give her housekeeping but it was a pittance and barely enough to keep the three of them going. To be honest Muriel was only able to make ends meet because of her parents and the money they were giving her every week to tide things over. Muriel's father really wanted to punch Arthur into next week but Muriel begged him not to for her's and the baby's sake. Her dad, Jonathan, would very often say to his wife Linda "I don't know why she doesn't leave him and come back home, we would support her." But as Linda explained "She is still in love with him at the moment and she won't have anything said against him, you will just push her away. Given time that will change." Linda's tone told Jonathon she had given him a warning but he also knew that Linda was right so he kept his mouth closed, for now at least.

It was only about a year after Arthur junior's birth that Muriel was pregnant again, which, again was another reason for Arthur to go out and get drunk, not that he needed an excuse. When their second child, a beautiful baby girl named Elizabeth, was born, Arthur was hardly around. He had started to allow the drinking to get even heavier to the point where it affected him getting up to going to work. Needless to say he lost a couple of jobs as a result, but now it wasn't just the drinking that was worrying Muriel. Arthur had also started to raise his hand to her so she went along trying not to upset him just in case he turned on one of the children. Muriel didn't tell her father because she knew he would want to knock him out, or "Punch his lights out." as they say in London. Deep down though she knew her parents had an idea of what was happening so she made sure that if Arthur visibly marked her she wouldn't pop around to her parents because they were forever looking her over to see if there were any bruises. Arthur applied for a job that entailed him doing long distance driving which, to be honest, suited Muriel down to the ground. It gave her time to herself, not having to respond to everything he told her to do. Arthur was away from Monday to Friday coming home at weekends, and even when he was home he would spend time with his cronies who thought he was such a nice guy. Muriel started to feel that Arthur had another woman but she tried to push the thought away because she didn't want to believe that he would do that to her on top of everything else. To add to matters, Muriel was pregnant again. What she didn't know was that Arthur had been seeing many women over the last few months on his journeys away, so his roving eye was back. Muriel would try not to think about that gut feeling she had for the sake of the children, especially now their beautiful little daughter had been born. Arthur had seen very little of his new baby girl and when he was home he expected Muriel to keep the kids quiet so he can have a rest. He had become one of the most unpleasant men and emotional bully that anyone could ever meet.

Back in those days there were no mobile phones to call your wayward husband on to check where he was. For many women, like Muriel, they had to get on with bringing up the family and not think about that gut feel that was niggling away at them. Women in similar circumstances would not openly tell anyone about how they were being treated because it was very much a mans world back then. Women weren't being heard and in many cases were treated like second class citizens. As Muriel and Arthur's marriage deteriorated it was no surprise to anyone that he was spending more and more time away from the family. His drinking took him further afield to Kilburn where there was a good, strong Irish community. They felt like a family because they understood each other's feelings about leaving their homes back in Ireland. It was here that Arthur met a lady who was in her 20's named Bernadette, a nurse working in a local hospital. It was clear to Arthur's friends that there was an attraction between the two of them which they all thought was great. They knew he was married with 2 children but Arthur's new found friends had pretty much the same ideas about women's position and role in life. Arthur's mates promised that they wouldn't say anything to Bernadette and in fact they coaxed him into making a play for her. Of course he neglected to tell Bernadette that he wasn't available, well at least for the first couple of months, but after that she started to get suspicious, so he told her. By this time she was very much in love and, as she said to her friends, "Well it's clear that he loves me more than he does his wife, otherwise he wouldn't want to be with me." and anyone that said otherwise would no longer be regarded as a friend.

Arthur had made up his mind, he was going to leave Muriel and live with Bernadette. To be honest Muriel wasn't that upset, in fact she was relieved because she had had enough of him and had grown to hate him. The only thing she did say was that she wanted child maintenance for their children and being the ever graceful person she was she let him know that he was welcome to see the children regularly. I'm sure you are not surprised to hear that Arthur never paid a penny of maintenance and he never put himself out to see his children but for Muriel none of that was a problem. She was far happier on her own than with "That tyrant." as she would say to friends and family. Arthur and Bernadette set up home together as husband and wife, back then living together was seen as shameful. All seemed great at first, Arthur didn't let his true colours show through for the first few months Even the regular drinking down the pub wasn't a problem because Bernadette could go with him as her friends would sometimes drink in there to. It didn't really affect them when Bernadette was pregnant for their first because she was still able to go to the pub with him, however that all changed when their little son was born.

Unsurprisingly my readers, the same old pattern was developing for Bernadette as it did for Muriel. Unfortunately for Bernadette they weren't married which made it harder for her to leave, not that Bernadette wanted to because she was so besotted with Arthur. Eighteen months after they had their first child, Kyle, they had another son, Aran and a daughter, Veronica, three years later. Throughout this period the same old behaviours of Arthur's started at first to slowly creep in, like spending all his free time down the pub, like barely giving Bernadette enough money to feed them all and this was only for starters. By now it was clear that alcohol had taken hold of Arthur, he was now an alcoholic but as you have probably guessed he wasn't a happy alcoholic, oh no, instead he was a moody and violent alcoholic who's personality could change in the blink of an eye. He would very quickly turn on Bernadette and by now it was getting to the point that he would find any fault he could so that he could start on Bernadette. To add to it all, Arthur's divorce had come through and they could get married for the sake of the children. Bernadette didn't really want to get married but because she had three children she felt it was for the best so she went ahead and became his wife. This was one of the loneliest times for her as her family in Ireland had turned their back on her when they found out that she was living with a man and having his children.

For years Bernadette put up with Arthur's awful behaviour which involved him hurting her physically, mentally and emotionally, not forgetting the womanising which had had started very soon after they moved in together. Most of the time he was either away working, that is if he managed to keep a job, or he was staying with another woman for a while, coming home, and there were times when he would simply disappear out for a "Quick drink." and not come home for days because he had caught a ferry back over to Ireland for a week or so. Alas he always found his way back home to Bernadette. To everyone in the neighbourhood he was seen as a charming man who loved his family, always working away to pay the bills and look after them. The neighbours truly believed that he would do anything for them and Bernadette was too afraid to say or show anything different.

So, she put on a brave face, smiled and got on with bringing her children up more or less on her own. Back in those days there wasn't the support they have today so as you can imagine a woman wouldn't leave her family home because she wouldn't really have anywhere to go. Bernadette stood in her kitchen staring out of the kitchen window into the back yard thinking and contemplating whether or not there was a way she could grab her children and leave, and as she thought about this she realised that her real and only option was to go back to Ireland with the children. She really didn't think that would work out because of how they feel she behaved back home. So with tears in her eyes and silent sobs, she realised that this was her life so she had better get used to it. For a while she did wonder if she should tell his drinking cronies about what he's really like. That thought didn't stay with her for long because she knew that if she did they would probably get him in a dark alleyway and beat him up properly. She didn't hold with violence so that was no way to go.

Although Bernadette enjoyed her children she rarely had the time to do very much with them. She was now a machinist working at home for a coat factory trying very hard to make ends meet and of course because she had taken this job in desperation, Arthur decided that he was going to cut her housekeeping. "If you're earning now you don't need my money do you." Arthur had said "Yes I do because you're not giving me enough housekeeping as it is, which is why I have taken on the job." Bernadette knew that speaking out like that would merit a slap for her, so normally she wouldn't answer back. Sometimes she just felt desperate, but because she did this time, she knew what was coming. To give you an idea of how bad Arthur had become, there was one day when she asked Arthur to take her shopping as she couldn't drive and she had a lot to get. He agreed to drive her, but in the next breath he said "Yeah I'll take you but you can pay me the petrol money for doing it." Bernadette couldn't believe he was going to charge her for taking her shopping to buy food for his wife and kids.

As each day dawned life with Arthur was getting worse and now that the children were growing up they were being terribly affected which naturally worried Bernadette but she really didn't know what she could do about it at this stage. There was now an added insult to injury for Bernadette because it appeared that Arthur had found a new love, and wasn't shy in saying this to her either. He would taunt her with words like "She's far younger than you, and she looks after herself too, which is more than you do." Bernadette just ignored him and cried her silent tears when he wasn't around. She didn't feel great about herself but she was bringing up three children on her own and was also working long hours with her job. There was part of her however that hoped he would leave her and the kids and go of with this new "wonder woman" because now her feelings for him had turned from love to hate, bitterness and resentment.

Bernadette had always said to herself that she would put up with Arthur hitting her, but if he ever touched one of the kids, that would be it. On the day that she had popped out to do some chores leaving the children with him coming back early only to find Arthur hitting the oldest son Kyle that was it! He had touched one of the children, "No one touches my children." she shouted as she promptly reached for the broom that was in the hallway and pinned him against the wall on the stairs. She gave him a good whack with the broom then drew a fist and punched him. He immediately went to hit her but she stood strong and proud, "I dare you to touch me or the children because if you do I will kill you." It was true that she didn't mean physically kill him but by saying that she knew it gave him the warning to be prepared for her to fight back because she had had enough. After that he walked out of the house went down the pub and that was the last time he ever lived with Bernadette and the family again. Oh he tried on a number of occasions to come back and was full of apologies and promises but Bernadette stayed strong sand and refused his lies.

Thankfully life changed so much for the better for Bernadette, and a couple of years after she had kicked Arthur out she met someone that was a true gent who wasn't a drinker or womaniser. He was happy to take on her three children and bring them up as his own. You wouldn't be surprised to hear that Arthur never bothered to see the children, or pay maintenance for them, but that didn't bother Bernadette as he she had done so long without it that she didn't want it, and now she certainly didn't need it. For Arthur however life was changing dramatically and not in a good way. He stayed with this "Wonder woman" that he had teased Bernadette about for a couple of years but by then another female had caught his eye and so the pattern started again. This time his new lady had two grown up sons who would lay into him if he so much as touched their mother.

As the years went by his drinking became heavier and he let himself go becoming a sad, pathetic drunk who had wasted his life trying to see the end of a glass, always thinking that the grass was greener on the other side when it came to relationships, but in the end he was left very much on his own. Nobody knows if he ever thought of his children but his children certainly thought about him, but never in a good way because they were angry at the way he treated their mother. One day whilst out shopping Arthur's daughter Veronica bumped into a friend of their dad's, Nigel, who lived locally. Curiosity was getting the better of her so once they got past the idle chit chat she asked "Have you seen anything of Arthur? Is he still the same old git that he always was?" Nigel stared at her for a few seconds and after what seemed like ages replied "You haven't heard?" "Heard what?" she replied, "I'm sorry but I heard he died a couple of months ago." Veronica stared at Nigel in shock because she didn't think she would hear anything like that. She was looking Nigel in the eye as she replied, "Dead, what from?" "Well, I think it was heart failure, or so I was told." replied Nigel. Veronica got as much information as Nigel had about her dad's death and rushed home to tell her mum. As she walked through the door Veronica shouted for her mum, "Mum, mum, where are you"? She heard a faint reply from the garden so she headed outside and sure enough there was her mum hanging out the washing as normal. "What's wrong?" Bernadette said as she turned her head to look at Veronica, "Well." replied Veronica "I've just seen Nigel Mure and he told me that "The old git" (meaning her dad) is dead." Bernadette stopped and dropped the jumper she was trying to hang out back into the basket, "What? You're joking." "No" said Veronica quickly, "He's gone." Bernadette couldn't believe what she was hearing or to feel as sad as she did, but at the end of the day she did share a life with him once and they did have three kids, even if he did forget about them half the time. Bernadette couldn't help but say what immediately crossed her mind, "Now he will pay the price because now he'll face up to how he lived his life here." And Bernadette was right, he was going to have to face the music as he reflected back on how he lived his life. Although he wouldn't be judged by those up there, he would be judging himself if he wanted to move on and continue to evolve. That will be painful for him thought Bernadette.

Arthur was so surprised when he found himself in the spirit world, not because he didn't think that it existed, but because he always felt deep down that he hadn't earned the right to walk through the "Pearly gates", instead he always believed that he would end up somewhere much darker. Before he died, he hadn't been feeling too great for a few days, there was something inside him that knew his time was coming to an end and that he was on his way out. Arthur looked around his new environment and soaked up the beauty and serenity. As he turned around, he was totally surprised because coming towards him were his loved ones wanting to greet him back into his spiritual home. He couldn't believe that they were all back together again. His mother, father, and his little sister who died young was there to greet him too. She adored him when they were all growing up together. Although it was lovely to see them all, Arthur was already wondering how they would receive him because he knew that he hadn't been the most caring or the most well behaved person in the world which was putting it mildly. So his greatest fears that he had always had but never showed when he was living a physical life was starting to rear their head as he was with his family once more, and those fears were rejection and criticism. Arthur had always had a huge fear of being rejected or criticised, and he carried this all the way through his earthly life. He wasn't quite sure where it came from but when he felt those insecurities in a situation he would reach straight for the bottle which, to him, was the medication he needed. Now he couldn't reach for the drink, and he couldn't run away, so the only answer was to look and learn how his behaviour had impacted others as well as himself.

Arthur spent some time with his family when they welcomed him back into the fold, and also told him they were not there to judge him. They said perhaps once he had seen and reflected back on the life he had just led, they could maybe discuss a few things, but for now they just want to welcome him back in his spiritual home. They also wanted to help him a little because they could see that deep down he knew he hadn't led the best of lives and he was showing his anxiety about being criticised. It wasn't too long before he saw his birth guide walking towards him and Arthur couldn't help but be scared so he took a deep breath and waited. As his guide, Vincent, came close he had the really strange feeling that his energy was familiar, it was like they had communicated before. Arthur was right because his guide had not only been his guide in the lifetime that Arthur had just left, he had also guided him in other lifetimes to. Vincent smiled as he got closer to Arthur, "Welcome back to your spiritual home Arthur, I have been waiting to greet you." Arthur replied suspiciously, "Thank you, I think. I don't mean to be rude but who are you? Have we met before? It's just that I feel as though I know you." Vincent was not dressed like a monk, so there were no special robes, in fact he wasn't dressed up at all really apart from what Arthur classed as the kind of working clothes that he himself had worn in his time as a lorry driver. It is said that if our guides come in official or religious robes, they have highly evolved in both this world and the next. They may choose to wear the kind of clothes that we ourselves had worn in our professions, so we feel on an equal level to them.

Vincent didn't answer Arthur's question, "Come, walk with me." he said softly, prompting Arthur to do what he was asked to do. Arthur thought he would get in what he wanted to say before Vincent stepped in so he started off somewhat defensively, "Ok I will walk with you but I will tell you that my family has told me I will be looking back on my lifetime back on earth, reflecting on the kind of life I led. I'm not willing to do that, so if you're here for that we may as well part company now." Vincent looked at Arthur "There is no need for you to feel threatened because it's only you that will judge your behaviour, I am not here to judge, I am here to help you." Arthur came back with a short, sharp answer still suspicious "Help me with what? I don't need your help, I'm back with my family and I'm doing OK." There was a long pause before Vincent replied "Don't you wish to see your earth family? It's OK, they won't see you." Arthur was definitely tempted, he couldn't help but admit that he did want to see his children. He hadn't seen any of them since they were young children and he wanted to see how they had grown. He was quite surprised by that because he never really thought about them when he was on earth but now all of a sudden he had heart pangs wanting to see his children. Arthur agreed that he would love to look over his five children. Again he was surprised as he looked over his two children from his first marriage, he felt his heart strings were being tugged. "Arthur Junior has done well for himself hasn't he, being an accountant, that's a good job with good prospects, and Elizabeth hasn't done bad either as a nurse. Yep they've done well." he said quite proudly. Vincent looked at him and asking rather sharply "Do you think you played a part in their success?" Arthur didn't know what to say because he knew he hadn't had any input into their childhood or education really, but he boldly answered, "Well I must have because they're part of me and I was around for the early part of their life." Vincent said nothing. "Oh look there's Muriel." he exclaimed as he saw his first wife with their children, "Wow she's still looking good and she's aged really well."

"They all seem really happy." he said quietly, then he saw a man joining them. It looked like they were all pleased to see him, especially Muriel, it was her second husband. Arthur felt sad thinking on what he had missed out on as he watched this picture of happiness develop before his very eyes. "It's funny really because I always thought that Muriel would stay single after I left, I never really thought she would meet anyone else." He continued, "Still as long as she's happy that's the main thing isn't it? It looks like I did her a favour by getting out of her life." Vincent sharply replied, "Do you really think you can take some pride in leaving her so that she could meet someone else?" Arthur really felt that and again didn't know what to say so he completely ignored it. Now it was time for him to look over his other three children and their mother Bernadette who had also remarried and was very happy with her second husband. As he looked over he saw that Kyle was a mechanic with his own garage, Aran was like his dad in as much as he was a lorry driver but was very happily married and faithful to his wife. Veronica had been a secretary but once she got married and started a family she stayed at home to be with the children. Bernadette, well she carried on doing part time jobs but her main role was being at home and being there for the children even if they were all grown up now. She especially adored her grandchildren who she looked after quite a lot.

As Arthur watched Bernadette and the family, he was privy to a conversation they were having about him which was very unusual as Bernadette didn't like him being mentioned but having just heard about his passing it was the topic of conversation. Kyle was telling the family that he had been thinking about him recently, even when he was asleep. Aran quite excitedly said "I've also been thinking of him over the last few days too, how weird is that?" They both looked at Veronica to see if she had been having the same experience but before they asked she cockily said, "No I haven't been thinking about the old git, I'm not interested in him at all." Bernadette stared at her children, "That's strange but over the last few days he has been on my mind too. Normally I never think of him or wonder what he's up to, but this week I kept thinking back to him wondering if he was alive or dead." Veronica replied, "Well, at least we know where the old bugger is now." Although Veronica was speaking harshly, acting like she didn't care, it couldn't have been further from the truth, she just didn't want to show it. All of them had a laugh at that, Bernadette saying, "I know he didn't want anything to do with you kids when he was alive, but I wonder if he will look down on you from Heaven?" "Oh God I hope not.", said Veronica, but Bernadette knew she didn't really mean it, she was just hiding the hurt she felt because her dad had abandoned them.

Arthur wasn't best pleased at the remarks that they were all making, he felt quite angry and it showed in his face. Vincent could see this, pointed it out to him and asked why. Arthur aggressively turned saying, "Of course I'm angry, there's absolutely no caring or gentle thoughts about me, not with either of my families." "Can I ask you why you would expect anything different?" asked Vincent, "After all in their eyes you abandoned them, which is never easy for anyone to accept at any age, but it is particularly worse for children as that has an incredible effect on them for the rest of their life." Arthur had

had enough of looking down on his family to see how they were doing, "I want to go now, take me away from here." Vincent respected his request which was no sooner said than done. The next thing Arthur knew he was walking towards a large, beautiful white building and although he didn't at that point know what the building was, he wasn't worried about going in. In fact as he looked around he saw beautiful landscapes and it all felt so peaceful. As they reached the door Arthur felt he had been there before and as they walked in, he realised this is where he had been when he returned from an earlier lifetime before the one he had just left. He knew now was time to look back on his life and reflect on all that he had achieved or not as the case may be Arthur looked at Vincent, "It's all coming back to me now, I remember this is the hall of records that we go to when we have returned from another earthly life." Vincent replied "That's right. I'm impressed that you have remembered being here before because there are many that have no recollection of the hall of records. It is often quite a shock that they can reflect and see certain parts of the life they have just led. Of course, for those who continue to evolve spiritually whilst living a human life will very much have the hall of records and its purpose in their memory because of the good work they had done whilst living a human life, with the support from their guides and teachers. Arthur looked inquisitively, "So let me get this straight, if I remember correctly, this is the place where I look at all of the mistakes I made in life? Like I really need to see those mistakes again and have it rubbed in my face." Vincent reassured Arthur, "No, that's not the sole purpose, we will take a look at all that you have learned and achieved. Nobody's life is only ever full of mistakes, there will be many achievements and experiences that you can learn from even now. By doing this work, you will also be helping us to understand life and the world as it is now." Arthur felt a bit happier as they walked through the door, he had a smile on his face, "Well, that's ok then." He felt like he was in control again.

As Arthur walked through the door Vincent immediately directed him to a large door on the right which opened allowing them to walk straight in. It was a large room filled with books, written records and many objects that once belonged to Arthur which were placed there to help him feel a bit more comfortable. As they walked towards a desk Arthur started to recognise some of his belongings. "Oh my God!" he exclaimed. His Irish accent started to grow strong again, which he had lost having lived in England for so long. "I recognise some of these things, it's my stuff. How did they get here?" Vincent once again ignored Arthur's question getting him to focus on what he was visually able to see. With that he saw himself as a child living the hard life that he had growing up with a mother who wasn't tactile or maternal in any way shape or form. Then there was his father who worked hard on the land, so when he came home he had no time for his two sons, (his sister died when she was 11 years old). "Oh there's my dad, bless him, it was lovely to see him when I arrived here, and there's my mother too, who is still the same as she was down there, unforgiving and cold." "Yes, that is sad." said Vincent, "Unfortunately your mother wasn't prepared to do the work needed to help her move on. So whereas most move forward, understanding more about themselves, sadly your mother will lack that feeling of unity, love, forgiveness and understanding that builds between loved ones already here and those that have yet to arrive." Arthur felt quite sad as Vincent explained this because at the end of the day he did, and still does love his mother even though when he was young he would try anything just to get some acknowledgment that he even existed.

Vincent pointed out to Arthur how much love he showed as a child and when his father wasn't tired he returned that love so there was a bond that grew between them back then. He also had a strong bond with his brother, James as they understood what each other was going through, but once Arthur moved over to England that bond died, and they lost contact with each other. Now it was only just starting to dawn on Arthur that it was his drinking and his behaviours that caused that rift. This was only the start of what Arthur was to learn about himself and the behaviours he used. It would include all that Arthur gave to others in his life, even though those that knew him once his drinking had taken hold of him would possibly think that he gave very little. In fact, there was another side to Arthur that they would have rarely seen, if ever. As Arthur was reflecting on what he was seeing Vincent could see the sadness in his eyes, "Arthur, we're going to look back now to the times before you began drinking as well as when you stopped drinking because you were trying to quit and lead a better life for the sake of you and your family. As a 14 year old lad you thought nothing of helping your elderly neighbours who struggled to keep their farm going because their son couldn't always do the work." Arthur looked and reflected back with fond memories of that couple because they always made him feel important, and worthwhile. "As an adult when you were with both your first wife and your second wife there were many times when you were sober that you would laugh with your family. You would work hard and because you had saved a little money by not drinking you treated them. You actually enjoyed taking an interest in your children and they do have some vague memories of those times. When it is their time to return to us their memories will become that much stronger. There were also the times when you helped out friends where you could." Arthur looked like he was listening, but Vincent knew that he wasn't really. He had to find out the reason why, "Why do you act as though you're listening to me and yet I know you're not?" Arthur chuckled and tried to make light of the situation replying flippantly, "I can see there's no pulling the wool over your eyes." but then told Vincent the reason why he wasn't really listening. "Look I know you're showing me all the caring things I did when I was there, but at the end of the day I can't change the bad things I did because they've happened. They've gone and I can't change them can I and to be honest, after hearing my daughter being so harsh about me, I'm not sure I would even want to try". Vincent quickly replied "That's all bravado Arthur, if they were to search within their hearts they would see that there are some sort of feelings there for you, or a sadness that you weren't part of their life." Arthur wasn't convinced "Yeah well, it wasn't nice to hear and see that!"

There were many other events both good and bad that Arthur was shown and he reflected on, what he saw was a person who was scared and alone who didn't know how to handle his emotions or the emotions of others. Vincent was pleased that Arthur was recognising many things about himself, even though it was quite emotional and hard for him to admit these things to Vincent or to anyone else for that matter, but he wanted to put the work in to try. Arthur looked at Vincent saying quietly "I really lost my way didn't I?" Vincent always being honest replied "Yes you did, but I can help you find your way back." This remark angered Arthur because he couldn't understand how he could put all this stuff right now that he was dead as he thought of it. He also couldn't see how it would help his children as they were alive and kicking and he was err, well, wherever he is because he was still not sure at this stage. There was just so much stuff that he had to take in and learn about what the spirit world was, who was here and what the hell Vincent kept spouting on about when he talked of Arthur's true self, his soul. And this lot is only the start he thought.

When Arthur was reflecting back on his life he really didn't feel good about himself. He wanted to give up looking back on his earthly life and get on with whatever punishment he thought they were going to give him for his bad behaviour. As Vincent and Arthur were walking in a beautiful garden showing the true perfection of nature's beautiful world on the other side of the veil and giving a feeling of great peace, out of the blue Arthur asked Vincent a question that he had been pondering on for a while now. He decided to get it out and ask his guide. "Vincent, as I look around here, I see beauty that is perfect in every way and for many I guess this would represent heaven, so tell me, if this is heaven then is there a hell and am I going to be sent there for all of the bad deeds I did when I was alive?" Vincent stopped immediately, turned towards Arthur and saw the look of fear on his face, "No, there is no hell, there is just this beautiful etheric plane where we all gather and reunite with our loved ones, our guides and our angels, not forgetting that just by being here we are back with our Father the Divine." That did it for Arthur who came back at Vincent straight away, "Look, I had religion forced down my throat when I was growing up, I turned my back on the churches, priests and all that they spout off, so you may as well understand that before we go any further." Vincent replied, "I'm not here to talk to you about religion, I'm here to help you come to terms with being here, and the reflections you make as you learn more about yourself."

Arthur calmed down as Vincent was talking, feeling more at ease now that his guide had explained everything to him. He felt pretty awful because of the way he jumped down Vincent's throat about religion, so he decided to quietly apologise. "I'm sorry for the way I spoke to you just then, it's just that I hate having religion preached to me." He continued "When I was growing up, I was brought up in a religious household and both parents preached constantly at us about God and sins etc… I decided then that I wasn't interested and trust me that hasn't changed." Vincent stood silent for a while before saying "Do you think perhaps because you constantly felt shamed in the name of God by your parents that you really struggled to even hear God's name?" Arthur looked to the ground, as much as he wanted to answer the question, he couldn't find the strength to speak, because he knew that Vincent was right. He felt bad about how he treated his wives and children and then left them with nothing but debt and a feeling of abandonment. The true reality was that he didn't want to face his sins and take responsibility because he believed that he was going to be punished by God.

Silence fell between them, until Vincent spoke, "You can't run from this forever, if you are seeking peace then you need to work with all this. If you don't wish to put the energy into it, I will respect that and leave you to it. Be warned though that the peace you're looking for only comes with the awakened light within us." Arthur, feeling defensive, and it showed, snapped back, "There you go again with your holier than thou words and attitude." Vincent stepped back and turned away as he felt there was nothing more he could do at this stage. Arthur, seeing him turning to walk away, panicked, "No, don't go, I'm sorry, I didn't mean to be so rude, please don't go, I promise I will make every effort to try to work with all this stuff." Vincent turned back, looking at Arthur, "It's not for my benefit that you need to reflect, I don't need to find peace, it's for you. It's for you to learn who you are, but I do respect that you have a free will so I would never try and impinge on that." Arthur didn't know what to say, but he did manage a quick and quiet "Sorry, yes I will work with all of this stuff that I have inside me. "Somehow Vincent wasn't convinced, because he knew that Arthur had to really want to help himself but was he willing to do that? Vincent reassured Arthur, "I can't force you to do anything as here in the spirit world, we have strong views that we cannot dictate or try to manipulate someone into doing something they don't want to do." Vincent continued, "We believe that with support, love and care, a person who struggled in their earthly life for whatever reason will make the decision to help themselves at the time that's right for them." He carried on, "We also know that the those who don't want to do the work they need when they arrive in the spirit world will not be happy as they see many of their loved ones move away from them because they are evolving, and for some, that is the time they start the work that brings healing to their soul in every aspect."

"Tell me my friend", said Vincent, "You seem scared of visiting your human lifetime to learn, work and heal whatever it was that made you so sad." Arthur paused for a moment before answering during which he decided that his only option was to open up and be honest with Vincent. "To be honest I'm scared of revisiting how I behaved because I know that it was pretty awful. I don't remember a time when I was happy including my childhood." He continued, "Our parents were quite distant towards both my brother and I; daddy was always working and when he came home he was too tired. Mammy, well, she never showed much affection. In fact she was pretty harsh. She saw my brother and I as workhorses that needed to work on our own small piece of land rearing lambs and running a smallholding. When we got home from school it was straight out to work on the land". Arthur sighed, "To be honest it wasn't a happy childhood at all. I have very few memories of laughter and fun times between us all. Daddy was better and did try but mammy wasn't interested, not even in my father I don't think." Vincent stayed silent for a short while before asking Arthur if he wanted to understand more about why he became the way he was by looking back to see the dynamics of the family. Arthur agreed and the next minute he knew he was looking straight back at himself when he was about 8 years old.

"Look Arthur there's you sitting at the kitchen table with your mother working away in the kitchen." said Vincent, "Do you remember that time in your life?" Arthur looked intently as he saw his mother making the dinner, his brother and himself sitting at the table. This picture spoke volumes because it was clear that Arthur's brother was definitely the favoured one in their mother's eyes. There was a lot of chit chat going on between James and his mother and it was clear to see that Arthur was left out of the conversation. In fact what was clear was that Arthur's mother spoke very differently to him than she did to his brother. With Arthur the only time she really spoke to him was when she barked an order at him, or to criticise him, whereas with James she spoke lovingly and joyfully. Vincent looked at Arthur and asked what was on his mind. "Tell me Vincent.", he said, "Has mammy done any work on what she was like when she was on earth? She did seem better towards me when she welcomed me back, but there was still a distance and no sign of an apology." "Well.",

Vincent said slowly, "Your mother is working and reflecting on certain things but at this stage she still isn't revisiting some of the behaviours she used towards others." Arthur wasn't surprised to hear that, "Hmmm that doesn't surprise me because it would mean taking responsibility and she wouldn't want to do that." As he said that he realised he was doing exactly the same thing by not wanting to see how he behaved and treated people. Vincent saw that this was a light bulb moment for Arthur and he didn't want to lose that moment, "I see you have realised the work you have got to do now Arthur, because in many ways, you repeated your mothers patterns with your families."

"Oh God yes.", replied Arthur, "I see it now. In fact I treated them worse than mammy treated me." It was clear to Vincent that Arthur was feeling such strong shame, and for the first time ever he was taking responsibility for his bad ways. Vincent ceased the moment, "It's so nice to see you taking responsibility for the way you were with your families, and I'm sure that at some stage you will have the opportunity to say sorry." Arthur looked at Vincent "How the bloody hell do I do that. I'm dead remember." Vincent ignored Arthur's outburst, "You will soon learn that there are many ways in which you can let your family know you're sorry as well as reassure them that you are supporting them from here." Arthur looked at Vincent, thought for a moment, and said "Even if I can say sorry to them do you really think they will believe me? After all I used to say sorry to both of my wives countless times and then go off and do it all again. I think believing me would be a very hard thing to do." Vincent was becoming more and more frustrated with Arthur because one minute he was prepared to commit to doing the work and the next minute he was fighting against him. Even though Vincent had evolved to a high level it didn't mean that he would be gentle and not speak his mind telling Arthur what he was feeling about Arthur's constant bad attitude. That's exactly what he did. "Arthur, I'm sorry but I am working hard to help you to settle back in the spirit world, but so far all I have met with from you is a brick wall that I can't break through. I have to ask you whether or not you want me to leave you alone, as it appears you don't want my company nor my help." Arthur was taken aback with Vincent's outburst and also with the question. He immediately felt vulnerable and rejected but he wasn't going to let Vincent see this. So his reply was once again defensive and also aggressive, "You can please yourself what you do, I didn't ask you to be with me." Vincent's response to was quiet, dignified and simple, "Ok, I understand that you don't feel you need me, and I do respect your free will to make your decision about whether or not you want my help, so I shall leave you to it, and go to someone who is ready to be supported." Vincent continued, "You see Arthur it is about being supported to help you to settle in or answer any questions that fledgeling spirits might ask." (Fledgling Spirit is the author's term for those who have just passed over and are going through the settlement period).

For Arthur the thought of Vincent leaving him to it made him feel quite afraid. He was going to be on his own so before he knew it he had blurted out, "It's ok for you, you probably had a good life when you were on earth, but I didn't, and because of it I ruined both my families' lives. The reality is that I don't deserve your help, and I don't deserve forgiveness." Finally Arthur was letting go. Vincent allowed a few moments to pass before responding, "So you don't feel you deserve help?, Hmmm I don't feel I can agree with you on that Arthur, because everyone deserves help." Arthur looked Vincent in the eye, "What even people like me?" Vincent smiled, "Yes, even you. So now you have to tell me if you want my help, and if not I will leave you to it." Arthur agreed that he needed Vincent's help and would like him to stay and help him settle.

After a while Arthur started to settle in really well. He was learning so much about himself and some of the reasons why he behaved the way he did, which was a big relief to him, and helped him to understand himself more. The biggest improvement was that he wasn't excusing his behaviour and wasn't trying to get out of taking responsibility for his actions which was a big breakthrough for him. Through all this learning he finally understood what it was like for his two wives. He knew that one day he would have to face both of them when they return to the spirit world, but for now he didn't have to focus on that. Only he did, because the day came that he was always dreading, he was standing in front of his first wife Muriel! When Vincent told him about Muriel's passing to spirit and suggested that perhaps Arthur could meet with her, Arthur just wanted to run and hide shouting "Not bloody likely. The last person she would want to meet is me. She will kill me." Vincent had a little laugh as Arthur said this and he was still chuckling as he replied, "I don't think she will kill you but she might want to have her say. After all don't you think she has a right to?" "Well, yes, I suppose so." agreed Arthur. Vincent looked at him, "It's time to make the peace."

The next minute Arthur knew, he was seeing Muriel walking towards him. He expected her to throw a punch at him, but instead she looked at him with a faint smile, "Hello Arthur." Arthur felt very nervous, he smiled back and responded with the same greeting to Muriel. Vincent stepped back, "I will leave you two here to have a chat." Muriel nodded thank you, but Arthur was so taken aback by seeing Muriel that he didn't respond or even notice that his guide had left them to it. God, she's as beautiful now as she was when she was young and I first met her, he thought. Her skin was still as fresh as it always was and she still had a very trim figure which he always loved. The same couldn't be said of Arthur's figure before he passed away because he became a quite chubby and had developed a beer belly. They both walked along side by side in the most beautiful open space that was filled with flowers, trees and all different kinds of little animals but they hardly noticed the scenery as they walked along. Arthur decided to break the ice, "What happened? I didn't think you would be here just yet." Muriel replied, "I had a heart attack and died instantly, which was a blessing for me but a hell of a shock for the kids." "Oh

I see." replied Arthur, "Have you checked in on the children since you got here?" he continued. Muriel looked at him snapping back, "Why?" and then she continued to tell Arthur a few home truths from her point of view. "Don't tell me you're worried about them, because it will be the first time ever." Arthur automatically felt defensive, he was just about to snap back when he remembered what he had learnt about the way he behaved in his earthly life, and the impact that he had, so he calmed himself, "Ouch, that's harsh but I deserve it." Muriel was dumb founded that he hadn't snapped back. Deep down inside she was disappointed that he hadn't because that would have been a good reason to have an argument with him and show him she's not scared of him anymore.

"Yes you do deserve it and a lot more besides." Muriel replied angrily. Arthur let her verbally lay into him as he knew she had waited a long time for this. When Muriel could see that Arthur wasn't going to respond defensively or argumentatively, she calmed down and as she did said quietly, "What did we do wrong? Why were you always either drinking, or pulling a new girl? Why weren't we enough?" That last statement really got to Arthur, and as he looked at Muriel with compassion in his heart, he replied "You were enough, you and the kids didn't do anything wrong, it was all down to me." Muriel didn't know what to say because she wasn't expecting to have this kind of conversation with him. Arthur continued to finally face the music by taking the opportunity to take full responsibility, "It was my drinking that really fuelled the way I treated you, Bernadette and the children they way I did." Muriel got quite angry because he mentioned Bernadette, almost shouting at him, "Don't you dare talk to me about her, tell me, was she inclined to steal other people's husbands?" "It wasn't like that." said Arthur defensively, "Bernie," as he used to call her, "Didn't know I was married when I first met her because I had told her that I was divorced. By the time she knew she had fallen for me hook, line and sinker." Muriel was shocked to find all of this out as she had spent so many years blaming the other woman. Instead of coming back with a sharp or nasty comment she listened to Arthur as he continued, "For what it's worth she hates me just as much as you do because I treated her the same as I did you." Muriel was pleased to see that finally Arthur was behaving in an adult way, shame it had to be after they had both died she thought to herself.

There were a lot of discussion and a lot of open talking that was needed which both Muriel and Arthur did and for both it felt very cleansing. They were never going to be buddies, but they weren't going to be enemies either.

One question that had bothered Arthur was what the children felt about him and in the end he asked Muriel the question. "Well, how do you expect them to feel about you? You were cruel to me, you had no time for the kids and then to add insult to injury you left us for another woman." Again Arthur felt a sharp pain from Muriel's words, but wasn't going to argue with her about it because she was right. Arthur replied "I know, I was a bastard and for that I am truly sorry. I have learned so much about the way I behaved most of the time and how I kept everyone at a distance by being selfish, controlling and a lot of the time a deserter who left his family to get on with it." Arthur wasn't expecting any compassion but he did want to let her know a lot of his problem was that he drank to feel somebody because he knew he was weak and couldn't stand the fact that both his wives were very strong on a lot of levels. At the end of the day he had an addiction that destroyed both of his families and in the end ended up killing him. Both Muriel and Arthur agreed that, although they had met up and had sorted out a lot of old feelings that both of them had been hanging onto, the only time they should unite is if one the children needed them. He knew that there was no way he could make up for the heartbreak he caused but he could try and guide the children and finally be there to help them where he can.

What was quite interesting but hurtful for Arthur was when his daughter Elizabeth from his first marriage went to see a medium in the hope that her mum would come through for her. The medium was aware that Muriel was there for Elizabeth and connected with Arthur. However when the medium shared that both parents were there, Elizabeth only wanted to hear from her mum, and not her dad. In fact, she was quite defensive when the medium mentioned him, "No way do I want to hear from him. He broke my mum's heart and didn't give us kids a thought."

Arthur wanted to speak to Vincent because he didn't know what to do about this situation. Vincent immediately came to Arthur and asked him to explain what had happened. After Arthur had explained everything Vincent said, "Unfortunately this is not uncommon when a parent leaves their family behind and expect them to get on with life without him or any help from him." Arthur was sad when he heard Vincent say this, "Is there anything I can do that may change Elizabeth's feelings?" "I'm afraid not." replied Vincent, "But you can be there for her now and guide her through troubled times. Whisper that you're sorry to the medium and let her tell Elizabeth that you will be there to support your daughter when she needs it. Let her tell your daughter and you never know it may bring comfort that you're sorry and want to help her now, but there are no guarantees. However, that's no reason to walk away again and let her get on with it. You need to really be there for all of your children without expecting a reward of any kind of help that you give. Just do it out of love and see where that takes them all." This is exactly what Arthur did, and as time went on and he watched down over his children he realised that although all of his children were doing well on one level, they all seemed to have emotional problems and could be quite erratic when it came to dealing with things. When it came to their feelings, he couldn't help but compare what he was like when he was their ages. He saw some similarities and some traits of his which he didn't like at all. Arthur realised that all of this erratic behaviour his children had was because of his own behaviours towards their mothers and of course the fact that he was not present in their lives for very long at all.

Arthur realised that this was going to be a long process, perhaps his children wouldn't want the apologies that he hoped he could give them through a medium, but it wouldn't stop him trying. He was determined to help all of his children where he could and do whatever he could for them. He also wanted to help Bernadette where he could because he had realised he owes her that. Arthur shared with Vincent how he was determined to bring peace to all of them even if it did take a while. He was OK because he had all the time in the spirit world before he went back for another lifetime. Finally he was going to be the father he should have been when he was still on earth.

Chapter 10

GEMMA

Gemma was a sweet old lady thought everyone that met her. She was incredibly proud to be classed as spiritual and she also had a great reputation in her early days as a medium. Gemma was the oldest of three girls her younger siblings being Grace and Gillian. Her parents, Hugh and Dolly, were quiet and very conservative in their way of living but very loving towards their three children. As a family all of them were strong and very family orientated. Gemma's family lived in the southeast of England, they really and truly had quite a good upbringing as children even though World War 2 had started. There were English planes and at times even German planes flying above them but life in their village carried on pretty much as normal. In many ways the family wasn't really affected the way many were until Hugh joined the army to do his bit for King and Country.

From the start Gemma's parents knew that she was a bit different especially when they had their two other children Gillian and Grace and observed the differences between their personalities. Gemma was always so serious about life and didn't really join in on the kind of games her sisters wanted to play. For example Grace and Gillian wanted to play with dolls, scooters, bikes etc. but Gemma kept herself detached from playing with her sisters. She used to say, "I'm too busy to be playing with you two because I am busy playing with my friends up in my bedroom." In fact Gemma never really bonded with her sisters. Dolly always felt as though Gemma had an old head on young shoulders and she really didn't have that childlike innocence her other two children had, the innocence Dolly believed that all children should have. Very often Gemma would come down for breakfast saying that she was tired because she had been kept awake by her friend who visits from heaven to play with her. Her parents always thought these were imaginary friends, so they never really thought much of it.

Gemma was only 8 years old in 1942 when she witnessed her first real spiritual experience, and what she saw never left her. It was in the height of summertime when, as she walked down the street after being in the local shop on the corner, she looked up only to see a plane flying over her. Gemma didn't know whether it was an English or German plane until she saw the bomb drop on her school causing the building to collapse into a load of burning rubble. It was a stray German plane that saw an opportunity to cause carnage before heading back to Germany.

Thankfully Gemma was far enough away to be safe but because it was a nice summer evening it was still light and she could see it all. There was no one in the school so there weren't any casualties. Sadly however, the two houses next to the school were also hit by the bomb and the people in the house were killed instantly. As Gemma stood in utter shock she had a feeling that the spirits of those who died were leaving their bodies. Before she knew it, she was having a truly spiritual experience as, although she couldn't see the bodies of those that had died under the rubble, she saw a beautiful strong light encircle the rubble. Next she saw five different and separate beams of light floating away from the carnage. She knew that without a doubt it was the souls of those who died. At just 8 years old you would think Gemma would be scared or upset, but not Gemma, she wasn't afraid because she understood exactly what was happening which was lovely. When Gemma returned home and tried to explain it to her mother, she saw the look on her mum's face that said she didn't believe her.

"Why are you looking like that at me mummy? I am telling you the truth, I promise." Dolly didn't know what to say or do, she sat and stared at her daughter for a few seconds before replying, "Sweetheart, I know that you think you may have seen and felt all that you say, but I hardly think it was from ghosts.

In times like this when we see horrible sights, it's very easy to imagine things that help us to cope." Gemma looked at her mother angrily, "I knew you wouldn't believe me, it's always the same, you never believe me, but you always believe anything that Grace and Gillian say to you." Gemma had a point, her parents pretty much believed whatever Grace and Gillian said but when it came to Gemma, they always treated her like she was making it up and said she had a "Very vivid imagination." Gemma huffed off to her bedroom talking to herself about how unfair life was, as she walked into her bedroom she slammed the door so hard that she was sure that her mother would hear it. Once she calmed down, she picked up a little book her mother bought her last birthday. She had read it many times and loved the story so much because she could relate to the little boy in the story that felt the odd one out within his own family. Gemma related to that little boy so much because that was how she felt. Although Gemma knew that she was loved by her parents, she always felt she was loved in a different way to her sisters.

As Gemma sat reading, she started to hear that all familiar sound of her "Imaginary" friend calling her name. Gemma looked up and saw Agnes standing there. Agnes was an 8 year old little girl who passed to the spirit world many years ago after a freak accident falling off a low wall that she was walking on and cracked her head which killed her instantly. Little Agnes also lived in Gemma's house and in fact she had the same bedroom. Little Agnes was dressed rather old fashioned Gemma thought with her white pinafore over her black dress. Agnes explained that was how children dressed back in her days which, according to her was "Many, many, many years ago." It was actually the late Victorian era, which, in the 1940's era was pretty modern history. Agnes had bonded with Gemma immediately and would visit her daily. When Gemma's dad went off to war, her mum, naturally, was struggling to keep everything going whilst bringing up the children on her own. Gemma was struggling also missing her dad because she always felt that he understood her more than the rest of the family, but even he would be hard pressed to believe what Gemma had just experienced! Gemma felt supported by her new friend Agnes and she loved to ask questions about "Ghosts" as Gemma would put it, and what it was like to be one. Agnes also loved Gemma's company and would be more than happy to answer and explain all that she knew. On that day when Agnes started calling Gemma, she was in no mood to talk telling Agnes to "Go away because I am reading." Agnes ignored Gemma and carried on calling her until Gemma relented, which she always did. As they chatted, Gemma told Agnes about what she had seen that day, and that she couldn't get the bright light out of her mind, "Was that light taking the dead people up to heaven?" Agnes wasn't too sure telling Gemma, "I don't know, but I think it would because I had a bright light around me when I died." Gemma was intrigued and carried on asking questions, "What's it like to die Agnes?" she asked. Agnes looked at her and thought about it for a second, "I can't really remember now, but I think all of my pain in my head stopped and I could breathe again. The only problem was when I woke up I couldn't see my mummy and daddy anywhere, but my nanny was there to greet me which was nice cos I loved my nanny." The questions kept flowing, "Do you grow up in heaven and turn into an adult the way we do down here?" Agnes replied, "Yes, of course we do if we want to, but I don't want to at the moment, I'm having too much fun with you and my other friends that I have here and in heaven." Gemma didn't know that Agnes had friends in both worlds, she immediately started to feel jealous of these friends. "I didn't know you had other friends." she said sharply, "I thought you only had me as your friend." Agnes replied equally sharply, "I am allowed to have other friends you know." Gemma didn't want Agnes to go away and leave her without a friend so she apologised and asked if they could forget it, which Agnes agreed too. Gemma and Agnes remained friends for a very long time even though Gemma was turning into an adult, she always had time for little Agnes.

The years flew by, Gemma's dad survived the war and came home but he was battered and bruised on every level of life, including his mental health, but they all managed to get by OK because they had to, sadly there wasn't really the help that is on offer today for mental health. As the years flashed by Gemma and her sisters turned into beautiful young women which was lovely for their parents to see, but there was still that distance between Gemma and her siblings. As Gemma grew older, in her sister's eyes, she became even more strange, they couldn't understand her not wanting to go out with a man and find a husband. Yes, to some degree she had become different in some ways. The truth was that she wasn't bothered about finding a husband because she somehow knew that she would be working with the spirit world so she couldn't afford to let a man get in her way of staying on her path. Dolly was always worrying about the reaction Gemma would have from people outside of the family and was forever telling Gemma, "Keep the fact that you talk to the dead to yourself because you may be regarded as a witch and there are still some laws around this that could get you into trouble." At that time what Dolly had said was true, but deep down Gemma felt her mum was more concerned about what the neighbours and her friends would think, not so much about what would happen to Gemma. It was different with her dad though because he understood more about the spirit world and life after death than some because he had seen it on the battlefields during the war. Hugh only spoke to Gemma once about his experiences when he told her of a time that he saw one of his brothers in arms get shot on the battlefield, "And it was like everything stopped for a short while and as my friend Donald fell, a beautiful ray of light came down, embraced Donald and started to float up. I could literally see Donald's Spirit lift up in the light and into the sky." He told Gemma, "It was at that point I stopped feeling afraid of death and dying because, if my number was up and it was time for me to go, I know I wouldn't be on my own, and that I would be looked after." Neither Gemma or Hugh could really explain the beautiful feeling that the strong and powerful light brought, the only way they summed it up together was that it was like this light was connecting to the souls of all those around them. Although there was only ever the one deep conversation they had, it did help Gemma to know that she wasn't the only one in her family to have these kinds of experiences.

Hugh and Dolly knew that Gemma would probably end up never marrying because she was too independent and head strong for any man to deal with. They encouraged all of their three daughters to focus on their studies, get their qualifications and work in an office as a secretary, which, back then, was seen as a good and high paid job which had great respect connected to it. They encouraged Gemma more because they felt she may end up on her own. So, even though Gemma felt it a bit of a chore to do studies that weren't connected to talking to the spirit world, she did feel that it was something she would need to do in order to look after herself in the future. When the time came and Gemma had all the qualifications she needed, naturally the next step was to look for a job that would suit her. The only problem was that there was nothing available locally, therefore she would have to look further afield, somewhere like London, which shocked both Hugh and Dolly as they didn't think she would like it there. Gemma had decided that she was going to move up to London and then find a job for herself, her parents agreed that they would support her financially for a while so that she could keep her head above water. It was pretty clear that both her sisters wouldn't need to be financially supported because they were happy living in their village and both of them were going strong with their boyfriends. It looked like marriage for them both was on the cards. Thankfully from the time the girls were born Hugh and Dolly had been putting money aside for their weddings so that it wouldn't be a big strain on their finances. They guessed that money was going to be needed for two weddings but they decided that money should be put a side for Gemma so that they can support her in whatever she decided to do with her life, and now it seemed that the day had come for Gemma to rely on the support from her parents for a while.

Although Gemma was nervous when she arrived in London, she was also really excited about what London would hold in store for her. Before Gemma was allowed to leave home her parents insisted on going up to London with her to find her a nice place to live. Although Gemma felt as though her parents didn't trust her to find a place for herself which annoyed her a bit, deep down she was quite pleased they were with her. Going up to London was quite a task, definitely needed preparation, even to the point of Dolly making cheese and pickle sandwiches and a flask of tea to eat and drink on the journey, so as they didn't have to pay out for a lunch as they had heard London was an expensive place to visit. Considering they only had a day to organise finding somewhere to live for Gemma, it didn't take too long to find rooms that were for rent. In no time at all they found themselves viewing some dingy properties at a price they could afford to pay for Gemma until she gets on her feet, they also viewed some lovely properties that they couldn't afford! However, they did manage to find a little room with a small kitchen in Shoreditch which was pretty close to the city so it would put Gemma in a good place for getting to and from work, so they snapped it up and paid a month's rent in advance. Now the next thing was for Gemma to find a job.

Before Gemma could leave home, there was one thing she had to do, and that was to say goodbye to Agnes. Gemma was going to miss Agnes as they had pretty much grown up together. Gemma had put off thinking about saying goodbye to her lifelong friend until now as she didn't want to get all mushy about it as she put it. As Gemma walked into her room, she called out for Agnes to come forward, and after a few times Agnes responded. "Oh, you've remembered I'm here then." said Agnes harshly. "Oh, don't be like that Aggy (that was

Gemma's nickname from Agnes), I didn't mean to ignore you these last few weeks, it's just that it's been so busy." Agnes asked, "What do you want then." This was the moment that Gemma dreaded, "I've come to say goodbye because I'm moving up to London today so I will only be here high days and holidays I'm afraid." Agnes didn't say anything although she did have a smirk on her face. "What are you smirking at." asked Gemma. "You really don't get it do you Gemma, It's not goodbye, it's never goodbye because I can meet you in different places. I'm not stuck here you know." Gemma had never thought about that before, she had always assumed that she could communicate with Aggy as well as feel the presence of other spirits because they're all connected to the house they live in. "What are you on about Aggy." asked Gemma, "Do you mean you can come to see me wherever I am?" Agnes laughed, "Yes of course I can." Gemma was pretty pleased that Agnes was going to be able to visit her. Suddenly Gemma felt insecure and scared about starting to talk with other spirit people. She turned around quickly and almost in a panic asked Agnes, "Aggy, will I be safe talking to other spirit people? I mean I don't want to get hurt by an unfriendly ghost when talking to them." Again Agnes laughed as she tried to comfort Gemma, "Don't worry, your guides won't let that happen. Anyway no one in the spirit world is nasty because they learn to go above that, in fact let me tell you there are very few spirit that would want to hurt you, and there are none that can. I thought you had learned all of this from me." Gemma was relieved, "Maybe I was blocking this stuff out because I thought I was opening up a can of worms."

Gemma was never afraid to talk about Agnes and how they understand each other to her sisters. Gillian in particular used to snap back at Gemma when she did bring Agnes up and give her some home truths as she would put it. "It's a shame you haven't put the same effort in being more of a sister to us as you do with your friendship with Agnes, if she really does exist that is." This argument was always the divide between the sisters, it certainly created a distance between them all, which naturally upset their parents. When it was time to say goodbye to her siblings Gemma felt uncomfortable, and yes, a bit sad, but she wouldn't let them see that. They had spent so many years together but there was no bond, and Gemma couldn't see the part she played in that as she had always believed that her sisters and her were on a completely different wave length to her. The truth was she had never given them the chance to be close to her. As Gemma went to walk out of the living room door where both her sisters were standing, she said to them, "Feel free to come and visit me.", and Grace whispered under her breath, "Don't hold your breath." Gemma couldn't hear what was said but she knew that it wouldn't have been anything nice.

Gemma could carry herself well and was quite confident using the skills that she had to be a shorthand typist. When she went for an interview, she could present and hold herself well. Of course she had great organising skills as she could be very bossy, so she was soon snapped up to work in the offices of a shoe manufacturers in the City, which was almost on her doorstep. Gemma loved her new job and her newfound freedom, she wasn't answerable to her parents. She felt quite independent even if the truth was that her parents were still heavily supporting her financially. Gemma got on quite well with the boss, as well all the other staff that she worked with, it really was the first time that Gemma felt comfortable with other people around her as she was mainly a loner. There was a lovely girl that was also a typist that Gemma got on particularly well with, her name was Shirley, and she had a nervous energy but funnily enough this didn't bother Gemma as she thought she was quite sweet. So, in no time at all and really for the very first time in Gemma's life she had made a friend with someone that was actually here on this earth.

It was a good few months before Gemma finally told Shirley about her ability to talk to spirit because she was afraid that she would lose her new friend. As it happened it turned out Shirley was very interested in ghosts and things as Shirley put it. "I very often get a feeling that someone's watching me, or that I'm not alone, and my mum does too." Shirley continued "In fact she's really good with the tea leaves, and people are always coming to see her for some help." Gemma was pleased that she had a friend with the same interests. It was lovely to talk about it because Gemma was missing Agnes, even though she had asked her to visit her, there was nothing, so it helped having a friend that she could confide in. Gemma knew that being able to talk to ghosts was very much frowned upon, you were seen as a witch or a charleton, and Gemma was neither. Even though Gemma now had Shirley to confide in, it didn't stop her from feeling lost without Agnes there, she kept going through the words that Agnes said to her just before she left for London, "You're a medium Gemma, you can talk to other Spirit too." How Gemma thought out loud, "How do I do this? Where do I go to get help and support with this?" Poor Gemma was feeling homesick and lonely so she decided to take the train back home Friday night to see her family and hopefully Agnes.

When Gemma arrived, she couldn't wait to give her parents a big hug because she really had missed them, to some degree she had missed her sisters to. When Grace and Gillian walked in they were a bit distant with her at first, but they could see that Gemma had changed a little, especially when it comes to talking about everyday life, she seemed more connected to the world and to them as well. Gemma wanted to know how the wedding arrangements were going for both of them, "Not long now." she said to Grace as she would be the first to marry out of the three of them. "It's going well thanks Gem, in fact I'm glad you're home because I have to get you fitted for your bridesmaid dress, the wedding is only a couple of months away so we have to get you organised." Gemma pulled a bit of a face, she didn't really want to be part of all this pomp and ceremony. Inside her head she was saying to herself, "Why can't they do us all a favour and run away to Gretna Green and get married."

What she was thinking and what she actually said was completely different, she smiled, "Oh how lovely, I shall enjoy getting dressed up for the day." Well, that was a big change as normally Gemma would have said absolutely no way was she getting dressed up all fancy, but for the first time ever she thought of her sister and realised how important all of this was to her. When Gillian heard her reply to Grace she couldn't help saying, "Yeah, right, you in a fancy dress, this I have got to see." Gemma said nothing but looked at her Gillian and scowled which said more than words could ever say.

Dolly had heard the response from Gillian, grabbed her on the quiet to warn her not to start anything and got her to promise that she would be on her best behaviour. Dolly and Hugh were so pleased to see their daughter, they could see quite a difference in her, and the difference was for the better. They all sat down to a lovely tea, a chat and a catch up, but as much as Gemma was enjoying being with her family, she couldn't wait to go into her bedroom and call for Agnes as she hadn't had any communication with her since she had left. "Aggy, Aggy", she excitedly called, but there was nothing. She called again but again nothing. "Come on Aggy stop sulking, I've missed you and have been looking forward to seeing you." All of a sudden she heard Aggy's voice say, "Well you've remembered that I'm here then." "Oh don't be like that Aggy you know I've missed you, and by the way why didn't you come to visit me?" replied Gemma. Aggy looked towards Gemma, "I did, I saw your new friend whatever her name is, and I could see that you weren't missing me at all." Aggy looked hurt and Gemma felt terrible because although she had missed Aggy to some degree she was also having fun making new friends and settling into her job.

"Aggy look, just because I don't live here anymore and I am making new friends doesn't mean to say I don't care for you. We've grown up together and we've got a bond that no one else can ever break, but I have to have a life other than you." Aggy knew this really but she did miss Gemma so much when she was not there. She knew that as much as they have a good bond the reality was that Gemma lived in the physical world and needed to live that life. Aggy, well she lived in the spirit world and couldn't share life with Gemma the way she would like to and she shouldn't really expect it to be that way either. Aggy started to smile , "OK I forgive you. So, tell me, what's life like in London?" she asked. Gemma smiled and started to tell her about her job, her new friend Shirley, how she believed in the spirit world very strongly and they seem to have so much in common. Aggy looked at Gemma commenting "But?" and Gemma continued "But I do miss my regular conversations with you and I miss the feel of spirit who come around me and make me feel as though they are looking after me. None of them seem to come to me anymore and I can't work out where I go from here." Aggy said nothing for a few seconds, "Gem, (Aggy's nickname for Gemma) Shirley holds the key, don't worry, she will unlock the door." As Agnes finished her sentence she looked directly at Gemma, "Treat her well." Gemma was confused, something she seemed frequently to experience with Aggy. There had been many times over the years when Agnes became serious, giving some very sound knowledge, advice and guidance from the spirit world. This was another one of those occasions. "What do you mean?" asked Gemma, "Just be patient and trust that you are on the right path, but just make sure whilst you're finding your path that you treat Shirley well." Sounding confused Gemma replied "OK, I will." Agnes wasn't convinced!

Gemma had a really great time back at home, spending time with the family and she didn't even mind being measured up for the long frilly dress she would need to wear for Grace's wedding. Her parents listened with great pride as Gemma talked about her new job and the feedback she was getting from her peers about how good she was. As Gemma was getting ready to go back to London on the Sunday, she made a point of calling for Aggy to come through because she wanted Aggy to promise to visit her in London, "And to quote your words

Aggy, I am a medium so I can connect with spirit wherever I am, so you have no excuse, do you?" Aggy laughed and agreed that she would do that. A few weeks went by, Gemma was still lost about how she could get some guidance and support as she tried to develop her abilities. One Monday morning, an excited Shirley walked into the office, rushed up to Gemma, and whispered in her ear, "You'll never believe where I went last night." Gemma turned her head slightly whispering back "Where?" As Shirley was about to give Gemma all the details their office manager called out "Ladies start your work, you're not here to gossip.", both the girls replied at the same time, "Yes Miss Flynn".

Shirley couldn't wait for lunch time so that she could give Gemma the run down on the night before. As soon as it hit 1pm all those in the office got up from their chairs and rushed to the front door, with sandwiches in hand and went to the park opposite to have their break. As Gemma and Shirley sat down on a park bench Gemma looked at Shirley, "OK then what's so exciting?" Shirley was so excited she spoke that fast Gemma had to tell her to slow down because she couldn't understand what she was saying. Shirley slowed down a little, "Well, I got together with a friend of mine on Friday evening and she was telling me about this place she goes weekly to receive messages from the spirit world, I think she called it a seance." Shirley definitely had Gemma's attention with this exciting news, "Oh wow, and……" Shirley continued "Well she asked me if I would like to join her last night, as it's not too far from where I live and I said yes." Shirley paused just when Gemma didn't want her to. "Shirley, did you go." "You bet I did, and it was brilliant." Shirley blurted out, "We all sat around this table in the dark and there were knocks, bangs and lots of other sounds, but what was really exciting was that my nan came through with such a lovely message for me. Oh Gemma it was wonderful." "Oh you lucky thing, I would have loved that." said Gemma with a hint of jealousy in her voice. But Shirley hadn't finished with her news, "Oh I haven't finished yet." continued Shirley, "Gemma, then when I told them about your experiences you have had from when you were young they were keen to meet you." Now it was Gemma that was the excited one, "Oh that would be great, I would love that, thanks Shirley, shall we go next Sunday?" Shirley immediately responded, "What do you think." and gave Gemma a little wink.

When Gemma got home from work that night she was thinking about the following Sunday and where she would be going. It dawned on her that Aggy was right when she said "Shirley holds the key." "Oh my gosh." she said out loud, immediately sat down, closed her eyes and asked for Aggy to come forward, which she did immediately. Aggy had a cheeky look on her face, "Hello, my you look happy Gem, what's caused that?" Gemma realised by the way Aggy was saying it that she already knew about her invite to a seance. "You already know don't you?" Aggy laughed, "Of course I know, I am one of the spirits that have been steering this with your guides." Once again Gemma had that confused look on her face, "Guides, what guides?" Abby explained, "The guides that are going to walk along your path of life with you, in fact there are some of them that have been doing that since the day you were born. You've felt them with you often and have told me that, you always knew there was more than one." Gemma decided to go with whatever Aggy said as she was feeling more and more confused every time Aggy spoke.

The week couldn't go by fast enough for the two girls, all week their chatter was about spirit and the seance that they were going to, then came the day. The girls didn't live too far apart and they had agreed to meet at the bottom of Gemma's road so that they could walk together along to Parkholme Road which was where the seance was being held. "There it is" said Shirley, that's the house we're going in." Gemma followed Shirley's finger as she pointed to the house. It was a big house with three levels and appeared to be quite bright and well maintained. "Oh, this is totally different to how I pictured it.", said Gemma, pleasantly surprised, "How did you picture it?" asked Shirley. "Well, I thought it might look a bit dark and spooky, you know, the kind of thing you would see in a film at the pictures." Shirley laughed, "Oh Gemma you and your imagination!" Shirley opened the gates and they both walked through. Gemma's heart was in her mouth, just as Shirley was about to ring the bell Gemma said, "Oh gosh I'm so nervous, are you nervous Shirl?" Trying to calm Gemma Shirley replied, "No not really, when I met the people last week they were all really lovely and very thoughtful." There were three doorbells to the side of the door with names underneath and Shirley rang the second bell down. That must mean that the house is divided into flats Gemma quietly thought. It appeared to be taking a long time for someone to open the door, whilst they were waiting Gemma called out to Agnes in her mind and asked her to be with her and keep them safe. No sooner had she said it than she felt the presence of Agnes. "Thanks Aggy." Gemma said in her mind, knowing that she was with her immediately put Gemma at ease.

At last, the door started to open and as it did a very smartly dressed gentleman greeted them into the hallway. "Hello Shirley." said this gentleman gently with an equally gentle smile on his face. Shirley responded "Hello Mr White, please may I introduce my good friend Gemma." Mr White looked at Gemma holding his hand out for her to shake it, "Hello Gemma, it's very nice to meet you." Gemma immediately reached her hand out to take his hand, "Hello Mr White, it's nice to meet you to." "Oh please." said Mr White, "Please call me Gregory, it's all very informal here.", and with that he started to walk towards the stairs, "Please follow me." They walked up to the middle floor which was where Gregory and his wife Meredith lived. When they reached his door he opened it, stood to the side and gestured the two girls into a very nicely decorated hallway. Once he was inside, he continued to ask them to follow him which they duly did. Gregory had stopped at quite a wide door and as he opened it, they saw a big round table that would easily fit about eight people around it. A little bit of panic in Gemma arose at the thought of so many being around the table. Gregory's wife walked up to the girls and greeted them. "Hello Shirley, nice to see you again, obviously you enjoyed last week because you have come back." Mrs White then looked at Gemma, "Welcome, you must be Gemma, Shirley told me all about you. My name is Meredith, I am married to Gregory." Meredith showed them where they should sit and asked if they would like any water, "Tea and biscuits will be given at the end of the séance."

Meredith started the conversation going by saying "So Gemma, Shirley says that you have been able to communicate with spirit since you were a child?" "Uh yes that's correct." replied Gemma slightly nervously. "Well, I say I can talk to spirits, I've really only ever spoken to one spirit that is connected to the house my family and I lived in, but I have always felt other spirit around me. So, my real experience is mainly one spirit called Agnes." Meredith didn't answer for a few moments, she seemed to be looking intensely at Gemma which made her feel uneasy. After quite a long pause Meredith said, "Don't question yourself my dear, you definitely have the ability." People started to take a seat at the table, the lights were dimmed but not out completely and Meredith started to ask people to "Please, all hold hands." Gemma became aware that as she held Shirley's hand on one side a lovely lady called Martha held her hand on the other side. Gemma's hands were a little bit clammy which embarrassed her a little because she was convinced that they would notice this and pull away from her. The reality was though that no one noticed because things were starting to happen around the table. The first thing that Gemma noticed was how the atmosphere had changed, it had become intense and hot around her. She was also feeling like someone was standing behind her but she couldn't be sure. Shirley was clasping Gemma's hand so tightly she had to whisper for her to her to ease off. Meredith sat with her eyes closed and for what seemed like ages there with nothing happening. Gemma was thinking, "Is this it?" but just then Meredith started to talk but she seemed to have a deeper more of a man like voice. This man was welcomed by those present as if they knew him well. Gemma could see Meredith's face, and when she looked at her, she saw a man's face over Meredith's face, almost like a mask being placed on her. This really freaked Gemma out and she started to panic, but then she felt Agnes near her whispering, "Don't worry, you're not in danger, you are very safe." Thankfully this calmed Gemma down because up until that moment she was about to have a panic attack.

This man who spoke through Meredith was speaking about the importance of evolution in both the physical world as well as the spirit world. As Gemma was listening to this she couldn't help but feel as though it was all a bit above her and was going over her head. As the seance continued there were also messages from people in the spirit world that were connected to those present, which Gemma and Shirley enjoyed listening to. All of a sudden Gemma heard her name being mentioned, "Hello Gemma it's your gran here, I just want to say how proud I am that you are here this evening because you definitely have the ability to work for spirit, just like I did when I was there." Gemma's gran then went on to talk about special memories, how she passed and who she had met that Gemma would know, or know of, that were also in the spirit world. All of this blew Gemma away, especially when another spirit came through for her and explained that she was Gemma's guide speaking through Meredith. She was introducing herself to Gemma because now was the time to become acquainted as it was time for Gemma to develop her abilities. Gemma's guide started a direct conversation with Gemma, "Good evening Gemma, it is so good to see you here and to finally let you know that I am to be a part of your life path now. My name is Petra, and I am one of your Guides. I am so glad you have joined this little group as they can support and guide you through your path as you develop as a medium." Gemma couldn't answer because she was so shocked by what was happening. Petra carried on to explain that Meredith was going to be her teacher and friend, and she, along with others would support her. Petra then left, just as swiftly as she came in. There was still a lot happening at the seance but Gemma wasn't taking it all in as she was still mulling over her gran coming through as well as her guide.

At the end of the evening, when it was time for them all to have a cup of tea, Gemma went over to Meredith to have a chat about what had just happened. At first Meredith was talking to the others in the group but as soon as she saw Gemma she walked towards her to have a little chat. "Well my dear, what do you think about what you experienced?" asked Meredith. Gemma replied, "I'm not too sure really, it was all so amazing and so surreal." Meredith nodded, "I know exactly what you mean, it was like that for me." Meredith asked Gemma, "Is this something that you want? I mean do you want to expand your knowledge and abilities to do some deep work with the spirit world?" Gemma didn't even have to think about that, as she knew she had been directed to this séance for a reason. "Oh absolutely Meredith." said Gemma, "I've been desperately wanting some guidance like this for a long time. Would I be able to join you all? I will be very committed to it." Meredith knew that Gemma should be part of their circle and welcomed her with open arms.

The girls didn't talk much on their way home because they were mulling it all over, but the next day when they were at work, they agreed to meet up that evening to have a good old chat about it all. Gemma also talked with Agnes who was there to meet her when she returned home after the séance. She helped to explain a lot to Gemma including how she can call upon Petra to blend with her and work as a team. "I'm so pleased that you're finally going to do something about working with the spirit world cos we need a lot more people like you, but don't forget who has always been here for you.", said Agnes half-jokingly although Gemma knew that she meant what she said, thinking "There's that warning again." Gemma decided to laugh it off, "As if I could forget you, you will always be in my heart." When Shirley and Gemma met up, they popped along to an ice cream bar for a milk shake and chat. Naturally they were both excited about what had taken place the night before. "And I couldn't believe it when my gran came through.", said Gemma excitedly. "I was always close to my gran, she understood me more than the rest of the family, and she could speak to ghosts, oh I mean spirit to. I must get used to calling them spirit and not ghosts." Gemma wasn't letting Shirley get a word in, "And to meet my guide was pretty amazing, I can't wait for next Sunday to see what happens next." Shirley didn't say anything, but she felt a little jealous or envious of her friend and her ability to speak to people in the spirit world. Although she was very pleased for Gemma, she did feel a bit left out. Gemma was still talking incessantly, "You're coming next Sunday aren't you Shirl." Finally, Gemma took a pause, so Shirley. jumped in quick, "Of course I am, you don't think I would let you go on your own do you, besides I want someone to come through for me. That would be lovely if they did."

For Gemma it had been a long week and a bit of a slow weekend because she just wanted Sunday evening to come around and when it finally did Gemma was counting the hours until the allotted time that her and Shirley would meet up and head over there. Both the girls were full of excitement and aspirations for the evening ahead. Gregory once again answered the door and led them up to his flat. Once inside the people from last week were already there and all smiled and said hello to Gemma and Shirley. Meredith came straight over to them and welcomed them, "Hello girls, lovely to see you both again, welcome to this evening's circle, let's hope it is as exciting as it was last week." With that Meredith turned to all the other circle members and asked them all to take the seats they normally sat in. Meredith beckoned for the girls to sit in the seats they had the previous week. Once again, they didn't have to wait too long until the atmosphere around them changed and they all started to feel the presence of spirit joining them. Meredith was once again in a trance, and it wasn't too long before Meredith's voice changed to a much deeper but not old voice. To the surprise of Gemma and especially Shirley the words that were coming out of Meredith's mouth were directed to Shirley. "Hello Shirl, it's great that you're here, I've been waiting a long time to see you. I'm doing fine, all the scars that I got on the battlefield at Normandy all disappeared as soon as I arrived here, and I could also see again, cos I had an injury that caused blindness just before I popped me clogs." Shirley didn't know what to say or how to answer because it was a total shock. Although she hoped her brother Terry would come through, now that he had it took her a few moments to speak. Gemma nudged and asked "Who's that?" "Umm it's my brother Terry." whispered Shirley. "Hello Tel, how's you? Mum will be so pleased you came through, I can tell her you're OK." Terry was still speaking through Meredith, revisiting memories they had together, and how old Shirley was. Shirley's brother Terry was a lot older than her, she was an unexpected but very welcome baby, so there weren't too many memories that Shirley held because she couldn't remember them although she did know, on another level, that she loved him very much. "He was only 18 when he died, and mum and dad were never the same again. Oh, I can't wait to tell mum", said Shirley emotionally.

There were a couple more messages come through Meredith and then the energy started to change, everyone was told to place their fingers gently over the table or just touch it lightly. As soon as they did the table started to creak, rock and move slightly. The girls couldn't believe it and were a bit worried about what could happen next, then they heard bangs, taps and different kinds of noises going on around the room. Now, although the room wasn't brightly lit, there was subtle lighting so the girls could see that nobody around the table were creating what was happening. "Well, that was a good night wasn't it?" Meredith said at the end of circle. "How did you find it girls?" Gregory asked. "It was amazing." replied Gemma, and Shirley agreed, "Yes it was amazing, thank you." When the girls were due to leave Meredith asked Gemma if she could have a quiet word with her which, naturally, Gemma agreed to but she was a bit apprehensive. Meredith looked directly into Gemmas eyes, "You my dear, have a wonderful energy, and you should be expanding you abilities further, so I am wondering if you would like to join my little group of beginners that meet here every Friday evening? I think you could learn a lot." Gemma was over the moon and didn't really have to think about it. She immediately responded "Yes please, that would be wonderful."

On the way home Shirley was so excited but also emotional about her brother coming through. "Oh Gemma, I'm so glad my brother spoke to me and gave me such a lovely message for mum." Shirley exclaimed, "We do miss him even though he has been gone a long while now. Mum will get a lot of comfort from this." Gemma put her arm through Shirley's as they walked home, "I'm so glad for you to Shirl." Shirley was curious about what Meredith wanted to talk about and asked Gemma outright, "What did Meredith want to talk to you about?" Gemma explained, "Oh, she wants me to join a beginners group that she holds every Friday to develop the abilities I seem to have." "Oh that's great Gem, I'm pleased for you, you definitely have the ability, well I think so anyway." Deep down though Shirley was a bit disappointed that she wasn't asked but was pleased for her friend because she knew what it meant to her.

Gemma was welcomed with open arms when she joined the Friday night group and she fitted in like a good glove fits a hand. At first it was all a bit daunting but as time went on she started to feel more confident with all that she was being taught. It wasn't long before practically every night was taken up either going to some sort of event that Meredith had organised, being at the Friday night circle and of course let's not forget Sunday evenings that Shirley and Gemma attended together. Shirley was noticing a change in Gemma, it seemed that now Gemma barely had any time for her anymore, apart from the Sunday night circle. When Shirley asked Gemma if she wanted to go to the pictures or even out for some fish and chips it seemed that Gemma always had something else arranged with her new friends. They did still get together for their brief lunch hour but even then it was all about circle, Meredith or another new friend and of course how wonderful spirit was at a meeting the night before. Shirley couldn't believe that Gemma seriously considered not travelling back to her parents home the night before Grace's wedding, instead she wanted to see if there was a train at a ridiculously silly early time on the morning of the wedding. Shirley pointed out to her how that would make her sister feel. "Ok, you're right, said Gemma, I just didn't want to miss my Friday night circle". Shirley looked at her friend in shock, she couldn't help but think how selfish she was being.

It was time for the three girls to get dressed and ready for the wedding. Naturally, as the bride, Grace looked absolutely stunning, but so did Gillian and Gemma in the long blue dresses walking behind Grace and holding her train as she walked down the aisle. It wasn't a posh wedding, everything was on a budget, including the reception which was back at Grace's mum and dads house, but even so, Grace's parents and her family did her proud. Although Gemma knew most of the people at the wedding, she didn't know all of them such as Gerry the good friend of her new brother-in-law, Anthony. Gemma had noticed him as soon as he arrived and she took quite a shine to him, it had to be said the feeling was mutual for Gerry as well. Once they were all back at the house for the reception, Gerry waited his time to go and chat with Gemma, as soon as he saw his moment, he seized it. He walked over to Gemma quite confidently, "Well you look as beautiful as the bride." Gemma turned and replied "Well, aren't you the silver-tongued guy." Gerry smiled, "Hello my name is Gerry, I don't think we have been introduced." "Hello Gerry I'm Gemma, Grace's sister." They immediately got on really well and were really at ease in each other's company which is unusual for Gemma because we all know how serious she could be. They started to talk about what they did for a living, "I'm a lorry driver for a large company that supplies spare parts for industrial machines, so quite often I have to go and drop off parts to companies just outside of London, as well as up north like Yorkshire, Manchester and around those kinds of areas." Gemma jumped in quickly, "Oh I live in London, in Shoreditch to be exact." Gerry looked at her, "Well fancy that, we should meet up one evening when I'm up that way, we could go to the pictures or something." "Ok, you're on." Gemma answered.

When Gemma got back to London she arranged to see Shirley to tell her how the wedding went and also about meeting Gerry. "Oh he's lovely Shirl, he's good looking, charming, and very funny." Shirley smiled, "He sounds lovely, are you going to see him again?" Gemma replied excitedly, "Well, I hope so, I gave him the phone number we all use on the landing back at my rooms and he said he would phone me." A week or so went by, and Gemma got back into her routine of going to Gregory and Meredith's as well as sitting alone many nights asking spirit to join her. She would especially ask for her guides to come through and talk to her, which they often did. So, although she thought about Gerry a few times once again she was more interested in working with spirit and Meredith.

To Gemma's surprise Gerry did call her one evening. announced that he was driving up to London the following day and asked how would she fancy getting together? Gemma immediately said "Yes I'm free tomorrow evening, what time and where?" When Gemma went to work the next day, she was full of beans. As usual Shirley and Gemma sat and had their lunch together while Gemma busily told Shirley all about Gerry and meeting him that evening. "That's great Gem, I'm sure you'll enjoy it, you will have to let me know how you get on tomorrow. Gem!", said Shirley apprehensively, "I was just wondering if you fancy doing something next Saturday evening? We haven't been out together for ages, and it is a Saturday evening, so we don't have to get up the early the next morning." "Yeah , that's a good idea Shirl, where do you fancy going?" Gemma said, all bubbly, which pleased Shirley no end as she had been feeling as though Gemma and her were drifting apart. "Well, there's that new dance hall in Hackney that's just opened up, I can't remember the name of it but the girls in the office said it's really good. You never know, you're good luck may rub off on me and I might meet the man of my dreams." and with that Shirley gave Gemma a wink.

Gerry was a bit early so he waited for Gemma to come out of her house where they had agreed to meet. As soon as he saw her coming out of the door, he said to himself "The wait was worth it, she's beautiful." Gemma almost skipped down the steps and out of the gate to meet him. She looked directly into his eyes, nervously saying, "Hello, have you been waiting long?" Gerry looked at her, a big smile on his face saying one word "Hello." he said nothing else. "Is there something wrong?" asked Gemma, "You are very quiet." "Oh sorry." replied Gerry, "No nothing's wrong, I was just thinking how lovely you look." Gemma gave a cheeky smile, "There goes that silver tongue again." Gerry took Gemma to a lovely little restaurant not far from where she lives, it wasn't posh but it was clean and it was in a price range he could afford. For Gemma, this was the first time she had been taken out for a meal on a date and she felt a little bit like a princess. They talked for ages, and after their meal they went for a nice walk down by a canal nearby. It was clear from the start that there was a chemistry between them, and both were falling for each other in a big way.

When Gemma saw Shirley at work the next day, she was full of beans as she told Shirley how wonderful her evening was, and how she was hoping that he could come back up to London soon so that they could see each other again. "Failing that I shall have to go back home for a weekend just to see him." Gemma said laughing. Shirley may have had a smile on her face but deep inside she was actually quite annoyed with Gemma. Any conversation with her now was about either her and her date, how she's getting on with Meredith and the group she has joined at Meredith's and then of course all of the details about how spirit were communicating with her and how much Meredith said she was growing and doing really well. So all of this didn't leave much room for Shirley anymore, and although her life wasn't overly busy, there are a few things going on in her life that she would like to share. Still, she thought, they could have a good old chat and some fun on Saturday when they head out to the dance hall.

The week skipped by for Gemma, and to top it all just before she left work on Friday evening she was called into the manager's office to be told that they are so pleased with her they were giving her a rise, a quite a nice one too, but what came with that was more responsibility. Gemma liked that word responsibility but really the word she was getting it mixed up with was control. Gemma liked to have control, in work and in her personal life, and now she was getting it. She was on her way up to being a personal assistant for the top man, which was a very big role to have. Gemma almost skipped to circle that evening which was pretty good for Gemma to, because the connections and information she was getting from spirit was incredibly strong. Meredith had nothing but praise for her. Yes, it turned out that Gemma really did have what it takes to be a good medium. After circle, as always, it was time for a cup of tea and a biscuit which gave them all the opportunity to have a chat about their experiences that night. As Gemma was sitting listening to one of the other members of the circle, Meredith walked over to Gemma, "Well done my dear, you were very good this evening." Gemma had a big smile on her face, "Thank you Meredith, it's lovely to hear that feedback." Meredith went on, "I have been asked to talk to a small group of people about spirit, the philosophy of spirit and of course my experiences. I would really like you to join me." Gemma was so flattered that Meredith wanted to involve her, that she immediately agreed to go before she even knew the day when this event was being held. "That's wonderful." exclaimed Meredith, meet me here at 5.30pm tomorrow and we can make our way across to the event together." Gemma's heart immediately sank as she realised it was the next evening and she was due to be going out with Shirley. "Oh gosh I forgot I'm supposed to be going out with Shirley," said Gemma Meredith looked at Gemma, "Can you cancel it? It's just that this event may be beneficial to you as you will meet some more people that can open up some doors for you on your spiritual path." How could Gemma resist that? So she agreed that she would cancel her evening out with Shirley.

The following morning Gemma walked across to where Shirley lived and as she rang the doorbell she thought that Shirley would be OK about cancelling their night out and would understand. She was in for a shock, because Shirley wasn't ok about it and let Gemma know it in no uncertain terms. At first Shirley stared at Gemma whilst listening to why she had to cancel the night out. She was weighing up whether or not she should say anything or just smile and accept it just as she always did. But no, she wasn't going to accept it this time, "You know I have listened to you spout on about different things, I have put up with you cancelling dates that we've made, I have listened intently to all of your wonderful news but not once have you asked me how I am, or what's new in my world. It's just always about you, and do you know what, I'm fed up with it and I think you're very selfish." Shirley continued, "As far as I'm concerned I will be pleasant when I see you at work, but that's it. I've just had enough, you're no friend. Oh and by the way I'm not coming to circle with you tomorrow evening, or any other evening for that matter." With that Shirley slammed the door in Gemmas face. Gemma was in total shock, as much as she wanted to say something to Shirley when she was having a go, she couldn't get the words together. Once Gemma composed herself she rang the doorbell again but didn't get an answer, so she headed back home. Much as Gemma was looking forward to the evening with Meredith and meeting new people, she was still a bit bruised from what happened with Shirley and she couldn't get her out of her mind. Gemma was sure that she could bring Shirley round if she popped over there again tomorrow to talk to her, she could think of nothing else but Shirley at that point. She was sure Shirley wouldn't miss circle tomorrow night because she loved it. Gemma was sure she would have forgiven her by then if she just said sorry and eat humble pie.

It didn't take too long for Gemma to focus on something as she met Meredith and Gregory and headed off to Bethnal Green for Meredith's event. It was an amazing night for all of them. Gemma listened to Meredith's first talk about spirit and her bond with them which was followed by a talk about the philosophy of spiritualism. Gemma found this amazing as she hadn't ever really heard about the philosophy of spiritualism at that stage. This philosophy though wasn't a human creation, it was all that Meredith had learned from the spirit world herself. Meredith followed that with a demonstration of mediumship, bringing through loved ones from the spirit world to those present. As Gemma watched this, she decided that she was going to be as good as Meredith, no matter what it took, she knew she had the commitment. "Oh, that was wonderful Meredith, you are amazing." Said Gemma like a teenager in awe of her idol. "Thank you Gemma, it was wonderful to have you along." replied Meredith, "In fact I would like you to join me on more of these events because I think you could learn so much. One day you can be up there with me." Gemma couldn't believe her ears, this was a dream come true, Meredith was taking her under her wing. On the way home Gemma hadn't had a thought about Shirley, until she was at the bottom of her street, when she once again thought she would calm down by tomorrow, she always had done.

The following evening arrived, Gemma waited at the place where she normally met Shirley until the last minute just in case she turned up, but there was no Shirley. On the way over to Meredith and Gregory's place, Gemma found herself getting angry now over Shirley's childish attitude as she saw it. "Blow her.", Gemma thought, "I can do without her in my life, I don't even see what her problem is." All these thoughts were running through her head. There was a big part of Gemma that hoped Shirley would already be at Meredith's and hadn't waited for Gemma just to spite her. "If that is the case." thought Gemma, "I'll give her a piece of my mind." When Gemma arrived, there was no Shirley. Meredith walked straight over to Gemma, a broad smile on her face, to greet Gemma, "It's a shame about Shirley isn't it?" Gemma was confused, "Sorry what do you mean?" Meredith explained, "Well that she isn't coming along to join us on Sunday anymore. She popped over earlier today to let us know. I thought you would have known." Gemma looked down to the floor, "No I didn't know, she was probably going to tell me in work tomorrow." "Yes she probably was.", agreed Meredith, "I have to say I'm not too shocked as her abilities weren't anything like yours." That was a lovely compliment from Meredith, but Gemma didn't really want to hear that right now. Gemma couldn't believe she would go this far with this silly mood that she was in at the moment. Monday arrived and Gemma couldn't wait to get to work to sort this problem out with Shirley but as she arrived, Shirley was talking to another of the girls that worked there. She took a quick look around, saw Gemma and smiled to acknowledge she was there but turned around and walked off with her new buddy. Gemma was actually far more upset than she thought she would be, but she wasn't giving up on making the peace with her friend. Now that she hadn't got Shirley to talk to, Gemma realised she was a good friend indeed. At lunchtime she saw Shirley walking on her own towards the office door, so she called her and asked if she could talk to her. "Why." asked Shirley, "I don't think we have anything to say Gemma." Gemma promptly said, "Oh come on Shirley don't you think you're taking this too far? I mean after all, it was only a silly little row." Shirley couldn't believe Gemma had just said that, she repeated Gemma's words back to her, "It was only a silly little row! You must be joking. For months now I have put up with you letting me down, never asking how I am, always expecting to do what you wanted to do and never really treating me as an equal. No Gemma, this isn't just a silly little row. I don't trust you anymore and I want to be with people who see me for who I am and as an equal, not someone who they can pick up and drop to suit them." Gemma's head was reeling, she couldn't say a word as she watched Shirley walk away and meet up with the same girl she was with earlier.

When Gemma tried to get herself into a peaceful place to prepare herself to speak with spirit, the one spirit she wanted to talk to at that time was of course Agnes. Agnes did come forward, "Hello Gemma." Gemma could sense her strongly now and as the two blended together Gemma immediately told Agnes what happened with Shirley and asked what she could do to make it up to her. Agnes had very little sympathy for Gemma because she had been doing the same with her inasmuch as she only ever asked her to come forward when Gemma wanted something. Agnes shared her views with Gemma, "What do you expect? You have treated her like she was there solely for you when you wanted her. In fact, you do the same to me, it appears you have outgrown those who truly care for you." Gemma couldn't believe how blunt Agnes was being with her, and how harsh she was with her words. Agnes decided she had said what was needed but just as she left her, she said "Maybe you need to do some thinking." Out loud Gemma shouted, "Maybe I should do some thinking? What a cheek." Gemma was annoyed and justified everything in her mind so that she didn't have to take responsibility for how she had been behaving. It was at times like these that Gemma normally cut off her nose to spite her face rather than really take a good look at how she had been behaving and sadly this was the path she was about to take again. As the evening wore on Gemma decided that it was good riddance to Shirley because now that she didn't have someone as immature as Shirley hanging around, she had a better chance of working herself up to the top of the ladder at work. She had also persuaded herself that Agnes would come back with her tail between her legs and apologise for what she said and all would be forgiven. Only that was never going to happen.

Gerry and Gemma were still seeing each other whenever he could get up to London, and Gerry was falling more and more in love each time he saw her. Gemma was very fond of Gerry too, but now life was getting busier and busier with Meredith and Gregory. They were doing far more talks and demonstrations, encouraging Gemma to join them as she was their protege. They could see a future for her as a medium and an oracle for the spirit world. In fact it got so busy for Gemma, when Gillian was due to get married, she really considered making her excuses in favour of attending a talk that Meredith was giving in a hall in Croydon. Thankfully Gerry managed to get her to see sense, reminding her that her relationship with Gillian was already strained and if she missed the wedding, world war three would break out not to mention how her mum would feel if she wasn't there.

Gillian looked beautiful, so did Grace and Gemma as her bridesmaids and everyone could see the pride in their parents' eyes. The wedding reception was in a room at the back of the local pub that Hugh used occasionally. There wasn't any dancing, but the guests did have a good old sing song around the piano and by the looks of it everyone had a good time. Later on that evening, when Gerry and Gemma were alone, Gerry commented on how lovely the day was, with that he reached for her hands and as he cupped them he got down on one knee, looked up into her eyes and asked, "Will you do me the honour of being my wife?" Gemma took a sharp intake of breath, stared at him, but didn't say anything. "Well, aren't you going to say anything?" Gerry said. "Oh Gerry, you've caught me by surprise, that's all. I don't know what to say, I need to think about it." Gerry was a bit shocked as well as embarrassed, as he got up off his knees he quietly said "What you have to think about? I thought we both wanted the same thing, but apparently not." Gemma tried to get Gerry to calm down a bit and get him to understand that it was just a bit of a shock, she just needed time to think about it Gerry agreed to give her time to think about it, but he felt quite confident that she would come around in the end. Gemma really wanted to share her news that Gerry had asked her to marry him, but she didn't want to share it with her family because they would try and talk her into settling down and moving closer to home. It's at times like this that Gemma missed her two close friends Shirley and of course Agnes. It didn't help seeing Shirley everyday getting on with her life, laughing with her new friends at work, but there was no way that she was going to go and apologise to neither Shirley or Agnes for that matter. Perhaps Meredith would be a good listener she thought. "Yes." she said out loud, "She's a friend."

Nervously Gemma approached Meredith, "Can I have a word with you please." She said. "Of course you can, what's the problem." Replied Meredith. Gemma told Meredith about Gerry's proposal, for a few moments Meredith stared at Gemma, finally saying "Oh, I see, and how do you feel about that?" Gemma noticed there was no smile on Meredith's face or sound of joy in her words when she asked how she felt. "Well, I'm not sure to be honest, I mean he offers security and love, and he's a lovely man." Meredith quickly interjected, "But how will he feel about your work with Spirit? As well as the different talks you will want to join me on, and let's not forget that we're training you to do these talks on your own, will he allow that?" Gemma hadn't thought about that side of things. In Gemma's mind Meredith's comments confirmed that she was convinced that she was destined to work on a very deep level with spirit. Gemma didn't want anything to get in the way of all that. Gemma saw Meredith as an icon and she didn't seem pleased about the proposal, in fact she seemed a bit angry about it, saying everything that she could to put Gemma off the idea.

Unfortunately Gemma listened to Meredith more than she would anyone else. So now, as a result of her chat with Meredith, Gemma had decided to turn down Gerry's offer of marriage. "I'm sorry Gerry I can't marry you, I'm not ready for marriage yet because there's too much I want to do." Gerry couldn't believe what he was hearing. "Like what? What do you want to do?" asked Gerry sharply, "What is it that you think I would stop you from doing." Gemma responded, "Well there's my work with Spirit, I wouldn't be able to go on talks in different parts of London, then there's my development circle, I'm learning so much from Meredith and I don't want to give it all up." Gerry looked down to the floor because his dream was that they would get married, live near their families, and have children, but none of this seemed to be in Gemma's dreams. He knew there was no point talking to her about it as they weren't even on the same page, deep down he had never taken Gemma's work with spirit as serious, so yes, all that would have had to stop. Gerry was hurt and angry, just before he walked away he looked at Gemma, "I really hope that all your dreams come true, but soley living to work with the dead will be cold and lonely at night when you have no one living to look after you, to hold you and comfort you in hard times. That's no life at all and I hope you don't live to regret your decision." With that Gerry walked away without looking back.

As she had with Shirley and Agnes, Gemma thought that Gerry's attitude was stupid and childish, she had decided that he would come to her before she would go to him. He really loved her, she thought, so he would see her side of things and they would carry on getting together every now and then. Every thought she had about Gerry, the situation and his reaction was very derogatory about him, she was laying the responsibility for their relationship breakdown completely at his feet. "He doesn't know what he's talking about." she said out loud and finished off what she was saying with "Yes, he'll come around to my way of thinking".

The years went by, but Gerry never did come around, in those awkward moments when they would run into each other either in London or when Gemma went back home all Gerry ever did was tip his hat and gave half a smile. He was married and had two children that were a credit to him and his wife. Gemma also did very well for herself as she managed to work her way up the ladder and became PA (Personal Assistant) for the top man of the Company. She made very few friends along the way and saw women of her age come and go, get married and have children. This included Shirley, who had married a lovely man that she met in a dance hall in Hackney. They had a lovely home and a beautiful daughter. Shirley wouldn't change her life for anything or anyone. Gemma had other fish to fry, and there was no marriage for her. All the while that her parents were alive, she would visit them occasionally and of course she would see her sisters at those times. They had very little to say as both of her siblings were proud to be married with children. In Gemma's world they weren't on the same level and they wouldn't understand her, so over the years her relationship with Gemma and Grace went to nothing. Even when they both passed away years later, she didn't feel any great loss, she just felt sorry for the relationship she never had with them. Again, she saw the deterioration of her relationship with her siblings as their fault for not putting the effort into it. Gemma continued to go to talks and demonstrations of mediumship with Meredith and Gregory and one day it was her turn to stand up there and demonstrate mediumship and give talks. She was a big success within the mediumship world and she herself began teaching fledgelings. The two consistent people that stayed with Gemma throughout her life until they passed was Meredith and Gregory. When they both passed away it turned out that they had left everything to Gemma, which was lovely, although she didn't need anything because she was a woman of financial independence in her own right.

When Meredith and Gregory first passed away, and although she missed them, Gemma wasn't too lonely, but as time went on and she herself became frail to the point that she couldn't teach any longer because of her health, for the first time ever she understood what Gerry meant about being cold and lonely. For days she wouldn't see anyone, and nobody was coming around knocking at her front door to see how she's doing. Yes, she had had plenty of students that supposedly thought she was the "Bees knees", but once they moved on they all seemed to forget about her. As the days turned into weeks, and the weeks turned into months, Gemma felt sad, alone and a bit angry with the spirit world as they appeared to stop visiting her also. She blamed them for her loneliness, and would very often go around her little old flat in need of great repair talking out loud, telling them how it was all their fault. "I gave up a normal life for you spirit, I put you before having a husband and children, you used to tell me this was my destiny, and now look at me." Over a period of time Gemma went out less and less but there was one neighbour that had noticed how frail Gemma was, but knowing how private she was, the neighbour decided not to say anything but she kept a close eye on her as much as she could. When the time came for Gemma to leave this world for the spirit world, she passed gently in her sleep. Sadly, because she was such a loner, she wasn't found for quite a few days when a neighbour reported to the police that she hadn't seen her about. Both the police and social services arrived, and once the police broke the door down, they found her in her bed, a lonely pathetic old lady that only a neighbour missed.

Gemma was excited to reach the spirit world where she met her guides, and her spirit team. She also saw her parents and her sisters walking towards her and she was over the moon. She also couldn't believe how young she felt, it was all so overwhelming and exciting, and she was looking forward to having time out with her guides so she could hear how wonderful she was as their representative on earth. Mind you for the moment she was just happy to see her family again and to enjoy her time with them. The time came for her to meet her guides and teachers, Gemma was over the moon to actually be with them on this side of the veil reflecting on her life. She was convinced that she had led a very spiritual life which she thought they would praise her for. As they looked back at Gemma's life her guides asked her what, she believed, was the main thing she really learned by having her human experience. She didn't waste any time reeling of loads of different things but the very last thing she said proudly was, "Well, I think it was how to be spiritual." Before she knew it, her guides were taking her back to times when she wasn't so spiritual to her sisters, to Shirley, and to Gerry, and even to her parents. "Well, I didn't wish them harm, and I was always there for them.", she said defensively. Her guides looked at her, "Perhaps you should chat to them all to find out what they feel." Gemma knew that this wasn't going to be the way she thought it would be. She realised at that point, that the time had come for her to receive some feedback on her life on earth, and this was going to be an uncomfortable ride.

"You never treated us like your sisters." said Gillian, now that she had started, she wasn't going to stop, "In fact you never really treated us like we were related to you, almost as if we weren't good enough for you. How do you think that made us feel?" Gemma was about to go on the defensive but her guide advised her that for once she needed to just listen. At the end of the conversation and just as Gemma could take a breath, who was there to talk to her but Gerry. "Hello Gem, it's been a long time, I bet you never thought you would see me up here.", said Gerry with a smile. "You're right I didn't expect you to meet me, how long have you been up here?" replied Gemma, Gerry responding, "Oh, not that long really, but long enough to meet up with a few of my family and friends, oh, and I've seen your family too." Gemma looked at Gerry, "How did life treat you Gerry? I thought about you a lot over the years and wondered how you were getting on." Gemma hesitated briefly, "Gerry, I've been learning how I managed to upset a lot of people when I was living my life on earth, I'm just wondering, do you still feel angry towards me to?" Gerry didn't say anything straight away, but when he did, Gemma didn't really expect what came out of his mouth. "Well, I was really angry with you at first because I felt like you led me up the garden path. I thought there was a chance for us, but then I realised that you preferred to be with dead people rather than being with me. But it turned out I had a lot to thank you for because it wasn't that long after I met the woman that I would end up spending the rest of my life with." Gerry continued, "She was totally different to you, warm, caring and considerate, I couldn't have loved her more if I tried. We went on to have three great children who I am so proud of." Gerry paused for a moment, "Gem, you did me a big favour turning me down, because I realised pretty soon after we split that it would never have worked between us."

Gemma was stunned by what Gerry had to say, "Was I really that cold?" "Yes Gem you were." Replied Gerry, "In your world a person only fitted in your life if you could control them, oh and you would have to be interested in the after life, it was a pretty hard life to try and fit in with you." Gemma reached out trying to apologise to Gerry, "Oh Gerry I'm so sorry, I had no…." Gerry interrupted, "Don't feel sorry for me, feel sorry for yourself and all the things you missed because you were so wrapped up believing that you were so special spirit had chosen you for their work and they didn't want you to live a normal life like the rest of us." Gerry finished off, "No Gem don't feel sorry for us, we ended up OK." Gemma couldn't help but feel tearful. She thought Gerry would need many years to get over her and now she knew different. She could see now just how people felt about her. Now she had to face up to it and learn exactly what she was like and it was a tough pill to swallow. After Gerry had walked away, Gemma felt alone and sad. For a short while she wallowed in her own self-pity. All of a sudden, she heard a voice she hadn't heard for a great many years, "Hello Gemma, do you want to play?" said Agnes in her mischievous and cheeky voice. Gemmas face lit up as she saw her dear friend Agnes in front of her. "Oh my God Aggy, I can't believe it's you.", said Gemma excitedly, "I'm so pleased to see you, and you've done your growing here haven't you?" Gemma, continued "Oh how I've missed you over the years, it was horrible not having you to talk to, I missed our giggles and the fun we had." Agnes responded, "Yes we did have fun didn't we, I did pop in on you sometimes, but you never felt my presence. Oh Gemma, life always had to be on your terms didn't it." Gemma snapped back, "Oh don't you start, I've had enough of you all ganging up on me, telling me how bad I was. Haven't you got anything nice you want to say about me? I mean there were people that were far worse than me." Aggy agreed with Gemma but she reminded Gemma how she thought her behaviour to others was OK because she was a spiritualist and she was working for the spirit world. "But it didn't represent us in the right way because you were selfish." said Agnes sharply.

Gemma wanted go away somewhere, lick her wounds and come back fighting, but this time she knew she couldn't do that. Instead she was going to have to do a great deal of thinking and saying sorry to those that will accept her apology. There was one final hurdle that Gemma felt she needed to get over and that was the conversation with her birth guide because she was sure there would be a few upsetting things said there too. Gemma's main guide, Walter, was assigned to her at birth, over the years he had tried to guide her, teach her, keep her safe and help her to develop her abilities, the only problem being that Gemma became a law unto herself very early on. "I know what you're going to say Walter." said Gemma quietly, "Where did it all go so wrong for me?" Walter didn't answer, instead asking her the same question, "Where do you think it went wrong? And why?" "When I let my ego take over as I was growing up." answered Gemma very slowly. Gemma knew she had to ask the next question even though she might not like the answer. "Was I right that my destiny was to work for the Spirit world?" "Yes." replied Walter, "But not to the degree that you took it to. Just think about it, did we really ask you soley to focus on the Spirit World? Where did we tell you that your work with us must be the only thing that you focus on? Where did we tell you that you shouldn't get married or have a family?" "Well, I can't remember that, but I got it from somewhere." said Gemma defensively. "I know we didn't say that." said Walter, "We want those who work for us to have a human life, to have a family, and to live a full life because only then can they understand what life is like and only then can they help us. We understand that while you're on the earth you have to find a balance, be earthly, as well as working with us as a team."

It was at that point that Gemma realised how much she had missed out on, and how much she didn't learn because of her own ego. Now she knew what she needed to do. She knew she needed to give life another go, be re-incarnated on earth as soon as she was permitted to. Meanwhile, she would have to eat humble pie and once more become the student. Only time would tell if she would succeed and live the spiritual life she tried so hard to find in her last lifetime. Let's hope so.

Lightning Source UK Ltd.
Milton Keynes UK
UKHW020747160522
403010UK00009B/121